Praise for the Novels
of Gail Fraser

The Promise of Lumby

"Readers who have traveled to Mitford with Jan Karon will find the trip to Lumby at least as pleasant and marked with a lot more laughter. If the world of cozy fiction has a capital, it's Lumby. Although I hesitate to use the overused word 'charming,' it most definitely applies to *The Promise of Lumby* and its three predecessors. Gail Fraser tells wonderful stories that have kindness at their core—and are a gentle reminder of the goodness in people's hearts. *The Promise of Lumby*, like the first three in the series, is a book I'll save to read again and again."
—Cozy Library

Lumby's Bounty

"A visit to the charming, whimsical town of Lumby is a refreshing change from our fast-paced lives. Challenged to host a hot-air balloon festival, its residents rise to the occasion: Lives change, love blossoms, a wild and irrepressible young man matures. A delightful read." —Joan Medlicott, author of *The Ladies of Covington* Series

"Drop in on the sweetest small town since Mayberry, where the worst people are still nicer than the best people you know, and life's problems are solved by a backhoe, an industrial sewing machine, or monks wearing light-up tennis shoes. Your own troubles will melt away. When they return—if you're a smarty—you'll visit the next warmhearted book in Gail Fraser's series and get lumbified all over again." —Bob Tarte, author of *Fowl Weather* and *Enslaved by Ducks*

"Lumby will astound readers with its sense of humor, quirky charm, its aura of magic and possibilities and happy (if unexpected) endings."
—Cozy Library

"Author Gail Fraser has the ability to take everyday life and make it interesting reading. *Lumby's Bounty* is a feel-good story by a writer who knows her audience."
—BookLoons

continued...

Stealing Lumby

In the tradition of Jan Karon's Mitford series, this engaging inside look at small-town life will draw a bevy of fans to its old-fashioned story combining a bit of romance, a bit of mystery, and a multitude of quirky and endearing characters." —*Booklist*

"There's a . . . quality to the writing that lends an unrushed, meandering feel to the narrative as evildoers are dispatched and equilibrium is restored. Fraser's story is pleasantly easy reading and as small-town cozy as they come." —*Publishers Weekly*

"*Stealing Lumby* is a classic cozy read, with good-hearted characters that face life's problems head-on. Readers can be certain that, despite heartache and loss, good will prevail and evildoers will get what they deserve. Although that doesn't happen often in the real world, at least not in the time frame we'd prefer, Lumby is a wonderful place where it does. I'm certain readers of the first book in the series, *The Lumby Lines*, will love *Stealing Lumby*." —Cozy Library

"*Stealing Lumby*, second in the Lumby series, is as delightful as the first. . . . Where else will you find a moose wandering around a village with a folding deck chair enmeshed in his rack? . . . I loved the blind horse being ridden by its elderly, almost blind owner. And how about the Moo Moo Iditarod? . . . It's fun to become a part of the village and listen in to their solutions—some of which make one laugh out loud, while others are wise and knowing, and some are just plain crazy. Which should make *Stealing Lumby* scamper to the top of your must-read list. After *Lumby Lines*, of course." —Bookloons

The Lumby Lines

"At a time when we seem to be taking ourselves all too seriously, Gail Fraser pulls a rabbit out of the hat that charms while it helps us relax. *The Lumby Lines* strikes just the right balance of playfulness, satire, and drama. A thoroughly enjoyable read!"

—Brother Christopher, The Monks of New Skete

"Unique. . . . You will be amazed by the great imagination of the author. . . . The reader is in for a treat. This book is a delight to read and one that you will thoroughly enjoy." —Bestsellersworld.com

"Gail Fraser has assembled a wonderful cast of characters and plunked them down in the middle of a beautiful town that rivals Jan Karon's Mitford for pure fun. Of course, there are obstacles to overcome, mysteries to solve, even some romance and reconciliation along the way to a very satisfying conclusion. Altogether a wonderful story, highly recommended." —Cozy Library

"*The Lumby Lines* goes straight to the heart. The simplicity, humor, and downright friendliness of the book make reading it a pleasure. . . . Readers will close this book with a sigh of contentment and a desire to visit Lumby again. The author has faithfully carved out a slice of small-town living and topped it off with a large helping of humor. This reviewer can't wait for her next visit to Lumby!"

—Christian Book Previews

"A setting reminiscent of Jan Karon's fictional village. . . . *The Lumby Lines* is a feel-good novel with lots of heart and angst. I was sorry to leave my new friends but have brightened since I learned that a sequel, *Stealing Lumby,* is coming soon." —BookLoons

Books in the Lumby Series
by Gail Fraser

The Lumby Lines
Stealing Lumby
Lumby's Bounty

THE PROMISE OF LUMBY

GAIL FRASER

NEW AMERICAN LIBRARY

New American Library
Published by New American Library, a division of
Penguin Group (USA) Inc., 375 Hudson Street,
New York, New York 10014, USA
Penguin Group (Canada), 90 Eglinton Avenue East, Suite 700, Toronto,
Ontario M4P 2Y3, Canada (a division of Pearson Penguin Canada Inc.)
Penguin Books Ltd., 80 Strand, London WC2R 0RL, England
Penguin Ireland, 25 St. Stephen's Green, Dublin 2,
Ireland (a division of Penguin Books Ltd.)
Penguin Group (Australia), 250 Camberwell Road, Camberwell, Victoria 3124,
Australia (a division of Pearson Australia Group Pty. Ltd.)
Penguin Books India Pvt. Ltd., 11 Community Centre, Panchsheel Park,
New Delhi - 10 017, India
Penguin Group (NZ), 67 Apollo Drive, Rosedale, North Shore 0632,
New Zealand (a division of Pearson New Zealand Ltd.)
Penguin Books (South Africa) (Pty.) Ltd., 24 Sturdee Avenue,
Rosebank, Johannesburg 2196, South Africa

Penguin Books Ltd., Registered Offices:
80 Strand, London WC2R 0RL, England

First published by New American Library,
a division of Penguin Group (USA) Inc.

First Printing, July 2009
10 9 8 7 6 5 4 3 2 1

The author gratefully acknowledges the right to reprint the smothered BBQ burgers recipe on pages 444–45, courtesy of Diane and David A. Nelson, and the variation of egg-bake recipe on pages 438–39, courtesy of Libby Nessle.

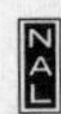

LIBRARY OF CONGRESS CATALOGING-IN-PUBLICATION DATA:

Fraser, Gail R.
The promise of Lumby/Gail Fraser.
p. cm.
ISBN 978-0-451-22696-9
1. City and town life—Fiction. 2. Villages—Fiction. 3. Eccentrics and eccentricities—Fiction. 4. Veterinarians—Fiction. 5. Northwest, Pacific—Fiction. I. Title.
PS3606.R4229P76 2009
813'.6—dc22 2009001306

Printed in the United States of America

In memory of Sister Katrina.
Dedicated to the men and women of New Skete.
Thank you for your friendship.

Acknowledgments

Special acknowledgment and the deepest of thanks go to Dr. Tom Wolski, a good friend, a great bass and a veterinarian extraordinaire, who compassionately cares for all of our beloved animals at Lazy Goose Farm. Tom's enthusiasm, patience and medical expertise made Tom Candor possible. If I ever need to kill off another panda, he will most definitely be the first person I call.

Also, all my gratitude and respect go to Nancy Coffey, a superb agent who steadfastly carries the Lumby flag so I can continue writing. The work she and her team have done on the novels and her ceaseless commitment to the series are deeply appreciated. And, once again, my deep thanks go to Ellen Edwards, a wonderful editor, and to the team at Penguin NAL.

Finally, I'd like to acknowledge all those readers who came up Farm to Market Road and have helped put our small town of Lumby on the proverbial map.

The towns, characters and events depicted in this novel are entirely fictitious. While there may be a town in this or another country called Lumby, its location and depiction are different from the town I describe within this and other Lumby novels. Any resemblance to actual people, events or places is entirely coincidental.

THE PROMISE OF LUMBY

LUMBY ANIMAL
CLINIC
OFFICE
REST STOP

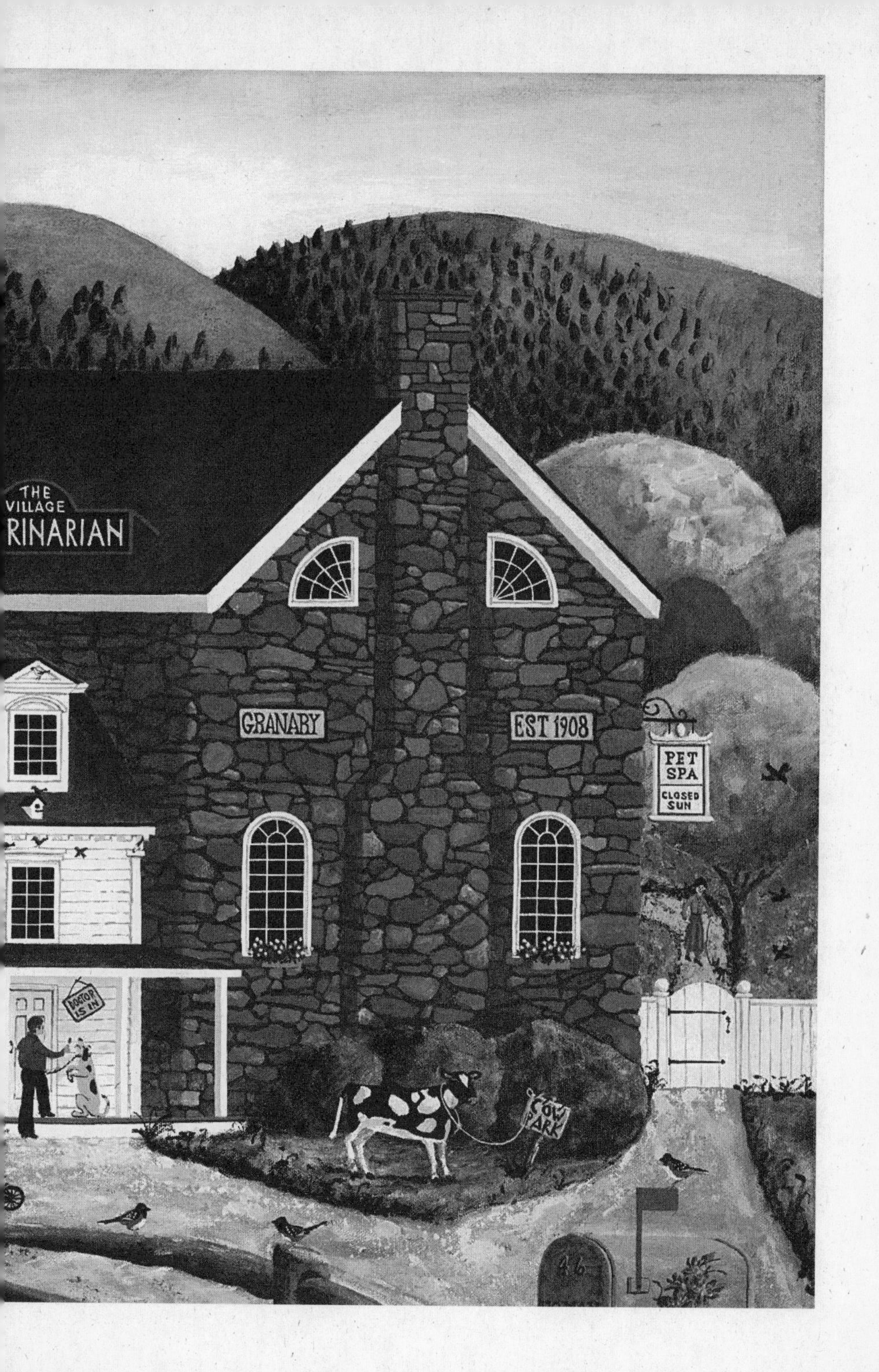
THE
VILLAGE
RINARIAN
GRANARY
EST 1908
PET
SPA
CLOSED
SUN
DOCTOR
IS IN
COW
PARK

Lumby
Cold Water
Pond
Red Moose
Mill
Barns of
Lumby
Montis
Abbey
Goose Creek
Fork River
To Trout Lake
Farm-to-Market Road
Woodrow
Lake
To Wheatley

ONE

Vial

Fifteen Years Earlier

Dr. Jeffrey Thomas Candor's life was abruptly redirected the afternoon of February 3 by a series of related tragedies that would have exploded through the national press had the storm of the century, which crippled the East Coast under as much as four feet of snow, not stolen the headlines. Afterward, events of the day were successfully buried for nearly twenty years until the residents of a small town unearthed the veterinarian's dark secret. But on that winter morning, the possibilities of the accidents as well as the distant town of Lumby were the farthest thoughts from Jeffrey's focused concentration.

Standing at the kitchen sink of his Redding, California, town house, Jeffrey looked out at the frozen yard. The boughs of the pine trees bent unnaturally, weighed down by needles encased in heavy ice. Frost glistened in the rising sun.

"The roads will be bad in the mountains. You should postpone your trip," he advised his wife.

Laura sat at the dining room table, staring into her coffee mug. "My parents are expecting us," she repeated without looking up.

"I told you, I'm sorry but I have no choice. The surgery is scheduled for this morning. You'll just have to go alone."

"So you've said," she replied indifferently.

Jeffrey studied his wife for a long moment and wondered if there was one irreversible moment that had broken their marriage. He thought back on the eight years of their relationship, as he had been doing with increasing frequency during the past few months. Where in the path of their togetherness had their roads separated? He was growing weary of trying to diagnose their discord, of trying to cure them as he would a critically ill patient.

Sensing she was being stared at, Laura glanced up. "What is it?"

Jeffrey sighed. "Absolutely nothing," he said sadly and then looked at his watch. "I need to get going. You'll be home by dinner?"

Laura glanced out the window. "I may spend the night there," she replied.

He was no longer surprised by such a vague response and had long since stopped questioning Laura about her unplanned absences. "Whatever you want," he said as he pulled on his trench coat. "Just let me know when you're on the road."

She nodded, still looking away from him.

As Jeffrey expected, the roads were slippery, doubling his commute time. Thirty minutes later, he waved to the guard as he drove past the gate of the staff entrance to the American Zoological Park. The veterinary clinic was located on the north side of the complex, so Jeffrey followed the park's perimeter road as he had most every day since joining "The Park" seven years ago.

Although in acreage The Park was only the sixth-largest zoo in the country, for nearly eight decades, it had enjoyed a renowned reputation for its captive-breeding program for endangered species. By adding Dr. Candor, the nation's preeminent Ursidae or bear veterinarian, to its staff The Park had become a prime destination for endangered animals from around the world that would have otherwise been sent to large zoos.

Jeffrey lowered the window a few inches and inhaled crisp air heavy with the scents of pine and fresh straw, of which he would never tire. The feral sounds of the enclosed animals were usually also good for his soul, but on that cold and somber morning most of the animals were still inside, so an unusual quiet hung over the exhibitions.

Walking into the small clinic, Jeffrey went directly to his office and immediately read through a long fax written in broken English that had arrived from China a few hours earlier. He withdrew a medical textbook from his briefcase and opened it to the same page he had studied the night before, once again scrutinizing the illustrations.

Jeffrey scanned the bookshelf for yet another reference that might be of help, but couldn't find what he was looking for. Crammed between and in front of the books were stacks of research papers and back issues of veterinary journals. Tucked in the corner of the top shelf was his University of California Berkeley undergraduate diploma, covered with dust.

A young man, one of Jeffrey's two vet technicians, knocked gently on his open door. "Jan and I are ready for you," he said. "I'm about to scrub and our girl is on the table, drowsy and ready for you to prep her."

"Good. I'll be right there," Jeffrey said, and quickly reread the fax one final time before going down the hall.

In the pre-op room, Jeffrey pulled a pair of blue scrubs from a box marked "Candor" stored above his locker. It was generally assumed that Jeffrey was issued his own scrubs because he was the medical director of The Park, but the more accurate reason was that at six feet five inches tall, he didn't fit into standard-sized garb. On the one occasion he had had to resort to using staff-issued pants, the bottoms came halfway to his knees.

After snapping on his gloves and pulling up his surgical mask, Jeffrey walked through the swinging doors. The compact operating room was flooded with fluorescent light. On the closest wall, four X-rays hung on a view box for Jeffrey to reference during the resection.

He glanced over at the narrow observation window and saw three men and a woman behind the thick plate glass. Jeffrey nodded to the executive director of The Park. Standing to the director's left was the chairman of the board, whom Jeffrey distrusted, and to the chairman's right the senior curator. With them was a small Asian man, who appeared to be taking notes.

"All okay, Doc," the second tech said, carefully watching the animal.

Jeffrey looked at the X-ray viewer and then down at the patient.

A beautiful two-hundred-fifty-pound giant panda that had been loaned to the zoo five years earlier lay motionless on the metal table with two sheets covering her body. Through a collaborative effort between the U.S. and Japanese governments, Ming had been successfully bred by artificial insemination in 1987. That year, she and her baby were more famous than many Hollywood movie stars.

The bold black-and-white markings on Ming's face made Jeffrey smile. She had always been a gentle animal, far more trusting of humans than was natural for her breed. During her stay at The Park, she had remained in good health—until recently, when she had suffered an alarming loss of weight. After monitoring her for several days, Jeffrey had run a battery of tests. An ultrasound had revealed a large mass in her upper intestine. In Jeffrey's opinion, all noninvasive efforts to correct the problem would be futile. He was about to perform the operation necessary to save her life.

Jeffrey glanced at the observation window and then at his staff, all of whom were wearing surgical masks. Tension gripped the operating room. "This is a simple operation, folks," he said. "Everyone take a deep breath and relax." He followed his own advice as he put the anesthesia mask over the panda's face. Only when he was sure that she was fully under did he pick up a scalpel.

During his career, Jeffrey had operated on most species of bears. In fact, the prior fall he had traveled to Washington, D.C., at the request of the National Zoo, to lead one of their more complicated surgeries on a pregnant polar bear. But he had never operated on a great panda or on an animal that was as critically endangered as this one. With only sixteen hundred pandas in the wild, and another one hundred eighty in captivity, the value of each fertile female was incalculable.

Jeffrey's hand was steady as he made a fourteen-inch incision in the animal's abdomen, cutting easily through the thick layer of fat. Once the blood was suctioned and the epidermal layer pulled back, Jeffrey changed scalpels and continued through the layers of dense muscle to reach the intestines. He glanced up at one of the techs, who, after studying the panda's vitals, nodded back.

Forty-five minutes later, the tumor was successfully removed and Jeffrey began cauterizing the numerous arteries and veins that had been severed. The surgery was going better than expected. Just as he picked up a suture needle to close the stomach wall, a woman rushed into the operating room. Not wearing any scrubs, she stayed near the door.

"Jeffrey, there's an emergency call for you," she said.

He looked up only for a second. "It can't wait?"

"He said no."

Tom assumed it was the call he had put through to China about Ming's operation. "Put it on the speaker, please."

Suddenly, the quiet of the operating room was broken by a voice booming out of the speakers. "Dr. Candor?"

Jeffrey continued suturing. "Yes, this is Jeffrey Candor."

"This is Dr. Wilson at United Hospital. Your wife has been in a car accident and is in critical condition. She's on life support. It would be best if you could come immediately."

Jeffrey's heart began to race and nausea came over him. He shook his head to clear his thoughts and glanced up at the clock, trying to calculate the minutes. "I'll be there in less than an hour."

Jeffrey knew better than to look at his two technicians, to see the alarm in their eyes, or worse, to allow them to see the alarm in his. Then everything began to move in slow motion; each suture seemed to take an eternity to knot. Jeffrey's eyes blurred and he felt sweat beading on his forehead. He couldn't help but look at the clock again.

Thirty agonizing minutes later, the final suture was tied and sterile bandages were taped over the incision. Jeffrey quickly removed his mask.

"We need to give her some antibiotics, but you can start waking her up," Jeffrey said as he crossed the room and reached into the drug cabinet. He grabbed a vial of clear liquid from the shelf and a syringe from the drawer. The simple act of loading a syringe, something he had done thousands of times before, served to calm his shaken nerves. Returning to the operating table, he quickly injected Ming and, without thinking, put the empty vial into his scrub pants pocket.

Jeffrey headed for the door. "You can reach me on my cell phone," he said.

"Let us know how Laura is," his vet tech said.

Jeffrey didn't take the time to change out of his bloodied operating garb. Storming through his office, he grabbed only his car keys, forgetting both his wallet and cell phone. Once outside, he immediately noticed that much of the ice had melted, and within minutes he was traveling eighty miles an hour down the freeway. An overpowering blend of fear and regret washed over him as his thoughts darted from one memory to the next. He and Laura had been so distant during the last six months, but he still loved her. Perhaps there was a chance for them . . . if she survived.

Arriving at the emergency room forty minutes later, he looked frantically for help, for someone who could tell him where his wife was.

"Dr. Candor?" asked a nurse in a white lab coat.

"Yes. How is my wife?"

"We have her stabilized," the nurse explained. "Her hip is fractured in multiple places. The surgeon requested an MRI after seeing the X-rays."

"When will they operate?"

"She'll be taken into the OR directly from imaging. But I need to tell you . . ." The nurse paused. "I'm sorry. She lost the child."

Jeffrey's eyes blurred. "What child?"

"Your wife was about ten weeks pregnant."

Jeffrey hunched over, as if someone had struck him in the stomach. "I didn't know."

"There's a doctor's conference room at the end of the hall. Why don't you wait there? The surgeon will be down as soon as possible."

"Thank you," Jeffrey said, nodding weakly.

In the empty lounge he sank into a chair and rubbed his eyes. It's true that time passes at different speeds, Tom thought. It slows down so we can remember each excruciating detail of horrendous events in our lives: the color of the walls, the coffee stain in the carpet, the noise of the water fountain, the betrayal of a wife.

Jeffrey wondered who Laura had turned to for the intimacy that had been missing from their relationship for quite some time. Who had made love to her and how would Laura look into that man's eyes and tell him that she had lost their child, a child conceived in an illicit affair?

Oddly, among all of the emotions that surged through Jeffrey, jealousy was not one of them. Nor was anger. What he felt was far worse: a dispassionate resignation, and chilled indifference that his marriage was over. At that moment, with this knowledge of his wife's unfaithfulness, all feelings he had for her were abruptly and permanently deadened.

He dug his left hand deep into his pocket and began playing absently with the small glass vial that had contained the antibiotics for the panda. Realizing what was in his hand, Jeffrey walked over to the trash can marked "Medical and Hazardous Waste." Just as he was about to throw the vial away, something on the label caught his eye: a small red line across the top of the text. He was confused; the label on the antibiotics vial had a green background, but this one was bright red—the color of warning. He read the label carefully: "Potassium Chloride." And then he realized that he had done something that every veterinarian has done at least once: he had grabbed the wrong vial. The tragedy was that this one time, with that extraordinary panda, he hadn't caught his error before injecting the drug into the animal.

In that instant, he knew Ming was dead. "Oh, God," he moaned, "what have I done?"

TWO

Christian

Present Day

Just south of the small town of Lumby, in the richly scented kitchen of Montis Inn, Pam Walker wiped her forehead and retied her apron strings, then tucked the end of a kitchen towel at her right hip. Mark, her husband, was bent over the larger of two stainless-steel farm sinks with one of his arms elbow-deep in water. For most of the evening, he had been trying unsuccessfully to repair the garbage disposal.

"What in the world did you put down this thing?" Mark asked, feeling blindly around the disposal blades.

"Nothing. Just scraps from lunch," Pam said.

With one arm still in the sink, Mark tried to reach for a screwdriver on the counter. The stronger he pulled away from the drain, the tighter the pressure seemed to increase around his wet wrist. "Honey, I think my hand is stuck."

Expecting another of her husband's ill-timed jokes, Pam didn't even look up from the stove, where she was busy cooking. "Stop horsing around, Mark. The dining room is still half full of hungry guests."

"No, seriously," he said, with enough panic in his voice to catch his wife's attention.

Pam looked at Mark trying to free himself from the sink and started to laugh. "You're kidding."

"Don't turn on the disposal!" he implored.

Pam walked over to their commercial refrigerator and searched for the lard.

"Here," she said, opening the small plastic bucket and scooping a cupful of grease into his palm. "Rub it on your other hand."

Mark did as instructed, and seconds later, his hand popped free, splashing water across the floor. He noticed Pam's reaction, and thought it best to head right for the mop closet.

"Don't worry," he said. "I'll wipe it up. It could have been worse—I could have lost an arm in there."

"Since you didn't, why don't you wash up and bring the desserts to table four? I still have one more entrée to go."

It was a night like most others at Montis Inn: controlled chaos among the understaffed and overextended.

Pam was so occupied with preparing the last dinner plate that she didn't notice Mark's return. He went over to the linen closet, which also served as the "wine cellar" for their small collection of grand cru wines, and pulled a bottle from the bottom row.

Returning to the kitchen door, Mark nudged it open with his toe while he uncorked the bottle, and peered out at the gentleman who was seated by himself at the table closest to the fireplace.

First and foremost, the man was distinguished-looking. Although small in stature and quite lean, he had a relaxed confidence about him. Most people who dined alone either kept their eyes glued to their plates or looked nervously around the room. In comparison, this man smiled after completing his appetizer of parsleyed escargot in simmered brandy. "Delicious," he said aloud, and then leaned back, crossing his legs and opening the newspaper.

His short gray hair and closely trimmed beard framed the intense blue eyes that Mark had first noticed when greeting him that evening. Before beginning to read, the man pulled a pair of silver-and-tortoiseshell glasses from the breast pocket of his crisply pressed striped shirt.

"You don't know who he is?" Mark asked Pam.

She wiped her hands on the kitchen towel. "Who?"

"The guest eating alone," Mark said. "He asked for a bottle of nineteen eighty-two Lafite."

Pam looked up in surprise. "Well, he certainly knows his wines—there's not much better than that," she said, beginning to stir the raspberry sauce that would be drizzled over the seared duck–and-vegetable confit. "Did you tell him we don't have that vintage?"

Mark let the door swing closed and walked over to the island. Carefully he popped the cork. "Indirectly. I suggested the nineteen eighty-two Château Palmer would better complement his dinner. That's the best bottle we have."

Pam felt a tinge of regret. "I thought we were saving that for our anniversary."

"Honey, it was on the wine list," he explained. "Sorry."

Pam pulled a hot serving platter from the range. "Do you really think it will go well with the duck?"

Mark shrugged as he removed a decanter from the shelf. "I have no idea. I've never tasted anything that cost this much." After pouring the wine into the crystal carafe, he sneaked another look into the dining room. "He looks familiar. Are you sure you don't remember his name?"

"I think his first name is Christian, but I'm not sure," she said as she began preparing the plate. "Two parties checked in at the same time, so I didn't have an opportunity to speak with him."

Across the dining room, a couple folded their napkins and pushed their chairs away from the table. "The Reynoldses are leaving," Mark reported.

"Would you clear their table after you serve the wine, please?"

Mark smelled the decanter. “I hope it’s not bad.”

“The meal or the wine?” Pam asked glibly.

“Your cooking is always outstanding. I’ve never seen anyone put more time and effort into a menu.”

“My problem exactly,” she said under her breath.

But Mark was already out the door. “Remember the bread!” she called out as loud as she dared, but he didn’t hear.

Pam took a deep breath and rubbed her neck, rolling her head from side to side as she exhaled. For three years she had been cooking breakfasts and dinners for the inn’s guests, and trying to keep up with her growing restaurant clientele, but each meal seemed progressively harder to put together.

“We need a change,” she said aloud, although no one was there to agree.

A minute later Mark came back through the swing doors, balancing a stack of plates on his right arm. Seeing the peril of Mark walking across the floor, which was still slick from the water and grease, Pam rushed over and grabbed the plates just as his feet went out from under him.

“Wow!” he yelled, grabbing the island countertop to halt his fall.

Pam shook her head. “Maybe you can mop up before it kills one of us. I’ll serve the entrée,” she advised before leaving the kitchen with the hot plate.

Entering the dining room gave Pam the sense of being magically transported from the heat and pandemonium of the kitchen to a quiet, inviting refuge where classical music played softly in the background. The Montis Inn restaurant was a spectacular example of relaxed elegance. From the hand-carved tables to the comfortable upholstered chairs, it was a room in which visitors wanted to stay and converse long after the meal was finished.

“Seared duck with raspberry sauce?” she said graciously, placing the plate in front of the last diner of the evening.

He leaned closer to the plate, appreciating the complex aromas. “It smells marvelous,” he said, looking up at her.

"A Montis Inn special," she said proudly.

Noticing that the other guests had left, the man looked at his watch. "I didn't realize how late it is. I'm sorry if I've kept you and your staff later than usual."

Pam smiled. "My staff is my husband," she said, refilling his glass. "And we normally don't leave the kitchen until midnight, so you have several hours to enjoy your wine."

"An outstanding selection," he commented. "It's a shame I can only drink two glasses. Why don't you and your husband join me?"

Pam was surprised by his invitation. Although their guests frequently asked her and Mark to sit and talk, such requests were mostly made only after the guest had been at the inn for several days and they had all become acquainted. It was Pam's practice to decline, not wanting to blur the line between host and guest.

But tonight was different; at some point during the past several hours, she had reached the limit of her tolerance for being the cook of Montis Inn. The thought of literally and figuratively throwing in the towel, if only for the rest of that evening, had never been more appealing.

Pam dropped her shoulders and sighed. "That would be delightful," she admitted. "Let me get Mark."

"And two more glasses," her guest reminded her.

Back in the kitchen, Pam quickly put together a plate of fresh baguettes and various cheeses from farms as close as Lumby and as distant as Italy.

When Mark and Pam joined their guest, he stood and extended his hand. "I'm Christian Copeland. I'm delighted to be here."

"Please sit and enjoy your dinner," Pam said, placing the cheese platter on the table.

Christian cordially pulled out her chair while Mark filled their glasses.

"Cheers," Mark said, lifting his glass. "This really is unexpected. I've always wanted to try this wine. Thank you."

Pam smiled at Mark. He was always charming with the guests.

And he still had the same rugged handsomeness that had first attracted her almost twenty-five years ago. There was more gray speckled throughout his thick brown hair, and several more laugh lines around his brown eyes, but overall the happiness they had found individually and as a couple at Montis was reflected in both of their faces.

"A perfect pairing for the meal," Christian said, tilting his glass sideways and turning it gently. "Very nice legs."

"Where?" Mark asked.

Christian laughed as he leaned forward to bring his glass closer to Mark. "The coating that clings to the glass as you turn it. Do you see those long streaks, the rivulets? Those are called legs," he explained.

Unlike the many wine connoisseurs who had dined at Montis Inn, there was no condescension in Christian's voice, just an open, easy warmth from a desire to share what he knew.

"The more rivulets, the higher the alcohol concentration. Occasionally, there's a relationship between legs and the quality of the wine, but I have seen quite notable legs from a mediocre vintage." He then righted his stemware and swirled the wine with an almost imperceptible movement of his hand. "This increases the surface area and oxygen—for the same reason you decanted the bottle. It releases more aroma and improves the taste." He took another sip. "Wonderful."

Mark's eyes suddenly widened. He pointed his finger at the man. "That's who you are!"

"Mark!" Pam couldn't believe he had been so rude.

He turned to his wife. "Do you know who this is?"

"Yes, Christian Copeland. He just introduced himself."

"Pam," Mark said, rolling his eyes, "this is *the* Christian Copeland."

Pam shrugged her shoulders in ignorance. "I'm sorry," she apologized to her guest.

"Copeland Vineyards," Mark hinted, "as in those four cases of merlot we have in our kitchen."

Christian nodded and smiled. "I'm glad you feel my wine complements your exceptional cuisine."

Pam blushed. "We're honored you're here," she said, stumbling over her own words.

"I assure you, the honor is all mine," Christian said. "I seldom have the opportunity to stay at such a beautiful inn unless I'm working."

"I've read some of your restaurant reviews in your magazine, *Vintner's Fare*. We have a subscription," Mark said.

"So, you're not here to write a review?" Pam asked.

"Correct," Christian said, taking another bite of duck. "This is just delicious." He paused for a moment, wiping the corners of his mouth with his napkin. "I'm in the area to look at land for some friends of mine who might want to start a vineyard up here."

Pam put down her glass. "In Lumby?"

Christian hesitated. "Not in the immediate area. They're still evaluating the feasibility, so I offered to come over and take a look at the soil."

"I would think it's too cold up here," Mark said.

"Not really," Christian said. "There are some excellent wines out of Canada from vines grown in harsher climates than this one."

"If you have any questions during your stay, please let us know," Pam offered.

Christian paused and put down his glass. "I'm curious about one thing. Why is there a plastic pink flamingo in front of your inn and why is he wearing shoulder pads and a football jersey?"

Pam and Mark laughed.

"That's Hank," Mark began. "He's Lumby's . . ."

"Mascot, in a way," Pam explained. "He's been one of our most esteemed town residents ever since he came from Amazon."

Christian raised his brows. "South America?"

"Oh, no, that would be too far for Hank to travel," Mark said. "He was accidentally shipped to Jimmy D's son from Amazon, the online bookstore."

Christian nodded, intently following the story.

"Hank's involved with most aspects of our town," Pam said. "In fact, he was directly responsible for petitioning the town council to plant several rows of aspen trees around the landfill."

"Oh, right, I had forgotten that," Mark said. "And he also made a substantial donation of Audubon books to the library. We assume he'll run for mayor next year, but I'm not sure I'll vote for him."

Christian stared at his hosts in disbelief. "But he's a plastic pink flamingo!"

"Well, not really," Pam said, politely correcting their guest. "He's Hank."

Christian leaned forward as if to keep his next question private. "So why the football garb?"

"Oh, that's easy," Mark answered, waving his hand. "The high school football team had a pep rally across the street last night and Hank drank too much soda to fly home."

Christian thought about that for a moment. "Oh. And why does he stay in Lumby?"

"I think he likes the remoteness and the mountains—he wants to be an eagle," Mark answered.

Pam added, "He's here a lot, so I think he likes the anonymity of our inn."

Christian smiled. "I'm certain any anonymity you've had in the past will vanish the minute your charming inn is introduced to the world."

Pam laughed at such an improbable thought. "We're so far off the beaten track, I'm sure that's one turn of events that we, and Hank, will never see at Montis."

THREE

Crates

Brother Michael had seldom seen such masses of travelers as those who were pushing their way through the baggage-claim area at Seattle–Tacoma Airport, grabbing suitcases, finding lost companions and calming hysterical children. The noise was deafening and the unruly suitcases slamming into his legs were equally painful. After standing in the chaos for two hours, Michael was exhausted from the assault on all his senses.

The younger monk looked helplessly at Brother Matthew, who was sitting quietly in the corner of the room, away from the maddening crowd. Matthew smiled and raised both hands, gesturing for Michael to lift his sign higher.

Brother Michael nodded and walked closer to the conveyor belt. Before raising the cardboard above his head, he reread the block print, which he had carefully drawn that morning, struggling with its correct pronunciation: Shou Macaque and Mei Macaque. When their Japanese visitors finally arrived, Michael wanted to welcome them by name.

Matthew watched for a minute, but realizing there was little help he could offer, he returned his attention to the newspaper that he had brought in anticipation of a long wait.

The Lumby Lines

What's News Around Town

BY SCOTT STEVENS October 6

A slow week in our sleepy town of Lumby.

Yesterday, the sheriff's department reported a rare occurrence of vandalism in Lumby: someone dismantled the three "No Parking" signs in town, leaving only metal posts. The perpetrator is assumed to have also been responsible for sawing off fourteen parking meters in Wheatley. Hours before this paper went to press, the undercover investigation of this reporter revealed that both acts were carried out by a new Department of Transportation employee who misunderstood his work directives. DOT says that it will be replacing the signs next week, and for anyone interested, job application forms are available at the post office.

The last Farmers' Market of the season will be held on November 9 to coincide with Lumby's annual pumpkin festival. This year's activities will include: pie baking, pumpkin decorations, family floats, the pumpkin diaper derby and, of course, the weigh-in for the biggest pumpkin (a minimum weight of 600 lbs. is required to enter). Also, and hold on to your seats, Mary Edwards will relinquish her crown to the newly elected Turnip and Pumpkin Princess at the end of the day.

The public phone booth on the corner of Main and Hunts Mill Road has recently been redecorated as a confessional by one of our more religious, if not industrious, residents. The booth is now draped on all sides with what appears to be dark red upholstery fabric, and a hole has been cut out of the phone booth's Plexiglas to accommodate a sliding lattice through which one talks. An ornate iron crucifx is hung over the grille and a wooden kneeler has replaced the metal seat.

Brother Matthew laughed gently and glanced up just as Brother Michael was enveloped by another planeload of passengers pushing their way into the baggage area. Matthew marveled at the diversity of people. How very small and far away their town of Franklin seemed right then.

Suddenly, three large blasts sounded over the intercom and one of the four conveyor belts started circulating luggage. Brother Michael walked into the crowd, holding up the sign. Some travelers cordially shook their heads, while most just looked away. Within a few minutes, the baggage-claim area was once again empty, leaving the two monks in silence.

Brother Michael walked up to Matthew. "Do you think we missed them?" he asked.

Matthew reached under his robe and withdrew a cell phone from his shirt pocket. "Perhaps they didn't make the flight. They should have been here an hour ago, even if they got held up in customs," he said, as he dialed the number for Saint Cross Abbey.

Brother Michael collapsed into the chair next to him.

Matthew spoke into the phone. "Do you know if they got on the plane? We're at the baggage claim now." He paused. "Why would they be in the cargo building? Ah . . . We'll head over there now. Thank you, John." Matthew turned off his phone. "They were on the flight, but it appears there was a problem with immigration, so our guests were brought over to the importation bay at the airline's cargo building."

"Is that far?" Michael asked.

"Brother John thinks it's about half a mile away," Matthew said as they headed for the exit and their van.

Although John was correct about the distance between the main terminal and the freight building, it took the monks fifteen minutes to drive down the thoroughfares and access roads around the airport.

"This is a nightmare," Michael said, while they sat in traffic. "I feel so sorry for them. They must be exhausted after such a long flight." He stared out at the stream of red brake lights. "What a fiasco."

Matthew looked over at his unnerved colleague. "You don't like traveling, do you?"

The deafening roar of an aircraft directly overhead delayed the brother's response. "Not when it involves airports and traffic jams and masses of people."

"Then why did you volunteer to go to New York City and represent Saint Cross Abbey at the Culinary Expo?" he asked.

"I knew that a trip like that would take too much of a toll on Brother John, and it was either him or me . . . and, of course, you're already overburdened with the monastery's other businesses."

The business and financial complexities of Saint Cross Abbey had, indeed, grown substantially during the past four years. Back then, just weeks away from declaring bankruptcy, the monks were blessed with a turn of fortune when Pam Walker lent them a much-needed hand. She defined a business and captured a market that would forever be linked to the brothers: Saint Cross Rum Sauce. From that starting point, the number of products they offered doubled and then doubled again, and before long, Saint Cross was a brand label being sold from coast to coast.

Around that same time, their business wealth took another unexpected leap when a kind benefactor by the name of Charlotte Ross willed the monastery a small company, National Gourmet Products, which she had quietly acquired after NGP's unsuccessful takeover of the rum sauce business.

Applying long hours, a strong work ethic and smart management to their enterprises, the monks continued to grow both the Saint Cross Sauce Company and National Gourmet Products until they produced more income than the monastery needed. After all debts were paid, the monks quickly channeled the remaining revenues into the Saint Cross Foundation, a philanthropic organization founded to offer assistance to those in need around the world. It was because of a Foundation donation that Brothers Matthew and Michael were weaving their way down the ramps and roadways at the airport that day.

Matthew pointed to his left. "I think that's where we want to be, and there's an access road over there," he said, putting on the van's turn blinker.

Confident that they knew where they were going, Michael placed the map on the backseat. "Does it seem odd to you that two missionaries were sent over so unexpectedly?" he asked.

"A little, I suppose. Since our foundation endowed their orphanages in Honshū, perhaps they want to build a stronger relationship with our community."

"And the two who we are picking up, Shou and Mei, are they monastics?"

"I really don't know anything about our Japanese visitors," Matthew admitted. "Their letter was written in such broken English it was almost indecipherable. In truth, I'm surprised that with all our translation problems, we're actually at the right airport on the right day to greet them."

"Do you know how long they'll be staying with us?"

Matthew shook his head. "They used the words *yǒng jiŭ* several times, which, I am told, means 'forever' or 'permanent,' but I think they were talking about our friendship and not the length of stay."

Matthew turned into the cargo parking area and pulled up next to a FedEx truck. The two walked quickly toward the freight office.

"Boy, I'll never complain about flying coach again," Michael said under his breath.

Walking inside, the monks immediately noticed two Asians in an adjoining waiting room. Both men sat motionless with their eyes closed. They looked quite old and, understandably, weary.

Brother Michael bent slightly as he approached them. They were very small, almost the size of children. "Mr. Mei?" Michael asked softly.

One of the foreigners opened his eyes and seemed startled to see a man in a robe standing so close to him. He shook the arm of his companion and then began speaking in a dialect that was so fast and so foreign, neither Michael nor Matthew heard one familiar word.

Brother Michael bowed lower. "Mr. Shou?"

The two men continued to converse between themselves, their voices becoming more agitated.

"Perhaps use their last names?" Matthew suggested.

"Macaque?" Michael asked.

One of the men jumped up, forcing Michael to step back. He began yelling at Michael and then gently popped Michael on the head with his small hand.

Michael turned to Matthew in dismay. "What did I say?" he asked, trying to back away from the man.

The tirade lasted for close to a minute and stopped only when an airline employee called out from behind the desk, "Brother Matthew?"

"Yes, I'm Brother Matthew."

"The monastery rang us and said you were on your way. Your cargo is over there." She pointed to what appeared to be two enormous dog crates stored in the corner of the cargo bay. "And that one as well," she added, gesturing toward another box, larger than the crates, marked "FEED."

Matthew stood speechless in the middle of the room.

Michael's thoughts were spinning, his eyes the size of saucers. "They put their monks in crates?" he whispered.

Matthew shook his head. "This can't be," he said, walking over to the carriers. He peered inside but saw nothing—the inside was almost pitch-black. A large sign was taped to the top of each crate: **"WARNING! LIVE ANIMALS!"**

Matthew looked over to the desk. "I think there has been a misunderstanding," he said slowly. "We are supposed to be picking up two visitors from Japan."

The woman flipped through a stack of papers and skimmed the top page for a second time. "Are you Brother Matthew from Saint Cross Abbey?"

"Yes," he answered.

She turned some of the pages that were stapled together and then looked at the crates. "No mistake. In fact, it appears from all of these documents that the Japanese government went beyond our requirements to ensure they were safely imported."

"They, who?" Michael asked.

She looked at them in surprise. "The snow monkeys."

The two monks glanced at each other before returning their stares to the crates. Just then, one of the animals moved to the front of the crate to look out. His pink face was surrounded by gray and brown hair. The expression in his large eyes looked almost human.

"Help me," Matthew said as he pushed one of the crates toward the door, where there was more light. Bending down, he looked in and saw a small creature cowering in the back corner.

"It's a monkey," he said in amazement.

Michael looked at the declaration, which had been stuffed in a clear plastic pouch attached to the crate's handle. "Actually, it's Mei Macaque," Michael said.

Matthew continued to stare at the small animal. "My word," he said softly.

"I'm so embarrassed," Michael said in dread.

"Why?"

Michael looked over at the Asians, who had already fallen back to sleep. "I just called those two men over there monkeys. No wonder they got so upset with me."

"An honest mistake," Matthew said, standing up, "as was mine when I thought we were picking up two missionaries."

Michael continued to watch the foreigners from the corner of his eyes. "What do we do now?"

Matthew raised his brow, as was his tendency when trying to think through a problem. "Quite an unexpected surprise." He chuckled. "I don't know what to say."

"Can we keep them at the monastery?" Brother Michael asked with youthful enthusiasm.

"Probably not," Matthew replied. "But I think it's best we begin our drive back to Saint Cross this afternoon and go directly to the veterinarian in Lumby. Dr. Campbell can examine them and, I hope, keep them in her clinic for a few days until we can determine what's best for our new friends."

FOUR

Stalls

In autumn, when the northwest winds bring cold, dry air down from Canada, the evening skies over Lumby become amazingly clear. For several nights each month, the full moon illuminates the mountains and rolling valleys with a haunting lambency. On such nights, in fall's gloaming, one is given a rare view of the region's spectacular beauty.

The steep walls of the Rocky Mountains rise to the west, well beyond the gentle and evergreened foothills that border the valley's twelve square miles of rolling pastures, agricultural fields and grasslands. At night, the jagged cliffs appear ominous, while the dark, verdant hills look more inviting, with moonlit waterfalls cascading into swollen silver streams.

On the south side of Mill Valley, named for the hundred-year-old bright red water mill rising from the banks of Goose Creek, sits Woodrow Lake. The calm waters of the seventeen-mile expanse reflect the stars' gleam and make the light dance on the surface, breaking into shimmering fragments at the inlet of the Fork River.

From the second floor of Montis Inn, Pam Walker gazed down toward the lake, her eyes following the taillights of a lone car that hugged the shoreline traveling south on Farm to Market Road. In the far distance she could see the amber glow of the small city of Wheatley.

"I'm glad you chose this room for your office," she said to her husband.

"Yeah, it's great," Mark replied, not looking up from his computer screen. "Did you want something, honey?"

"Do you have today's paper?" she asked, glancing around the room.

Mark pointed behind him. "On the chair."

"We received a gift from Christian Copeland this afternoon—two cases of his vineyard's 1991 Reserve. It came with a very nice note," Pam said. "I thought I'd send him a thank-you card along with a copy of *The Lumby Lines*. He was so charmed by it during his visit."

"That's nice."

The Lumby Lines

Sheriff's Complaints

BY SHERIFF SIMON DIXON October 3

5:04 a.m. Deer vs. Ford F150 on State Road 541 one mile east of Priest's Pass. Guardrail totaled but no injuries.

7:11 a.m. Jogger reported an excavator owned by NW Builders was stalled and blocking traffic at intersection of Main and Loggers Road.

8:21 a.m. Woman at Bookstore reported that Hank and mannequin from Lumby Sporting Goods are loitering by the front door.

8:24 a.m. McNear reported that someone defaced his prize pumpkin.

9:32 a.m. High School reported full power outage. Students dismissed early.

10:07 a.m. Resident at 91 Loggers Road reported several windows on south side of house just shattered. No one injured.

10:07 a.m. Resident at 88 Loggers Road reported explosion next door. All windows in house broken.

10:08 a.m. Owner of NW Builders reported accidental overuse of dynamite at demolition site at 90 Loggers Road. Requesting police protection from angry neighbors.

11:41 a.m. Man reported goat stampede on Windlock Trail by Katie Banks's farm. Call put in to Katie to let her know they're out again.

1:59 p.m. LFD reported power restored at High School.

2:17 p.m. Lumby Septic requested EMS assistance to extricate employee from tank in Jimmy D's backyard.

3:52 p.m. Wilson girls reported that while on break, elk walked up to hot apple cider stand and drank the pot dry. Elk has since left premises.

4:21 p.m. Cindy Watford reported flock of "something like a thousand" homing pigeons landed on car that is not hers.

5:22 p.m. Young Timmy Beezer reported finding prehistoric dinosaur bone in Cooper's cow field.

5:23 p.m. Resident reported shooting horse in rear after mistaking it for large coyote. Dr. Campbell summoned.

7:18 p.m. Man reported tree house on fire from barbecue mishap.

Still leaning against the window casement, Pam looked across Farm to Market Road. Within the past month, she and Mark had finished building a large arena located directly behind the smaller barn. Both were well positioned on the land they had acquired after renovating the old monastery, situated halfway between the orchard and Woodrow Lake.

Construction had been a trying four-month effort due to the size and complexity of the structure: a two-story barn, two hundred feet long by one hundred twenty feet wide, with a raised monitor roof running along the length of the ridge. The monitor resembled a two-hundred-foot-long cupola, seven feet high with twenty-eight windows on each side, which allowed natural light to flood the arena.

By the time the last nail was hammered, the arena had twenty-six twelve-by-twelve box stalls and, at the far end, another seven fourteen-by-fourteen stalls. The center arena was large enough for both equestrian dressage and jumping competition. "Pity neither you nor I know how to ride," Pam had commented to Mark when she saw the finished barn. Her next query followed suit: "So, what exactly are you going to do with all this space?" A month later, Mark had not yet answered that question, other than introducing the idea of buying another draft horse.

Although the large barn was dark both inside and out that night, exterior floodlights from the small barn lit enough of the area for Pam to see the outline of the new building.

"When will the lights be working in the new barn?" she asked.

"In the next couple of days," he replied absently, still studying his computer screen.

"Why don't you have Mac do it? She'll be here tomorrow morning."

Mark looked up. "Why is Mac coming?"

"Before I can hire a chef, we need to take care of that," she said, pointing directly upward. "If we finish off the third floor, we can reduce the salary we pay by offering room and board."

"You really want to do that?"

"Hire a chef or convert the third floor into a chef's apartment?"

Mark raised one shoulder. "Both, I guess."

"If we're really going to make a go at having a five-star restaurant here, I can't do it alone." Her voice cracked. "I keep trying harder and harder, but it's too much for me to manage."

Mark thought about what Pam had said. Although they had talked about the possibility of hiring someone to manage the kitchen, perhaps he had underestimated her urgency. "Honey, if that's what's best for you, then you should do it."

Pam immediately felt relieved. "Thank you."

Mark returned his focus to the computer screen and his eyes widened. "This is amazing. Do you know you can buy a bobsled team on eBay?"

Pam raised her eyebrow, wondering what her husband was up to. "Why would anyone want to do that?"

"I don't know, but they have one for sale for, like, three million dollars. And there's an uneaten pancake that was served to Pope John Paul." He paused as he read in silence. "Honey, how about this for our courtyard: a life-sized statue of Michelangelo's *David* made of Jell-O?"

"That's disgusting," she said.

Mark winced. "Not as gross as a thirty-nine-inch toenail."

"What in the world are you doing?"

Mark pushed his chair away from the desk. "Shopping around for some winter items we need: those covers we put on the outside hose faucets so they don't freeze—that sort of thing. Maybe even a Christmas present or two."

"Nothing made of Jell-O, I hope." She laughed and drew back the curtain a little farther. Pam looked out over their orchard and saw that the back fields were clearly visible in the moonlight. The dozen tall white beehives, which were usually concealed by summer's heavy foliage, looked almost iridescent.

"Wow," she whispered. "Now that all the leaves are down and the trees are bare, you can even see the beehives. Do you think the bees are more active during a full moon?"

Mark glanced up at his wife. She looked stunning standing by the window with the moonlight shining down on her. Beautiful signs of maturity were coming through—some gray hairs among the blond, and more laugh lines around her blue eyes. At forty-eight, she still had a tall, lean athletic body, and was as smart as she was beautiful. He smiled, feeling his good fortune in life. "Not now. It's too cold."

"It is chilly," Pam said, pulling her sweater around her waist. "Why don't you make a fire in the fireplace?"

Mark returned his attention to the computer. "I don't want to burn down the inn."

"What?" Pam asked in alarm.

"When I opened the damper this morning, part of a nest dropped down from the flue. I think a raccoon moved in during the summer. What's that company we use for the chimneys?"

"Ashes to Ashes. I'll call Graham tomorrow," she said, looking at her watch. "It's almost eleven, are you coming to bed soon?"

"Yeah, soon," he said to appease her. "This is incredible." He paused. "I just found the government-surplus Web site."

Pam walked over and put her arms around her husband's shoulders, kissing him on the back of the neck. "You're like a squirrel hoarding for winter. No army fatigues, promise?"

"Not to worry," Mark said, brushing off the idea. "You would have to be nuts to buy two hundred pairs of camouflage pants."

"Come to bed soon," she said as she put on her jacket.

She walked outside to the front porch, where the brisk air caught her by surprise. Pam pulled her collar up tightly around her neck. Instead of returning to the residence, though, she crossed the road and began to walk up into the orchard. She knew the grounds of Montis as if she had lived there all her life. Spread before her were ten well-maintained acres on the east side of Farm to Market Road, where seven buildings stood, and another twenty acres of orchard directly across the street. The additional land they had acquired two years ago lay below the orchard and above Woodrow Lake. Surrounding their property on three sides was dense forest that the monks had used for hunting a century before, when Montis was a simple abbey.

Crossing the road and walking partway up the hill, Pam turned and looked down at the inn. Gentle floodlights beamed upward, lighting the one-hundred-year-old stone facade of the community house. They had bought Montis four years before. During the first summer, she and Mark had lovingly restored the original chapel into what became the main building of their country inn. A short distance behind that stood the old monks' sleeping quarters and private annex, which Pam and Mark had converted into a series of guest suites. The other significant restoration was in the large building at the back of the compound, which stayed as the dining room and grand kitchen. Two smaller buildings, the library and their private residence, completed the complex that they now called home.

From the field, Pam could see the lit paths traversing the courtyard. Lights remained on in the guest quarters, where several couples were staying. Smoke rose from the chimney at Taproot, which they had named their small house.

Pam knelt on the cold ground and blew warm air into her cupped hands. During rare private moments such as these, she would reflect back on her prior life, or "Phase 1" as she and Mark had come to call it, the fifteen-year period when she had sacrificed almost all she had for a large consulting firm in Baltimore. Those were her corporate years, when she had no choice but to dig deep every day to stay one step ahead of brilliant colleagues and aggressive competitors.

In retrospect, though, as grueling as it was, that tenure was also an extraordinary opportunity to be her best on an international playing field. Before becoming a partner in the firm, she had seen the world outside her own country as a vague abstraction. Then, as she began to travel, first to Europe and South America and then extensively throughout Asia, each country became unique and better understood. In one six-month period, she had traveled the entire Pacific Rim.

Pam laughed to think that after all those miles, she and Mark had found themselves in the small, sequestered town of Lumby. Life took unexpected turns, indeed.

She heard voices coming from the inn's courtyard. Two guests who had checked in the day before were walking from the library to the guest annex, holding hands and laughing. Pam smiled. It pleased her to share Montis with others, to help create wonderful memories that their guests would cherish in years to come.

A strong breeze blew over the valley, cold enough to force Pam to return to Taproot. Walking back into the residence that she and Mark had shared from the beginning, she marveled at the good fortune in their lives. Although it was their original intent to live in Taproot only during the restoration of the larger buildings, they had come to love the rustic abode. The front door opened to a large room the Walkers had turned into a living room and spacious kitchen with a wood-burning stove and a large oak table. It was, Pam thought, the most comfortable room in Montis Inn.

Once inside, Pam closed the damper of the wood-burning stove and turned off all but one living room light. It was midnight and she headed to bed, knowing that she would need to be in the main kitchen by seven to prepare breakfast for their guests.

FIVE

S-4081

When Pam woke the next morning, it was obvious that Mark had not come to bed the night before. And although it was unusual for him to be absent while she prepared the morning meal, Pam assumed that he had lost track of time and fallen asleep on the bed in his office. Had she known that he was still on his computer, actively engaged in a high-stakes auction, she would have been deeply concerned.

Instead, she single-handedly prepared a breakfast in a style for which the historic hotel had become famous. On that specific morning, the guests of Montis Inn were treated to an impressive assortment of coffees and teas served with fresh fruit compote, followed by poached eggs and baked cinnamon French toast filled with spiced apples. Plates of thickly sliced Canadian bacon and homemade coffee cake were also placed on each table. There was a good reason for their restaurant's outstanding reputation among the small number of people who knew about it.

A tap sounded on the kitchen door.

"Come in," Pam said, assuming it was the last of her guests wanting to make dinner reservations.

Mackenzie McGuire walked in, her unruly red hair stuffed under a cap with loose strands falling around her face.

"Mac!" Pam said in delight, and quickly looked at her watch. "Come in, come in." She waved to her friend.

"I'm running early this morning, but I can come back later if it's more convenient," Mac said.

Pam dried her hands on a towel tucked under her belt. "Not at all," she insisted. "Sit down."

Mackenzie was one of the first Lumby residents the Walkers had met after buying Montis Abbey. Mac came highly recommended as the town's finest carpenter and general contractor, so Pam and Mark had hired her to lead the monastery's restoration. From that first day, there had been an instant rapport among all of them, and over the years, Mac had become their good friend.

At forty-two, Mackenzie was a very attractive woman, although both she and Pam freely used the expression "a diamond in the rough" to describe her. In deference to her job, which kept her fit regardless of what she ate, Mac wore baggy carpenter overalls on a daily basis. And to control her naturally curly hair, she frequently donned a baseball cap. Most of the time, either the brim of her cap or her ill-mannered hair cast her freckled face in shadow, but her eyes attracted the opposite sex; they were as pale blue as her hair was red.

"This kitchen always smells so amazing," Mac said, pulling up a stool to the island.

Pam grimaced. "Thanks. I haven't seen you in weeks. How is everything?"

"Other than my son coming of age, life's good."

Pam turned from the stove, where she was preparing a country stew for that evening. "What's wrong with Terry?"

"Nothing really," Mac said, pushing a loose strand of hair back under the cap. "He just seems to be partying too much with way too many girlfriends."

Pam raised her brows. "Girl*friends,* as in more than one?"

Mac nodded. "More than several, from what I can determine. Between the girls who call him until all hours of the night, and the young ladies he brings home after the movies, I can't keep track."

"Sounds like your ex-husband when he was young," Pam suggested carefully.

"In this one area, Terry's behaving exactly like his father," Mac agreed. "And that's what concerns me. Terry never had a strong male role model and he may have some wrong ideas about women. I've overheard a few of his conversations and I'm disappointed that he's so thoughtless and flippant about the girls' emotions."

"Why don't you sit him down and talk with him?"

Mac shook her head and several more wisps of hair shot out from under her cap. "It's not that easy. We have an amicable relationship right now—almost a friendship. Although he's still living at home, he's a legal adult. A while ago, he and I had a huge brawl, and from that moment on, I agreed to let him be," she said with full regret. "He's on his own, and to step in as his disapproving mother and start reprimanding him would just push him away."

Pam shrugged. "Maybe he needs that more than a free roof over his head."

Mac dropped her head. "You're right, but it's easier said than done, especially when I'm working with him on several jobs. He's so mature in so many ways, but he has some really mistaken ideas about relationships. I wish I could be a better role model."

"You're a great role model," Pam argued.

Mac grimaced. "I haven't been on a date in years."

"Not because of you," Pam commiserated. "It's just that Lumby has only a few eligible bachelors."

"A few?" Mac looked at Pam and made a zero sign with her fingers. "Try none."

Pam threw the towel over her shoulder. "Is it really that bad? I suppose I never gave it much thought."

"You're lucky you don't have to. Believe me, I have and it's not too promising out there." Mac paused. "But I do wish I could show Terry that there's much more to a good relationship than a few hours of partying."

"I'm sure he'll grow out of it," Pam said, trying to sound encouraging. She lowered a plate heaped with golden brown French toast in front of Mac. "Until then, this will make you feel better. Two of our guests left for the mountains before breakfast, so there are enough leftovers to feed an army."

Mackenzie eyed the scrumptious offering and laughed. "We need to have more meetings at the crack of dawn."

Pam poured her a cup of coffee and then returned to washing dishes while Mac ate.

"How do you stay so thin with all of your great cooking?" Mac asked as she poured syrup from a warmed pitcher.

Pam brought a finger to her lips as if revealing a secret. "I actually get tired of my own cooking."

"But this is delicious," Mac said. "I hear your restaurant is getting great reviews."

Pam smiled. "Locally, it is. But serving more than our lodging guests is turning out to be a challenging business." She paused before sharing her plan. "I think we're going to hire a chef."

Mackenzie's brows rose. "Wow, I'm surprised. I thought you loved cooking."

"I did," Pam said, and then immediately corrected herself. "I *do,* but this has become a full-time job and nothing else is getting done at the inn. I have no time for the guests, and everything else that needs my attention is being ignored."

Mac wiped her mouth with a napkin. "What about Mark?"

Pam laughed. "I love the man dearly, but believe me, the world is a safer place when he's not in the kitchen."

"But can't he pick up some of the other responsibilities around here?"

Pam nodded. "He does, to some degree. As you know, Mark is a . . ."

"Free, creative spirit?" Mac offered.

"Yes, exactly! So, bookkeeping and handling the details of multiple reservations don't really play to his strengths, if you know what I mean. It's best if Mark stays occupied with all of his special projects around Montis."

"Such as the new barn?"

"Speaking of which, you did a beautiful job building that," Pam said.

Mac beamed. "Thank you. It must be a dream to use."

Pam looked sheepishly at her friend. "It's still empty, except for a few sheep and our horse."

Mac looked flabbergasted. "Empty? But there's enough room for all the animals in the state. I thought Mark wanted some horses and llamas."

"He does. And I'm sure he'll get to it as soon as he comes out of his office," Pam said. "He's been working on the Internet for the last few days."

"Does he know you want to bring in a chef?"

Pam began stacking clean plates from the commercial dishwasher. "He does now. I just put in some chef-wanted ads online and in a dozen newspapers around the state. But I need to do some organizing to make the job more attractive to the applicants. Look at this," Pam said, opening the door of the back closet. Stuffed inside from floor to ceiling were wine bottles. "If a qualified applicant saw that, he would turn around and walk out, and I can't afford to let that happen. The demand for great chefs is so much higher than the supply." She slammed the door in frustration.

"So you want me to build you a wine cellar?" Mac asked.

"Oh, no," Pam said. "Our idea is to have you convert the top floor of the main building into a fully equipped apartment where the chef could live. It would be ideal if we could find a husband and wife who would both like to work at Montis, but either way, the person will need his or her own space and we just can't afford to give up any of the guest rooms—although we're rarely fully occupied, we need all the money the rooms can generate."

"We can take a look at it this morning," Mac said. "But I won't be able to begin the job for another two weeks. Dr. Campbell has asked for some repair work at her vet clinic on Main Street before she gets any serious buyers."

"I heard a rumor that she's going to retire," Pam said, placing a clean pot on the back stove.

"It's no rumor," Mac said. "She already sold her house just outside town, and is actively looking for someone to take over her vet practice. The clinic is great—The Granary is one of the finest buildings in town, and she did a terrific job redesigning the large addition ten years ago."

Suddenly, the kitchen door swung open and Mark ran in, his eyes glinting with pleasure. "Honey! You're never going to believe what just happened!"

Mac started laughing. "Well, good morning to you too," she said.

"Oh, hi, Mac," he said, and then quickly turned back to Pam. "Honey, I won!"

Pam eyed him suspiciously. "Won what?"

"I won the bid—a six-hour auction that started at three this morning. Okay, maybe it was a typo, and it should have been a sixty-hour auction, but it's over with and I won! It was incredible!" He was speaking so fast, Pam had a hard time following his words.

"What did you buy?"

"S-4081," he said. Mark yanked a printout from his pocket and handed it to Pam. "S-4081 from the government auction site," he repeated, making it sound very proprietary.

Pam unfolded the wrinkled paper and read the description. She fumbled for a stool to sit down. "You bought a *motorcycle*?" she asked.

"Well, not just *any* motorcycle," Mark quipped. "It's a World War II 1944 BMW R75 sidecar motorcycle. And it only cost thirteen hundred dollars!"

Pam looked at the photograph and then up at her husband. "But, honey, it has no wheels."

Mark took the paper from her. "Well, that's why I got it at such a great price! You'll see. Next week, you and I will be scooting around Montis on this thing. It'll be great."

Pam gave him a cold stare.

"Oh, and . . . ," Mark said, scrambling to think of a functional purpose for his new toy, "I can fill the sidecar with hay for the animals. I'm sure it will cut the time I spend in the barn by half."

"In that new barn that's sitting practically empty?" Pam challenged.

"Yeah, but that will change really soon."

Pam rolled her eyes. "So you're going to get some animals to justify your motorcycle?"

"Yeah, that's it," Mark said tentatively. "Oh, and I got you an apiary."

Pam frowned. "How can one buy an apiary?" she asked doubtfully. "And why would it be on a government-surplus site?"

"Don't know, but you'll love it," Mark said with a broad smile.

SIX

Bobbing

Sheriff Simon Dixon shook his head as he walked up the steps to the police station. In the seventeen years that he had gently watched over Lumby and its residents, perhaps he had never come across anything more odd. In the center of the intersection of Main Street and Farm to Market Road sat a concrete cistern five feet high and thirty feet in diameter, filled to the brim with water. Faded block letters on the tank's side spelled out: **ROCKY MOUNT**. A few dozen pale yellow rubber chickens and ducks bobbed on the surface.

At the shallow end of the tank—if a cistern does, in fact, have a shallow end—stood Hank. Watching over the activities through a pair of dark sunglasses, Hank adjusted the strap of his broad-brimmed straw hat so deftly that no one took note. Covering his lower torso and athletically sculpted legs was a pair of Bermuda swim trunks. A beach towel hung around his neck. Hank glanced over at a few rubber ducks that had invaded his private pool and were making their way over to his side. Hank gave some thought to starting up a conversation, but the idea of fraternizing with fowl was almost inconceivable to such a noble bird.

Since his arrival several years ago, Hank had filled the position as the town's talisman, serving as a barometer and occasional devil's advocate of public opinion. Soon after settling into Lumby, he was selected as an altar boy in the Presbyterian church, and then led protests against deforestation at Lumby Lumber. Frequently seen about town as an icon of appropriate if not stylish fashion, he was looked up to by townsfolk as the embodiment of their own quirkiness.

Simon was still laughing when he walked into the police station.

Dale Friedman, Lumby's young deputy, looked up from his desk. "Morning, Simon."

"Good morning, Dale. Do you know anything about the cistern in the middle of Main Street?"

"Yep," Dale answered casually. "It appears to belong to Rocky Mount. Their town supervisor called this morning asking if we had seen it. Seems some kids made good on the high school football team's bet. It was a great game last night. You should have been there. Twenty-one to twenty."

"And the losing team had to deliver a cistern to the winning team?"

"I think it involved a little more than that. Seems the Rocky Mount boys were goaded into disassembling part of the town's water tower as well."

"Are their other cisterns still in place?"

"Actually, no. The smallest of Rocky Mount's cisterns showed up in the center of the university quad in Wheatley, and the Rocky Mount sheriff is still trying to determine the whereabouts of the third."

Simon looked out the window. "How on earth did they haul it here and get it filled with water so quickly?"

Dale shrugged his shoulders. "Kids are dangerously industrious when they put their minds to something."

"And what are the rubber chickens doing in there?" Simon asked.

Dale didn't look up from his paperwork. "Probably keeping the rubber ducks company."

Simon was unsure what dumbfounded him more: forty rubber chickens and ducks floating in a concrete cistern in the middle of town, or his assistant's nonchalant response to the bizarre event.

"And . . . ?" Simon encouraged.

"That's about all I know."

Simon scratched his head. "You know what?" he said. "I'm going to let you manage this situation."

"Not a problem," Dale said, jumping up out of his chair.

Several motorists blasted their horns in protest at the road obstruction. Although Lumby's low traffic volume had never warranted a traffic light, four years prior, the townspeople had voted overwhelmingly at their annual meeting to have one installed at the intersection of Main Street and Farm to Market Road, directly above where the cistern was now situated. It was a sign of the times, some thought. But shortly after the light was hung, it suffered from technical difficulties, blinking irregularly for weeks and then ceasing to operate altogether. A few years later it was repaired only to die another premature death. Shortly thereafter, as a joke, some teenagers replaced the red filters with blue.

So, on that morning, the cistern was clearly interrupting the pace of traffic set by the erratic blinking of the blue traffic light.

Another car horn blew.

Simon laughed. "I think you're being paged."

Suddenly, there was a bang directly above Simon's head. He looked up just as a large chunk of plaster dropped from the ceiling and hit his shoulder. He covered his head, waiting for another boom, but none followed.

"What in the world are they doing upstairs?" he demanded.

"Don't know. It's been going on all morning," Dale replied as he headed out the door.

Just as the door slammed, another crash came from the post office overhead. Simon thought it best to get out of the danger zone and went back to his office to place several calls to Rocky Mount. After advising their sheriff that Lumby would assist with but not lead

Lumby Landfill
Lumberyard
Mineral Street
S & T's Soda Shoppe
Jimmy D's
Brad's Hardware
Wools
Feed Store
Goose Creek
Hunts Mill Road
Lumby Elementary
Holy Trinity Church
South Grant Avenue
Loggers Road

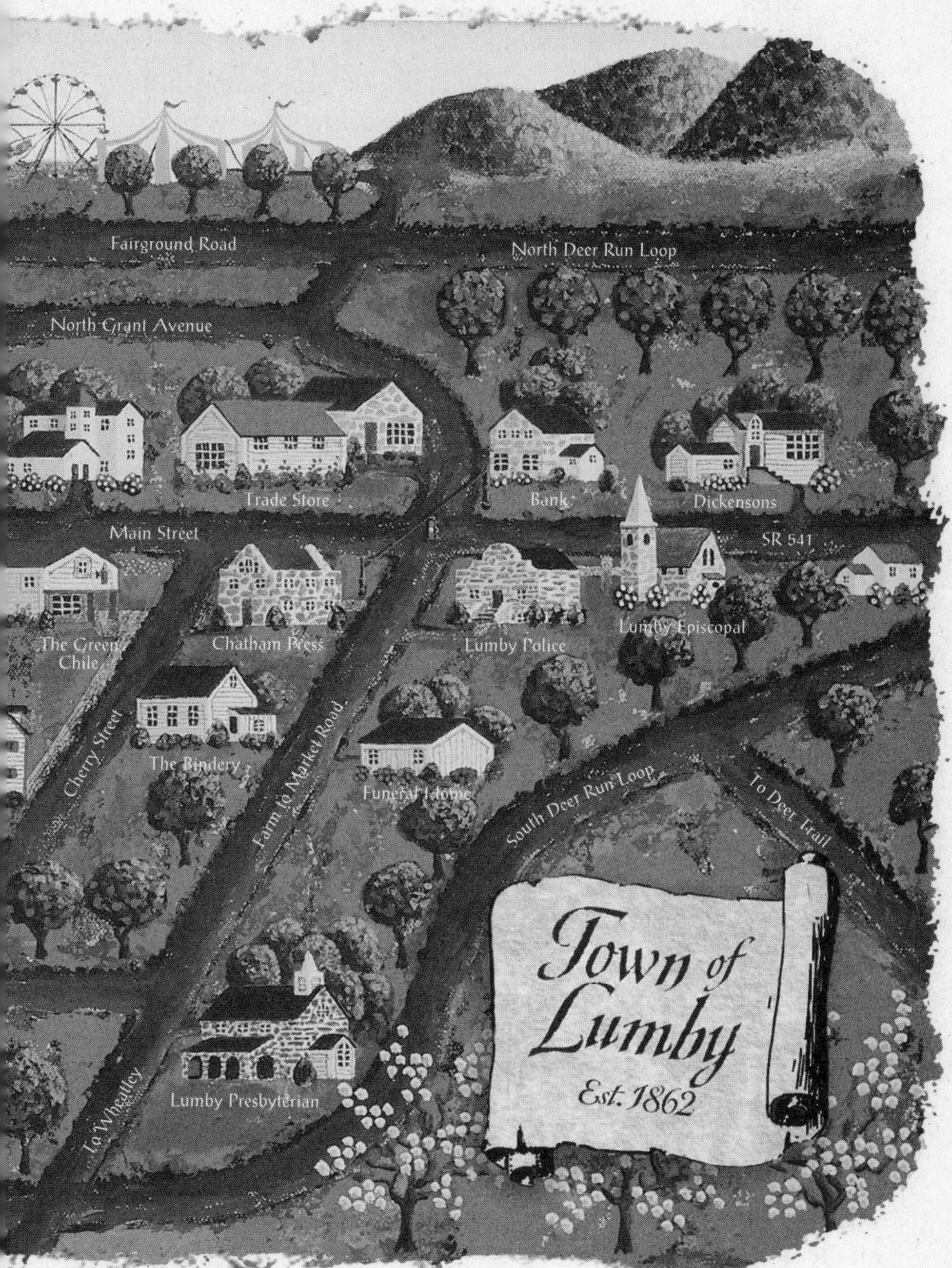

Fairground Road
North Deer Run Loop
North Grant Avenue
Trade Store
Bank
Dickensons
Main Street
SR 541
Lumby Episcopal
The Green Chile
Chatham Press
Lumby Police
Cherry Street
The Bindery
Farm to Market Road
Funeral Home
South Deer Run Loop
To Deer Trail
Town of Lumby
Est. 1862
Lumby Presbyterian
To Wheatley

the effort to relocate the cistern back to Rocky Mount, Simon walked outside to check on the progress of draining the tank.

Simon immediately saw Scott Stevens, a reporter for *The Lumby Lines,* standing next to Dale trying to get an interview. Scott, who had been known to embellish the more uneventful stories to which he was assigned, picked up and inspected one of the rubber chickens. By the time the story went to print, would Scott have discovered the missing corpse of Jimmy Hoffa under the floating flock?

A pedestrian approached the cistern and laid a wreath against it, which Hank scrutinized. Scott seized the opportunity to question the young lady, leaving Dale alone to direct traffic around what was quickly becoming a sacred albeit inconvenient monument. It was, after all, Hank's private swimming pool.

A passing driver threw flowers onto the bathing chickens.

Directly across the street, several onlookers sat on the stone steps of Lumby's bank while more pedestrians gathered in front of Chatham Press on the other corner of Main and Farm to Market.

"Someone should get Jimmy D," a man in the growing crowd called out to Simon.

"So he can serve Hank a shot of brandy?" a woman asked back.

Another woman in the front of the crowd added, "Hank might need it—he looks pretty cold in there. I think his beak is turning blue."

The crowd broke into laughter and cheers.

Hank blushed.

Lumby's only school bus maneuvered slowly around the cistern, allowing the children to peer out the window at the bizarre sight. One child threw his math book into the water, sinking two chickens with it. Hank glared at the insolent youth.

Otherwise, the town was going about its usual morning activities. Several merchants who had been temporarily distracted by the water tank returned to sweeping the never-ending autumn leaves off the sidewalks in front of their stores and restaurants.

Most of the brilliant summer awnings and streetlight banners had already been rolled up and stored away for the winter, and the last remaining August summer flowers in their raised beds had been replaced with hardy mums. The reading benches in front of the Lumby Bookstore as well as the café table before Gabrielle Beezer's restaurant, The Green Chile, had been moved inside. Trails of smoke rose lazily from shop chimneys, and the calm and torpor that came with winter had begun to descend on their quaint village.

A teenage boy who had been sent over from Dickenson's Grocery Store ran toward the intersection carrying a large piece of cardboard. Before Dale had time to respond, the boy taped the sign to the side of the cistern and ran off.

Dale stepped up to read the notice.

PERDUE STUFFERS ON SALE TODAY
AT DICKENSON'S $2.00/lb

"How's it going?" Simon asked as he walked up behind Dale.

"As well as can be expected," Dale answered. "They're bringing a sump pump and hose from the fire station, so we'll have it drained in no time. Removing it is another story—the concrete alone must weigh two to three tons." Dale scratched his head.

"Let's call Beasley and have him bring over his excavator. For the time being, we can put the cistern behind the Feed Store. No reason why we should spend tax dollars taking it all the way back to Rocky Mount."

"Smart thinking, Simon," Dale said, patting his boss on the back.

Terry McGuire strolled up with his arm around the waist of a very attractive teenage girl. "It looks like you have a problem here," he ribbed Dale.

"Nothing we can't handle," Dale said while directing traffic around the cement tank.

Terry walked around the cistern. "They certainly did a fine job," he said.

The sheriff's ears perked up; perhaps Terry knew the particulars of last night's activities. Simon regarded the young man with a critical eye. Terry had changed markedly since graduating from high school a few years prior. He had physically filled out and was looking more like his father every day—except, of course, for the vibrant red hair he shared with his mother. He had become a very handsome young man with a responsible attitude toward the construction work he did with Mac.

Terry leaned over and kissed the girl on the neck. "Come on, Sam," he said, leading her away.

"Hold on, Mr. McGuire," Simon said, grabbing the young man's jacket. "Do you have a minute?"

Terry slipped his arm from Samantha's waist. "Wait for me at S&T's," he told the blonde with a wink.

After Terry's companion walked away, Simon said, "I don't recognize your friend."

"Samantha Dorset. She just graduated from Rocky Mount," Terry replied, as he watched her sashay down the street.

"A very attractive young lady."

"I'm not sure about the lady part, but she's hot," Terry said, smiling broadly.

"Your girlfriend?"

Terry looked alarmed. "Not! Just friends with privileges."

Simon crunched his eyebrows. "Privileges?"

Terry rolled his eyes. "You know. Privileges. I'm just sliding with no commitments."

Simon frowned. "I certainly hope young Samantha Dorset knows that."

"What if she doesn't?" Terry asked with a cynical edge to his voice. "They want to be taken out, and I've got a great-paying job. All I need now is my own place, if you know what I mean," he said, jabbing Simon in the ribs with his elbow.

"Unfortunately, I think I do know what you mean," Simon said. "Do you know anything about the cistern?"

Terry shrugged his shoulders. "Nothing really. Sam's friends told us it was a bet between the captains of the football teams, but I don't know who brought it over."

"That's what we had heard," Simon said. "Terry, were you involved?"

"Definitely not!" Terry protested. "I don't do childish pranks anymore. I've got too many other irons in my fire."

"That I see," Simon said. "Just make sure no one gets burned in the process."

Terry looked down the street to where his date was sitting on the bench waiting for him. "They're big girls. They can take care of themselves."

"Sometimes they don't, Terry," Simon said sternly. "You need to step forward and show the same responsibility toward them that you show in your work."

But Simon's words fell on deaf ears as Terry was looking at Samantha and thinking about more important matters of the moment.

SEVEN

Granary

A familiar van slowed down as it approached the intersection. Simon squinted, trying to see who was in the car, and then smiled when he recognized the driver. "Brother Matthew!" Simon called out as the vehicle pulled up beside him.

The driver's-side window rolled down. "An odd place for a cistern, I would say. Is the town having water problems?" Matthew asked.

Simon laughed. "Not even close. So what brings the both of you to town?"

Brother Michael rolled his eyes. "It may be stranger than the explanation you have about those rubber chickens," he replied.

"We were hoping to see Dr. Campbell," Matthew added.

"She should be at the clinic," Simon offered.

A car behind the van beeped twice.

"We'll try to stop by before we leave," Brother Matthew said with a wave as he merged into Main Street traffic.

The west side of town, where the stores end, is anchored by some of the more prominent buildings. On the right side of the road at the corner of Mineral and Main sits Jimmy D's, the popular tavern, which is owned by Jimmy Daniels, also the mayor of Lumby. Directly across the street is the historic Feed Store, which for the past hundred years has provided the townsfolk with most anything they need for farm and animal.

Next to the Feed Store, set well off the road on a lot substantially larger than any other, is one of the more interesting buildings in town: the old stone Granary. It began as a gable-roofed stone barn that held the harvested crops that the Feed Store would sell for the farmers. When bagged animal feed from national distributors finally made its way to Lumby, The Granary lost its singular purpose and stood empty for well over ten years.

Then, in the nineteen forties, the two-story stone structure was purchased by Charlotte and Zeb Ross, owners of a growing orchard business in Rocky Mount. They lovingly added on a wing that was larger than the original barn, and converted the combined structure into a beautiful grand house on Main Street.

By the time Dr. Campbell purchased it in the early nineteen eighties, The Granary was one of the most architecturally significant buildings in downtown Lumby. The gabled side of the original granary faced the road, with a large chimney running up the center of the exterior wall. Flanking the chimney were words carved in flat stone: "GRANARY" on the left and "EST 1908" on the right.

Connected to the back half of The Granary was the newer wing, which extended out to the left and offered a long, inviting covered porch and a steep roof with several dormers. One of the few additions Dr. Campbell had made was a large cupola topped by an iron weather vane depicting several barnyard animals. Her other addition was a charming sign that she had had painted directly on the house siding: "LUMBY ANIMAL CLINIC."

Driving past Brad's Hardware, the monks turned their van around so they could park directly in front of the vet clinic on the same side of the street. Brother Michael jumped out and strolled up the front walk, observing a huge draft horse that was tied to one of the many iron-post hitches in front of the clinic.

At the bottom of the steps were empty U-Haul book boxes and

thicker china cartons. Brother Michael ran up the stairs and peered through a window. He turned around, shrugging his shoulders. "No one's here," he called down to Matthew.

Matthew stepped out of the van and bent over, stretching his stiff back. "I'm sure someone will be along in a minute. Let's wait," he said as he walked over to the mare and rubbed the animal's nose.

Michael, returning to the horse, looked at the thin rope that tethered the large animal. "She could break this with one gentle tug," he said, running his hand along her thick mane.

"An amazing animal," Matthew replied.

"One wrong step with her hoof and your foot would be crushed," a woman's voice warned.

Matthew turned around. "Mackenzie McGuire," he said, raising his arms. "How wonderful to see you again."

"You too," she said, giving each man a warm embrace.

The year before, Mackenzie and her son had spent several months working at Saint Cross Abbey, during which time Mac had become very good friends with the monks.

"So what are you doing in town?" Mac inquired.

"Seeking Dr. Campbell's advice," Matthew answered. "Do you know if she's around?"

"Ellen went to the bookstore but will be back in a few minutes," Mac said. "I'm taking a break if you'd like to join me," she offered as she sat down on the front stoop.

While Brother Matthew and Mackenzie got caught up, Michael strolled around to the side of The Granary, admiring the architecture. He immediately noticed the carpenter saws and tools lying on the ground close to several newly constructed stalls. He also noticed a recently added metal roof and extensive gutter system overhead.

"Quite the projects you're working on," Michael said when he rejoined the others.

"With Ellen's plans to—" Mac began, but then caught sight of Dr. Campbell strolling down the sidewalk, engrossed in a book. "Speaking of the saint, there she is now."

Dr. Campbell was so caught up in her reading that she didn't see them.

"Hello, stranger," Matthew called out.

She looked up, waved, and quickened her pace. "Well, if it isn't the brothers of Saint Cross," she said, beaming.

Brother Matthew noticed the book she was holding. "Greece?" he asked.

"I'm preparing," she said quickly. "What a surprise to see you here. What brings you to Lumby?"

"Your assistance, if you have a few minutes," Matthew said.

"I'm all yours," she offered, placing the book on the stairs before Brother Matthew led her back to the van.

"What a magnificent animal," Michael commented as they passed the sleeping mare.

"She's for sale if you're interested," Ellen said.

Matthew looked at her in surprise. "But haven't you had her since she was a foal?"

"I have, but change is coming," she said.

When they reached the van, Matthew opened both back doors so Ellen could see the crates inside. "So, what do you have here?" she said, peering in. Then her whole body froze. "Oh my!" she whispered. "These are Asian snow monkeys!"

"So we concluded," Matthew said. "They were sent to us as a gift by government representatives in Japan and we obviously have neither a facility nor the knowledge to take care of them. We thought maybe you could help."

Ellen continued to study the small creatures. "Do you have their importation papers? It will show their inoculations."

Michael ran to the front of the van and pulled a stack of papers off the dashboard. "Here is everything that was given to us," he said, handing her a pile of wrinkled documents.

Ellen scanned the pages. "Well, let's get them inside for an examination."

Matthew and Michael picked up the first crate and gently carried it into Ellen's clinic. Passing through the large reception area, Ellen led them to the largest of three examination rooms.

"Why don't you bring the other in?" Ellen advised. "The poor animals must be exhausted and terrified. They'll be calmer if they're kept together."

Ellen reviewed the import records again while Matthew and Michael brought in the second crate. "Unfortunately, I don't read Japanese so a lot of this is Greek to me," she admitted, laying the stack of papers on the counter behind her.

Matthew laughed. "Neither do we. In fact, we thought we were picking up two monastics at the airport."

"If you could stay over in the corner," Ellen suggested as she put on a pair of heavy gloves.

Then, with amazing speed and calm, she unlatched the first crate's door, reached inside and took hold of the monkey. To everyone's surprise, it didn't struggle. In fact, the animal remained relaxed in her hands as it was taken from the enclosure. When she held the mammal in front of her, the snow monkey reached out to touch a strand of her hair.

Ellen laughed. "Just amazing," she said. "It appears you were given someone's cherished pets. This monkey is incredibly tame. Here," she said, passing the monkey to Michael. She then opened the second crate and withdrew the other animal, which was as calm as the first.

Ellen quickly examined the monkey. "Very dehydrated, which is to be expected from such a long ordeal, but she looks to be in great health. If you have no objections, I suggest we keep them here for a few days to rehydrate them and stabilize their eating. That would also allow me to watch them more closely," she said, looking at the snow monkey in wonder. "They're so much more beautiful than I ever imagined."

"They certainly are," Michael said, playing with the one he was holding.

"We have a larger issue, though," Matthew began to explain. "We have no facility to keep them at the monastery. We were hoping you could provide a long-term solution."

Ellen held a stethoscope up to the monkey's chest. "Oh, I would take them in a heartbeat if I was staying."

Matthew regarded the veterinarian in confusion. "If you were staying where?"

Ellen looked up and blushed. "I'm sorry. I assumed you had heard. I'm retiring in a few weeks and will be leaving for a long-anticipated trip to Greece. Then I'm moving closer to my family in Colorado. The practice has been for sale for several months and I'm just finishing packing up my home."

Matthew looked startled. "Ellen, I'm so surprised."

"I've been here for close to thirty years. After my husband died, my kids suggested I move closer to them. Now the time has come to take them up on their offer."

"But what will the town do without you?"

Ellen shook her head. "I've been asking that very question, but no one seems to believe I'm actually going to retire."

EIGHT

Pulleys

With the monkeys in good hands at Dr. Campbell's clinic, and after bidding goodbye to Mackenzie, Brothers Matthew and Michael left The Granary by way of Main Street to Farm to Market Road.

At the intersection, Dale Friedman and Simon Dixon were still trying to resolve their mounting problem. During the time that the brothers had visited with Ellen, several more supporters had weighed in on the matter by throwing even more rubber duckies into the cistern. Another more creative youth had added his three-foot-tall acrylic Godzilla, which Hank didn't like at all.

A paperboy ran out of the Chatham Press building with an armful of newspapers. After placing half of his payload into the newspaper rack on the corner of Main Street, he darted out into the street and ran up to Simon.

"Mr. Beezer asked that I give you this," the boy said as he handed the sheriff a copy of *The Lumby Lines*.

Simon looked up at the second-floor window of the Press building and saw Dennis watching the events unfold from his office. No doubt his friend was going to have a fun time reading the letters to the editor about the cistern. Had it not been for the column space needed for other regular features, Dennis would certainly have included several of them in the next issue.

The Lumby Lines

Lumby Forum

An open bulletin board for our town residents

October 10

The Lumby Chicken Association just chose Gainesville, Georgia (the fried-chicken capital of the world), for its Winter Poultry Farm Tour: $113 for 4 nights and 3 days with a guarantee to visit at least 7 different chicken farms! Call Stanley to sign up.

If you're interested in sizing up your gourd before the pumpkin festival, call McNear at his farm and he'll send his wife out.

SWM seeks someone of opposite sex. No real requirements at all. Call Phil 925-3928.

Since most members never understood the rules, the Lumby Chess Club has renamed itself the Lumby Scrabble Club. Anyone is welcome to join, especially if you can bring a dictionary.

Free Rabies Shots! Last offer before Ellen Campbell retires. If you're frothing at the mouth, be sure to stop by The Granary.

Hookers tea party this Saturday night. Bring yarn, needles and accessories.

Don't let isolation ruin your life—the church will help. Come by the Presbyterian church for Sunday-night potluck dinner—prayer and meditation to follow.

Free to any home. Cat that strays and neutered like one of the family.

Dickenson's Help Wanted: Girls to stack fresh fruit and produce at night.

The women of the Episcopal church have cast-off clothing of every kind. They may be seen in the basement on Sunday after the choir sings the last hymn.

S&T Thursday Night Dinner Special: Chicken $4.00, Beef $4.50, Turkey $3.00, Children $2.00

After leaving Lumby, the brothers of Saint Cross Abbey headed to their next stop of the afternoon, one that both always looked forward to: Montis Inn.

For almost a hundred years, Montis Abbey was the monastic home for a small contemplative order of monks that specialized in calligraphy. Matthew had spent most of his adult life there and, with the other brothers, had penned some of the finest artwork in the country.

But it was the Montis orchards that held the fondest memories for Matthew. While he lived there, the quiet and solitude of the fields lured him each evening, even in the harshest of winter weather. And it was during those hours, feeling so small in the shadows of the great

Rockies and under the expansive sky, that Matthew felt closest to God. During the inevitable moments when he questioned the depth of his faith and the religious commitment he had made in his life, he simply had to walk the rows of apple and pear trees, and his belief was restored. How he secretly longed for such a personal sanctuary at Saint Cross Abbey.

In the courtyard of Montis Inn, Pam Walker was well under way with her autumn yard cleanup when Brothers Matthew and Michael turned into the drive. Recognizing the Saint Cross Abbey van, she waved to them and laid the rake on top of the growing pile of fallen leaves.

"What an unexpected surprise," she said.

"I hope we're not interrupting your work," Matthew said, giving her a big hug.

"You are and I'm so glad of it." She laughed, rubbing her sore back. "Would you like to come in for coffee?"

Matthew looked at his watch. "Unfortunately, we don't have time today. We were hoping to find Joshua here." Joshua Turner was a former monk and Matthew's longtime friend.

"He and Mark are down at the stable involved in a new project," Pam said, rolling her eyes.

"Don't tell us. Mark finally bought the llamas to fill that huge new barn of yours," Brother Michael guessed.

"I'm afraid not. As much as I don't want a herd of animals down there, that would be better than the stalls standing empty as they are now," she said.

"Dare I ask what has caught Mark's attention?" Matthew asked.

Pam smirked. "A World War Two sidecar motorcycle."

Matthew couldn't restrain himself. "And I thought people became more predictable with age."

"And more mature, but not Mark," Pam added. "Pray for me, please," she pleaded, putting an arm around her dear friend.

Michael was much more intrigued. "An old motorcycle. Really?" he asked.

Pam looked exasperated. "Yes, my dear husband bought a sixty-year-old BMW with no wheels from a government-surplus Internet site. The guys are down at the small barn making room for it right now."

"He can put it in a stall," Matthew proposed.

Pam shook her head. "I told him that's not an option. Our new barn cost too much—I don't want leaking oil all over the place."

"So is he going to refurbish it?" Michael asked.

Pam frowned. "The only thing he knows about motorcycles is where to put in the key."

"I don't think military bikes had keys," Michael said. "Too easily lost on the battlefield."

"Why don't you go on down and tell him that?" Pam suggested.

Matthew looked longingly across the street and up into the fields. Some of the trees were still full of fruit that would be harvested within the coming weeks.

"Do you mind if we walk through the orchard on our way down to the stable?" Matthew asked.

"Not at all," Pam said, picking up her rake. "And please take some apples back with you."

Wanting to give the older monk time alone, Michael said, "I'm going to stay and talk to Pam for a minute. I'll meet you down at the barn."

Although Matthew would not have objected to Michael's company, he welcomed the chance for solitude.

"By the way," Matthew called back to Pam, "if you're available the day after tomorrow, you may enjoy coming to Saint Cross with Joshua. There's a meeting scheduled for eleven o'clock that we would appreciate having you attend. It will be most interesting, I assure you."

"I'll plan on it," Pam said, waving to him.

Matthew's spirits lifted as soon as he crossed Farm to Market and began the gentle ascent to the higher pastures. Every few minutes, he looked back at Montis and saw Michael and Pam still immersed in conversation. Woodrow Lake, to the south, appeared calm and inviting. As he walked down the well-mowed rows between the fruit trees, going deeper into the orchard, he spread his arms so he was able to touch the outstretched branches on either side.

In the upper field, the meditation bench that Matthew had constructed twenty years earlier was still in place, although now covered with wild vines. After clearing it off, he sat on the sun-warmed stone and closed his eyes. Matthew was now in his late sixties and beginning to feel his age. But being back in the orchard strengthened him. When he died, he thought, he would want to be buried here, amongst his beloved trees and very close to God.

Down in the barn, Joshua Turner leaned out of the window of the Jeep. "You're going to kill yourself," he warned.

Mark looked down from the hayloft and tried to remember why they had built a barn with a second floor well over twelve feet off the ground—ten would have been much safer. He tightened the harness around his waist and glanced up at the four steel pulley wheels that were bolted into the crossbeam of the barn's ceiling fifteen feet away from the end planks of the loft. The rope attached to his harness was thrown over the beam with the end tied to the bumper of the Jeep. In his hand he held another rope that needed to be threaded through the four wheels to support a cradle for the motorcycle so it could be lifted off the ground during the winter season.

His eyes once again followed his harness rope over the beam and down to the Jeep, which was parked by the barn doors.

"It'll be great," he called down to Joshua.

Before Joshua could reply, Mark leapt off the loft's floor and into midair. He immediately dropped several feet but then his body jerked upward when the rope tightened. After swinging wildly for a few seconds, he came to rest hanging twelve feet off the ground and directly aligned with the pulleys above.

Mark looked up to the ceiling. "The rope is holding just fine. Now back up the Jeep."

Joshua put the car in gear and slowly reversed it out of the barn, pulling Mark upward toward the crossbeams.

"That's good!" Mark yelled as he neared the top.

But Mark, who was well out of sight by now, didn't yell loudly enough for Joshua to hear.

"Stop!" Mark yelled louder, as his head hit the truss.

Joshua slammed on the brake just before Mark's body was crammed up against the roof trusses.

"Are you all right?" Joshua called out.

"Okay." Mark cringed. "Give me a minute."

After catching his breath, Mark took the loose rope and threaded it through each of the pulley wheels. He grabbed the end and tied it to his harness. "Okay, I'm done," he called down.

Joshua inched the Jeep forward, lowering Mark to the ground.

Before Mark's feet hit the floor, he was untying his harness. "Was that great or what? Here," he said, passing Joshua the end of the heavy rope that was now looped through the pulley wheels attached to the crossbeam.

Joshua pulled on one end and watched the rope run smoothly through all four wheels.

"When we put the motorcycle away for the winter, we'll just harness it in the ropes, give a pull and suspend it until spring. Since Pam was a little annoyed about the whole bike thing, better out of sight and out of mind. And we won't lose any space for hay."

Joshua glanced over at the empty stalls. "Speaking of hay, where are the animals?"

"I turned them out a couple of hours ago," Mark replied.

"But, Mark, I hadn't finished mending the fence when you called me over," Joshua said, running out the back of the stable. He looked up into the pasture. "They're gone."

"I'm sure they headed up to the orchard to eat some fermented apples. I'll join you as soon as I straighten out these ropes," Mark said, just before he tripped over a web of knots he had just created in the ropes.

NINE

Confession

As Joshua hiked up the hill toward the back field, he caught a glimpse of three sheep running nervously along the tree line. The front sheep stopped, looked around and then darted across a row of pear trees and back into the adjoining forest.

Joshua shook his head, thinking of the many times he had gone in search of stray beasts from the Montis barnyard. He had always enjoyed working for Pam and Mark—they were good friends as well as generous employers. And the arrangement he had had with them during the previous three years had given Joshua time to complete his doctorate degree at the University in Wheatley. But now change was approaching, and soon he would be leaving Montis to begin his career.

Joshua was deep in thought when he reached the farthest pasture.

"A shepherd who has lost his flock," a man said.

Joshua jumped, startled by the voice. He glanced around but didn't see anyone.

Brother Matthew, still seated on his old bench, waved his arm. "Over here."

Joshua finally spotted Matthew sitting alone in a small alcove along the forest edge. "Matthew! You scared the life out of me!" he said.

The monk bowed his head in teasing reverence. "Forgive me, my son."

Joshua laughed and walked up to his old friend. Although he was not tall, Joshua had a casual, self-confident stride. His thick sandy auburn hair had grown longer since the last time Brother Matthew had seen him.

Joshua and Brother Matthew had first met more than twenty years before at Montis Abbey, when a very young and rebellious Joshua was delivered to the monks after breaking through the ice during a midwinter midnight drunken swim in Woodrow Lake. To everyone's surprise, including his own, Joshua had remained at Montis for twelve years before realizing the time had come to walk a different path—one that ultimately led to a wonderful marriage to Brooke and an education in agricultural engineering.

"I was planning on coming to see you at Saint Cross tomorrow," Joshua said.

"I hope you do. The brothers need your help in thinning the woods next to the pond," Matthew said, sliding over. "Would you like to sit?"

Although the stone looked uncomfortable, Joshua accepted. Once next to Matthew, he realized how perfectly the stone bench had been placed so long ago; from it, one could see a panorama of the Montis property, Woodrow Lake and the gentle skyline of the small city of Wheatley.

"So, what brings you to Montis?"

"We met with Dr. Campbell in Lumby this morning and thought we would briefly stop here," Matthew explained.

Joshua knew Matthew too well. "And the orchard called to you?"

Matthew nodded. "It did indeed."

"I know the feeling. I don't understand why you refuse to plant fruit trees at Saint Cross," Joshua said in his direct manner of speaking. "You have such good soil at the monastery, you could have a tremendous orchard."

Matthew closed his eyes and took a deep breath. The smell of the ripened apples brought back so many fond memories.

"Many reasons, I suppose," he said. "To plant and manage so many trees would be too demanding for our community—we're getting older and just aren't as physically able as we once were." He paused and then added, "It would be too selfish of me to suggest the idea just because I enjoy walking through the fields. And it gives me all the more reason to come and visit all of you." He then abruptly changed the subject. "I assume those were sheep from the Montis stable?"

Joshua laughed. "Yes, the flock that is in my charge, I'm ashamed to admit." He looked down at the barn and saw that Mark had all but tied himself up in rope. "But my graduate work is coming to an end, so my herding days are numbered."

"You sound like Ellen Campbell when she makes reference to her retirement—happy but sad as well," Matthew commented.

Joshua dodged the comparison. "I heard that she may be leaving but no one seems to believe it. Did she mention anything to you?" Joshua asked.

"Yes, and there were packed boxes at The Granary."

"I'm sorry to hear that," Joshua said. "She has been a wonderful vet for the town and a good friend. She was also a great help in my graduate work."

Matthew raised his brows. "But isn't your concentration in agriculture?"

"Yes, but that overlaps with animal husbandry, especially in my field of genomic biology."

Matthew shot Joshua a confused look.

"Agricultural engineering," he clarified. "How we genetically engineer crops can directly impact the animals that consume them. And Ellen was always open to the benefits of what we're trying to accomplish."

"Aren't most veterinarians?"

Joshua considered the question. "I suppose they are, but some side with the purists."

"Purists?"

"Those who believe that we should leave nature well enough alone and never tamper with genetics. They think we're playing God."

Matthew nodded. "A strange line coming from a man who almost became a monk."

"Life does offer us unexpected ironies, doesn't it?"

Matthew looked carefully at his close friend. "Given your tone, I think you might be talking about something else?"

"Ugh." Joshua groaned softly, running his hand through his hair. "That's a hard question to answer." He watched the sheep move out of the woods and begin to graze under an old fruit tree. "I would have to say all is not well."

Matthew remained silent as he shifted to a more comfortable position on the stone bench.

"In a few months, I will be completing my doctoral work," Joshua began.

"I heard from the Walkers that your dissertation received national accolades."

Joshua nodded. "To my surprise, it did, and it caught the attention of some key individuals in both academia and research. I've received a few offers of employment to begin as soon as I complete my obligations at the university in January."

"All of that sounds very encouraging," Matthew said.

"If one wanted to go into teaching or lab work, it would be."

"Ah," Matthew said, finally understanding Joshua's predicament. "Therein lies the problem?"

"Therein," he said with a weak grin. He got up from the bench and began pacing back and forth. The sheep looked up for only a moment.

Joshua continued. "Four years ago, when I was working at Charlotte Ross's orchards and just before I first met Brooke, I got the idea to go back to school. I wanted to use what I loved about the land and agriculture to somehow better the world. I thought I could solve famine by bioengineering new strains of wheat and corn that could sustain drought and disease." He chuckled as he remembered those earlier, more idealistic days. "I saw myself walking through the fields in some impoverished province of China, helping the local residents plant the seeds and harvest more than they ever thought possible."

"An admirable dream."

"It was . . . and still is. But I realized, a little too late, that very few in my specialty actually get their hands dirty out in the field."

"Literally and figuratively," Matthew added.

"Exactly. And even if there was that opportunity, after marrying Brooke, I would never consider leaving her for even a short time."

"I see," Matthew said as he watched his friend tread over the same path, to and fro. "So, what is it that you want to do?"

Joshua stopped in a heartbeat and looked over at Matthew. "As stupid as it sounds, I just don't know, and I find that almost intolerable. I was so certain of my choice when I decided to leave monastic life, and then even more sure when I asked Brooke to marry me. But now I don't feel strongly about anything in my professional life. In fact, I almost cringe at the idea of being relegated to some white-walled corporate lab or classroom all day." He started walking again.

"Some paths are easier to see than others."

"But some paths need to be taken regardless. I have an obligation to Brooke—she supported us while I was in school and now I need to toe the line."

"I'm sure that's not how she sees it," Matthew offered.

"I'm sure she doesn't either," Joshua said. "But we haven't talked about it. I can barely admit to myself that I might have made a mistake about going to graduate school. I want to have some answers in place—to be able to tell her what our future looks like—before I speak to her."

"Are there alternatives? Perhaps a compromise?"

Joshua dug his hand deeper in his pockets as he considered the question he had asked himself a hundred times. "That's what I haven't figured out. Over the past four years I've really enjoyed working at Montis. It's so important that I can see and touch the results of my labor, and that I know after a hard day's work that there's something to show for it." Instead of walking in a straight line, Joshua began turning outward, forming a circle. "I also enjoy the personal connection—helping people I know and like."

Suddenly, a yell came from the direction of the barn. Clearly Mark had run into trouble.

Joshua laughed. "And knowing they need my help as well." He quickly became serious. "But I'm sure I have more to offer than the work I do here. I want to do more . . . to use what I've learned."

"Just not in a Chinese rice paddy," Matthew said.

"No, not halfway around the world. When I look at the options, perhaps a faculty position is the best there is," he said. "My dissertation received quite a few honors, so I would think several schools may want to interview me."

"That is, only if you want to be interviewed," Matthew replied.

TEN

Cornered

Jimmy Daniels and Simon Dixon walked out of Jimmy D's and crossed Main Street.

"The Granary has always been one of my favorite buildings in the village," Jimmy D said as they approached the front path to Dr. Campbell's office. "And it's a perfect spot for a veterinarian's office."

"I agree," Simon said, looking up at the beautiful stone facade. "It's sad Ellen is leaving."

Jimmy grabbed Simon's arm and stopped him in his tracks. "Don't say that! She's not going anywhere," he insisted.

Simon countered with his usual voice of reason. "It's her decision to retire."

"But we're here to convince her otherwise," Jimmy said, lowering his brow. Jimmy was determined to keep Dr. Ellen Campbell in his town. And although he was a good albeit unconventional mayor, his stubborn streak was a mile long.

"No use of duct tape to tie her to the chair," Simon teased.

Jimmy glanced over at Hank, who was perched on a rocking chair, standing vigil until someone would listen to him about the town's need for a new veterinarian. Ever loyal to Ellen, though, Hank still wore his moving-van overalls, now covered with foam packing popcorn.

"What's he doing here?" Jimmy asked, nodding at Hank.

"Don't know," Simon said. "Maybe just helping her pack."

Hank was so frustrated that he became tongue-tied.

The front door opened just as Jimmy and Simon reached the porch steps. Ellen stepped out carrying two moving boxes.

"So it's true? You really are retiring?" Simon asked.

Ellen's excitement was clearly visible. "After thirty years here, I am indeed."

"Here, let me help you," Jimmy offered, taking the boxes from her. He slid around her and walked back inside.

"Wait a minute, Jimmy. Those are going to my car," Ellen said.

But Jimmy was already heading toward her office. Her door was closed, which was highly unusual.

"Be quick," she said as he opened it. "I don't want them to get out."

After all three scooted into her office, she closed the door behind them and looked around.

Jimmy squinted. "Do you have some clandestine project going on in here?" he asked as he set the boxes on a side chair and began removing the books, placing them back on the empty bookshelves.

Suddenly, a monkey jumped from the top shelf and landed squarely on Jimmy's head, grabbing a handful of hair with one hand and one of Jimmy's ears with the other. As the animal tried to balance himself, he pulled that much harder on both.

"Samson! Leave Jimmy alone!" Ellen said as she ran over and gently snatched the monkey from the mayor's head. Unfortunately, Samson didn't want to let go of his ear.

"Ouch!" Jimmy yelped.

"Oh, it's just a little monkey," Ellen said, cradling the animal in her arms. She walked over to the other bookcase and called to the other. "Come here, Delilah."

The second monkey scampered down and crouched on Ellen's shoulder.

"Let me put them away before Jimmy becomes fatally wounded," she teased, disappearing around the corner.

When Ellen returned a minute later, Simon pulled out her desk chair. "Here, Ellen, come sit," he offered. "Would you like some coffee?"

She looked suspiciously at the two men. "Why do I feel like prey being led to the den?"

Jimmy flashed a broad and, Ellen had to admit, endearing smile. "We thought we could help you."

"By unpacking the boxes I just packed?" she asked.

"Ellen, our favorite veterinarian," Jimmy began.

"Your *only* veterinarian," she corrected him.

Jimmy ignored the comment. "Perhaps you haven't thought this through."

Ellen grinned. "Only every day for the past two years."

Jimmy repositioned more books on the shelves. Ellen turned to Simon. "Can't you arrest him for doing that?" she teased.

"I'll be surprised if that's the least of his crimes today," Simon replied. "He really is determined to change your mind."

She shook her head. "It's not going to happen," she promised.

"But it's so sudden," Simon said more softly.

"Sudden?" Ellen said in a perturbed tone. "I told the town council a *year* ago that I would be retiring this month. And I reminded them again at the June meeting."

"Yeah, but that was aeons ago," Jimmy groused.

Ellen cocked her head. "So, your complaint is that I gave the town *too* much notice?"

There was silence in the room.

Finally Simon said, "We just never thought you would actually leave."

"Well, I'm sorry, gentlemen, but I've given my fair share to Lumby. I'm sure the town will continue just fine without me."

"But that's the point," Jimmy said as he unwrapped diplomas lying at the bottom of the box. "If you leave . . ." He stalled for time. "If you leave, we can't build the zoo we always wanted."

"*When* I leave," she interjected. "And what zoo are you talking about?"

"You know, the one that everyone's been discussing," Jimmy bluffed.

"In your dreams, Mayor," she replied.

Jimmy decided to take another tack: guilt. "If you leave there will be no one to care for the animals. You know better than anyone how dependent on you the farmers are."

Ellen looked sympathetically at Jimmy and then shrugged her shoulders. "I've done what I can to bring in another vet. I've run advertisements online and in all the newspapers throughout the region. And I've already reduced the price of my business down to where I'm almost giving away the practice and taking a loss on The Granary. I don't know what else I can do."

"You can stay," Jimmy pleaded.

"I can't," she said, trying to soften her tone. "I've worked hard all my life—I deserve some time off."

Hearing the resolve in Ellen's voice, Jimmy stopped unpacking and slumped against the windowsill. "We didn't come here to change your plans," he said.

Ellen glared at him.

Jimmy blushed. "All right, maybe we did," he confessed, "but our intentions were honorable."

Simon added, "Obviously, the town hasn't prepared for your retirement as well as you have. Is there something we can do or some compromise that can be made to limit the impact of your departure?"

"I've already talked to Dr. Gardner down in Wheatley about taking over my patients. He's agreed and I'll be transferring all of my files to him before I leave. Also, I've hired Mackenzie McGuire to make all the repairs to The Granary and the main house. I've even asked her to do some additional work in the back of the clinic to make it more salable." She paused. "But, in truth, if I don't get an offer for the practice fairly soon, I'm going to rent it out as a residential property and ask Joan Stokes at Main Street Realty to manage it for me."

"And that would be a one-year lease?" Simon asked.

"Yeah, it would have to be," Ellen said.

Jimmy rubbed his eyes. "So, if you don't sell it in the next few weeks, basically there won't be a vet clinic to use, so we probably won't get another vet for at least a year."

Ellen gave it a moment's thought. "That's probably true, unless the new vet wants to build another animal clinic. But that would be highly unlikely because the volume of business in town just wouldn't pay for it."

Another long silence followed as each considered the future of The Granary.

Jimmy jumped up from the windowsill. "Well," he said with forced optimism, "that means we just have to find a vet."

"I'll certainly do anything I can to help," Ellen said. "If you come by later today, I'll give you a list of all the ads that I've run in the last three months."

The front door chime rang. "Ellen? Are you here?" a man called from the lobby.

"Coming," she called back. "You're going to have to excuse me. And no more unpacking my stuff," she added as she left her office.

Jimmy looked at Simon. "She's really leaving."

"She is indeed," Simon replied.

In the lobby, Chuck Bryson, a longtime resident and good friend to them all, held a large owl limp in his arms. It was breathing shallowly and a small amount of blood trickled from under its wing.

"I found her over by Goose Creek," Chuck explained.

Dr. Campbell gently lifted the owl. "It looks like she may have been shot," she said, walking into the exam room, where she laid the owl on a stainless-steel table.

Jimmy and Simon joined Chuck at the door. Ellen was amazingly proficient as she examined the wounded animal. "She has some buckshot in her wing. I'm going to have to X-ray her to see how many pellets are under her skin, and then I'll take her into the operating room." She looked up at Chuck. "I'll call you this afternoon." And then she disappeared with the owl into the back room.

"Where are we ever going to find such a great vet?" Jimmy asked rhetorically.

Chuck raised his eyebrows. "So, Ellen is definitely leaving?"

"Unfortunately," Simon answered. "And it seems she's done an admirable job in trying to sell her practice, but there's just no interest, and time is running out."

Chuck glanced around the lobby of the clinic that he had come to know so well during his thirty-year friendship with Ellen. He owned a menagerie of animals and had spent more time than most at The Granary.

After having lunch at Jimmy D's, Chuck returned to The Granary to check on the owl. Seeing that Ellen was already in surgery to remove the gun pellets, he wrote her a brief note asking her to call him. On his way out, he ran into Joshua walking up the front steps.

"Well, if it isn't Chuck Bryson. I haven't seen you in weeks," Joshua said.

"The bees are quiet and you haven't needed me in the apiary," Chuck replied. For many decades, he had enjoyed sharing his expertise in beekeeping with the monks and then with the Walkers. Joshua had been a good apprentice over the past several years.

"You taught me too well. We haven't had any major problems with the hives this fall."

"Come sit, young Joshua," Chuck said, taking a seat on the top porch step. "I have a proposition for you."

Joshua looked intrigued. "And what would that be?"

"I was at Berkeley last week," Chuck began.

"I thought you had retired from teaching physics at the university."

Chuck laughed. "Not yet. I still teach one class and oversee four doctoral students who are working on their dissertations. Anyway, I read in the faculty newsletter that there's a symposium on wheat genetics at Berkeley in the next few weeks. I can't remember the exact date, but a few of the lads from Europe will be joining some of our researchers and representatives from major chemical companies to share notes."

"I hadn't heard about that."

"No surprise," Chuck said. "The university is underplaying the forum."

"They don't want protesters," Joshua guessed.

Chuck nodded. "Probably. I need to attend to some business on campus and thought you might like to fly with me to San Francisco and attend the symposium. During the trip you can tell me what you're planning to do with this great education of yours."

Joshua regarded Chuck out of the corner of his eye. "I'm not sure what's worse: confronting the protesters or facing that question."

"Ah, not to worry, young Joshua," Chuck said, smacking his friend on the shoulder as he stood up. "The answer will come in due time."

ELEVEN

Article

"This is great," Mark said from the backseat of the Jeep, where he was playing with their two Labs. "It's been months since we've gone to Saint Cross."

Pam slowed the car as they entered the small village of Franklin. "Honey, we were just there two weeks ago delivering more apples," she corrected him.

"Yeah, but that didn't count," Mark objected. "We didn't spend any time with the guys."

"They were praying," Pam explained to Joshua, who was seated next to her.

Joshua laughed. "And you didn't stay for vespers? What a surprise."

"I didn't want to press my luck with God," Mark said.

Joshua squinted at him. "Someday you need to explain your rather unique perspective on religion."

"I'd like to hear that one too," Pam added. "And I wouldn't be surprised if the Great Pumpkin has something to do with it."

When it was obvious that Mark was too involved with the dogs to explain his spiritual views, Joshua picked up the paper lying on the dashboard.

Pam glanced over at the headline of the lead article. "It's pumpkin time. Are you going to the festival this year?"

Joshua grinned. "Brooke wouldn't have it any other way. It's one of her favorite Lumby traditions."

The Lumby Lines

A CONSUMER REPORT

BY CARRIE KERRY October 8

GBF-9500: After being a passive observer at prior Pumpkin Festivals, last winter I found some spare testosterone and decided to join the big boys in town by planning to grow a mammoth gourd this summer. My competitive juices flowing, I did what reporters do best: research.

And what I found was a load of information pertaining to gargantuan vegetables: seeds that are the size of my thumb, special fertilizers, bizarre ritualistic watering techniques, sunning theories, hanging apparatuses (to hammock or not to hammock, that appears to be the question), and a small group of relentless people who are so deeply engaged in the challenge to grow the biggest that every additional pound of pumpkin is considered a matter close to life or death.

So, after sowing these extraordinary seeds in modified soil and fastidiously watering at 3:14 each morning, by late August I had a 234-pound pumpkin whose single vine and enormous leaves engulfed my entire backyard.

When my pumpkin stopped growing for no apparent reason, I researched further and found several references that supported the premise that passing a low-level electrical current through a pumpkin would significantly increase its growth rate.

So, I decided to take the radical step and purchase a GBF-9500, which is generally used by chiropractors on their patients' back muscles. As I discovered, it's more of an electrical-pulse stimulator—think non-vibrating vibrator—that transmits electrical pulses through six-inch electrode patches that I adhered to the outside of my pumpkin.

The machine makes NASA's work look like child's play: dual channel, multimode, a pulse of 50–300(uS) with variable contraction times from 2 to 99 seconds, generating an "asymmetrical square pulse wave," as stated in the brochure. Whatever. All I know is that it jump-started my plant's growth and added another 300 pounds to my pumpkin.

The GBF-9500 is extraordinary, and I'm sure it could cook a French stew and cure the plague if given the opportunity. So, overall, I give it a rare rating of five out of five bananas.

The sleepy two-block town of Franklin was all but deserted. A half dozen shops that were frequented only by its few residents and the monks of Saint Cross Abbey were mostly empty. Shortly past the last store, Mark, Pam and Joshua saw the familiar sign "Leaving Franklin—Please Drive Gently." Another mile farther down the road, they came to the entrance to Saint Cross Abbey.

Mark, who had been lying on his back roughhousing with the dogs, sat up when Pam turned the Jeep into the private drive. He looked down the narrow road that led to the main chapel. "So, Joshua, do you miss being a monk?"

Joshua surveyed the well-manicured grounds. "Aspects of it, I suppose," he answered. "There is a quiet rhythm to a contemplative order that's very comforting. But I never felt the joy as a monk as I do with Brooke."

"I'm sorry she couldn't come with us today," Pam said.

"I am too. Ever since the partners of her architectural firm announced their plans to retire, she's been working incredibly long hours," Joshua said.

Pam drove the Jeep behind the annex and parked by the side entrance.

"Okay," Mark said, crawling out of the car. "I'll be with Brother John if you need me." Clipper and Cutter jumped out and dashed into the woods to explore the new environment.

"I thought you were going to help me mark and cut trees," Joshua said.

"Well," Mark stalled, trying to think of a good excuse, "I think Brother John is in more need of my assistance."

"To test his latest rum sauces?" Pam asked in a disapproving tone.

Mark shrugged. "If that's how I help best," he said before scooting away.

"Sorry about that," Pam said to Joshua. "I can help you after the meeting."

"It's really not necessary. Several of the brothers have offered to lend a hand," he said.

Just then Brother Matthew opened the annex door. "It's chilly out here. Please come in."

Before anyone could react, the Walkers' two Labs bolted between the monk's legs and ran into the building, disappearing down the hall.

"Come here!" Pam called out. But they were already long gone, probably heading for the kitchen. "I'll get them in a minute," she promised.

"Not to worry," Matthew said. "I'm sure John will corral them as soon as they cross paths."

Pam grimaced. "Let's hope."

Joshua leaned into the backseat and collected his gear. "I'm going to get to work. Would you let Michael know that I'll be down in the south field?"

"He should be down there shortly," Matthew said.

"Great. See you in a few hours," Joshua said.

"I'm so glad you came today," Matthew said, holding the door for Pam. "It should be an interesting discussion."

"Anything I should know in advance?" she asked.

"I think this is something one must experience firsthand with no preconceptions," he said.

She raised her brows and grinned. "Sounds intriguing."

As the two walked through the community room, Pam noticed Brother Michael seated at the small desk talking on the phone.

"We'll wait a minute for Brother Michael. He's just wrapping up his call," Matthew said.

They could easily overhear his conversation.

"Thank you again for the article," Michael said. "It will give our foundation tremendous coverage. . . . Have a good day."

Michael replaced the receiver and joined Pam and Matthew.

"Did the interview go well?" Matthew asked.

Michael nodded. "I think very well, although it was much longer than I expected."

Matthew explained to Pam, "A freelance reporter is writing an article on our philanthropic initiatives around the world. He feels he can place it in one or perhaps two publications."

"Actually, Matthew," Michael said, "he's submitting it to a dozen. *International Philanthropy* has already bought it and is taking it to press tomorrow. They had planned a feature article on the Gates Foundation, but needed to push that out, and we were slid into its place."

Matthew raised his brows. "So, we won't have an opportunity to review the article?"

"I don't think there's any need," Michael said. "He's written a few articles about Saint Cross in the past and has always been very supportive. The questions were run-of-the-mill. He began with our rum sauce business and then made some queries about National Gourmet Products, but his focus was on our philanthropic foundation—how we identify gift and grant recipients, what is the nature of our microlending, those types of questions. I told him about Brian Beezer's recent successes down in South America."

Pam's ears perked up when she heard Brian's name. "How is he doing?" she asked.

"Well," Matthew said, "Brian's come a long way in a short time and we've certainly benefited from his energy and entrepreneurial spirit."

"That's good to hear," Pam said. "So, how large is the circulation of the magazine?"

Michael looked at Matthew. "What do you think, millions? I think they publish it in nine different languages."

"I believe so," Matthew said. "Michael, there was nothing out of the ordinary about the interview?"

"Not at all. In fact, to add some color and make the article more current, I told him about the delightful snow monkeys that were given to us as a gift from Japan. I said that we deeply appreciated their generosity and are enamored of the charming animals, and that demonstrations of such global brotherhood fuel our outreach efforts all the more."

"Very good," Brother Matthew said.

Pam nodded. "A magazine that goes to all corners of the world and has both religious and secular readers must have a tremendous impact on the monastery."

"One would think so," Matthew said, leading Pam and Michael down the hall. "We have never been in this specific magazine before, but there are many publications which include articles that only a handful of people might actually read."

"That's unfortunate," Pam said. "I would think one word in the right place could bring tremendous exposure to Saint Cross and might result in additional contributions to your foundation's endowment."

Michael laughed. "We wish it were that easy, but it's highly improbable."

Suddenly one of Pam's dogs darted around her legs and disappeared around the corner.

"I'll go get him," she said.

"No, no, let them explore," Matthew said, opening the door to Chapter Hall. "Our meeting is about to begin."

Chapter Hall was one of the most beautiful rooms in Saint Cross. The carved vaulted ceiling reflected a craftsmanship that could no longer be found. It was the room in which the monastic community gathered for weekly spiritual readings as well as each morning to discuss the day's schedule. The core of the abbey, it ranked in importance only after the large church and the monk's private chapel.

In the large room, twenty-seven monks sat in quiet meditation, preparing themselves for the coming discussion. The tables had been rearranged into two rows diagonal to each other to facilitate more open discussion. Pam took a seat at a table in back.

Brother Matthew stood at the front of the large room and put his hands together at chest level. "Thank you all for coming," he said slowly. "I believe I have already shared with you the little I know of today's meeting. Monastics from an abbey in Oregon have requested an hour of our time to present an idea. Since I know nothing about the nature of their proposal, several of us agreed to invite Pam Walker to sit in on our discussion." He looked at Pam and bowed slightly. "Pam, thank you for coming," he said before sitting down.

The door opened and two women entered the room. Pam guessed one to be in her midthirties and the other in her midfifties. They wore similar attire: black slacks and long-sleeved cotton shirts of dark colors. Each wore a crucifix hanging from a chain around her neck.

The first woman, a stout brunette with heavy glasses, was carrying what appeared to be an open crate of wine bottles. The second, obviously the older of the two, held a stack of pamphlets and a plant whose roots were wrapped in burlap. When she saw Pam she hesitated for a moment, clearly confused as to why a woman was sitting among the monks.

"I am Sister Claire," the elder began, looking first at Brother Matthew and then glancing across the room. "Thank you for seeing us. Sister Kristina has joined me to share with you an idea we have."

Pam studied the woman, who easily held everyone's attention. Despite being no taller than five feet four inches and quite lean, she had a commanding presence. Her silver hair had been roughly cut, with bangs hanging just above her light hazel eyes. Claire's voice was clear and articulate, reflecting both intelligence and honesty, and she stood with the ease of someone who was comfortable with herself.

"Our monastery, Saint Amand, located in northern Oregon, is a community of sixteen sisters and four novices," Claire began. "For the last twenty-two years, it has been our religious and spiritual home and, through our vineyard, has given us the opportunity to build a substantial and quite profitable business. In fact, we produce some of the highest-rated wines in the Northwest, although our volume remains quite small."

Claire placed the small plant on the table in front of Brother Matthew. She then went around the room and set a bottle of wine on each table.

Pam assumed the sisters had come to Saint Cross to ask the brothers to use the abbey's national distribution system for their wine. A reasonable request, Pam thought. She quickly wrote "Commission? Royalties?" in her notebook.

"We find ourselves in the unique position of"—Claire paused—"looking for a new home."

Pam looked up, raising her brows. That was unexpected.

Sister Claire continued. "We have outgrown both our land and our buildings. If we expand our monastery, we will have to reduce the acreage allocated to our vineyard. Although it would be most logical to stay in Oregon, one of the sisters, who has been following your philanthropic efforts, suggested that we meet with you."

An older brother interrupted. "This is very interesting, but I'm at a loss as to how any of it relates to Saint Cross."

Sister Claire waited for a moment before answering. "We think it may be to the benefit of both communities, yours and ours, to consider a . . . partnership of sorts."

"Partnership?" Brother Matthew asked.

"We have come to learn that there are eighty acres behind your monastery that could be purchased from one of the local farmers. If we were to buy the land, the sisters could build a new monastery that would accommodate our growing numbers, and offer twice the land for cultivation."

Pam watched Claire closely, and her fascination with the sister quickly developed into admiration. For Claire to come into an unknown environment and suggest such an idea as confidently as she had showed tremendous inner strength.

"When appropriate, we could share some or all religious services with the monks of Saint Cross. Our discretionary profits would go to Saint Cross for your philanthropic efforts. In that way, we can ensure that the small money we have to give is put to the best use."

Suddenly two black Labs lunged into the room, so excited they were almost flying. Tails wagging, they bounded from monk to monk, slobbering and panting. Pam jumped up and tried to grab Cutter's collar, but he was too fast. In a flash both dogs darted back out of the room, and the hurricane was over.

"I'm so sorry," Pam said before resuming her seat.

"God's creatures." Claire smiled. Returning to the business at hand, she glanced around the room and saw the shocked expressions of several of the monks. "Please understand that this idea was not developed quickly or taken lightly on our part. We have prayed and deliberated over this problem for more than a year and have only recently concluded that a . . . partnership, if you would like to call it that, may be a truly viable path to follow."

When she stopped speaking, the room fell silent. The monks continued to stare at Sister Claire, and to her credit, she didn't speak just to fill the void. She stood tall and allowed the idea to settle like dust after a windstorm.

After a very long minute, Matthew cleared his throat. "Well," he said, drawing out the word as long as possible, "in truth, I'm at a loss. We have never considered expanding our community to include sisters, so this is quite new territory that you have presented."

"We understand," Claire replied. "Our intent was to place the idea on the table and answer whatever initial questions you may have. In consideration of our suggestion, let me give you a folder that includes detailed information about our monastery and wine business, and if appropriate, we can provide financial statements for the past five years. I feel that the first step, though, is to determine if the general concept is one that your community would like to pursue."

"That, in itself, will require lengthy discussion among the brothers, especially if there are strongly opposing views," Matthew responded.

"As we had," she agreed. "We know this will be a long process and understand that, unless the suggestion is immediately rejected, we will need to spend far more time together, individually and collectively both here and in Oregon, to ensure that there is a spiritual synergy between us."

Matthew nodded before picking up the folder.

Seeing that several brothers were looking at the handout, Sister Kristina stepped forward to explain. "We tried to collect all pertinent information about us in those pages. It even goes so far as to share with you the high-level economics of our wine business so you feel comfortable that we will not be turning to Saint Cross for financial support at some later date."

"I must admit, you have certainly given us something to think about. May I ask how long you will be in the area?" Matthew asked.

Sister Claire nodded. "We plan to leave the day after tomorrow."

Brother Matthew stood and walked to the front of the room. He towered over Sister Claire, but the relaxed gentleness within both people seemed to create a perfect balance.

Brother Matthew shook Claire's hand. "Thank you again for coming. If you let us know where you are staying, we will call you tomorrow morning."

After the sisters left, Matthew said, "Well, at the very least, that was quite interesting."

A few monks laughed.

"Although I am at a loss for an opinion, I am amazed that such a life-altering proposition came to us so unexpectedly," Matthew said, sounding more philosophical than conversational. "We will each need to meditate and pray on this subject."

Brother Marc added, "Our decision, either way, will have tremendous implications."

"For us and for the sisters," Brother John added.

Brother Aaron, who at seventy-eight was one of the oldest members of the community, leaned forward. "I suppose that's one of my concerns," he said thoughtfully. "If they moved here, would we, in a sense, become our sisters' keeper?"

"It appears not financially," Matthew answered. "I feel confident that they would not misrepresent their business. If all would like, and if Pam agrees"—he looked up at her—"perhaps you can review their books."

She nodded.

"But there would still be a responsibility for them," Brother Steven said.

"As with any person with whom we have a relationship," Brother John answered.

"We would be two separate communities but religiously connected?" Brother Aaron asked.

"That would be my assumption," Matthew said.

He looked around the room, considering how best to lead the large group in discussion so that, at some later date, a consensus could be reached. It would no doubt be a tremendously difficult debate, with different opinions possibly polarizing the monks. Brother Matthew was painfully aware that such a proposition could deeply divide the community. He sighed, struggling to find the words to begin.

"Well, I say let's do it," Brother Michael said lightheartedly, startling Matthew with the speed of his suggestion.

"I agree," Brother John said immediately.

Suddenly, many of the monks voiced the same opinion.

"A fine addition to Saint Cross," an older brother said.

Matthew struggled not to reveal his utter surprise. "Are there no concerns?" he asked.

"Certainly there are," Brother Marc said. "More than we could discuss in three weeks, but not so many as to dismiss the possibility. I suggest we move forward and invite the sisters to stay with us for a while. We, in turn, should visit their monastery in Oregon."

"Agreed," Brother John said. "We should take it one step at a time, but let's take the first step now."

"Are there no dissenters in the group?" Matthew asked, and waited for several moments. He smiled when everyone remained silent. "Very well then, I will call Sister Claire and ask her to return. Marc, perhaps you and Aaron can join me for that discussion."

"Do let us know if they bring more merlot," another brother joked.

Suddenly there was a rapid knock on the door.

"Come in," Matthew called out.

The door swung open and Joshua almost ran into the room. "I'm terribly sorry for interrupting your meeting, but there's a problem," he said quickly. "Mark is locked in the walk-in refrigerator."

Several of the monks started to laugh.

"Keep him there," one of them teased.

"I think his lips are turning blue," Joshua pleaded.

Brother John got up. “There’s a red release button to the right of the door. Didn’t he see it?”

“I don’t know. All I could see was that he was trying to hold on to several boxes of rum sauce while pounding on the door,” Joshua said. “From what he was yelling, it seemed like he was more claustrophobic than cold.”

“Good thing you came along when you did,” Brother Marc said, as Brother John and Joshua left to rescue their friend.

“Perhaps this is a good time to break,” Matthew suggested. “We’ll plan to continue our discussion after dinner tonight.”

After all the other brothers had left Chapter Hall, Matthew took a seat across the table from Pam. “Your thoughts?” he asked.

She shook her head. “Like you, I don’t know where to begin. I would never have guessed it.”

“Nor I.” Matthew chuckled.

“But I liked Claire a lot. And I like the fact that they seemed to have thought through the idea from every angle. Do you want me to look at their books?”

“I hate to impose yet again, but we would deeply appreciate your opinion.”

“It’s no imposition at all,” Pam said. “Well, let me go see if my husband has frostbite.”

Matthew smiled. “For such a nice fellow, he does seem to get himself in the strangest predicaments.”

TWELVE

Yellow

The caravan that had been dispatched from the naval yard in Bethesda, Maryland, consisted of one black Hummer and a twenty-foot semitrailer flatbed attached to a black cab in front. Both vehicles had darkly tinted windows and the objects being transported were draped with a heavy black tarp strapped down with metal cables. The trip across country had been uneventful until the payload neared its first stop at Farm to Market Road, just north of Wheatley.

Seeing a string of brake lights ahead of him, the driver of the Hummer slowed his vehicle. He leaned out the window, trying to see beyond the traffic jam.

"What the hell . . . ?" the driver said to himself.

His radio speaker crackled loudly. "Hansen, what's the delay?" asked Rupert, who was driving the flatbed directly behind the Hummer.

"A moose," Hansen answered in disbelief. "There appears to be an adult male moose standing in the middle of the road about fifty yards ahead. Half a dozen cars are pulled over in each direction."

"Well, blast your horn," Rupert advised.

A child jumped out of a van from the other side of the road and ran up to the moose, holding out an apple. The moose smelled the fruit, licked the boy's arm and then began strolling up the road, staying very close to the center lane.

"Hi, Howard," someone yelled from another car.

"Blow your horn," Rupert repeated over the radio.

Hansen was unsure if Howard was the boy or the moose. "I don't think so," he replied.

The traffic began to inch forward with the moose leading the way. As oncoming cars approached the meandering animal, they drove onto the grass, keeping well off the asphalt, which gave the moose full berth to venture wherever he wanted. A half mile down the road, just as Woodrow Lake came into view, the moose broke unexpectedly into a loping trot. He crossed the road and disappeared into the woods that surrounded the southern coves. Traffic picked up immediately.

Twelve miles later, the caravan reached the bridge at Fork River, which was engorged by the fall rains. There, the road began a slight ascent, passing the northern end of the lake. The stone inn of Montis was in clear view.

"We're in sight of the first drop-off," Hansen radioed back to the other driver.

Suddenly, a man wearing a bright yellow parka darted out from a small dirt driveway on Hansen's left and ran into the road, waving his arms widely. Thinking the man was about to run in front of the Hummer, Hansen slammed on his brakes, which created an unnerving chain reaction that ended with the flatbed. The cables surrounding the payload strained against the forward momentum.

"This is where you want to be!" the man yelled out, still swinging his arms in the air.

Hansen rolled down his window. "Mark Walker?"

"That's me," Mark said with a huge grin. He pointed to the dirt road. "In here."

The Hummer pulled forward, allowing the flatbed to back into the driveway. Hansen pulled in behind him and parked his SUV.

Mark ran up to the Hummer. "Boy, you guys really look undercover. Are you from the surplus warehouse?"

"Delivery duty. My name is Hansen. That's Rupert," he said, pointing to the flatbed.

"Don't tell me. They're code names," Mark said, winking at the man. "I won't tell anyone. Is that my motorcycle back there?"

Hansen picked up his clipboard and rummaged through the papers. "Payload 9233," he read, "is a nineteen forty-four BMW R75."

"This is *so* cool," Mark said.

"Sir, where is your drop point?" Hansen asked.

"What's a drop point?"

"Where we discharge the payload," Hansen advised.

"Oh, we're just going to put it in our barn for now. We've rigged up a great pulley system. You can just back in over there," Mark said, pointing.

Hansen looked skeptically at Mark. "You will need to sign the attached before taking delivery. Additional signatures will be required for the transfer of ownership." Hansen passed Mark a stack of government documents. "We advise that each page be reviewed in full."

Mark riffled through the papers. "But there are dozens of pages here—and it's all small print. It would take me a week to read it," he complained.

"Initials are required at the bottom of each page before unloading, sir," Hansen counseled. He then looked at his watch. "And the semitrailer needs to depart for Seattle by fourteen hundred."

Mark looked at the flatbed once more. He knew this was when Pam would scream caution. But this was the U.S. government. Their bureaucracy was there for a reason, and they would never lead a private citizen astray, would they?

"Okay," Mark said, "where's the pen?"

After Hansen retrieved the signed documents, he directed the truck to back up toward the barn. Joshua, who had been waiting by the barn doors, guided the driver as he reversed down the long road. Mark ran alongside.

"This will be a breeze," Mark called to Joshua. "Just get it over the pulley."

"Not a problem," Joshua said.

Mark tried to look under the tarp, but it was too tightly strapped down. It was obvious that there was more than just a motorcycle. The front-most object was a long, round cylinder.

"So, what else do you have under there? A missile?" Mark joked.

Hansen remained expressionless. "It would require a security clearance for me to answer that question, sir."

Walking next to the flatbed, Mark tried again to lift a corner of the tarp.

"I wouldn't advise that, sir," Hansen said.

Mark's eyebrows rose. "You *do* have a missile under there, don't you?"

"Wow!" Joshua yelled out when the back of the flatbed was well inside the barn.

Once the engine was turned off, Hansen began unclamping the metal straps. Mark grabbed one end to assist.

"I'm sorry, sir," Hansen said. "Please back away until your payload is ready to be unloaded."

Just as Hansen began to pull back the tarp, Pam walked in.

"Great timing, honey. It's here," Mark said, with boyish excitement. "And there's a real missile too," he whispered.

They watched as Hansen rolled the tarp off the old motorcycle.

Mark's mouth fell open. "Wow. It's yellow."

"So I see," Pam said without enthusiasm.

Taking a closer look at her husband's purchase, Pam saw that the photograph had been accurate—it had no wheels. And the 1944 BMW R75 was, indeed, bright yellow, almost the same color as Mark's parka.

Other than missing a few parts, the vehicle appeared to be in good condition, although both Pam and Mark noticed several small holes in the sidecar.

"Bullet holes," Pam said under her breath.

The motorcycle was resting on three metal brackets. Hansen jumped up onto the flatbed and removed the nylon straps that were securing the bike and sidecar to the flatbed.

"Can I get up there and put the ropes around it now?" Mark asked.

Hansen extended his hand and easily hoisted Mark onto the flatbed. Joshua passed him the ropes, which he wrapped around the body of the motorcycle.

"Okay, here's the plan," Mark said. "I tied the rope to the fender of the Jeep. Pam will back it up just enough to lift the motorcycle a few inches off the trailer and then you guys just pull it forward and out of the barn. Then Pam will ease the Jeep forward until the bike is lowered to the ground. Josh, you and I can grab some hay bales to support it on each side."

Joshua nodded. "That just might work."

"This is so perfect," Mark said. "Okay, let's lift it up."

Hansen stepped out of the barn as Mark jumped off the trailer. Pam was in position behind the wheel of their Jeep. Mark looked up to ensure the rope was passed through all four pulley wheels, and then followed it to the end, where it was tied to the front bumper of the Jeep, at the opposite barn door.

"All right, as soon as we lift it up, you'll drive the flatbed out," Mark told the driver as he climbed into the cab of the semitrailer. "Okay," Mark called to Pam. "Is everyone ready? On three. One . . . two . . . three."

And then, to everyone's amazement, the unloading began exactly as Mark had planned. Pam slowly reversed the Jeep, the ropes went taut and the motorcycle with the sidecar attached lifted gently off the supporting brackets. Mark waved his arm to the truck driver, who pulled the flatbed out of the barn. Pam continued to back up until the motorcycle was eight feet off the ground.

"Pam! Stop!" Mark yelled out.

Pam stepped on the brake so hard that a strong jolt shot through the rope. Suddenly the sidecar detached from the motorcycle and crashed to the ground, leaving the motorcycle swinging in midair.

Mark ran toward the broken sidecar. "Joshua, help me move it out of the way."

Once the wreckage was pushed aside, Mark called over to Pam, "Honey, come forward slowly."

Joshua kept his eyes on the Jeep while Mark watched the bike.

"Mark," Joshua said with concern, "it looks like the knot on the bumper is coming loose."

Within two seconds, the rope untied itself and slipped through the bumper. The end flew up toward the barn roof and the motorcycle crashed to the ground.

Everyone stood in stunned silence. Pam jumped out of the car and ran to Mark's side.

"Wow, did you see that?" he finally said. "That was incredible. And it's still in one piece! These things are built like tanks!"

Hansen walked up holding out a clipboard. "Please sign here for your second payload."

"Second?" Mark said.

"The apiary," Pam reminded him.

"Oh, right," Mark said, signing the papers.

Hansen jumped back on the trailer and pulled the tarp farther back to expose two dozen enormous panels of wire mesh. Each panel, which lay flat on top of the other, looked to be about fourteen feet long and eight feet wide.

"Where are the beehives?" Mark asked.

"Beehives, sir?" Hansen said.

"The apiary," Pam offered as clarification.

Hansen looked at his clipboard. "Payload 9234," he read, "is an aviary."

"No, I bought an *apiary,*" Mark said, enunciating the "p" very clearly.

"No, sir. This is an outside *aviary* originally constructed for the National Zoo in Washington, D.C."

Pam looked at Mark in disbelief. "You bought me a two-thousand-dollar *birdcage*?"

THIRTEEN

Reservations

It was midafternoon by the time Pam left Mark and Joshua at the barn. As each of her long strides took her farther from the commotion behind her, she once again struggled to calm her frustrations. Although she loved her husband deeply, and was continually amused by his childlike fervor, his impulsive involvement in anything and everything that caught his attention had cost them dearly since coming to Lumby. While Pam didn't want to curb his enthusiasm, at some point she would have to rein in his spending. But not that afternoon—there were larger issues to resolve.

Walking the short distance up the road to the inn, she mentally reviewed what she would serve for dinner that evening. Although only four lodging guests had confirmed their restaurant reservations at the inn, there were also two people coming at six o'clock and another party of four arriving half an hour later.

Pam looked at her watch and quickened her pace. The demands on her time had become unnerving. She was no longer enjoying the dream of their "Phase 2" and occasionally wondered if returning to a corporate job would offer some relief from the stress she was feeling. To deepen her dismay, Pam had not yet received one résumé or inquiry in response to her ads for a chef.

Without realizing it, Pam began jogging the last several hundred yards to the inn, which only magnified her sense of urgency. Circling around the main building, she stopped in the courtyard, trying to decide if she should shower and change before heading to the main kitchen. No, there wasn't time. It seemed that there was never enough time.

Pam paused in the dining room only long enough to take note of necessary preparations for that evening. Although the tables were already set, new candles and fresh flowers were needed to be put out. Hopefully Mark wouldn't be too much longer at the barn and could lend a hand.

Still focused on the dining room, Pam backed into the kitchen by pushing the swing doors with the backs of her elbows. She gave one final scrutinizing look around the room, nodded with satisfaction and turned into the kitchen.

"Oh!" she yelled out, startled to see a huge man standing in front of the refrigerator, leaning against the open door with his back to her. Pam quickly looked around to see if there were any others in the kitchen. She swallowed, trying to get over the feeling that her heart was in her throat.

"Excuse me," she said loudly.

When the man turned around, he seemed even larger, with a tremendous stomach that hung out over the top of his pants and long grizzled hair pulled back in a rubber band. His sideburns were untrimmed, as was his mustache. His wrinkled clothes looked as if he had slept in them, and his eyeglasses, which he repeatedly pushed higher on his nose, were visibly scratched.

"Can I help you?" Pam said forcefully.

"Just looking around," the man said. "Seeing what kind of place you have here."

Pam stayed by the door, caught between irritation and intimidation.

"Who are you?" she demanded.

The man pushed the refrigerator door closed so hard that bottles shook within it. "Cutty," he said. "You the kitchen help?"

Pam flushed with anger. "You could say that. What are you do—"

"Tell me where they keep the wine, sweetheart."

"Who the hell are you?" Pam yelled.

"I'll take my business up with the boss, darling."

Pam took several steps forward and stood as squarely as she ever had. "I *am* the boss, and I don't like being called 'sweetheart.' "

The huge man visibly shrunk. He pulled out a crumpled piece of newspaper from his pocket. "You're Pam Walker?" he asked sheepishly.

"I am," she said. "Do you mind telling me who you are and what you're doing in my kitchen?"

"I'm sorry," he said, trying to tuck in his shirt before going over and shaking Pam's hand.

His palm was greasy.

"Darryl Cutty, but everyone calls me Cutty." He handed her the newspaper. "I came about the job."

Pam immediately thought Mark must have advertised for a stable hand and forgotten to tell her.

"What job?"

"For head chef. This is the Montis Inn restaurant, isn't it?" he asked. "You have a nice setup here."

Pam's jaw dropped and she stared at the man in disbelief. "You're a chef?" she finally asked.

"Yeah, I've flipped some burgers in my time," Cutty replied, hitting his nose with his fist for effect.

Pam wanted the discussion to be over. "I'm sorry. We do more than flip burgers here. We're looking for a professionally trained chef who can bring his own style of cuisine to our restaurant."

"Don't have my own cuisine, but I can make a great stew," Cutty said.

"I'm sorry, Mr. Cutty," she said, opening the door. "Thank you for coming, as unexpected as this was. If we ever decide to bring in a sous chef, we'll advertise again."

"Well, if you want to call my employer—"

"Mr. Cutty, if you'll excuse me, I'm awfully busy. After reviewing our menus and house specialties, which you can see on the Montis Inn Web site, if you're quite sure you have the qualifications to meet and better our standards, please mail us a résumé and we'll contact you if we are interested."

"Well, thanks for talking with me. You got a nice place here," the large man said as he pushed his way through the swinging door.

Pam watched him shuffle across the dining room and out the main entrance. As soon as she heard the door close, she grabbed a stool, because she was shaking from the encounter. Once she sat down, all of the built-up adrenaline rushed from her body. She leaned forward and rested her arms on the island countertop, then laid her head in her hands. For several minutes she stayed hunched over trying to calm her nerves.

Suddenly, from behind her, a man's arm grabbed her around the chest. When she felt his breath on the back of her neck, she panicked but didn't scream. Instead she grabbed a fork lying near her hand and just as the male was putting his lips on her skin, she jabbed the utensil into his forearm.

Mark shouted in pain and yanked his arm away. "What did you do that for, Pam? Are you crazy?" he yelled.

She spun around and saw her husband holding his arm, wincing in pain.

Pam was mortified. "I'm so sorry," she said, and burst into tears.

Mark was baffled. "Wait a minute. I'm the one who just got stabbed. Why are you crying?"

She pushed out the words in between gulps of air. "I thought you were the man."

"What man? The large fellow I saw get into his car?"

"He was here about the job and . . ." Her voice trailed off.

"I thought he was the plumber fixing the garbage disposal," Mark said. "He was a *chef*?"

"No, I don't think so," Pam said, shaking her head. "The whole thing was awful. And then you grabbed me."

Seeing the pained look in Pam's eyes, Mark gently wrapped his arms around her and drew her close. After holding her tightly for several minutes, he finally felt her breathing slow. "It will be all right," he whispered. "I'll be your full-time help until we hire someone."

"You don't know how much that means to me," Pam said.

The phone rang on the desk in the far corner of the kitchen.

"I'll get it," he said, letting her go. Picking up the phone, he said, "Montis Inn . . . Yes, it's still open. . . . Your name?" Mark listened for several minutes. "We would definitely like to talk with you. . . . Great. We'll see you in about thirty minutes."

Mark, beaming, hung up the phone. "Our problems are solved, honey. That was André Levesque, the chef at Cedar Grove Inn in Wheatley."

"Wow! That's where we used to stay when we came here for vacation." She grinned. "They had spectacular food."

"He's been the chef there for eight years and is on his way up to talk with us."

"That would be a dream come true," Pam said. "Let me run over and take a quick shower." She glanced up and down at Mark's dirty, grease-stained work clothes. "You might want to do the same."

"Honey, he's not interviewing us. We're interviewing him."

"Don't be so sure," she said, running out of the kitchen.

∾

At three forty-five, Pam heard a car pull into their small parking area. Prompt, she thought as she walked out of their private house to greet André Levesque. The man stepping from his car was well dressed with a European flair; he wore loose black pants with a strong crease down the front, a brilliant red shirt, a black flannel blazer and what appeared to be a signature accessory—a long scarf in a pattern of red and black. He was shorter than Pam by several inches, and very trim. By his ease of movement, Pam guessed that he was in better shape than her husband. But, in Mark's defense, André was probably in his midthirties, at least ten years younger than Mark.

"Welcome to Montis Inn. I'm Pam Walker," she said, shaking his hand. She quickly noted André's clean hands and manicured nails. "I'm so glad to finally meet. My husband and I were guests at Cedar Grove Inn several times before we found Montis."

"Thank you," he said with no French accent. Standing in the courtyard, André circled around Pam, examining each of the buildings in the charming complex. "What you've done with the old monastery is nothing less than miraculous. I had feared the old ruin had seen its final days."

Pam laughed. "I'm sure a lot of folks thought the same. Why don't we go to the living room where we can talk?" she said, leading him to the main building. "I understand you graduated from The Culinary Institute of America."

"In Hyde Park, New York," André replied.

"Did you join Cedar Grove from here?"

"No, I went to Le Cordon Bleu for a year and then worked in Paris before coming back to the States."

Pam stopped at the bottom of the front steps. "With your background, why did you come to Wheatley?"

"Because I still have a lot to learn. I'm still developing my own signature. When the time is right, I plan to open my own restaurant."

"Where?"

André looked up at the stone manor and then back at Pam. "Perhaps Boston, but I haven't decided. That won't be for another five years at least, so there's plenty of time to think about it."

In the living room, Mark was standing by the fireplace, tending to logs he had just lit.

"Mark, this is André Levesque."

"Great you came," Mark said. "So, you're French?"

"My parents were French-Canadian but my grandparents were both from France," André said.

"Have a seat and make yourself at home," Mark said as he straightened the magazines on the coffee table and replaced loose sofa pillows. "We're very shorthanded right now."

Pam laughed. "What that means is that Mark hasn't gotten around to straightening up in here."

Mark sat next to Pam and put his arm around her shoulder. She couldn't hide her impatience.

"So, you're thinking of leaving Cedar Grove?" Pam asked.

"Not my own doing, I'm afraid," André answered.

Never one to mince words, Mark asked, "They've fired you?"

"Oh, absolutely not," André answered with a soft chuckle. "The Dwyers have accepted an offer for their property and will be selling it next month. We've been told that the new owners will be reverting it to a private residence."

Pam exhaled a breath of relief. "So what are your immediate plans?"

André leaned back in his chair. "Interesting question. I wasn't expecting this crossroad for several more years." He stared out a window. "I used to work in Boston, so that would be a possibility, but I think I want something quieter, something that would offer the free time for me to develop my autograph."

"Autograph?" Mark asked.

"A culinary signature," André explained. "A taste, preparation and presentation that are uniquely mine."

Just then the phone rang. Mark jumped up and ran out to the lobby. Pam and André could easily overhear lodging reservations for the following night being made.

André continued. "Perhaps the sale of Cedar Grove is a good thing—forcing me to move on. It was becoming increasingly difficult to find my own time. They are always fully booked and their restaurant serves fifty at their two seatings each night."

Pam nodded. "I had forgotten they have two seatings for dinner."

"Five thirty and seven thirty," André said. "It would be unmanageable otherwise."

Pam rolled her eyes, knowing just how unmanageable open reservations were. "How many rooms do they have at Cedar Grove?" she asked.

"Sixteen," André said.

"Similar to Montis," Pam said.

Mark strolled into the living room and was about to fall onto the sofa when the phone rang again. "Excuse me," he said, heading back to the lobby.

"We're almost never fully booked," Pam quickly said. "Lumby is really out of the mainstream for vacationers and our restaurant only has a small local following."

"What meals do you serve?" André asked.

"A full breakfast only to the inn guests, although we do occasionally have drop-ins whom we try to accommodate. I would probably continue preparing those. And then dinner Tuesday through Sunday."

"Sunday brunch?" he asked.

Pam nodded. "Yes, between twelve and three but we generally only have six to eight diners."

The phone rang again. Mark looked around the corner at Pam, clearly baffled by the number of calls they were receiving. Pam shrugged.

"The phone seldom rings," she explained to André. "We could go a full week without a single reservation."

André looked toward the lobby, listening to Mark's conversation.

"A party of twelve for Sunday brunch? . . . One o'clock . . . Your name please? . . . Fine, thank you."

Pam jumped when the cell phone in her pocket vibrated just as the fax machine started. "I'm so sorry. This really isn't what it appears," she said to André before answering her phone. "Montis Inn. Yes, we have vacancies. . . . I'm sorry? . . . Yes, we do have three adjoining suites." Pam grabbed a pencil off the table and scribbled on a piece of newspaper. "Bob and Karen Hartman for four nights. . . . If your dog is well behaved, yes, with an additional deposit . . . And your credit card number please?" Pam quickly jotted down the numbers. "We'll see you tomorrow afternoon, Karen. Have a good day."

André stood up just as Mark walked into the living room. "I'm sorry," André said. "You both seem quite pleasant and you have a gorgeous inn, but this obviously isn't a good fit. If I go to another private hotel, I want it to be quiet enough to test my recipes in the kitchen."

Pam panicked. "We're quiet!" she asserted.

The phone in the lobby rang again. She gave a long, false laugh. "Mark, disconnect it," she said under her breath. She turned back to André, desperately needing him to reconsider. "This has never happened before," she said urgently, "and I have no idea why it's happening now."

"Montis Inn," Mark was heard saying from the lobby. "Dinner for six this evening? . . . At the chef's table in the kitchen?" Mark stepped around the corner and gave Pam a bewildered look, to which she shrugged her shoulders. "I'm sorry. We really don't offer that at this time. Your name please? . . . Great. We'll see you at six thirty. . . . As well as tomorrow night? . . . Yes, we can seat you at the same time. . . . No, our wine cellar can't be conveniently toured."

Pam turned bright red. "Our wine cellar is in a pantry in the kitchen."

André smiled. "I've been there before," he said empathetically. "Whatever works."

"Are you sure you don't want to see the kitchen?" she pleaded.

André looked at Pam and tilted his head as if he were reconsidering. "Thanks for your hospitality, but I don't think so. When Mark gets off the phone, please tell him I said goodbye."

And as quickly as Pam's hope had blossomed, it deflated as she watched André Levesque walk out of Montis Inn.

Mark returned and looked around the room. "Where's André?"

"Gone," Pam said, falling back onto the sofa. "First thing tomorrow morning, we're going to place a help-wanted ad in every paper we can think of."

An hour later, a couple walked into the lobby with luggage in hand. "I can't believe we're actually here," the woman said with giddy, nervous laughter.

The man gently hit the bell on the front desk, then turned around and peered into the living room. "It's exactly like he said," he commented.

Mark ran down the stairs two at a time, almost tripping on the last tread. He grabbed the banister just in time. "Welcome to Montis Inn. Can I help you?" he said.

"We'd like to check in, please. Margaret and James Edwards," the man said, reaching into his back pocket for his wallet.

Mark shuffled through the papers in the check-in basket and pulled out their reservation form. "If you could complete this, I'll run your credit card."

As her husband filled out the form, the wife stepped up to the desk. "I know this seems silly, but would you sign this please?"

Mark looked up. She was holding a rolled-up magazine just inches from his face. Mark unrolled the magazine and amazement filled his face. On the cover of Christian Copeland's *Vintner's Fare* was a photograph of Montis Inn, under which in bold type the copy read: **"THE BEST UNDISCOVERED TREASURE IN AMERICA."**

FOURTEEN

Tom

Upon arriving in Rocky Mount, most newcomers describe the town as "small," as in: a small airport, a small downtown and a small coffee shop. However, after leaving the main (albeit small) thoroughfare and turning west onto State Road 541 toward Lumby, visitors take in a scene of infinite vastness and natural beauty, with thousands of acres of untouched forest. Approaching Lumby, most are struck by the quaintness of the village, and within minutes, by the quirkiness of its residents.

On this particular afternoon, the cabdriver looked at his passenger in the rearview mirror. He was an unusually tall man in his mid-forties with wiry silver-gray hair who had sat quietly since leaving Rocky Mount airport. Although the driver had tried to engage him in conversation, the passenger's responses were polite but brief. The only time he spoke was when he asked the driver to slow down on a hairpin curve at Priest's Pass because he had spotted a grizzly foraging next to the road.

"Howard must still be on Farm to Market," the driver said as they neared the town.

The passenger leaned forward. "I'm sorry?"

"Our moose," the driver said. "Generally, we see him near Priest's Pass."

The man thought for a moment. "That seemed to have a much higher elevation," he observed. "I saw snow up in the mountains. By this time of year, the moose have probably migrated to lower ground for the season."

"Makes sense," the driver said. "I heard he was causing some traffic jams down near Woodrow Lake."

"Ah," the passenger said, turning his shoulders to get a better look out the window.

As they approached the village, a formidable sign on the right side of the road said "Welcome to Lumby—Home of the Pumpkin Festival." If that wasn't odd enough, under the sign stood a plastic pink flamingo dressed like a scarecrow, with hay protruding from under his dungarees. He was sitting on what looked to be an enormous pumpkin.

"Where do you want to be dropped off?" the taxi driver asked.

"Anyplace where I can get some lunch," the passenger replied.

"S&T's makes the best sandwiches in town."

The taxi slowed at what appeared to be the only main intersection. The traffic light glowed a constant blue on all four sides. The man looked at the street signs: Main Street and Farm to Market Road.

One block farther, the taxi pulled over in front of a charming restaurant. "That will be twenty-two dollars."

Once out of the cramped confines of the backseat, the man stretched his long body. He raised each arm above his head and bent to one side and then the other, loosening the sore muscles in his back.

S&T's Soda Shoppe was almost empty, so the stranger, a particularly good-looking man, was quickly noticed when he took a seat at a middle booth.

"Something to drink?" Melanie Gentile, the waitress, asked.

"Coffee, please," he said, scanning the menu. "And I'll have a cup of corn chowder and tuna on white toast, please."

"Coming right up," she said with a pleasant smile.

While waiting for his food, the man read a copy of *The Lumby Lines,* which he had picked up at the door.

The Lumby Lines

Sheriff's Complaints

BY SHERIFF SIMON DIXON October 10

12:14 a.m. Owner of Wayside Tavern reported two riding lawn mowers chasing each other down State Road 541.

12:19 a.m. Owner of Wayside again. Patron complaining of broken arm after falling off riding lawn mower. EMS dispatched.

12:38 a.m. Bartender at Jimmy D's reported lawn mower blocking front entrance. Owner cannot be found.

6:55 a.m. McNear called with complaint that someone had cut the vine of his pumpkin festival entry.

7:01 a.m. Cindy Watford reported that a colony of "at least a hundred" rabbits was in her doghouse and refuse to come out. Her miniature poodle has nowhere to sleep.

7:42 a.m. NW Builders reported excavator hitting main water line on Loggers Road. LFD dispatched.

11:11 a.m. Cooper reported smoke coming out of silo #4. LFD dispatched.

1:58 p.m. Gabrielle called. Two sets of dentures found in customer's water glass. Will turn them in to Simon this afternoon.

2:29 p.m. Resident on Cherry Street reported geese in sauna.

2:39 p.m. Town dump reported trash on Farm to Market from broken hydraulics on Dumpster. Clean-up crew will be sent out shortly.

5:02 p.m. Resident reported Hank and Sporting Goods mannequin sitting on steps of Presbyterian church. Mannequin not appropriately dressed.

11:52 p.m. Call from Jimmy D's. Man injured by lit cigar in his buttocks.

11:54 p.m. Call from Jimmy D's. Man injured from lit cigarette in his ear.

11:58 p.m. Patron at Wayside Tavern reported stolen riding lawn mower.

Turning to the next page, the stranger studied the advertisements and town forum with unusual intensity. He then removed an envelope from his coat pocket and looked at the brochure inside, taking special notice of the address listed.

After lunch, he crossed the road and walked west along Main Street, stopping at every store to look in the windows. Two blocks farther, he spotted his destination: a beautifully restored granary with a charming veterinary sign hand-painted on the siding.

From the sidewalk, he took several minutes to study the building. He had not been misled. The photographs in the flyer were an accurate representation—it was, indeed, a stunning clinic with an architectural craftsmanship he seldom saw in his profession.

The visitor walked up the stone path, pleased to see several metal hitching posts secured deep in the ground. He knocked on the front door, but there was no answer. After waiting for several moments, he opened the door and called in, "Hello?"

The clinic, he assumed, was closed, so he took the opportunity to have a look at the building.

The man circled around the outside of The Granary and came across a row of horse stalls. Newer wood planking and steel hinges indicated that quality work had recently been done on them. Continuing to the back of the building, he examined the condition of the siding and the windows. Looking up at the second floor, his eye caught a flash of color up on the roof. Stepping back, he was immediately struck by the sight of a woman with vibrant red hair standing on the shingles, apparently looking into the top branches of a tree in the backyard.

After a few seconds, she pulled a folded card out of one of the many pockets of her overalls, studied it and then looked up again.

Tom followed her gaze, and caught sight of what was holding her interest: a brilliantly colored bird about eleven inches in length that was boring a hole into the side of the upper trunk of the tree. It was primarily blackish green in color, with a gray collar, a pink belly, a black rump and a red face.

The woman again looked down at the card she was holding, turned it over and studied the other side. She then stepped close to the edge of the roof and stretched her neck to get a closer look at the bird.

"A Lewis woodpecker," the man called up to her.

Mac was startled by the voice and had to catch her balance by stepping on the gutter.

"What?"

"It's a Lewis woodpecker, probably an adult male."

Two questions were rushing through Mac's thoughts: How did he know that? and Who was this man?

She held up her laminated sheet before putting it back in her pocket. "It's not on my reference card."

"Probably because it's not very common. You're lucky to have spotted it," he said.

She moved across the roof with amazing ease and confidence despite the alarmingly steep pitch.

"Are you a birder?" he asked.

"All my life," she said. "When I'm working on a roof, I see lots more birds than I do from the ground."

"A good vantage point," he agreed.

She straightened her back and looked around. "It certainly is."

"I didn't mean to interrupt," the stranger said, "but would you know if the clinic is open?"

"I think Ellen is home. You can go inside and call her if you have a sick animal," Mac suggested.

"No, that's all right. Sorry for interrupting," he said, before turning to walk away. "Very nice work you did on the stalls," he added.

Mac watched the man. "Can I help you with something?" she blurted out. "I'm about to take a break."

He turned and looked up at her again. "Actually, I was hoping to meet Dr. Campbell."

Mac slid her hammer into the tool belt that hung around her waist. "Give me a minute," she said. "I'll take you inside." She stacked several loose shingles together and climbed down the ladder with impressive grace. Once on the ground, she was struck by how tall the man was.

"Doesn't the height bother you?" he asked.

Mac was going to say, "Not at all. I like tall men," until she realized he was talking about the roof. She blushed. "There are wonderful views from up there," she said as she removed her gloves. "I'm Mackenzie McGuire."

"I'm Tom Candor," he said, shaking her hand.

Mackenzie looked into his hazel eyes and studied his face. He was attractive, but there was little warmth about him. He had no laugh lines.

"Let me show you in," she said, leading him through the back entrance of the clinic. "So, Tom Candor, what brings you to Lumby?"

He didn't reply.

"I'm sorry. Was that too presumptuous a question?" she asked.

"Not at all," Tom answered politely, but still he didn't answer the question.

In the lobby of the clinic, Mac called Ellen. While they were speaking, Tom walked into one of the examination rooms. Clearly, no expense had been spared on the equipment there: the stainless-steel exam table was hydraulically controlled, the flooring was nonporous acetate and the sink faucet was controlled by a foot lever so one's hands could remain sterile. The size and position of the drawers and cabinetry were well thought out and of premium quality.

Mac stood in the doorway, watching Tom. "Ellen will be here in a few minutes. She said to make yourself at home."

Tom felt as if he had been caught prying and quickly walked out of the exam room. "An occupational hazard," he explained. "I'm always interested in seeing how other clinics are organized."

"Are you a veterinarian?" Mac asked, taking a seat in the waiting area.

Tom continued to pace around the lobby. "Yes, I am."

"Ah, so that's why you could identify that bird."

"Not really. I've never had to treat one. But I have been watching birds since I was a young boy."

He was polite, but Mac sensed either through his tone or his body language that he would prefer to end the conversation.

The door flew open and Terry McGuire walked in with a young woman following close behind him. "Hey, Mom," he said, throwing her the keys to her truck, and then taking the hand of his companion, "the generator is fixed and I brought it around back."

Mac stood up. "Tom, this is my son, Terry. Terry, this is Tom Candor."

Terry stretched out and shook his hand. "Are you new in town?" he asked.

"Just visiting."

"Tom is a veterinarian," Mac explained.

"Too cool," Terry said, with youthful energy. "Are you going to buy Doc's clinic?"

The directness of Terry's question caught Tom off guard.

"Terry!" Mac admonished. Continuing in a more cordial tone, she asked her son, "Are you going to introduce us to your friend?"

"Yeah, this is Jennifer," he said bashfully. "Jen, this is my mom."

Mac rolled her eyes at her son's lack of social graces. "Nice to meet you."

Jennifer blushed and gave a little wave. "Hi."

"So, what are the two of you going to do today?" Mac asked, trying to sound casual.

Terry shrugged his shoulders. "I haven't decided."

"What would *Jennifer* like to do?" Mac said, prodding her son to think about his date before himself.

"Whatever I do," Terry said, throwing his arm around the girl's shoulder. "Let's go, Jen."

The two were off in a flash, leaving Mac flooded with guilt and embarrassment. She looked out the window, her gaze following the youths as they walked across the street and into Jimmy D's. To her disappointment, Terry didn't hold the door open for his date, but instead barged through before her.

Mac turned and looked at Tom Candor, who had also been watching them. "He's having a hard time coming into his own," she explained. "When he was a child he thought as a child—"

"But when he became a man, he put away childish things," Tom completed.

Having someone complete her sentence sent chills along Mac's arms. "I wish it was that simple for him," Mac said. She had an urgent desire to tell Tom that Terry's behavior was her fault, that she had forgotten to teach her son all of the lessons one would otherwise learn from the father that Terry had never had.

But just then the door to the clinic opened and Ellen walked in, wearing her usual smile. "You must be Tom Candor," she said.

"I am," he replied, shaking her hand. "Thanks for coming in to meet with me."

"I'll get back to work," Mac said, retreating through the back hall. "Nice meeting you, Tom Candor."

"The same," he said as Ellen led him into her office.

Shutting the door, she offered him a chair while seating herself behind her desk. "So, what can I do for you?"

Suddenly a monkey jumped down from the bookcase, scampered up Tom's leg and grabbed his private parts. He then sat on Tom's chest and pushed his derriere into Tom's face.

Instead of yelling out in either pain or surprise, both of which would have been justified, Tom calmly but firmly took the monkey's hand and pried its fingers free. He then embraced the monkey with both arms, rendering the animal immobile.

Tom looked around the room. "Where is the female?"

Ellen tried not to look impressed. "How do you know there's a female?"

"He would never have done that if a female wasn't close by," Tom said, looking around. "He's just proving his dominance."

"Delilah!" Ellen called out, tapping hard on the table.

The male monkey tried to squirm out of Tom's embrace, but he held the animal expertly. Tom turned and watched another monkey crawl halfway down the bookshelf and pause.

"Come quick," Ellen prompted.

Without warning, the monkey leapt through the air and landed on Ellen's desk. Tom let the male loose and he jumped from Tom's lap to join the female.

Tom's eyes were wide with interest. "They're amazing," he said. "I haven't seen snow monkeys in decades."

"They're here as a gift to the monks," Ellen explained.

"Monks?"

"That will take a few minutes to explain. Let me put them in another room." As Ellen left, Tom took note of the empty bookshelves. "So, where were we before we were interrupted?" Ellen asked when she returned.

Tom looked her squarely in the eyes. "I may be interested in buying your practice."

Ellen let out a laugh. "Well," she said, "this is quite unexpected."

"Is it still for sale?"

"Absolutely. I'm just surprised because I know most of the vets in this part of the state, but I don't remember us ever meeting."

"No, we haven't. I'm currently living in Maine."

"Well, how you came to hear about my small clinic must be an interesting tale."

The bell on the front door chimed. "Excuse me," she said, getting up. "My assistant is off today."

"Ellen?" called a man from the lobby.

She opened the door and saw Jeremiah Abrams standing by the front desk. "Jeremiah, over here," she said, waving to her almost-blind friend. "What's wrong?"

"Am I interrupting?"

"Not at all. My favorite clients always come first," she said, putting her arm through his. "Where is Isabella?"

"Hitched outside. She's farting something awful and I think she may have diarrhea."

"Well, let's take a look," Ellen said, leading the old man across the wide front porch.

Tom Candor followed several steps behind them.

Ellen placed a hand on Isabella's mane and slid it down her back and then to her side. She took the stethoscope hanging around her neck and put it in her ears, warmed the other end with her breath and laid it against the horse's coat. She worked smoothly and quickly. After listening to the mare's heart, she moved the stethoscope to her stomach.

Suddenly, Isabella did what Jeremiah had complained about, and passed an enormous amount of gas.

"Holy!" Ellen laughed. "That's quite the odor!"

Jeremiah, who was standing by Isabella's head, rubbed her nose. "You can smell it a mile away."

"You need to go over and get some horse grain at the Feed Store," Ellen explained. "They have a new stock boy and I bet he gave you rabbit feed by accident."

"I pointed to the bag I wanted—it's always over in the corner."

"Jeremiah, if the boy didn't know you or Isabella, he probably grabbed the wrong bag. But Isabella will be fine as long as we get her on a good diet," Dr. Campbell said as she untied the harness reins from the hitching post. "Do you want me to go over there with you?"

"That's not necessary," the old man said as he led his mare away. "I'll just talk to Sam."

After Jeremiah left, Ellen dashed inside and picked up the phone, dialing a number she knew by heart.

"Sam? This is Ellen. . . . Good, thanks. . . . Jeremiah is on his way over. I think your new stock boy sold him rabbit feed like he did before. . . . Yeah, she has the same symptoms. Would you make sure that they deliver your premium equine feed to his farm today? And also, if you would, take away the old feed—he's really too blind to tell the difference between the bags. . . . I appreciate that. . . . Oh, and why don't you send me the bill this time? . . . Thanks."

She hung up and turned to Tom Candor. "Are you a small- or large-animal vet?"

"I'm licensed for both, actually."

"That helps with this type of practice. You'll certainly see everything here, from a pet turtle to a moose."

"Howard, I assume."

"So, you already know about Howard?" Ellen laughed. "God forbid if something should ever happen to him. He's so beloved, I think he almost beat Jimmy D for mayor last year. Why don't I make a fresh pot of coffee and we can pick up where we left off?"

FIFTEEN

Peanuts

That evening, Brooke and Joshua Turner sat at the front corner table in The Green Chile, talking quietly. They were waiting for Pam and Mark to arrive before ordering drinks, but their friends were already twenty minutes late. Both Brooke and Joshua were famished and had all but finished the freshly made nachos and salsa that the owner, Gabrielle, had brought to their table.

"It's nice to have a minute alone," Joshua said. "We haven't seen much of each other lately."

Brooke laid her hand in her husband's. "I'm sorry," she said. "I never thought that the retirement of the firm's two senior partners would put such demands on my time."

"Well, we just need to get out more often." He leaned over and kissed her lightly. "You still love what you do, don't you?"

Brooke was surprised by the question. "Well, that came out of nowhere."

"I was just thinking about you and the firm this afternoon."

Brooke took a bite of a nacho. "I love being an architect. I always have. And the firm is one of the best in the state. It was easier working for myself, but there are a lot of benefits to having colleagues around. I'm sure the firm will change after the partners sell it, so ask me again in six months."

"I don't think one can ever find the perfect job," Joshua commented.

Brooke studied her husband for a minute. She had noticed in subtle ways that recently he had not been as happy and lighthearted as he normally was. "You seem more serious lately, ever since you finished your dissertation."

"I've just been thinking about my career," he said.

"That's right. January is right around the corner."

Joshua nodded. "Despite so many years of looking forward to completing my doctorate, right now I really don't want this time of my life to end."

That came as a surprise to Brooke. "Why not?"

"What comes afterward seems so daunting. I could easily send out a thousand copies of my résumé to anyone who would read it—universities, large corporations, small research centers—but I'm not sure what job I should be going after." Joshua squeezed his wife's hand. "And then there's us, and our home here. Sometimes I just want to bury my head at Montis and continue working there forever."

"But you could be making ten times what Mark is paying you now."

"I know," Joshua said. "It occurred to me the other day that other than living as a monk at Montis Abbey for twelve years, I've only had hourly work that I've loved. I've never had to deal with building a career."

The door chime rang when Pam and Mark walked into the restaurant.

"We're so sorry we're late," Pam said, pulling up a chair next to Brooke and giving her friend a hug.

"The inn has been unbelievably busy the last few days," Mark added.

"I noticed a lot of cars there this afternoon," Joshua mentioned.

"This is just the beginning of it," Mark said.

Pam laid a copy of *Vintner's Fare* on the table. "Christian Copeland wrote a very complimentary piece on Montis and the phones haven't stopped ringing since."

Brooke picked up the magazine, flipped to the article and began reading silently. "This is wonderful."

Gabrielle approached the table. "Margaritas for everyone?"

"As strong as you can make them," Mark said.

Pam's cell phone rang in her purse.

"Don't answer it," Mark said.

Pam glared at him. "That's what he's been saying all day." She retrieved her phone. "Hello? . . . There are more in the side table by the front door. Okay. Call if you need help." Pam put the phone away. "June is holding down the fort for us this evening."

"Isn't that your new cleaning lady?" Brooke asked.

"Yeah, but she's also covering the front desk when we're gone," Mark said. "We're in dire need of help."

"We interviewed the perfect chef from Cedar Grove down in Wheatley—"

"I thought he was arrogant," Mark interjected.

"Well, it doesn't matter. When he saw all the commotion at our place, he ran for the high country," Pam said.

"He was a bit too much of a Francophile if you ask me," Mark added.

"We're not asking you," Pam shot back.

Brooke raised her brows. "So you're really going to bring someone into your restaurant?"

"Absolutely," Pam said. "Why do you say it that way?"

Brooke grinned. "I just can't see you turning over the spatula to a total stranger."

Pam was defiant. "Just watch me."

Brooke patted her husband's arm. "Well, if you can't find anyone, Joshua might be interested."

"What a great way to waste a Ph.D.," Mark quipped.

"It may tide him over until he decides what he wants to do with his life," Brooke explained.

Joshua blushed. "It's not that bad," he protested, and then noticed everyone was staring at him. "All right, it is, but I just need to make some hard decisions."

"You sound like a man being dragged to the guillotine," Mark said.

Gabrielle approached and placed four glasses on the table, then poured margaritas from a ceramic pitcher while telling her guests the specials for the night.

"Saved by tequila," Joshua said, trying to sound jocular. "Drinks for all."

While they were ordering, Jimmy D walked into the restaurant and joined Ellen Campbell, who was sitting with a tall man at one of the back tables. It was obvious they had just finished their dinner. Jimmy was his usual, gregarious self; his lighthearted voice could be heard over the restaurant's hum.

Brooke nudged Pam's arm. "Ellen's new boyfriend?" she asked with an exaggerated leer.

They all laughed.

"I don't think so," Pam whispered. "There's too much of an age difference."

Brooke glanced casually over her shoulder. "He looks to be in his midforties," she commented.

"And she's around sixty?" Mark suggested.

Brooke leaned toward Pam. "He's really good-looking."

Joshua glared at his wife. "You women are all alike."

Gabrielle walked up to their table and placed large dinner plates filled with extraordinary appetizers in front of them. "Well, you four look like you're having fun tonight."

"We are," Brooke said, winking at the husband.

"I'll be right back with your tortillas and another pitcher of margaritas," Gabrielle said.

Brooke pulled on her sleeve and nodded toward the other side of the restaurant. "Is that Ellen's new boyfriend?"

Gabrielle leaned closer. "No. I hear he's a veterinarian from Maine who might be interested in Ellen's practice."

"Wow," Brooke said, and looked again over her shoulder.

"That would be wonderful," Joshua said. "The town needs a vet, and I know Ellen is going to Greece with or without a replacement."

Pam and Joshua also glanced toward Ellen's table as she and her friend were preparing to leave. Jimmy slapped his hand on the stranger's shoulder.

As the group passed their table, Mark caught Ellen's attention. "Hi, Doc. I left a message at your office a few hours ago. Our draft horse was lame this morning. Perhaps you could stop by Montis in the next few days and look at her?"

"I'm doing farm rounds tomorrow morning and could be there at about ten, if that works for you," Ellen said.

Mark looked at Joshua and nodded. "That would be perfect. Thanks."

Jimmy came up from behind her. "Ellen, I'm taking Tom for a tour of our great town. Would you like to come?"

She rolled her eyes. "I'll see you tomorrow," she whispered to Mark, and followed the others out the door.

At the Montis stable the following morning, Mark lay on the ground, studying the motorcycle's new front wheel.

Pointing to a small plug, he called over to Joshua, "What do you think this is for?"

Joshua glanced over from the horse stall. "I have absolutely no idea."

"What's your best guess?" Mark pressed.

"I don't have one. I know nothing about motorcycles."

Mark hit the metal rim with his palm. "But you repaired our tractor."

"No," Joshua corrected him. "All I did was add oil. Didn't Dakin's Garage overhaul the bike?"

"Yeah," Mark said, standing up. "But he said to get to know the motorcycle before I take it out on the road."

"Did he give you any paperwork?"

"He printed off an owner's manual that he found on the Internet."

Joshua leaned out of the stall. "And have you read it?"

"It's in German," Mark replied, "so I'm flying by the seat of my pants."

Joshua laughed. "That may be the most prophetic thing you've ever said. By the way, where are the aviary panels?"

"I used the tractor and dragged them over to the arena," Mark answered. "That thing will be huge once it's assembled."

"And Pam's still not impressed?"

Before Mark could answer, a woman's voice filled the barn. "This has got to be one of the most amazing motorcycles I've ever seen," she said.

Joshua got up and walked out to the barn's center aisle. Ellen Campbell was standing next to Mark, looking at the BMW. She ran her hand along the rim of the sidecar.

"Absolutely amazing," she said, circling to the front. "Was it used in the Korean War?"

"I have no idea," Mark said.

"Just unbelievable," she repeated.

"Mark bought it on the government-surplus Web site," Joshua explained. "In addition to having no wheels, it fell apart when we unloaded it from the trailer."

"Who put it back together? Dakin's Garage?" Ellen asked.

Mark glanced at her. "How did you know?"

"He's the only one crazy enough to try to rebuild a World War Two bike. Have you started it yet?"

"I'm just about to," Mark said. "Do you want to watch?"

Ellen rubbed her hands together. "I wouldn't miss it."

The man Joshua had seen with Ellen the night before stepped out of her SUV.

"Joshua and Mark, have you met Tom Candor?"

Joshua shook Tom's hand. "Nice meeting you. I understand you may be interested in Ellen's practice?"

"Yes, a definite possibility," Tom said. "Are you the stable hand?"

Ellen chuckled. "No, he's just our resident doctoral candidate with spare time on his hands." She bent down and looked inside the sidecar. "And Mark Walker owns Montis Inn," she added.

Mark gave a quick wave as he continued to study the motorcycle.

"So, you wanted me to look at the mare?" Ellen said.

"In the far stall," Joshua said, leading them across the center aisle.

"Tom, I need to talk with Joshua for a minute. Can you handle this?" Ellen asked, gently pulling on Joshua's arm so he would let Tom proceed on his own.

Tom unlocked the stall door. "Any history I should be aware of?" he asked.

Ellen thought for a moment. "Nothing in particular—an otherwise healthy six-year-old mare."

"And her name?" Tom asked.

"Peanuts," Joshua said.

"My wife's idea, not mine," Mark called out.

Tom disappeared inside, with Ellen watching intently through the barred opening. Tom stood and watched the mare for a moment, then slowly approached her with his hand outstretched, his palm open. He said the mare's name as he placed his hand on her neck and moved it forward to her halter. He then led her to the corner of the stall, where he attached a lead from the hitch ring to the bottom of the halter.

Joshua stepped toward the stall door to offer assistance, but Ellen held on to his shirttail. "Did you want something?" he asked.

Ellen raised her finger to her lips. *"Shhh,"* she whispered, never taking her eyes off the new veterinarian. "Let's watch."

Tom's examination of Peanuts reflected not only his comfort

around large animals, but also a wealth of knowledge and skill that one could only gather through decades of practice. He had demonstrated the same level of competence at the three farms they had been to earlier that morning.

After examining the mare in the stall for several minutes, Tom slid the door open and led the horse into the aisle. Handing Joshua the lead, he requested that the animal be trotted away for twenty yards and then trotted back toward him. Ellen watched Tom watch the horse move out.

When Joshua returned, Tom picked up the front leg and again examined the hoof.

"Navicular syndrome, I would say," he said.

Ellen raised her brows. "Interesting," she said, as she looked closer at the hoof and felt the pastern. She quickly made the same diagnosis.

"I'm unfamiliar with that," Joshua said, returning the mare to the stall.

"The navicular bone distributes weight between the coffin and pastern bones," Tom began to explain. "Do you have a piece of paper? It's much easier to explain if I can draw you a diagram. And, Ellen, do you mind getting some Phenylbutazone out of my bag?"

When Ellen reached her car, she looked back and saw Tom and Joshua sitting on the steps of the hayloft, engrossed in conversation. Tom had found a thick marker and was drawing the anatomical structure of a horse's hoof and pastern on an old newspaper. Joshua was, as always, actively asking questions.

Sadness swept over Ellen, so deep and so fast that she had to fight back sudden tears. Although she had been preparing herself to leave, she had not prepared herself for that moment, for that change of guardianship when she would have to hand over the reins and let another veterinarian pick up where she was leaving off.

Mark sat down on the bike. "Hey, Doc, you want to try sitting next to me?"

She wiped away a tear and forced a broad smile. "I would love to."

At the far end of the barn, Joshua and Tom watched Ellen crawl lithely into the sidecar. Her knees jutted up in front of her chest.

"Wait. Something's by my feet," she said. She reached forward and blindly grabbed an animal with feathers. The chicken made a racket as it was displaced from its new roost. Letting it fly to the ground, Ellen stretched out her legs.

"This is quite roomy," she said.

Joshua and Tom looked on. "Quite supple for someone her age," Tom said.

"She never ceases to amaze us," Joshua said. "I understand you're from New England." He was hoping to find out more about the stranger.

"Not originally, but for the last several years I've been helping an old college friend expand his small-animal clinic in Maine," Tom answered.

"And originally?" Joshua asked. "You seem to have more of a West Coast accent."

Tom looked over at the motorcycle. Ellen was still in the sidecar and Mark was turning the front wheel with the handlebars. "They seem to be kindred spirits," he said.

Joshua studied Mark for a moment. "They are. Neither can turn away from a new adventure."

"Is Mark married?"

"Yes." Joshua nodded and smiled. "To a very patient woman. And you?"

"I wouldn't want to bore you with such a long story," Tom said, skirting the question. "Ellen seems to be well respected in town."

"Everyone adores her. I don't think any of us has really accepted the fact that she's leaving." Joshua paused. "Are you seriously interested in her practice?"

Tom rubbed his hands together. "Possibly."

"And have you ever worked in a small town?"

"Not as small as this one. Lumby seems quite . . . unique."

Joshua laughed. "An understatement. I'm assuming Ellen has told you just how quirky our town is?"

"She's given me a clue."

Tom scanned the newspaper he had just drawn on while Joshua continued to watch his two friends explore the bike.

"She's quite something," Joshua said softly, almost to himself.

Mark had put on a helmet and was handing one to Ellen. "You want to take it for a spin?"

"It would be an honor," Ellen said, pulling the helmet down over her head.

"Mark, perhaps you should take it out alone for the first time," Joshua cautioned.

But with the helmet on, Mark didn't hear his friend's warning. He turned the key, expecting backfires and large plumes of smoke, but to everyone's surprise, the engine turned over perfectly. Mark beamed and gave Joshua the thumbs-up.

Within seconds, Mark and Ellen were jettisoning down the driveway like a bolt of lightning, with Ellen waving both arms in the air, screaming for joy.

Tom laughed. "Have you known her long?" he asked.

"At least fifteen years. We first met when I was a monk here at the monastery. She's been a good friend ever since and offered invaluable help while I was working on my dissertation last summer."

Tom was surprised. He had thought Ellen was simply pulling his leg when she said Joshua was a doctoral student. "In what?"

"Agricultural. Genetic engineering," Joshua said.

Tom creased his brow. "Ah."

Joshua thought he heard a tone of disapproval. "Do you know much about it?" he asked.

Tom nodded his head slowly. "I'm aware that there are some who believe that genetically manipulating plants and animals for the betterment of man is considered acceptable."

Looking at Tom now, Joshua saw a very different side to the veterinarian. "And you don't approve?" he asked.

Suddenly the motorcycle rocketed up the dirt road and tore through the center aisle of the small barn, almost running over Joshua's foot. Exiting the building just as quickly, Mark then made a hard right, barely missing the side of the large arena. Ellen's laughter echoed.

"Actually I don't," Tom said. "I think a lot of problems that animals face today arise from human interference, from pesticides in the grain to steroids injected into their bodies."

"I agree, but that seems very different from engineering soy to be able to naturally combat a virus that plagues half of Asia. The genetically altered bean could allow us to feed millions who are now starving."

"How can something naturally combat a virus if you've engineered it to do just that? Isn't that an oxymoron?" Tom challenged. His voice was neither loud nor agitated, but it was obvious that he stood strong in his belief.

"A poor choice of words, no doubt." Joshua blushed slightly. "But not to use our intellect and technologies to help those who can't help themselves seems a greater crime."

"Then we agree to disagree," Tom said, and returned to reading *The Lumby Lines.*

The Lumby Lines

Lumby's Giant Pumpkin Weigh-Off

BY CARRIE KERRY October 10

Although there has been fierce disagreement among town residents, the Pumpkin Festival committee has completed its review of Mr. McNear's complaint and has decided that the weigh-in will definitely use Dr. Campbell's transportable equine scale, which will accommodate pumpkins of sufficient girth and weight up to 2,400 pounds.

Recapping the official rules:

1. All pumpkins must have been seeded, grown, cared for and entered into the competition by the contestant.

2. Each contestant may enter no more than two pumpkins. Each household may enter no more than four pumpkins.

3. Pumpkins must be at least 50% orange to cream yellow in color.

4. The pumpkin must be healthy, sound, not hollow, undamaged, disease-free, and free of rot, holes, cracks and large soft spots.

5. The vine must be trimmed to within one inch from the stem of the fruit.

6. Contestants are responsible for bringing their pumpkins to within fifty feet of the scale. The weigh-in staff will then use a forklift with a custom-designed pumpkin harness to place the entry on the scale.

7. Pumpkins must be removed from the fairgrounds within two days of weigh-in. (Simon Dixon reminds all participants not to abandon your pumpkin at the fairgrounds as some did last year.)

Prize money: 1st . . . . $1 per lb
2nd . . . . $.50 per lb
3rd . . . . $.25 per lb

Good luck to all growers!

SIXTEEN

Roots

Snow had already fallen on the peaks of the mountains surrounding Saint Cross Abbey, and to combat the cold, warm fires burned in most of the woodstoves and fireplaces throughout the annex and community building. It had become a time of quiet self-reflection as each monk more seriously considered the sisters of Saint Amand's proposition and deliberated upon the future of their monastery. Those autumn days would also be remembered for the brothers' introduction to the fine wines offered by their new friends.

In Chapter Hall, the members of the abbey's core council gathered after vespers. The group of four monks, who were selected each year by the community at large to address monastic issues and opportunities, stood by the open hearth talking softly. The men looked up when someone knocked on the door.

Sister Claire walked in, her hands deep in her pockets. Kristina followed several steps behind her. "A chilly evening," Claire said, joining the monks by the fire.

Kristina raised her palms to the flames. "It must be brutally cold here in February."

"As well as several months before and after," Brother Aaron commented as he leaned over to place another log on the grate.

"I'm sorry we're late," Claire said. "I was on a conference call with one of our distributors in Oregon."

"All is well, I hope," Brother Marc said.

Claire raised her brows. "Yes, but as we approach the holidays, there are always unexpected problems to resolve."

"As with our businesses," Matthew said as he led the group to the table closest to the hearth. "Our rum sauce sales increase tenfold during the last two months of each year, with the rest of our products easily doubling. And although we know what to expect, we're always scrambling this time of year to meet the demand."

"Better that than not enough demand," Kristina added.

"Agreed." After everyone was seated, Matthew bowed his head. "Lord, as we take these next steps in contemplating the opportunity that lies before us, please grant us wisdom to follow your word. Amen." He paused for a moment before continuing. "I believe the goal of this evening's discussion is to finalize our plans for the next two weeks." Although he spoke softly, his deep voice resonated against the wood ceiling of Chapter Hall.

Claire nodded in concurrence. "During the last two days, I've spoken with most of the sisters at Saint Amand. I think it's safe to say that all are interested in cautiously moving to the next step," she said.

"Cautiously?" Marc asked.

Claire nodded. "Two of the elders voiced concern about the composition of your local soil because it would have such an impact on the success of our vines." She rubbed her hands together. "No matter how thoroughly we test the dirt and how accurate the lab's analysis is, we won't really know about quality until we finally harvest the grapes five or six years from now."

"It's a gamble," Brother Aaron acknowledged.

"It is," Claire agreed. "But we're working on ways to reduce that risk. Kristina recently suggested that instead of selling our property in Oregon, we retain partial ownership of our current vineyard during this transition to Saint Cross. That would allow us to continue our wine production, albeit at a lower volume, while keeping our label active until our first vintage here." She took a deep breath. "So, yes, I believe we are ready to proceed to the next phase of . . ."

"Exploration," Brother Marc offered.

"Very good," Claire acknowledged with a grin. "I was going to say due diligence, but that sounds awfully cold, doesn't it?"

"Given that both monasteries have significant business ventures to consider, the term is not inappropriate," Matthew assured her.

"But that's my fundamental concern," Brother Aaron interjected. "In my mind, what's far more important than either of our enterprises is knowing that each monastery will be spiritually stronger from the merger. We've spent more time discussing our respective cash flows than our theological similarities and differences, haven't we?"

Matthew nodded slowly. "We have, and that is a legitimate concern."

Brother Aaron leaned forward and continued his thought. "I don't think we're deliberately ignoring that aspect, but it's certainly being overshadowed by what might be perceived as the more practical discussion."

"I agree with that as well," Claire said. "We are, first and foremost, a religious order, and the joining of our two communities should serve God more fully. However, the value of our labor is what's given us the financial independence to continue our religious mission."

Brother Matthew folded his hands. "So as we continue down this path, we will first consider our monastic lives and sacraments, followed by our secular objectives."

Aaron sighed in relief. "If our beliefs remain first in our intent, then I remove my objection, and agree with the others that we should continue."

Brother Matthew opened a worn leather portfolio that lay on the table, and glanced at the paper inside it. Turning to the sisters, he said, "In our meeting last night, our community discussed how best to proceed. It was agreed that three of us will accept your offer to travel to Oregon and become more familiar with your community and your services."

"Whom will you be sending?" Sister Kristina asked.

"Brother Aaron, Brother Marc and myself," Matthew answered.

"That's wonderful, Matthew," Claire said, visibly pleased with the news. "I'm so glad you'll have an opportunity to see our abbey firsthand."

"We look forward to it," Matthew said. "I believe you had originally suggested that we join you when you drive back to Troutdale?"

"If you would like. The four sisters who will be coming to visit Saint Cross could arrive as early as the day after tomorrow." Claire looked at Aaron. "They very much want to participate in all of your services and monastic duties during their stay."

Brother Aaron relaxed his shoulders and leaned back. "We welcome them. And I appreciate your saying that."

"If there are no objections," Claire continued, "I'd like to be here when they arrive. But we can leave the following morning unless you need more time to prepare."

"Not at all," Matthew said, writing some notes on a fresh piece of paper. "So, we will plan to leave Thursday morning."

~

Two days later, the sisters arrived at Saint Cross with warm albeit understated fanfare. Claire spent most of the day orienting the entourage to the monks' schedule, and showing them the adjacent land on which the sisters would build their future home. Sister Kristina, who would be staying at Saint Cross, offered her limited knowledge of the area and quickly stepped forward to fill Claire's absence.

As Claire closed her suitcase the following morning, she knew she was leaving the sisters in good hands. After matins, the Saint Amand van was packed and she and the three monks bid farewell to Saint Cross Abbey and to the frigid air that had settled on Franklin the night before.

The five-hundred-mile drive to Oregon was uneventful and enjoyably quiet. Aaron stretched out across the last row of seats and slept most of the way. Marc looked out the window in silent wonder as they drove through the different landscapes between Franklin and the Pacific. Brother Matthew sat in the front seat, sharing the driving with Claire.

An hour outside of Troutdale, Claire asked to drive so Matthew could better appreciate the beautiful views as they passed Mount Hood. Matthew was struck by the gentleness of the terrain compared to the rugged mountains surrounding the monks' town. Also, everything here was more verdant—there had not yet been a hard frost, so the autumn flowers retained their color, and the trees still had their fall foliage.

Matthew rolled down his window and inhaled deeply. The smells were different from the dry, thin air at Saint Cross. Here, there was a heaviness that could be attributed to the winds carried in from the ocean.

"Will our lack of humidity be of concern for growing grapes?" he asked.

Claire shook her head. "No, we don't expect it to be. Actually, there are several fine vineyards due north of you in Canada, with drier air at even higher elevations." She paused for a moment, thinking. "But one never really knows until the grape is harvested. We would probably need an irrigation system, which we don't have now."

Approaching Troutdale, Claire turned off the main road and began winding through the rolling hills of northern Oregon. After several miles, Matthew saw the sign for the monastery, a small, unpretentious plaque indicating that Saint Amand was two miles ahead. Just past the sign, the asphalt turned into a well-maintained dirt road.

After making a sweeping curve around the base of a hill, Claire pointed ahead. "You can see the steeple of our abbey through the trees."

Matthew looked toward where she was pointing, but saw only rows of grapevines. A few seconds later, he caught sight of the roof.

"Is all that your land?" he asked.

"Most of it," Claire answered. "We lease eight additional acres on the east side of our property line." She looked out the window and reminisced. "This is our home. It's our history."

"You sound sad."

Claire offered Matthew a weak smile. "Uprooting is never easy, is it?"

He thought about her comment. "No, it's not," he replied. "Several of the monks, myself included, moved from Montis Abbey to Saint Cross many years ago. Although they are only an hour's drive apart, a few of the brothers didn't want to make the change, so they left monastic life altogether."

"That's one of my concerns," Claire admitted. She looked in the rearview mirror and saw that Aaron was still asleep. "Is he well?" she asked softly.

Matthew looked back at his old friend. "He is close to eighty and very tired."

"We'll try to make his stay here as restful as possible. Perhaps the change of climate will do him good."

Claire turned the van into the driveway. The approach to Saint Amand was at least a mile long and took them through dense evergreen woods before they reached a clearing. The monastic compound consisted of five buildings spread across two acres of impeccably maintained grounds.

"The guest annex is the smallest building to your right," Claire explained as she drove slowly past it. A hundred yards farther up the road was a utilitarian-looking building with large doors on overhead rollers. "Our processing building," she said.

Following the circular drive, they passed in front of three buildings that appeared to be connected. The center building was obviously the chapel with a grand steeple and belfry. Attached to it on the right, Claire explained, was the community building, and on the left, the sisters' private annex.

Claire circled the car around and retraced their steps, bringing the brothers back down to the guest annex. As soon as she parked, the men got out and stretched their legs before gathering their luggage.

A sister, whom Matthew guessed to be in her thirties, walked out the front door of the guesthouse. Although she was wearing simple black slacks and a white cotton shirt, Matthew couldn't help but notice how stunningly beautiful she was.

"Welcome to Saint Amand," she said, easily picking up the two suitcases that Matthew had taken out of the van. "I'm Sister Megan."

Sister Claire introduced each of the monks. "Sister Megan will show you to your rooms," she said. "If you're not too tired, please join us for vespers at five thirty. Supper is served at six thirty."

"If you would follow me," Megan said, leading them to the annex.

Matthew continued to stare at Megan. "I'm sorry to be so bold, but have we met before?"

Megan looked carefully at Matthew's face. "I don't believe so."

"You look so familiar."

Megan walked in the front door. "Well, perhaps you'll remember. We have prepared rooms for each of you."

"That's not at all necessary," Matthew said.

"It's a rare occasion when the guesthouse is empty and we can offer private quarters to our guests," she said in a singsong manner before showing them to each of their sleeping cells.

Even her voice sounded vaguely familiar to Matthew.

After ensuring that Marc and Aaron were settled, Matthew closed his bedroom door, sat down on the corner of the cot and tried to remember where he had seen Megan. He closed his eyes and concentrated on her voice—a voice he was sure he had heard before.

At Saint Cross Abbey, Brother Michael stared at the large stack of mail that had just been delivered to the monastery. Although he had volunteered to handle all correspondence during Matthew's absence, he had never imagined that it would require an hour each day to simply sort through and separate the secular from nonsecular mailings, and those for their gourmet-food business from the monks' foundation.

On that day, the mound was twice its normal size, stuffed with countless religious magazines, which all seemed to arrive within a day or two of each other.

Michael picked up the top magazine, *American Monasticism.* As he skimmed the index of articles listed on the front cover, a title caught his attention: "The Gift of Snow Monkeys." Flipping to page eighteen, Michael began reading. The reporter who had interviewed Brother Michael the week before had written an eloquent and, more important, accurate story. The article ended with a quote from Brother Michael: "We will be forever grateful to a small village near the Nagano Mountains of Japan for their gift of two snow monkeys. We already feel so fortunate to be in the position of helping others, but when such heartfelt generosity is extended to us, it delights us and can be nothing less than glorious in God's eyes."

International Philanthropy, the next periodical on the stack, was one of Michael's personal favorites. Again, he saw the title "The Gift of Snow Monkeys" mentioned on its cover. Quickly turning to the page, he skimmed the article thoroughly enough to know that it was the same one. Michael smiled. Brother Matthew and the monks would be delighted with the coverage, since all too frequently any mention of Saint Cross got buried under the magazine space given to larger monasteries and religious organizations.

The next journal, another international publication with a smaller circulation of two million, didn't have Saint Cross and their snow monkeys as their cover story, but did run it at the centerfold. Tremendous placement, Michael thought.

For the next fifteen minutes, he collected all the publications that carried the article: fourteen in all.

Just as he was about to tackle the business envelopes, Brother John's voice came over the intercom. "Brother Michael, you're wanted at the front door. DHL requires a signature for an international overnight delivery."

Michael hastily stacked the pile of mail and ran downstairs. Opening the door, he saw a man with strong Middle Eastern features standing in front of a crate that was almost as tall as he was.

"Brother Michael?" he asked in such broken English and with such a heavy accent that the monk's name was barely recognizable.

"Yes, I'm Brother Michael."

Immediately the man began speaking what Michael assumed was tremendously fluent and, more to the point, fast Arabic. When it became obvious that Michael didn't understand a word he was saying, the man pushed a clipboard and pen at him, pointing to an empty box on the first page that was otherwise filled with Arabic type. The man repeated the same word until Michael penned his signature.

After Michael signed whatever document it was, the man gave the brother a wad of folded papers and ran back to his truck. Only then did Michael notice that there were four other men waiting in the vehicle. When the driver got inside, they all started talking Arabic at once, several of them smiling and waving as the truck drove off.

Intrigued as to what was in the box, Michael tried peering through several of the small ventilation holes on the front. Not able to see anything, he examined the sides and then the back of the crate, where he found a small latched window at eye level. Above the window, a much larger latch secured the back panel to the rest of the crate. Opening the window, Michael put his head warily inside and was suddenly eye to eye with a baby camel. The distressed young animal was more startled than Michael and proceeded to do what angry camels do best: spit.

SEVENTEEN

Vespers

After showering and donning their cassocks for vespers, the monks enjoyed a leisurely walk through the Saint Amand compound. The sisters' small church was dwarfed by massive evergreens on three sides, and carefully protected by their strong boughs. Brother Matthew paused for a moment, struck by the glaring contrast between their monasteries; where Saint Cross was built of large blocks of stone, the chapel at Saint Amand was crafted from red cedar that glowed warmly in the setting sun. The builders' attention to the smallest details, from the design of the wide soffits to the window trim, was impressive.

Sister Megan approached the men as they were admiring the carved front door. "Did you have an opportunity to rest?" she asked.

"We did, thank you," Brother Aaron replied.

Brother Marc took a deep breath. "This is a beautiful building."

"Yes, it is," she said, looking up at the roofline. "We built it eighteen years ago."

Matthew watched Megan carefully, hoping he would see a mannerism that would trigger his memory. “Your local carpenters have a great eye for detail,” he said.

Megan laughed gently. It was a unique laugh that Matthew had most definitely heard before.

“Those *carpenters* are all inside praying,” Megan said, “but I’m sure they would appreciate the compliment.”

Matthew’s eyes widened. “You built this yourself?”

“Well, my contribution was no more than the others, but yes, the sisters built everything here,” she said, scanning the complex.

“Without assistance?” Aaron asked.

Megan lifted her shoulders. “Very little, actually. We brought someone in to pour the concrete foundations and drill the well, but that’s about it.”

“That’s amazing,” Matthew said.

“It’s been a wonderful adventure and we’ve learned so much from working together,” she said, and then paused for a long moment. “Some wonder how we could ever leave.”

“I’m sure that decision won’t be an easy one. Did you grow up in this area?” Matthew asked, searching for a clue as to how they might have met.

“In northern California. I wasn’t one of the founders of Saint Amand, but it certainly is my life now.”

Bells began to ring throughout the monastery.

“Shall we?” she said, opening the door.

Inside, the church was flooded with natural light coming through large windows that spanned the two opposite walls. There appeared to be no separation between the interior space and outdoors, giving one a sense that they were praying under the trees.

The chapel was surprisingly small for such a large order, with no more than thirty chairs positioned tightly together. Matthew more deeply appreciated Claire’s prior comment that they had long since outgrown their abbey.

The sisters were already seated, deep in prayer and meditation.

They all wore straight black robes to the floor with no belts. Several local parishioners were seated in the back rows. Sister Megan showed the monks to their seats and then joined the others. Claire was seated in front of the altar.

The bells chimed again.

Vespers began with a prayer spoken by Sister Claire, followed by a reading from the Bible and more prayer. During the thirty-minute service, different sisters approached the chantry to offer selected readings. The format was surprisingly similar to that of Saint Cross, barring one significant difference; while all services were sung in chant at Saint Cross, there was only intermittent singing by the sisters. But when they did sing, it was a glorious sound that brought smiles to the monks' faces. After years of listening to only tenors, baritones and basses, they found the soprano and alto voices music to their ears.

What a glorious addition that would be, Matthew thought to himself.

After vespers, Claire escorted her guests to the dining room, which was crowded with four tables, each seating eight. Two long serving consoles flanked the far wall. On all accounts, the order of Saint Amand had, indeed, grown larger than its facilities.

"For this food we are about to receive we give thanks. Amen," Claire said. "Before we begin, I would like to welcome our guests from Saint Cross Abbey, Brothers Matthew, Aaron and Marc. They will be on retreat with us for at least a week. So, please welcome them and share with them your prayers and chores."

The supper was outstanding and showed a culinary expertise that would rival Brother John's best menu, with Matthew taking note that no wine was served. Afterward, the men were invited for coffee in the living room, but all three were too exhausted from the trip, so instead, retired to their rooms. They felt very much at home in their firm beds and modestly decorated bedrooms.

The following morning deep bells chimed throughout the abbey at four thirty. Matins were at five a.m., followed by an hour of silence before breakfast. The breakfast was as hearty and as well prepared as dinner the night before.

After breakfast, the brothers were invited to sit in on the community's morning meeting, which the monks found very similar in structure and process to their own; the sisters, led by Claire, discussed the chores that needed to be done and any unique obligations or conflicts for that day. Before the closing prayer at the end of the meeting, Claire asked Sister Megan to show the brothers around the compound. The brothers left the room with a sense that Saint Amand was, in fact, exactly as Claire had presented it: a deeply spiritual, well-grounded and carefully managed monastery.

The tour offered by Megan was an insightful one but it gave Matthew no further clues as to how he knew her.

Walking through the facility, Matthew was struck by the impeccable cleanliness of both the grounds and the buildings, which surpassed even the high standards at Saint Cross. Megan attributed some of their diligence to the fact that Saint Amand was an operating vineyard frequented by tourists.

"So, how do you sustain a contemplative environment if your grounds are open to the public?" Brother Aaron asked.

"It's a challenge at times," Megan said, nodding toward a group of four visitors who had just emerged from the chapel. "They're generally interested in the vineyard and the wine cave, which really is a misnomer since we don't produce the wine here."

Megan pulled open the sliding door to the processing building and the smell of fermenting grapes rushed over the monks. Walking in, they saw close to a dozen sisters working at various posts; some were packing grapes into large wooden boxes while others were moving crates around with a forklift.

"This is a busy time for us," Megan explained. "We're just finishing the harvest."

"So there are no vats?" Marc asked.

"No, we only grow and harvest the grapes here," Sister Megan explained. "Our crop is sent about twenty miles away, where the grapes are crushed, pressed and filtered before being stored in casks. And then, at the right time, the wine is blended, bottled and shipped out. We'll bring you there tomorrow if you'd like."

Matthew turned to Megan. "So, who would process your wine if you were to move to Franklin?"

"That's a good question. Sister Kristina is very close to becoming a master winemaker, so we could conceivably integrate that step into our new facility. Or we could find another facility that has enough surplus capacity to handle our volume."

"Is your wine made only from your own grapes?" Brother Marc asked as they walked through the building.

"It depends on the year, the size of our harvest and the quality of the grape," Megan answered. "Occasionally, we will buy grapes from other vineyards to add to our blends. We even sell our grapes when there's a surplus."

By the time Megan finished the tour of the cave and the Saint Amand wine cellar, all of the monks' questions had been answered. At noon, they made their way back to the dining room, where the community came together for an informal meal.

Claire arrived a few minutes late. Quickly gathering her lunch, she sat on the bench next to Brother Matthew. "I trust you found Megan's tour interesting?" she asked, tasting the soup.

"Very insightful. You must be proud of Saint Amand."

"We are," she said, glancing at the other sisters. "I was hoping you and I could meet after lunch, but it seems now I'll be tied up for about an hour. Perhaps you would enjoy a walk through the vineyard?"

"A good recommendation," he said, trying to rub his back. "I'm still stiff from the car ride."

In between spoonfuls of soup, Claire drew a diagram of the monastic grounds on the back of a napkin, noting buildings that were now familiar to Matthew. She also included the acres that were designated for their various grapes. "If you follow this path," she said, "it will lead you to the far end of our vineyard.

Very few visitors ever find their way back there. I can join you there shortly."

After lunch, following Claire's directions, Matthew found a path behind the chapel that would lead him through the planted fields. It was a beautiful fall day with an azure sky and a gentle breeze just strong enough to rustle the trees. Majestic Mount Hood with its snow-covered peak loomed in the distance.

When Matthew walked into the vineyard and strolled between the long rows of cultivated vines, he was instantly swept away by the same feeling he had whenever he was in the Montis orchard. He reached out his arms so that his fingers ran gently across the grape leaves. As different as they felt and as foreign as the smells were to Matthew, he found the same calm there that he had always embraced among his cherished fruit trees. He closed his eyes and was transported to a place that brought him great happiness, to a time when he was a young novice working in the apple groves at the small monastery in Lumby.

Matthew bent over and cradled a small cluster of grapes in his palm. He gave the fruit a quick tug as one would do when picking an apple, and to his surprise the stem held firm. As he applied more pressure, the ripe grapes exploded in his hand, sending pulp in every direction. He tasted small pieces on his hand and immediately spit out the bitter fruit.

He had much to learn about these grapes, Brother Matthew thought as he wiped his hands on the grass and tried to brush off the grape remains from his pant legs before continuing his walk.

Farther up the path, Matthew found a wooden bench well hidden by surrounding foliage. There, he sat for the next hour in quiet meditation, his body warmed by the afternoon sun.

Claire coughed as she approached. "You look deep in thought." She then saw his hands and pants. "And a little messy at that. Don't tell me you tried to pick some grapes?"

Matthew laughed. "I did, indeed, and look where it got me."

She smiled as she brushed some grape pulp from his shoulder.

"The vines and stems are too fibrous to pick by hand. We use what's called a harvesting knife," Claire patiently explained. "It has a three-inch high-carbon curved steel blade that hooks around the vine on a small handle. It takes some practice to make a clean, quick cut."

"Even with my mishap," Matthew said, "your vineyard is splendid. It reminds me of the fruit orchards I tended for many years."

"I would be delighted to teach you all I know about grapes."

"And wine, I hope," Matthew teased.

Claire nodded. "Of course. One must never forget about the wine."

Sister Claire had such an honest and caring demeanor that Matthew understood why the community had elected her a prioress. They both looked out across the vineyard. Most of the grapes had been cut off the vine but the leaves remained. The old trunks were massive and twisted with their branches reaching out horizontally along the wire trellis. As with any orchard, the history and life of the crop was as rich as the fruit it produced.

Matthew stood and inhaled deeply. "The aromas are so succulent."

"Composted matter and fermenting grapes that have fallen off the vine," Claire said.

Matthew picked up a handful of dirt. "Your soil is surprisingly rocky. I would have expected a rich, dense loam."

"The rock determines how quickly the water can get to, and then drain away from, the roots, both of which influence the growth of the vine. Grapes like to have dry feet." Claire pushed her bangs from her eyes. "Soil is a topic that fascinates vintners as much as the grapes they produce. Even the color of the soil affects the ripening of the grape."

Matthew dropped the pebbly soil and brushed his hands together. "And you think there is good soil in Franklin?"

"We *know* there's that possibility," she corrected him.

A stronger gust of wind rippled through the rows as Matthew and Claire strolled toward the monastery.

"I am surprised you're willing to leave all this behind," Matthew said.

Claire touched his arm. "Please don't think of it as an easy decision for us," she said. "In fact, it has been our hardest challenge since first coming here twenty years ago. But you've seen the size of our chapel and community house—they were built for a community half our size. We need twice the building space and could easily use four times the land for our vineyard." Claire paused for a moment. "We have put off the inevitable for eight years."

"Are there no other alternatives?"

"If we want to continue to grow, I'm afraid not. We have had endless meetings with engineers, but most solutions are either unfeasible or prohibitively expensive. We then tried to purchase adjacent property but the owners have no interest in selling, regardless of the price."

"So your final recourse is to move?"

"Yes," she said. "Once that was accepted by the sisters, it was only a question of where."

They continued walking down the path in silence.

"It's not easy, is it?" Matthew finally asked.

"The thought of leaving?" Claire looked up at him and smiled. He was one of the few people who could understand her position. And Claire trusted him, although she continued to keep her most personal thoughts about the move to herself.

Matthew shook his head. "No, the responsibility of leading the community."

"It's not meant to be easy, is it?" she asked.

Matthew chuckled softly. "No, I suppose not."

They continued to walk the acreage for another hour—a prior and a prioress, peers and friends with a unique appreciation of each other's lives. Sometimes they would stroll in silence and other times Claire would explain something about the vines. As the sun began to set, the two monastics headed to the chapel for vespers.

After another delightful dinner, Matthew called Saint Cross

Abbey. Brother Michael picked up the phone. "How are things going?" Matthew asked.

"Great," Michael said. "The sisters are very kind. And I can't tell you how nice it is to hear female voices in our service."

"Our thoughts as well," Matthew said. "Is there anything you need to discuss with me?"

"No, not really. The Christmas catalogue was delivered yesterday—it looks very nice," Brother Michael said. "And most of the fall shipments for our rum sauce were picked up this morning."

"That's encouraging. Anything else?"

Michael thought for a few seconds. "We received a call today from DHL. They wanted to be sure someone would be around tomorrow to receive a package from New Zealand."

"Did the person say what it was?"

"He was laughing so hard I couldn't quite understand."

"Well, whatever it is, I'm sure you can handle it," Matthew said.

Had Brother Matthew had any idea what was inside the six-foot-high crate that would be delivered the next day, he might have advised Michael to close the gates and lock the doors.

EIGHTEEN

Garlic

The Lumby Lines

What's News Around Town

BY SCOTT STEVENS October 14

An exciting few days in our town of Lumby.

Our great Pumpkin Festival has once again provided the thrills of major cosmopolitan living, with only a handful of mishaps. (Get-well cards for Ron Cooper can be sent to Room 318 at the Wheatley Regional Hospital—goes to show that you shouldn't put your foot on the scale when your pumpkin is being lowered into place.) Many agree the most spectacular moment was when the fireworks exploded prematurely while still inside one of McNear's giant pumpkins, blasting it to brightly colored smithereens. Another spectacular image was when the high school physics club attached helium balloons to one of the weigh-in entries. After ascending sixty feet, the balloons began to pop, sending the 800-pound pumpkin through the new roof of Lumby Sporting Goods—no injuries except a broken leg on their mannequin. A more detailed report will follow in next week's paper. Oh, and the winner of this year's weigh-in? None other than Jeremiah Abrams with a 932-pound pumpkin. His secret: "Isabella's manure, and that's the only thing it's good for." In second place was Chatham Press's very own Carrie Kerry with a 802-pound pumpkin, the growth of which she attributes to her GBF-9500.

Dr. Ellen Campbell received via Federal Express two chimpanzees from a zoo that has closed in northern Idaho. The curator had read about Ellen's caring for the snow monkeys and thought his chimps would find an equally comfortable home in Lumby. When asked about her plans for the new arrivals, Ellen said: "They're Tom Candor's concern now."

The new ad for a chef at Montis Inn drew numerous inquiries and several applicants. Hank stood by the entrance door of the Montis Inn restaurant and waited patiently for the next aspirant to arrive. That morning, he had personally greeted two chefs (or, in fact, one chef and one college student) and more were on their way. To welcome the nervous interviewees, Hank had dressed appropriately in a white chef's jacket and hat, which he thought was unnecessarily puffy. Hanging from one wing was an All-Clad frying pan and, from the other, a well-used spatula.

Pam and Mark sat in the dining room, comparing thoughts about the last candidate.

"Too young and immature," Mark said as he tried to balance a spoon on a fork that he had wedged between the salt and pepper shakers.

Pam watched her husband and bit her lip. "Too inexperienced," she said, drawing a red line through that résumé.

"Did you like Mr. Keller?" he asked.

She thought for a moment. The older gentleman—Pam guessed him to be in his late sixties—was amicable and conversant.

"I'm not sure," she said. "He seemed to emphasize game, venison, buffalo and elk, which would be interesting, but he didn't offer anything original in their preparation."

"Twice he suggested working part-time," Mark commented.

Pam was surprised. She didn't think Mark had been listening that carefully. "That's a deal breaker in my opinion. I want someone who will give one hundred percent, not fifty percent." Pam red-lined that résumé and put it at the bottom of the pile. "Coming in next is Allison Daley."

Mark leaned over on the table. "I'm starving. Do we have time to grab lunch?"

Pam glanced at her watch. "She should be here in a few minutes. We can ask her to prepare something if you want." She reviewed her résumé once again. "She's had solid kitchen experience but always as a sous chef. I wonder why she never stepped up to head her own kitchen."

"Hello?" A timid, high-pitched voice came from the entrance. "Is anyone here?"

"Come in," Pam called out.

Mark and Pam turned toward the door. The woman who walked in was slight, weighing no more than a bird, and looked almost gaunt. She was twenty-nine, although Pam would have guessed her age to be closer to forty.

"I have an appointment at one o'clock," she said.

"Allison Daley?" Pam asked, shaking the woman's thin hand. "Please sit down. I'm Pam and this is my husband, Mark."

Allison sat on the edge of her chair, anxiously rubbing the palms of her hands on her knees.

"Is everything all right?" Pam asked.

Allison's gaze darted between them. "Yes, fine. You have a beautiful place."

"Thank you," Pam said, starting to feel nervous just sitting next to the restless woman.

"Have you had lunch?" Mark blurted out.

"No," she answered. "I really don't eat much."

Mark stood up. "Well, we haven't and my stomach is growling. Why don't we go into the kitchen and we can talk while you and Pam make a sandwich or something?"

Pam joined Mark's lead. "What a great idea. Maybe cooking in different surroundings will give you an appetite." Pam glanced over at her husband as he led the way through the dining room.

In the kitchen, Pam grabbed two fresh aprons and towels. "Apron?" she offered.

"No, thanks. Don't use one."

"Okay," Pam said. "The refrigerator is stocked with just about any ingredient you might want. All the containers holding leftovers are marked and are on the top two shelves. Fresh meats are on the third shelf, fish and poultry on the fourth and vegetables in the four drawers. Why don't you take a look and see if there's anything you can work with?"

Allison opened the door and stood motionless for a minute. She turned around. "Well, what do you want?"

"Surprise us," Mark said with a broad smile.

"Do you have a standard cookbook or house sheet?"

"House sheet?" Pam asked.

"You know," the woman said, "a cheat sheet of your recipes?"

Pam looked dumbfounded. "No, we don't have one of those. Everything I cook is from memory or experimentation and is one of a kind."

"Oh," Allison said, turning back to the refrigerator.

"There's wonderful filet mignon, or leftover Tuscan roast pork that you can jazz up," Pam said, getting impatient.

Allison took out the jar of mayonnaise and shut the door. "Do you have any cans of tuna fish?"

"Over in the pantry," Mark said, pointing to the closet. "I love tuna salad on toasted country French with thinly spread honey mustard. Pam throws in the kitchen sink and then tops it off with a touch of raspberry-walnut vinaigrette."

Pam brought out a stainless-steel mixing bowl along with three plates. She also took four different loaves out of the bread drawer.

Over the next few minutes, Mark and Pam watched Allison make tuna salad with two ingredients: tuna fish and mayonnaise. She looked at the breads on the island and asked, "Do you have any white bread?"

Pam shrugged. "Sorry, no Wonder Bread here. Why don't you use the Artesian Bole? It's the round loaf."

Allison globbed a scoop of tuna salad on the bread and spread it with the back of the spoon and then covered it with another slice. She passed the sandwich to Mark.

"Oh, okay," Mark said, clearly disappointed that he wasn't getting his normal culinary feast, which Pam made out of the simplest of ingredients.

Pam and Mark ate as quickly as possible, trying to make their way through the awkward conversation in between bites. Allison never tasted her own sandwich.

"Well, it's been interesting having you for lunch, Allison," Pam said, bringing the interview to a close. "We have several applicants to interview and will be making a decision over the next week."

"Then I look forward to your call," she said, once again raising her voice at the end.

After Allison left, Mark went back into the kitchen with Pam on his heels.

"Would you *please* make me something good?" he begged as he sat down on a stool. "I'm still starved and that sandwich was worse than what I make."

Pam stood behind him and put her arms around his shoulders. She kissed him on the ear. "How about I make you an early dinner that will knock your socks off?"

"Promise?"

"Guaranteed," she said, resting her head on his back. "I'm exhausted. That interview was painful."

Mark rubbed her arms. "Is anyone else coming today?"

"One more and she should be a little closer to what we're looking for. She's appeared on Food Network a couple dozen times. I recognized the photo on her résumé. She's actually coming with her husband."

Mark picked up the pile of papers Pam had left on the island. "Is this them?" he asked, looking at a photo of a man and a woman at the top of a résumé. "I don't know about her, but I've seen him before."

She looked over his shoulder at the photograph. "You know him?"

Mark shook his head. "Well, I don't know him, but he's a regular on that morning show on NBC. He does those two-minute demonstrations," he explained.

Pam took a closer look at the photograph. "Are you sure?"

"Absolutely."

"I'm totally confused," she said, taking the papers from Mark. She went over to the small desk and dialed the number on the résumé.

"Diane? This is Pam Walker. No, we don't have to cancel, but there may have been a misunderstanding. Mark thinks it's your husband who might be applying for the position. That's where Mark saw him, on NBC. . . . Oh, I see. I'm sorry there's really no possibility we would hire two chefs, unless it's a two-for-one offer," Pam tried to joke. "Oh, we could never afford sixty thousand a year for both of you. . . . That would just be your salary? And what would your husband's pay be? . . . Eighty thousand? But we're a very small inn. We don't bring in nearly enough business to cover even one of your wages. I'm so sorry."

Pam dropped the receiver and collapsed in the chair. "Ugh," she moaned. "What a fiasco."

"Come on, let's go down to the barn," he said, trying to cheer up his wife. "I'll give you the ride of your lifetime on my bike."

Although riding on a motorcycle was the last thing Pam wanted to do right then, she certainly loved her husband for trying to lift her spirits.

ꟹ

An hour later, Pam was glowing. "That was great!" she exclaimed after their wild drive around their property.

To Pam's amazement, she had found riding in the sidecar of the BMW totally exhilarating, so much so that she asked Mark to teach her how to operate the motorcycle as soon as they had a free afternoon.

"It was amazing!" Pam said, still feeling the adrenaline rush. "How fast were we going? Seventy or eighty?"

Mark put his arm around her. "We might have gotten up to forty at best, honey."

"It felt like we were flying!"

As the Walkers crossed the courtyard, they greeted their lodging guests, occasionally stopping for cordial albeit quick conversations.

Once alone, Pam put her hand under Mark's arm and they walked side by side. "I'm glad the restaurant is closed tonight. I'm covered with dust and all I want is a long shower."

Behind them, a car pulled into the parking lot. A man got out and came toward them. "Excuse me," he called out.

Pam and Mark turned together and saw André Levesque jogging toward them.

"I hope you don't mind me dropping by unannounced."

"Not at all, but in truth," Pam said, "you're the last person I expected to see today."

"I can understand that. But if the chef's position is still open, and if you're interested, I'd like to talk with you about it."

Mark looked at him suspiciously. "Why the change of heart?" Although Mark had nothing specific against André, the man had so disappointed Pam the last time he was at Montis, Mark had his guard up.

"Someone I respect suggested that the two of you have one of the finest small inns in the country."

"We think we do," Pam said proudly. "But if you're looking for quiet, we can't offer that right now. We're actually overrun in both the inn and our restaurant."

André continued. "And he said that I would be making a critical mistake by not joining your team if given the opportunity."

"Is this someone we know down in Wheatley?" Mark asked.

"No," André said. "The recommendation came from a close friend of mine, Christian Copeland."

Mark was surprised. "You know Christian?"

"For over ten years," André said, nodding. "And he said I'd be making the mistake of a lifetime if I didn't come here."

Pam looked at Mark and then back at André. "I have an idea: I promised Mark an outstanding dinner tonight. If you're free for the evening, how would you like to join me in the kitchen and we can pull something together?"

André smiled broadly. "That's the best invitation I've gotten today."

An hour later, Pam and André were working side by side as if they had cooked together for years. André took the lead, and after evaluating the foodstuff in the refrigerator and pantry, suggested a menu for that evening, which they jokingly called "Mark's carte du jour."

There was an unspoken choreography between André and Pam that was so smooth and perfectly timed it was as if they were dancing together in the kitchen. As André stepped away from the stove to get additional spices, Pam moved forward to continue pan-searing the lobster. When she reached down and opened the oven door, André bent over her to stir the rice.

In no way did they interfere with each other's efforts and not once did Pam question or disagree with André's choices or decisions. In fact, during that one evening of cooking with André, Pam learned more about French cuisine than she had by trial and error in the four years since buying Montis Inn.

When Pam asked André to select a bottle of wine from the closet, he took the liberty of pulling two bottles of merlot from a Copeland Vineyards case that he had spotted underneath the desk. He uncorked both an hour before dinner was served.

Pam was so overjoyed with what André had pulled together that she handwrote the menu for Mark:

First Course:	*Beet mousse with caviar and citrus salsa and carpaccio of herbed roast baby lamb with tabouli and drizzled rosemary mustard sauce*
Second Course:	*Pan-seared lobster with ruby port reduction on charred onions*
Main Course:	*Pepper-encrusted filet mignon with caramelized endive and chestnut puree*
Dessert:	*Chocolate crème brûlée*

By the time the three were enjoying the main course, Mark and Pam knew they had found their chef, but there were many details that still needed to be discussed and agreed upon.

"This is incredible, André. I've never had such a great meal here," Mark said.

Pam rolled her eyes and smacked her husband on the arm.

"Oh, sorry, honey, but it's really outstanding," Mark said, taking another bite of filet.

"Your wife is an outstanding sous chef," André said, nodding at Pam. She was honored to be considered sous next to such an outstanding cuisinier.

André lifted his glass. "To Christian Copeland, for bringing us together."

"To Christian," the Walkers said in unison.

NINETEEN

Influence

On the southwest corner of the intersection of Main Street and Farm to Market Road is the Chatham Press building, which houses one of the oldest businesses in Lumby. Owned and managed by three generations of Beezers, the company provides the town's residents with their local paper and a well-stocked bookstore. In addition, but frequently overlooked, Chatham Press also owns The Bindery, a highly reputable publishing and bookbinding operation located a half block down the road.

Dennis Beezer had assumed leadership of Chatham Press and its various enterprises after the unexpected death of his father, William Beezer, several years before. Under Dennis's stewardship, the company had sustained strong circulation levels for *The Lumby Lines* and a healthy cash flow from the Lumby Bookstore. It had significantly increased revenue from The Bindery by critically selecting and publishing several books, with some achieving national recognition.

Dennis sat in his second-floor office as his staff worked on *The Lumby Lines.* Scott Stevens was meeting with the paper's photographer and layout editor about the next issue. It was a day like most others.

The Lumby Lines

Sheriff's Complaints

BY SHERIFF SIMON DIXON October 16

8:42 a.m. NW Builders reported that several large stones from their rock-blasting excavation landed on a nearby SUV. No injuries.

8:58 a.m. Lumby Feed Store reported that Hank and mannequin with broken leg are upstairs in theater watching unscheduled movie.

8:59 a.m. Resident at 42 Fairground Road found three giant pumpkins in his driveway, blocking garage. Needs assistance moving them so he can get to work.

9:45 a.m. Doc Wallace reported two gurneys missing from supply room of Lumby's Urgent Care.

10:22 a.m. High School request EMS assistance. Student may have broken wrist in unauthorized gurney race down hallway.

11:47 a.m. Moose damages car State Road 541.

4:02 p.m. Presbyterian church reported finding five-hundred-pound pumpkin stuffed into Dumpster.

5:31 p.m. Patron at Jimmy D's reported chimpanzee in men's room.

5:32 p.m. Resident reported smoke coming out of Porta Potty #3 at fairgrounds. LFD dispatched.

5:47 p.m. Deer vs. Honda at MM 3 on Farm to Market Road. Honda won.

6:22 p.m. Cindy Watford says that the horde of rabbits that was in doghouse is now in her garage.

Dennis smiled when he saw Jimmy D walk through the double doors. They had been close friends for longer than either would care to admit, and their fraternity had smoothly weathered all the storms that came their way.

"This is a surprise," Dennis said, waving Jimmy in.

"I was having lunch at The Green Chile and your wife sent me over with this," Jimmy said, placing a small brown bag on the publisher's desk.

"One of Gabrielle's new recipes, no doubt," Dennis said, peering into the sack. "Have you tried it?"

"Sure have and it's great, as always."

"Every time our son goes away, she redirects all of her extra energy into her cooking."

"How is Brian doing?" Jimmy asked. "We don't see him around very much anymore."

"He's maturing faster than I ever thought possible," Dennis said, sounding like a proud father. "He's really coming into his own, thanks to Brother Matthew."

"So, he's still working for the monks?" Jimmy asked.

"He is," Dennis said, smiling. "I would never have thought that my son would be so closely tied to a monastery, but he seems absolutely committed to helping them with their philanthropic projects. He was in Brazil, but the monks asked him to return to Lima, Peru, to oversee their annual grant distribution there. It's amazing to see him step up and assume that kind of responsibility." Dennis paused. "The last time he was here, on his own volition he met with the admissions department at the university to discuss fast-tracking a degree in international economics."

"We always knew he was one of the brightest kids around," Jimmy said.

"But it wasn't until he found a worthwhile direction that *he* realized it."

Jimmy leaned back in his chair and threw a dart at the board hanging on the wall. He stood and looked more closely at where the metal tip had landed.

"Ten dollars to hit the bull's-eye with your eyes closed," Dennis goaded. "From the chair."

"Not a problem," Jimmy said. He sat down, straightening the feathers. He studied the board, aimed, closed his eyes and tossed the dart.

"Pay up," Dennis said, before the dart even hit the board.

The dart was a quarter inch outside the red zone.

"I'll subtract it from you bar tab," Jimmy said.

Dennis took a piece of paper from his drawer and wrote "$10—darts" at the bottom of the list. "So, why the visit?"

"Just a social call."

Dennis smirked. "No, seriously. Why the visit?"

Jimmy played with a dart between his fingers. "Well, it's about the new veterinarian."

Dennis looked surprised. "I didn't know we had a new vet."

"We don't yet," Jimmy replied, shifting in his chair. "That's where you come in."

"I'm not following."

"Here's the plan. If you write an article about how great this guy, Tom Candor, is," Jimmy explained, his voice rising with excitement, or possibly desperation, "then he can't help but buy Ellen's clinic. Folks will be knocking on his door as soon as they read your endorsement."

"Endorsement?" Dennis asked. "From the paper?"

"Yeah, something like that," Jimmy said, speaking much faster than normal. "People respect your opinion. They'll do whatever you say."

Dennis burst out laughing. "You want me to strong-arm our readers into taking their sick pets to this guy, Candor?"

"Well, not in so many words, but that's the general idea," Jimmy said. "If Tom sees lots of people lined up outside The Granary, I know he'll take the bait."

Dennis squinted. "Hook 'em?"

"Exactly," Jimmy said, slapping his palm on the desk. "So, you can make it a real fluff article—no deep exposé about boring stuff."

"You're unbelievable," Dennis said as he pulled out the small Lumby phone book and dialed the number of Dr. Campbell's vet clinic.

"Ellen? It's Dennis. Is Tom Candor with you by any chance?"

There was a short pause while Ellen passed the phone to Tom. "Hello?"

"Hi, Tom, this is Dennis Beezer. I don't believe we've met. I'm the publisher of our local paper. I'm working on an article about Ellen's retirement and the clinic's change of hand. If you have no objections, I'd appreciate a few minutes to talk with you."

"Unfortunately, I really don't have any time right now," Tom replied.

"I'm sure you're busy, but perhaps five minutes?" Dennis said.

There was silence over the phone. "Thanks for the offer, but I'm just walking out the door for farm rounds with Ellen."

"It doesn't have to be today, and I can certainly work around your schedule," Dennis offered. He shrugged his shoulders at Jimmy, who gave him an encouraging nod. "If you buy The Granary, the article may act as a nice introduction of you to our town."

Another pause. "If we can keep it to five or ten minutes," Tom said.

"That would be great. Why don't we meet for a cup of coffee at my wife's restaurant, The Green Chile, at three this afternoon, if that works for you?"

As Dennis hung up the phone, he shook his head. "Well, that was a struggle. I hope he's more interested in talking with me this afternoon."

Jimmy brushed off Dennis's concern with a wave of his hand. "Oh, don't worry—he's a great guy, and honest as the day is long. He just needs to get to know you. Believe me, he's exactly what this town needs." Jimmy headed for the door. "Remember, put a nice spin on it."

"As in lie when and where necessary?"

"Well, not exactly. But don't piss him off. Ellen has one foot out the door and our town would be crippled without a vet."

~

That afternoon, Dennis was talking with Gabrielle when Tom Candor walked into the restaurant. Dennis looked at his watch: two fifty-eight. He admired a punctual man.

"Tom Candor?" Dennis said. Shaking his hand, Dennis noticed that Tom was slightly taller than him, which was rare. "I'm Dennis Beezer. Let's take the back table," he offered, leading the veterinarian away from the windows in front. "Thanks for taking time out to talk."

"I'm afraid I'm quite a boring subject," Tom said.

"Your interest in The Granary is one of the most intriguing news bites our town has had in months." Dennis laughed, trying to lighten the atmosphere. "Have you ever lived in a small town?"

"A few but certainly none as small as Lumby."

Dennis removed a pencil from his pocket and began taking notes. "I understand you're from Maine. Do you own a practice there?"

"No. For the last three years, I've been on staff at an emergency animal hospital outside of Bangor. One of my old friends is expanding his practice and I was just lending a hand."

Dennis scratched some words onto the paper. "And before that?"

"That's where it becomes boring," Tom said congenially. "I had my own office for several years, and then worked at a few different clinics." Tom took a sip of his coffee. "So, how long have you been in Lumby?"

Tom's question took Dennis by surprise. "All my life. My grandfather founded the Chatham Press, which went to my father and eventually fell into my lap."

"And do you like it here?" Tom slipped in before Dennis could turn the tables.

Dennis wondered if Tom's questions were part of his effort to truly determine if he would be interested in living in Lumby or if he was simply being evasive. "Lumby's certainly unusual, but I suppose there isn't any other place I'd rather be. There's a good-heartedness in our small town that is seldom seen nowadays."

"With all the crime in a big city, I find that comforting. It's the promise of a place like Lumby that so many people want. I know I'm one of them."

"The promise?" Dennis asked.

"The promise of a new start, a happier life," Tom replied.

Dennis laughed. "Well, sometimes Lumby is a little too quirky for some. So, you are a large- and small-animal vet?"

"I have licenses for both from the state."

"Do you have a preference?" Dennis asked, his pencil at the ready.

"Not really, but if I had to narrow my practice, I would probably specialize in large animals. If anything, I like being outside more than in the lab or exam rooms."

"I envy you. The only time I'm outside is when I'm walking between the Chatham Press and here. So, where did you go to school?"

"Berkeley," Tom answered, "but that's ancient history."

Just then young Timmy Beezer ran through the kitchen door carrying a shoe box, which he immediately put on the table in front of Tom.

"Are you the new animal doctor?"

Tom smiled warmly. "I am. And what's your name?"

"Timmy Beezer," he said. "Would you tell my folks that I should get a puppy?"

Tom laughed. "Well, that's a serious responsibility but I'll make the suggestion."

"Okay," Timmy said. "And can you look at Toad, my turtle? He didn't eat his lettuce today."

Tom lifted the lid of the shoe box and picked up the turtle, turning it gently on its back. Seeing that it was dead, he quickly put it back in the box and replaced the lid.

"You know what, Timmy?" Tom said. "I think I should take Toad back to my clinic to see if I can get him eating again. Why don't you and your mom stop by tomorrow?"

"Okay. Bye, Toad," he said, patting the shoe box. And then the boy was off on another adventure.

"Dead?" Dennis asked.

"Quite," Tom said. "Do you want me to replace him with a healthy turtle?"

Dennis looked toward Gabrielle. "No, I don't think so. Tommy's not that attached to it."

"Well, come by anytime and I'll gently break the bad news to him. But right now," Tom said, standing up, "I need to cut our conversation short. I'm sorry. Ellen is expecting me back in a few minutes." He extended his hand. "Thanks very much for the opportunity."

Dennis reeled back at the abruptness of Tom's exit. "Perhaps we can have a longer chat if you decide to buy Ellen's practice?" he said, walking Tom to the door.

"Actually, I bought it last night."

For the third time in ten minutes, the experienced journalist was taken by surprise. "Well, congratulations," Dennis said. "If there's anything I can do to help, please let me know."

"Thanks very much. I'm sure we'll see each other around town."

As Lumby's new veterinarian walked out the door, Gabrielle slipped up behind Dennis and put her arm around his waist. "That's just wonderful. He seems like such a nice guy."

Dennis squinted as he watched Tom walk to the intersection, heading away from The Granary.

Gabrielle knew her husband's silence meant something. "You certainly seem less than thrilled."

Dennis continued to stare at the stranger as he crossed the road. "I don't know. Something doesn't feel right. That was one of the least informative interviews I've had in a long time."

"But Jimmy wanted fluff anyway," Gabrielle said, trying to ease his concern.

"And fluff he shall get," Dennis said, before leaning back and kissing his wife. As he straightened, he spotted Terry McGuire walking hand in hand with a young woman whose hair was dyed almost as red as his own. They ran across Main Street, heading directly toward The Green Chile.

"Seems Terry has a different girlfriend than he did yesterday," Gabrielle said under her breath. "And don't give me the 'It's a guy thing' or 'He's just sewing his wild oats' excuse."

Terry opened the restaurant door just enough to lean in. "Have you guys heard when Brian is coming back?"

"Good afternoon to you, Terry," Dennis said.

Gabrielle stepped forward. "Why don't you two come in for some iced tea?"

"Sorry, Mrs. Beezer," Terry said more politely. "I have to get over to Brad's Hardware before it closes—you know, work and all. Do you know when Brian will be home?"

"We haven't heard," Gabrielle said. "The last postcard we got came from Peru."

"Well, if you talk to him, tell him to call me. He's missing out on a wild bunch of action."

Gabrielle bit her lip.

"We will," Dennis said just before Terry bolted away from the door.

TWENTY

Trajectories

Walking back to his office, Dennis stared at the ground as he recalled his conversation with Tom Candor. Something felt off other than Tom's apparent evasiveness—it wasn't necessarily wrong, but just not right. However, he couldn't put his finger on exactly what was nagging him.

"You look deep in thought," Simon said, walking up behind Dennis.

Jolted out of his daze, Dennis looked up and smiled. "How's your day going?"

"That's an interesting question. I just issued a summons to Don Wilbur."

Dennis stopped in his tracks and cocked his head. "But Don's been dead for over three years."

"Those were the exact words I used down at the county office in Wheatley."

"Don't tell me. It's another property-tax bill for his cemetery lot?"

Simon laughed. "A little more convoluted than that, but still utterly absurd. So, how's business treating you?"

"Having its ups and downs today," Dennis admitted.

Suddenly there was a large explosion coming from farther down the road.

"What in the world . . . ?" both men asked as they started running up Main Street.

Simon was the first to reach the crosswalk at Farm to Market Road and immediately saw that a manhole cover, three feet in diameter, was wedged into the crushed roof of a car parked in front of Dennis's office.

Several pedestrians had already gathered around the car. Hank stood under a nearby tree, wearing a Hard Rock Café T-shirt. His eyes were big with fright—he had just crossed over that very manhole while escorting the mannequin home. Had the explosion occurred seconds earlier, Hank would have been crushed between metal and metal. Life is so unpredictable, the flamingo thought.

"I don't think you want to see this," Simon called back to Dennis, who within seconds was standing next to him, breathing heavily.

Dennis yelled out, "Oh, no! This can't be!"

Although the automobile's front door was grotesquely twisted under the caved-in roof, anyone passing could still discern the custom logo: "The Chatham Press."

"New company car?" Simon asked.

"It *was,*" Dennis said in exasperation. He looked across the street and saw the uncovered manhole. "That thing must have flown twenty feet over and at least ten feet in the air. What on earth happened?"

Simon was already heading toward the sewer hole.

"Is anyone down there? Is anyone hurt?" Simon yelled into the pitch-black hole.

Everyone near him stopped talking.

"Is anyone hurt?" he repeated in his loudest voice.

Still, no response.

As he straightened, he smelled a faint, familiar odor. Simon breathed in deeply and then his eyes widened in alarm. "Gas!" he yelled. "Everyone out of here, now! Dennis, call the gas company. Tell them to close the main valve."

Suddenly, a second explosion rocked the ground. A hundred feet down Main Street, a manhole cover in front of the library projectiled into the air with tremendous force. It shot up at an angle, reached its peak and then hurtled back to earth, landing on the roof of a small yellow Honda parked on the other side of the road.

"No—no!" Dennis groaned. "Not Gabrielle's car!"

"Dennis, make the call!" Simon yelled.

But within seconds, Lumby's one and only fire truck could be heard a few blocks away. Simon looked over and saw Dale running out of the police station.

"They're on their way," he shouted.

Unfortunately, Dale had called the fire department, not the gas company, which would result in a near-fatal delay.

Tom Candor was standing at the front window of the animal clinic, now *his* animal clinic, and thinking about his good fortune. In Lumby, he could start a new life far removed from his past. It was a small town, and he had been warned on several occasions that Lumby took some growing used to. But how peculiar could this charming little village really be? He might enjoy the oddity of it all and would try to fit right in.

Tom was jolted out of his reverie with the first two explosions. Hearing the fire truck sirens, he ran out to the sidewalk and saw two crowds, one in front of the Press building, the other in front of the Mexican restaurant.

Suddenly, a third explosion blew Tom off his feet and onto his back, which provided a perfect vantage point as, not more than eight yards away, a manhole cover blasted out of its casement and jettisoned through the air toward The Granary. Tom watched in horror as the mass of steel slammed into the exterior stone wall of his clinic. Although much of the momentum was absorbed by the impact, the manhole cover broke through the wall and continued to travel inside, bursting through the old floor of the second story and making its way down to the refurbished horse stalls below.

Immobilized with shock and pain, Tom stared in disbelief at the gaping hole in the wall. A woman's voice behind him called out, "Are you all right?" But other than offering a weak wave, he was too dazed to reply.

Not until the woman came up next to him could he pull his eyes off his building. Mackenzie hovered over him, her red hair blowing wildly in the fall breeze. Terry McGuire stood right behind his mother.

"Tom?" she asked. "Are you okay?" She had placed her hand gently, almost tenderly, on his shoulder.

Tom stared at her in disbelief. "Did you see that? It was . . . beyond belief." He looked at the open sewer hole and then traced the path the massive cover had traveled from the ground into the side of The Granary. "How could it have gone that far?"

"It had to be a gas leak," Mac said. "We were just coming out of the library when the first one blew."

Terry didn't know what to make of his mother's sudden interest in Tom Candor's well-being. Or was it that sudden? he wondered. He looked at his mother with new eyes and saw something he hadn't noticed while they were together at the library, and hadn't seen in the last five years: his mother was wearing a hint of makeup.

"It broke the stone," Tom said, still dazed.

"The structure was originally built as a stocking barn for grain. The walls are pretty thin," Mac explained.

Tom stood up slowly and looked down the street. "Was anyone hurt?"

"No, just a few cars," Mac relied. "Are you sure you're okay?"

"Mom, he's fine." Terry sounded agitated. "I'm out of here."

Tom watched Terry storm away, and then looked up at Mac, who was also looking at her son. "Be honest with me," he said. "Does this sort of thing happen on a regular basis in Lumby?"

"Which, my son's rude behavior or UFOs flying across Main

Street?" Mackenzie tried to hide her embarrassment. "Usually not the latter. You look a little shaken. Do you want to go inside?"

He scratched his head. "I'd prefer to look at the damages. This may be a painfully obvious question, but are you available to do some repair work?"

"I was actually headed over here to talk to Ellen about some work she wanted me to finish. But then I heard that you're the new owner."

He raised his brows. "Wow, news travels fast."

Mac smiled. "When there are only three blocks in town, you can count on it traveling faster than your manhole cover."

Tom exhaled, releasing the tension in his body since the explosion. "I'll keep that in mind."

"Anyway, I thought you might want to see the final project Ellen had planned." She paused. "But it seems you have more urgent problems to deal with now."

"That I do." Tom grimaced.

"Before we look at the scene of the accident, I'd like to show you something," Mac said, leading him to the back of the building. Her thought was to first show him a small, manageable project before taking on the manhole disaster. Pointing up to the soffit, she said, "I was going to remove the old gutters, replace the rotted fascia and then install a wider gutter system that actually works. The roof catches so much water back here that it overflows the gutter and gets behind those backboards."

"Is it necessary?"

Mac thought for a moment. "Certainly within the next year. The longer you wait, the more damage will be done to the wood."

"What would the cost be for the gutters and molding?"

"I quoted Ellen nine hundred dollars," she said, taking a copy of the proposal from her folder and handing it to Tom. "But if you don't want a fixed price bid, we can work on an hourly basis."

"And what's your rate?"

"Forty dollars an hour."

"That's more than what I get paid!" Tom admitted.

"But I'm *really* good," she teased him.

He grinned. "I don't question that for a second. Are there any other outstanding projects you suggest to keep The Granary in the best of condition—it's a fabulous reminder of days gone by."

Mac liked the fact that Tom appreciated the clinic for other than professional reasons, and it meant the world to her that he was soliciting her opinion.

"Not really," she answered. "Ellen did a great job of maintaining the building, and before putting it on the market, she gave me the last of the higher-priority projects."

"And the repair of the new hole?"

Mac walked inside the front-most horse stall, stepping around wood fragments that were scattered everywhere. She jumped up on the manhole cover, which had landed squarely in the berth, and looked up through the hole in the ceiling.

"Amazing," she whispered.

"Repairable, I assume," Tom said.

"Oh, absolutely," Mac said as she stepped out of the stall. "I can patch just about any hole you have in your life, Dr. Candor."

TWENTY-ONE

Sanctuary

Mac walked to the front porch of The Granary and sat down on the first stoop. "If you could just give me some information, I'll get a quote for the repair to Jimmy by the end of the day."

"Why Jimmy?" Tom asked.

"I'm sure he'll want to gather up all of the repair bills before submitting them to the gas company. Hopefully that will be the last of flying manhole covers, for a while anyway." She winked.

Tom sat next to her as she opened her folder and withdrew an insurance-claim form. "What name should I use?" she asked.

Tom looked confused. "I don't understand."

"The property owner's name—is that you or Ellen?"

"Well, we signed the papers last night," Tom said, "so you should use mine."

"Wow," Mac said in surprise. "We assumed it would take months for someone to finalize the purchase."

"Not when the practice has had one owner for as long as this one did," he said. He looked up and down Main Street. "And I don't think it can get much better than this."

Mac turned her attention back to her paper. "Full name?"

His pause, unnoticeable to Mac, felt like minutes to him. "Thomas Candor," he answered. Although he had changed his legal name long ago, occasionally he was still caught off-guard by the question.

Mac kept her face down and her pen poised above the form. "Married?"

Tom was dumbstruck. "Why is *that* relevant?"

Mac looked up at him, blushing more than she would have thought possible. "It's not," she confessed. "I was just interested."

Tom grinned. "No. But I was married once, years ago. And you?"

"I've been divorced for quite some time." She looked down the street and saw that a crowd still surrounded Gabrielle's smashed car. "The town really supported me during my first few years here and offered me more jobs than I could possibly handle."

"Doesn't that have more to do with you being one of the best carpenters in the area, as Ellen keeps reminding me?"

Mac pulled her hair back with one hand. "Ellen was one of my first customers when I took up carpentry. We've had a great friendship ever since."

"So, do you see your ex-husband much?" he asked.

"Never," Mac said, looking down and knocking her boots together. "He didn't want to be harnessed with a wife and son, so when he turned his back and left, that was the last time we ever saw him."

"Is that a good thing?"

"For me, probably, but certainly not for my son. He would have benefited from having a father around to help him become a man." She looked over to Tom. "And you?"

He was unsure what exactly she was asking, but assumed it was about his own failed marriage. "It was a long time ago," he said quickly while fighting the urge to shut down the conversation as he always did when someone asked about his past life. "We came together when we were quite young and just grew in different directions."

"Are you still friends?"

"No. At the time of our divorce, I would say we were acquaintances at best," was all Tom could bring himself to share.

Mackenzie liked the fact that Tom didn't talk badly about his ex-wife. "Do you have any children?" she asked.

Tom's body, and expression, went taut.

Seeing his reaction, Mac recoiled. "I'm sorry. I'm asking too many questions."

Tom took a deep breath. "No, we had no children, just two very busy careers," he said. Glancing over at Jimmy D's, he saw three people looking back, obviously watching him and Mac. "This really is a small town, isn't it?"

Mackenzie followed the direction of his gaze. "You have no idea. But they're such good folks here. Their behavior may be off-kilter sometimes, but most everyone has good intentions."

"Although I feel as exposed as that hole in the side of my barn, I love small-town living," Tom admitted. "Since there's nowhere to hide, you have no choice but to be yourself."

"Why would anyone want to hide anyway?"

"Anonymity, perhaps," Tom replied.

Mackenzie laughed. "Anonymity is a concept that hasn't quite come to Lumby. Maybe that's why I also love living in a small town—everything is front and center." As she stood, she patted Tom lightly on the knee. "And it doesn't help that we're sitting in one of the most beloved buildings on Main Street." She glanced over at the large front porch. "It certainly has always been my favorite. Its architecture is as interesting as its history. There's only one thing missing."

"Birdhouses," they both said at the same time, and burst out laughing.

Catching his breath, Tom said, "I noticed Ellen hadn't hung even one birdhouse out back."

"She thought there were already too many animals hanging around," Mac said.

"Well, that's something we need to correct right away."

"I have at least a dozen at home that I can donate to the cause. I save the best scrap lumber and make them for a sanctuary not far from here." Her face lit up. "In fact, how would you like to join me tomorrow? You'll see one of the largest natural colonies of mountain bluebirds in the state."

Tom jumped at the invitation. "I'd like that. What time?"

"How about seven thirty?"

"I'll bring the coffee and scones."

"Then it's a date," she said, blushing at her own choice of words.

The Lumby Lines

Lumby Forum

October 16

Can't beat these prices: Stuff for free! Free rabbits for pet or pot, as many as you want. I've been invaded. Call Cindy Watford. 695-0491

Pumpkin mash. See Mrs. McNear @ the farm.

Other: Used chicken coop good for 20 hens. One year lease $2.00 or sale for $8.00.

For Rent: Unfinished garage still available from last summer. Livable. $15/mo. In high demand. Call now before it's taken.

Six empty beehives. 925-5253. Does not include any bees because they've taken off somewhere.

Certified piano teacher for your kids any age 12–14. Please telephone 925-0174.

Swap for winter months: I have one-room rustic cabin. No electricity but extension cord can be run from street post. Outhouse fully operational. Will trade for 2-bed Florida condo. Heated pool a must. Call Phil 925-3928.

Wanted: Female soul mate to come with me to Florida for winter. Call Phil 925-3928.

Mother-in-law finally passed. RV in backyard now seeking responsible tenant. 1 bath 1 bed. Very quaint bordering on charming. $55 per month. 925-4439.

Wife allergic to dog, so need to get rid of the bitch. Good hunter but needs to be spayed. See Charlie at the Wayside any night except Tues.

Wools Inventory Sale!!! Special on croc garden shoes and men's swim trunks.

10×70 Barn on Hunts Mill Road between Lumby Lumber and town landfill. Aromatic with lots of birds to watch. 925-4338 anytime.

Palm Reading $10 Fortune-telling $12. Joy at 14 Cherry Street behind the barber.

For sale: 10 chessboards for $10 each or will swap for same number of Scrabble boards. Come by Lumby Scrabble Club any Tues or Thurs nite 9–11 at library.

The following morning at seven fifteen a.m., it became readily apparent that Tom Candor and Mackenzie McGuire had something else in common: they so much hated being late that they were constantly early for everything.

When Mac pulled up in front of The Granary, the sun was just breaking in the east. Tom was sitting on the front-porch steps, swinging a large picnic basket between his legs. He had pulled up the coat collar around his neck to ward off the morning chill. Mac rolled down her window.

"I'm fifteen minutes early," she said as he jogged down the walkway.

"Well, then, the scones will be that much warmer when we eat them. Good thing S&T's opens early," he said as he opened the passenger door. Before getting in, he asked, "Other than coffee, is there anything else you need?"

The small, thoughtful gesture touched Mac's heart. "Binoculars?"

"Got 'em in here," he said, tapping the picnic basket, which he then placed on the backseat. "Along with a camera and the Audubon field guide."

"Then I think we're ready for quite the adventure," Mac said, not fully realizing how prophetic her statement would prove.

During the hour drive north to Bryson's Bird Sanctuary, Mac and Tom shared lighthearted conversation and much laughter. It had been so very long since a man had captivated Mac's interest to the point that she lost all track of time. She was being swept away in the excitement of firsts—first smile, first date, and the possibility of a first kiss.

While Mac told Tom stories of some of Lumby's more quirky moments, he found a warmth deep in his heart that had been absent for much of his life.

". . . and then Isabella trotted through the front door and right up to the bar, where she passed so much gas and—well, you know—that the Wayside had to close for two days. Poor Jeremiah was never allowed back." She paused. "Personally, I think that's why no one voted for her during our mayoral elections."

"You mean voted for him, for Jeremiah."

Mac shook her head. "No, actually it was Isabella's name that was on the ballot."

What surprised Tom more than what Mac said was the fact that she said it without blinking an eye.

"Here we are," she said, pulling the car off the road.

"Where?" Tom asked, looking for some indication of their journey's end. "We're in the middle of nowhere."

"This is Bryson's Bird Sanctuary," Mac said.

Tom shook his head. "We haven't seen a soul on the road for the last thirty miles. And there's no sign. How would anyone know there's a bird sanctuary here?"

"Well, there's no need for a sign," Mac said, leading Tom to a narrow path directly across the street from where she had parked. "Everyone knows that this is Chuck's land and that he donated it to the Nature Conservancy."

"Everyone?" Tom teased.

"Well, everyone who has any business being here. Chuck personally invites those he wants to visit here."

About a half mile hike from the road, they came to a large clearing that Tom guessed to be at least fifty acres. A crystal-clear stream bisected the field before it broadened out and formed a marshland at the far end of the pasture. Three solid-oak picnic tables had been set up in a manicured, well-protected area in a grove of large evergreens. Tom placed the picnic basket on the closest table.

"Do you mind if we have some of that coffee?" Mac asked, eyeing the wicker basket.

"Absolutely not, I'm starved," he said, as he began to unpack.

He had brought not only coffee and scones, but also fresh strawberries, vanilla yogurt and a bag of granola, which he had made the night before. Mac sampled it before Tom poured a large amount into bowls and topped the granola with the other ingredients.

"Delicious," she said.

Tom passed Mac her breakfast, all the while keeping one eye on the open field, hoping to spot the mountain bluebird that Mac had talked about.

"There!" he said softly, and grabbed the binoculars.

But instead of looking into them himself, he gave them to Mac. "On the tallest shrub by the bend in the stream. There are four or five of them."

Mac looked through the lenses. "I see them!" she whispered, spellbound by the birds.

"Don't move!" Tom warned, grabbing her arm.

She immediately dropped the binoculars and turned to look at him. "What?" she whispered.

He chuckled. "So much for following directions. There's a black bear about thirty yards away."

She followed Tom's stare to the tree line on the north side of the clearing.

"Is it too late to ask if you brought a gun?" Mac asked under her breath.

"Just a tad," he said softly. "Okay, here's the plan. On three, we're going to jump up on the table. Clap your hands and stomp your feet and make as much commotion as possible. He'll be more scared of us than we are of him."

"I seriously doubt that," she said.

"Trust me," he said, taking her hand for only a second. "Ready?"

Mac nodded.

"One . . . two . . ."

Suddenly there was thrashing in the woods close to the bear, and from the high brush, a moose charged out, tossing his head and moving his enormous antlers to and fro. The bear turned on its hind legs and darted away from the stream, disappearing into the woods.

"Look," Tom whispered, pointing to the marsh area.

What had gone unnoticed by both Tom and Mac was a small female moose standing knee-high in the bog area. When she looked up, green vegetation hung from her mouth. The male moose bellowed and stomped the ground. The female bit into another clump of wet grass.

"Unrequited love?" Mac asked.

"She may be too young."

Without warning, the female bounded out of the marsh with surprising speed, given her size. The large male tossed its head one last time and went in hot pursuit.

"Wow," Mac murmured.

"That was amazing. Did you get a chance to see the birds?"

"No." She shook her head. "And my hands are shaking so much, they would be a blur."

"Let me help you," Tom said, moving directly behind her. Reaching over her shoulders, he lifted the binoculars hanging from her neck, and held them up to her eyes. She felt his breath on the back of her neck.

"There're still two or three on the same shrub," he said. "Do you see them?"

She lifted her arms and placed her hands on his so she could adjust the height of the binoculars.

"There they are!" She watched in fascination. "I've never seen a more vibrant blue."

"Neither have I," he said, as they both continued to stare at the exquisite birds.

Tom slid his hands off the binoculars and rested them on her shoulders. Mac's heart skipped a beat. What was she getting herself into?

TWENTY-TWO

Rhea

Brother Michael enjoyed the drive back to Franklin after spending the afternoon in Wheatley meeting with retailers for the monks' rum sauce. Although the Saint Cross monks owned a prominent gourmet-food company, and distributed their products nationally, the brothers always met personally with the local buyers and those who had supported their business when it was in its infancy. As Michael would attest, it was as enjoyable for him to make the business calls as it was for the small stores to be visited by the increasingly popular monks of Saint Cross Abbey.

The only disappointment came when Michael visited Cedar Grove Inn and was told by his good friend Pat Dwyer that he and his wife had sold the inn and would be retiring to Flagstaff, Arizona. The monks were not only losing a loyal customer, but they would also miss the Dwyers, whom many of them had known for more than thirty years. Truth be told, Brother Michael would also miss the outstanding meals he was always offered whenever he dropped by.

However pleasant the visits of that day had been, Michael was glad to be pulling into the driveway of Saint Cross Abbey. Most of the autumn leaves had fallen, but there was still a smattering of color in the hills behind the monastery.

Approaching the crossroad in front of the main building, Michael saw a large piece of splintered wood lying by the side of the dirt road, so he pulled over and stopped the car. When he got out, he realized that it wasn't just one piece of wood, but the entire area was littered with broken boards. Had a wooden pallet from one of the flatbeds owned by a local farmer fallen off when food was being delivered? Thinking about various explanations for the wood being there, Michael began collecting the scraps into a large pile.

He looked around when he heard a car backfire, and saw a dilapidated van turn into the drive. With its broken muffler and burning oil, the van offended all his senses.

The driver reached the crossroad, where Michael's car was parked, and came to a stop. The window rolled down and a hand waved. "Where's Matt?" the man yelled out.

Brother Michael took several steps forward so neither would have to yell to be heard. "I'm sorry. There is no Matt here."

"Yeah, there is," the man corrected him. "It's on the bill of lading." Leaning over to the passenger seat, he scavenged through his papers and extracted a shipping order. He examined the addressee. "Matthew is his name."

Brother Michael nodded. "Ah, Brother Matthew. I'm sorry. He's in Oregon."

"Don't really matter to me. I still gotta make this delivery," the man said.

"What is it?"

"None of my business, but I'll need some help getting it out of the van."

Michael pointed to the man's left. "Please follow that road around to the back of the abbey. I'll meet you there in a minute."

"We'll need a couple more guys. That sucker's heavy," the man said as he drove off.

And, indeed, the driver was right. With Brothers John and Marc on one side, and Michael and the driver on the other, they were barely able to lift the crate out of the van.

"What a racket," the driver said as soon as the crate was on the ground.

Brother John looked at Marc, who shrugged his shoulders. The driver jumped back in his van and turned on the ignition. When the van backfired, a plume of foul smoke enveloped the monks.

"That's the nastiest smell," John complained as the van drove past them.

Although the fall breeze cleared the air, an odd smell still hung in the air. John inhaled again and frowned. What he had thought were fumes from the car were actually coming from the crate.

"What *is* that smell?" he asked.

Just as Brother Marc put his ear up to the crate, a deafening screech came from within, sending him off his feet, his backside hitting the ground. "What in the world . . . ?" he said.

"Whatever it is, we need to get it out of there," Michael said.

John headed to the shop for a hammer.

Marc stood and brushed the dust off his pants. "Poor thing. It must be terrified."

"It's a bird," Michael stated as he pulled a long feather from between two pieces of wood.

"But the crate is three feet tall," Marc said.

"All right, then, it's a really big bird."

"Here," John said, running up to Marc and passing him a crowbar, "let's get the top off."

While Mark loosened the planks on one end, John was able to remove a few boards from the top of the other end, making a narrow hole. Suddenly, a bird poked its head through the opening. The animal was beautiful, with black and white markings on its face and a patch of translucent blue feathers on its crown. Its long, thin neck was an iridescent green that blended into and became a brilliant ultramarine blue. The monks stared in utter surprise.

Without warning, another screech came from the animal, ten

times louder than the first. It sounded like the screams of a cat in heat.

Michael tried to peer into the crate, but kept a safe distance from the bird's large beak. "Can you remove that board?" he asked John.

John wedged the claw of the hammer under the wood. Just as he was breaking it free, the bird jabbed its beak into John's forearm. To John's credit, he didn't pull away until the plank was loosened enough for him to pull it off.

Although it was dark inside the crate, Michael could see some of the animal's body. "It's a peacock! Go ahead and let him out."

"Do we know who it's from?" Marc asked, pulling at more planks.

Michael shook his head. "The driver left no papers."

"Get some grain from the kennel and try to distract him while I pry the crate open," John said.

Within minutes, the peacock was free. It showed its appreciation by spreading its elaborate tail. A palate of blue and green concentric circles covering the tail opened before the monks' eyes.

"That's so awesome," Michael said.

"Why don't you take the grain and lead him into the kennel?" Brother John suggested. "You can put him next to the rhea."

"Who's Rita?" Michael asked.

John rolled his eyes. "This isn't the first delivery of the day."

"Did you see the wood out front?" Marc asked Michael.

"Yeah, I was gathering it into a pile when that driver showed up. Was it from a broken pallet?"

The peacock screamed again, bringing several brothers who were inside the building to the windows.

Marc laughed. "We only wish. It's a thank-you from a village in Bolivia where Brian Beezer just spent the week."

John explained further. "The wood in front is the remnants of the crate that was destroyed by the rhea when it was trying to escape. Go see for yourself."

Too intrigued to notice the brothers' growing irritation about the onslaught of animals, Michael headed off to see the latest addition to Saint Cross. Every few feet, he shook the tin can that contained the grain to entice the glorious peacock to willingly, and hopefully quietly, follow him across the back of the stalls.

As soon as Michael pulled the kennel door open, different noises erupted. He led the peacock into a kennel with fresh cedar chips spread two inches deep. As he was securing a pail of fresh water, a kick came from the other side of the wall, followed by another kick.

Michael closed the kennel door and looked around the corner. Expecting to see a mule, given the forceful strikes, Michael was amazed to see another bird, of sorts. This one was at least five feet tall and covered with shaggy gray plumage. Its huge eyes were disproportionate to its small head. "An ostrich," he said to himself.

"A greater rhea, to be precise," John said, startling the monk.

"I thought you went back inside," Michael said.

"It's getting late, so I thought I'd give you a hand with the feeding," John offered as he went into the first kennel, where the baby camel was sound asleep. Now that he was well fed and warm, he had stopped spitting and was a delight to have around.

"The brothers are beginning to wonder what your plans are for all of your animals," John said.

Michael raised his brows. "*My* animals?"

"Generally speaking, yes. Most of us see them as a result of your interview," John explained. "There's no accusation, just a question of stewardship."

Michael grinned. "You mean, who's going to clean out the kennels every day?"

John laughed. "That certainly came up in the discussion. But I think we're all wondering what you're going to do with your growing herd."

Michael knelt down and rubbed the camel's neck. "I don't think that's my decision. They were gifts to all of us at the monastery."

The rhea kicked the wall again and the peacock responded with an ear-piercing screech.

"There are those who feel the animals can't stay here," John said gently.

"Why not?" Michael asked. "They would be a delight to have around. Let's just wait until Brother Matthew returns. He'll know what's best."

The greater rhea kicked one final time, and the door gave way. The bird sprinted out of the enclosure before Michael or John knew what had happened. Had either monk known that the animal could top speeds of thirty miles an hour, they would have called for reinforcements.

&

High in the hills above Saint Amand Abbey, Brother Matthew stood in the vineyard. He leaned back slightly to be washed by the warm autumn sun and, inhaling deeply, savored the scents carried on the gentle breeze. Since arriving at the sisters' monastery, his long solitary walks through the fields had offered more peace and calm than he had known in years. They helped in lifting the heavy burden he always felt as abbot of Saint Cross.

As he resumed his stroll, he extended his arms in both directions, his fingertips touching the leaves of the trellised vines. How wonderful it would be to have such a vineyard in Franklin. He would certainly visit it daily if the sisters had no objection.

But therein lay his deepest concern about this trip and the sisters' proposed merger: he would personally so enjoy having cultivated fields behind Saint Cross monastery that he feared he couldn't be objective in leading the brothers to a decision.

"May I join you?" Sister Claire asked as she approached.

Brother Matthew graciously waved her over. "Please. I was just praying for direction," he said, smiling.

"Is there anything I can help with?"

Matthew trusted Claire's intent and knew her question was asked for his benefit and not her own curiosity. He looked down on the small woman, who exuded more inner strength than most men three times her size. "Perhaps you can," he began thoughtfully. "I'm struggling with how best to separate my personal desire to have such a vineyard at Saint Cross and the objectivity I need to facilitate an open discussion with the brothers."

Claire remained quiet, giving Matthew time to continue.

"I can't remember if, as abbot, I have ever faced such a conflict of interest, where my own desires fought against what I knew was best for the monastery."

"So, you feel the merger is not in the best interest of Saint Cross?"

Matthew stepped back, realizing what conclusion she had unintentionally drawn. "No, definitely not. I certainly didn't mean to suggest that it's a bad proposition." He paused for a moment. "I don't know why it came out like that."

"Perhaps because you won't consider the possibility that your personal interests could also be in the best interest of the abbey?"

"I see them as mutually exclusive," he concurred.

"But do they have to be in opposition?" Claire questioned as they began walking down the path between two trellised rows of grapevines.

"No, of course not," he answered. "But I suppose that feels more safe. Have you ever had a similar conflict of interest as prioress of Saint Amand?"

Claire's laughter was open and honest as she placed her hand on Matthew's arm. "Every day."

He was relieved to hear her answer. "Really?"

"Contrary to your apprehensions about the sisters moving to Franklin, I deeply believe that it's the right thing for both communities, but—" She stopped midsentence.

"But?"

"I don't want to leave Oregon," she said, dropping her head. "I've even gone so far as to consider separating from Saint Amand to join a nunnery down in Eugene."

Matthew was too shocked to reply.

"I trust this is said in confidence," Claire added.

"Absolute confidence," Brother Matthew assured her. "But I'm so surprised."

"So was I. I never realized how anchored I am to the Pacific Northwest. I was born in Portland, and educated at our state university. All of my family lives within a few hours of Troutdale, so I would be saying goodbye to them as well."

Matthew put his arm around her shoulder, trying to physically support her in her private struggle. And at that moment he realized how much he would miss not having Claire in Franklin. He had found a soul mate, someone who could understand the uniqueness of his responsibilities to a monastery and to God.

The chapel bells rang out, announcing that vespers would begin in ten minutes.

"Thank you," she said, squeezing his hand.

After vespers, Matthew retired to his room without seeing the message that Brother Michael had called from Saint Cross with a slight problem. And by morning the message was already buried deep under newer messages and incoming mail. It would eventually resurface the following week, several days too late to protect Saint Cross from the apparent arrival of Noah's ark.

TWENTY-THREE

Intentions

The Lumby Lines

Letter to the Editor

October 17

PROTECTING OUR INHABITANTS

far be it from me, hank, to throw fire on the fuel, but as a tax-paying (in the loosest sense of the word as i have managed my finances with hawklike acuity so as to avoid undue levy) citizen of our fair town, i feel a stand needs to be taken against the increasing dangers in our streets.

last week, as many of you witnessed, i stood at death's doorstep as a near victim of the unleashed flying manhole covers. had i escorted my companion back to her residence at the lumby sporting goods store a few seconds earlier, the most unfortunate of events, my decapitation, would have followed.

and who would have been there for medical treatment as our beloved doctor ellen campbell has one foot out the door on her migration to greece for the winter? to whom do we turn? some stranger named tom candor? who exactly is this man and why haven't any of us been allowed to interview him?

although it is premature to structure a political platform, the growing support, nay, insistence, for my candidacy affords that opportunity: as mayor, i would ensure that pieces of the road don't endanger endangered species and townsfolk alike, and if that so happened, my proposed health-care program would ensure everyone's access to the finest of practitioners whether he be called ellen campbell or tom candor.

—hank

When Mac arrived at S&T's Soda Shoppe, Tom was seated at the back booth reading a copy of *The Lumby Lines*.

He looked up and smiled when he saw her approach. There was a natural, unpolished attractiveness about her—a health and vibrancy that would only be diluted under heavy makeup. Her hair was neatly constrained by a large barrette.

"I'm glad you could join me," he said.

"I'm glad you made the offer," Mac replied, looking at the menu.

"I wanted to thank you for taking me to the sanctuary." He hesitated. "I can't tell you how much I enjoyed it. Definitely one of the best days I've had in a very, very long time."

Mac looked into his eyes and smiled. "For me as well."

"Would you like to take me back one evening this week? Perhaps I could impress you with a great wine served in paper cups?"

Mac laughed. "There are a lot of ways you've already impressed me." She blushed. "It's a great time to see the bald eagles that live up there."

"Then it's a date?"

"Consider yourself dated," Mac teased.

For the first time since meeting him, Mac saw a beaming smile that warmed Tom's entire face.

"So," Tom said, straightening up, "would you please tell me something?"

Mac laid the menu down, expecting to be asked a significant question.

"Who's Hank?" Tom asked. "I just read his letter to the editor and I'm a little confused."

Mackenzie laughed, a sound that delighted Tom. "He's our flamingo, who thinks he's a bald eagle."

"Your pet?" Tom asked.

"Oh no. He's a resident of Lumby. He's actually more involved in the issues of the town than most other locals."

"And he's running for mayor?"

"Oh, that could be just talk," Mac said as she waved her hand, appearing to dismiss the idea. "All I know is that he would need to change his position on commercial zoning to get my vote."

"Do you have any idea how peculiar your town is?" Tom asked.

Mac grinned. "Oh, I think Lumby's pretty normal, but its residents can certainly be a bit eccentric."

Without being asked, Melanie brought Mac a Diet Coke as she had been doing for the past fifteen years. "Would you like something to drink?" the waitress asked Tom.

"Coffee would be fine."

Mac put down the menu. "If you haven't had lunch here, I strongly recommend their soups and hot sandwiches."

After ordering, Mackenzie pulled a piece of paper from her coat pocket, laid it flat on the table and began to explain to Tom what would be needed to restore The Granary after the "flying manhole incident" (as it would be referred to in the coming years). As Tom asked questions, Mac provided detailed answers, and when she was unsure, she said so with a promise to look into the matter.

That, in itself, was tremendously appealing to Tom. He knew very few women, or men for that matter, with the self-confidence to say, "I don't know but I'll find out."

"What wonderful chowder," Tom commented. "I haven't tasted anything this good since leaving Bangor."

"Do you miss Maine?" Mac asked, picking up her sandwich.

Tom shook his head. "I was only there three years, and all along I knew it was a temporary move, so I never dropped anchor."

Mac frowned. "Why do I get the feeling that everywhere you go is temporary?"

"I'm not quite sure," Tom said. "Why do you?"

"From what you've told me, you seem to be indifferent about your past, so I assume you were never really tied to any one location."

Tom quickly corrected her. "I felt at home in California."

"Where you went to college?"

"And worked, yes."

"Were you married then?"

Tom flashed a glance at Mac, but she was looking down at her plate and never saw his reaction. For close to twenty years, he had reinforced a shield around those years. From the moment he had packed up his personal belongings and driven out of the small city of Redding, California, Tom all but erased every last detail of that part of his life. He had, in fact, become another person.

But he was keenly aware that upon signing the purchase papers for The Granary, a new chapter in his life had begun and the rules that had governed his relationships since the accidents could no longer apply. Turning his back on the past or fabricating a part of it or simply moving to a new town was no longer possible.

"Yes," he finally answered without looking up, "that's when I was married."

An awkward silence fell between them as Tom shifted in his seat. Sensing his unease, Mac said, "I shouldn't have asked. Sorry."

Tom looked into her eyes, and for the first time since standing alone in the hospital two decades before, he wanted to share the unbearable secret he had shouldered for so long. The burden of sustaining the pretense had become too heavy to carry and he felt that it would surely suffocate him if he couldn't release it.

"We were together for eight years," he volunteered, his voice so low and soft that Mac had to lean forward to hear. "On February 3, 1989, she was in a serious car accident during an ice storm." He paused and felt the pain wash through his body.

Mac's expression softened as she listened to the tragic story. "I'm so sorry," she said.

"She lost the child she was carrying."

Instinctively Mac reached out and touched Tom's hand, which had been lying on the table. Without thinking, he took hold of her hand as if it were a lifeline.

"It wasn't mine," he said, his voice suddenly chilling.

Even though Mac was confused, she held back in asking any questions. She somehow knew that Tom would tell her his whole story when he felt ready.

"It was a very bad day," he began, then paused for several moments. "There was an accident at the zoo—I made a horrendous mistake." The words just rolled off his tongue. It was the first time he had ever mentioned the calamity that had followed the panda's surgery.

When he finally looked up at Mac, his face was drained. And then he looked down and realized he was still holding her hand. Tom panicked and quickly drew away. "I'm sorry. I just can't," he said as he stood up.

Before Mac could say a word, Tom darted out of the restaurant.

ᔕ

Up the street, on the second floor of the Chatham Press building, Dennis Beezer put aside the galley he was proofreading and turned on his computer. The two-minute search he did on Tom Candor while writing the brief article about Ellen Campbell's retirement reaped no results, which wasn't necessarily surprising if Tom had been a small-town veterinarian his entire life. But just to confirm his premise, Dennis searched on "Ellen Campbell DVM Lumby" and found one reference to her practice being for sale.

Using his standard search engine, Dennis entered "Tom Candor DVM" and waited. Within seconds seven hundred results came up, but it was apparent from the first few listings that all the results had "Candor" as a noun and not a surname. He then searched on "Tom Candor Bangor Maine," "Tom Candor DVM New York," knowing that was a long shot, and "Tom Candor DVM California." There were many hits on Candor, California, but still, there appeared to be no relevant results.

For the next ten minutes, Dennis tried different search engines, using various combinations of the name. He remembered that Tom had attended the University of California, Berkeley, so he entered "Candor DVM Berkeley" and finally had a hit. But it was for a Jeffrey T. Candor who had graduated in nineteen seventy-six. Perhaps this was a brother, he thought and, on a long shot, searched "Jeffrey T. Candor DVM." To Dennis's amazement, eight thousand results were returned.

Scrolling through the pages, Dennis scanned each group of ten listings. Almost all the entries were newspaper articles that carried the same headlines: "Panda Killed by Renowned Vet." From Dennis's quick review of a few articles, he got the gist that in nineteen eighty-nine, Jeffrey Candor, whoever the man was, injected a lethal drug into an invaluable panda bear during an operation at one of the country's most prominent zoos.

How tragic, Dennis thought. Clearing his screen, he resumed his search and entered "Tom Candor Veterinarian" and still got nothing. Dennis looked at his watch and began to rush. He was due over at The Green Chile in a few minutes. Another dozen searches showed little more than what he had already seen.

Perhaps he was wrong. Perhaps Tom Candor was just who he said he was: a small-town vet who came to Lumby at just the right time. He hadn't given anyone reason to question his motives or ability. And Ellen Campbell was always so thorough—surely she'd checked every one of his references.

What Dennis didn't know was that, to the contrary, Ellen was so busy preparing for her own departure, after seeing Tom work with her clients and her clients' animals, she felt comfortable enough to sell him her practice without verifying any of the information he had given on his résumé. In fact, his résumé was accidentally discarded the afternoon he arrived, when Ellen was cleaning out the last of her files.

Dennis pushed his chair away from the desk. As he pulled on his coat, he entered one final search: "Thomas Candor Veterinarian." There were numerous results, and he selected the most probable.

As he clicked it open, the phone rang. On the other end was Gabrielle, asking if he was on his way. Without turning back to his PC, Dennis bolted out the door. Had he waited mere seconds for the *US Veterinary News* page to open, he would have been staring at a large black-and-white photo of the man he knew as Tom Candor. Below it was the headline:

Jeffrey Thomas Candor Pleads Guilty
License Revoked for Seven Years

While Dennis was having lunch with his wife, the computer timed out and shut itself off, erasing the image of the veterinarian whom Dennis now considered above suspicion.

TWENTY-FOUR

Exposed

Near dawn the following morning, the lights along Main Street had shut off and the sun was just beginning to peep through the windows of The Granary. A few minutes before the alarm clock sounded, Tom leaned over and hit the OFF button. Although he was now sleeping in his own bed, and was surrounded by a few familiar pieces of furniture that had been moved in over the past few days, Tom had gotten no more than an hour of sleep that night.

Two thoughts had been running through his mind: his walking out on Mac the day before, and F. Scott Fitzgerald's quote, "In a real dark night of the soul, it is always three o'clock in the morning, day after day."

At some point during the long hours of early morning, Tom had realized that the time had come to allow someone into his life, to share his most protected secrets, and he wanted that person to be Mackenzie McGuire.

After quickly showering and dressing, Tom ran across the street and waited patiently outside S&T's until their doors opened at six a.m. After buying a half dozen muffins fresh from the oven, Tom drove over to Mac's house.

No one replied to his knock. Thinking that Mac might be upstairs, he opened the door and stuck his head in.

"Mac? Are you home?" His voice carried through the empty house. "It's Tom Candor."

When there was still no answer, Tom let himself in. He found the kitchen and left the muffins on the table. "I'm so sorry—Tom," he wrote on the bag before leaving.

Walking through the living room, he was startled to come face-to-face with a shirtless Terry McGuire creeping down the stairs, a young lady tiptoeing several steps behind him.

Both men froze, trying to assess whose behavior was more egregious: Tom's for apparent trespassing or Terry's for . . . apparent trespassing.

"Dr. Candor!" Terry said.

"Terry," Tom returned in a parental tone.

Terry quicky told the woman, "Okay, Julie, thanks for coming over. I'll see you later."

She looked crushed at being dismissed so coldly. "Will you call me later, Terry?" she asked.

"Yeah, maybe," he said.

The girl stood awkwardly on the stairs.

"You really should go, Julie," Terry repeated.

Fighting back tears, she grabbed her jacket from the banister and ran outside. Before Tom could say anything, Terry asked, "Is my mom here?"

"No," Tom answered, still looking past the open front door. "I just left something for her on the kitchen table."

"You're not going to tell her about this, are you?" Terry asked. "I mean, you shouldn't be in here either."

Tom looked carefully at the young man. Under the thoughtlessness and immaturity, there was probably a good heart that needed some direction. "It's none of my business," Tom said as he walked out the door.

ꩰ

When Tom arrived back at The Granary, he immediately heard Mac hammering on the roof. Walking around back, he found her looking very much like she had the first time he saw her.

"I was just at your house," he called up to her.

"We must have passed each other on the road," she said without stopping her work.

"Do you have a minute?" he said. "It's hard to talk with you up there."

She waved and carefully made her way over to the ladder and down to the ground. "You went over to my house?" Mac asked as she removed her gloves. "What's wrong?"

"I wanted to talk with you—to explain," Tom said, driving his hands deep into his pockets. "I'm so sorry I left yesterday."

"I was worried about you. Are you all right?" she asked.

Tom laughed. "That's not an easy question to answer." He towered over Mackenzie, but there was such a gentleness about him, she never felt intimidated by his height. Tom rocked slightly, shifting his weight from one foot to the other.

She reached out and touched his arm. "What is it?" she asked tenderly.

It felt like a lifetime, so many years of painful loneliness since he had opened himself up to another person. The energy it took to hide past disappointments and tragic secrets had worn on his spirit, and it wasn't until that moment, standing in front of Mac, that he wanted to shed all his mistakes, the way someone would remove a soiled, wet shirt.

When he began talking, his voice was deep and slow. "There are so many things about my past. I'm not who you think I am."

Mac stepped back, not expecting such a confession.

Tom looked around to ensure he wouldn't be overheard. "My name was Jeffrey Thomas Candor. I was the medical director at the American Zoological Park." And then he began to speak more quickly, as if wanting to disclose every detail of his past in a split second. "The morning of my wife's car accident, I was at The Park operating on a giant panda. She was the only breeding female our country had at the time. The operation was complex, but it went well." He paused, replaying the scene in his head as he had a million times since that day.

"As I was suturing up the incision," he continued, "I received an emergency call over the intercom. It was the hospital saying that my wife, Laura, was in critical condition. I fought every impulse to rush, but I didn't. I know I didn't until the last stitch was tied and Ming was bandaged. After finishing the surgery, I went over to the medicine cabinet for a vial of antibiotics. I rushed back to the operating table and gave her an injection. Instead of waiting to see how she came out of the anesthesia, I left for the hospital. What I didn't realize until it was too late was that I had picked up a vial of potassium chloride, which killed her within minutes." The pain in his eyes reflected the remorse and guilt from which he had never been able to escape.

Tom stopped speaking for a moment, waiting for Mac to respond, but she gave him a chance to continue.

"When I arrived at the emergency room, they were preparing Laura for surgery—her hip was fractured in several places. I was told that she had lost a child, but Laura and I had not been intimate for close to a year. I knew neither of us was happy in the marriage but I didn't think she was so unhappy that she would break the sanctity of our vows." He breathed in deeply. "Within a matter of hours, I lost my marriage and my career and brought incalculable harm to a great zoological institution."

Tom's shoulders dropped. The years of pent-up tension flowed from his body. Revealing the secrets he had spent a lifetime protecting was so exhausting that he didn't have the energy to remain standing. He quickly sat down in the threshold of an empty horse stall. Mackenzie remained motionless, but continued to watch him.

Tom rested his arms on his knees. "That night I knew my marriage was over and the following day I was terminated at the zoo. A week later, the Board's inquiry concluded that I was negligent during the surgery, which I had admitted to all along. My veterinary license was revoked for seven years. Although I stayed by Laura's side immediately after the accident, she hated everything about her life. The night before I moved out, we had a gut-wrenching argument. Her last words as my wife were, 'Don't you *ever* blame me for what happened in the operating room—that was entirely your own doing, and you have to live with that every day just the way I have to live with the loss of my child.'

"Given how things ended between us, the separation was painless, and the divorce papers were signed as quickly as possible. And I began living a transient life, not staying in any one place too long. I legally changed my name and worked for several small clinics in Colorado as a veterinary technician, mostly cleaning kennels and washing dogs. When my license was finally reinstated seven years after the incident, I worked at a large clinic in Utah that was owned by a former colleague at the zoo."

Mac finally interrupted. "Why didn't you start over again with your own clinic?"

He tilted his head, considering the question. "I suppose I didn't have the energy or courage. And the guilt was still so overwhelming. I wanted to lose myself, and in Utah, I was able to disappear from my past for some time. And then, three years ago, a college friend asked if I could give him a hand in Bangor, and that was where I received the flyer about Ellen Campbell's clinic."

Mac was surprised. "Who sent that to you?"

"I don't know, but it was addressed to J. Tom Candor, so it was someone who knew me before the accident." He sighed heavily, dropping his head forward.

Mac felt the weight of his confession envelop her. "I don't know what to say. I'm so sorry, Tom."

"I am too," he muttered. "More than you'll ever know."

As Mac began to think through the complexity and gravity of his admission, tears came to her eyes. "So you've been alone all these years—ever since the accident?"

He slowly nodded his head. "Very alone."

Small realizations popped into Mac's head like fireworks going off in sequence: the lack of laugh lines around his eyes, his skill at evading questions and those times he had pulled away from her.

"I'm so sorry," she repeated as she wrapped her arms around him as tightly as she could.

He melted in her embrace and found refuge in her understanding and love.

For several minutes they stood together, silently holding each other. Finally, he spoke. "Just please tell me that you will keep this in confidence."

Without considering the consequences of what she was about to say, Mac replied, "Of course, you have my word."

As everyone in Lumby knew, and as Tom would soon discover, when Mackenzie McGuire gave her word, it was unbreakable.

TWENTY-FIVE

Prudence

Tom took Mac's hand and then covered it with his own. He wanted to return his arms around her, to pull her near and tell her how she had saved him by not turning away when she heard his darkest secrets. Instead, she surprised him by standing on her toes and kissing him passionately on the lips.

"You're a good man, Tom Candor," Mac said, meeting his gaze.

"Sometimes it's easier to believe otherwise," he said.

She squeezed his hand. "What's important is what you know in your heart to be true."

"This knife has been in me for so long, I don't even recognize it's there." He put his hand on her back and brought her close to him. "But you know the truth, and you're still here."

"I always will be," she said.

He kissed her hand. "I left something in your kitchen for you."

She pulled away, raising her brow in curiosity. "What would that be?"

"Your favorite muffins," Tom replied. "Assuming they haven't been eaten."

"Oh, was Terry there?"

Tom suppressed a chuckle. "You could say that. I ran into him when I was leaving."

"He must have just been getting up," she said.

"Whatever he was doing, it wasn't alone," Tom said, trying to soften the blow.

Mac pulled away. "What do you mean?"

Tom kept hold of her hand. "I ran into him and Julie coming downstairs."

Mac frowned. "Who's Julie?"

"I think last night's date."

"He must have come in after I went to bed," Mac explained, trying to clear her thoughts. "What did you say to him?"

Tom paused, keeping hold of Mac's hand. "We shared just a few words. But perhaps he would benefit from your giving him a strong sense of direction," Tom said gingerly. "He's treading in dangerous waters. I know—I was his age once."

Mac pulled her hair back but didn't reply.

"I'm sure it can't be easy. But he looks up to you, which I would guess is half the battle," Tom offered.

"Sometimes it's easier to look away and ignore his behavior," she said slowly, regretfully.

"I remember my father's lectures as if they were yesterday, so if there's any way I can help you, let me know."

Suddenly a man's voice called from the front of the clinic, "Is anyone here?"

Tom jumped away from Mac, as if caught in a compromising position. "Back here," he called, taking a few more steps backward, separating himself farther from Mackenzie.

Although she partly understood his reaction, his quick retreat after such a personal moment couldn't help but sting.

When Jimmy jogged around the corner, Mac forced a smile. "Well, if it isn't our fine mayor."

Jimmy cautiously scanned the tree limbs above his head.

Mac shot him a puzzled expression. "Looking for friends up there, Jimmy?"

He pulled his collar up around his neck. "No, but every time I come here, one of those monkeys attacks me."

"They're inside," Tom said.

"Good," Jimmy replied. "Because I'm here on important business." He saw Tom's alarmed reaction. "Oh, don't worry," Jimmy said, slapping his shoulder. "We're not going to shoot you or anything. We just want to have the party tomorrow night, if that works for you."

"What party?" he asked.

"Your shingle party, of course," Jimmy said with some bravado.

Mackenzie laughed when she realized what long-standing town tradition Jimmy was about to dredge up. "Of course," she said. But then she looked at Tom and remembered his confession along with her promise, and her smile faded.

"Would someone let me in on the secret?" Tom asked.

"Absolutely," Jimmy obliged and began a long speech. "Although there is debate as to when the first shingle party took place—some say nineteen thirty-two and others insist it was nineteen thirty-three—all agree it was the summer that Jed Prudence came to town with nothing more than a horse, a small bag of clothes and what was more valuable than either: a pair of clipping shears. He was, in fact, a traveling barber who had ventured farther north than his regular route and had stumbled upon this charming village. Lumby was still quite small, but it was a prosperous community, and Jed liked the stone buildings that anchored the two main streets. Furthermore, all of his purchasing needs were met at the Lumby Feed Store at the west end of the village.

"After spending three days cutting the hair of most every resident, from children (four cents) to centenarians (six cents) and trimming the locks of men and women alike, he came down with a vicious cold that settled in his chest and led to pneumonia. The townsfolk took pity on the poor man and moved him from the hayloft of the Feed Store, where he had been sleeping for free, to an empty room above what was then the telegraph office. There he gradually recuperated, growing stronger primarily from the charity of the other vendors in town.

"After he fully recovered, his other talent for shearing animals was discovered and put to use in the heat of the summer. As August passed, the townsfolk grew more dependent on Jed's services and the merchants realized that he was a man who could help grow the town of Lumby. So, they collectively assigned the vacant room above the Lumby Smoke Shop—which is now the Candy Store—to the town's new barber. And the next day all of the merchants gathered on the sidewalk while Jed was upstairs trimming the mayor's beard, and hammered a shingle by his door:

JED PRUDENCE
BARBER

"And to this day, when a new store proprietor comes to town, the merchants as well as most of the townsfolk gather to hang a shingle. It's our way of welcoming a stranger into the heart of our town," Jimmy said. "And you are the guest of honor tomorrow night!"

Tom glanced over at Mac, but he didn't make eye contact because she had turned away a second earlier.

"That's really not necessary," Tom said. His well-constructed plan of telling the residents of Lumby about his past in due time was unraveling. First there was his confession to Mac and now this. He intended to eventually tell everything that had happened, but not for a few months, after relationships were well established and time had allowed trust to build. Until then, his objective was to stay clear of situations in which he would have to omit a fact or, worse, outright lie. And the shingle party was one of those situations, given all of the questions that would inevitably be asked about the town's new vet.

"That's a very nice offer, but I really don't think so," Tom said.

"We insist," Jimmy said cheerfully. "It's really nothing you can escape from." He had no idea how true his words were.

Tom thought quickly. "So, it will only take a few minutes?"

"To hang the shingle, yes," Jimmy answered. "But the party lasts all night."

"The party?"

Mac finally looked at Tom. "They've become black-tie events," she explained. "About ten years ago, someone who had just come from a wedding wore a tuxedo to a shingle party and it caught on. There are so few opportunities for the women to dress up that the ladies of Lumby banded together and wrote a new dress code."

Tom smiled weakly, looking totally helpless. "I don't know what to say."

"No need to say anything," Jimmy assured him. "The party will start about six p.m. Gabrielle is providing the food and I'll be bringing the beverages. Simon and Dennis will be here a few hours earlier to lift the tents."

"Tents?"

"Just a few, which we'll put in front of the clinic. The women asked for that as soon as they started to wear nice gowns. You know, bird droppings and all."

"Ah, bird droppings," Tom repeated.

Jimmy shook Tom's hand. "I can't tell you how happy we are that you're making Lumby your home. These are such good, decent folks. They deserve someone like you."

It had been years since Tom had felt so small. "I hope I can live up to everyone's expectations."

"Just be yourself," Jimmy said, walking away.

Tom leaned against the barn wall. He rubbed his eyes with the palms of his hands, trying to relieve the pressure in his head. "What have I done?" he mumbled.

Mac was motionless, trying to think through the ramifications of Tom's guise. "I'm wondering that as well," she confessed, sitting down on a rung of the ladder. She looked over at Jeffrey Thomas Candor and wondered how she could keep Tom's confidence without being deceitful to all those in Lumby, whom she had come to love and consider family.

Feeling trapped and frustrated, she climbed the ladder and began ripping off pieces of gutter.

"Mac?" Tom called up to her.

"I don't know if I can do this. Not now," she implored, and worked her way to the far end of the gable.

TWENTY-SIX

Green

"Hey, honey," Mark called out to his wife from their bedroom at Montis Inn, "can I use your computer?"

Pam was sitting at the kitchen table thumbing through monthly bills. She looked in his direction. "Why?" she asked suspiciously. "You hate my computer."

Mark stuck his head out the door. "Yeah, but mine's acting all weird. I think there's something wrong with my Internet connection."

Pam narrowed her eyes. "What settings did you change this time?"

"It was broken before I messed around with it, really," Mark said, backpedaling as quickly as he could. He had repeatedly sabotaged his own computer by either attaching odd peripherals he bought online or downloading software that was supposed to supercharge the technology. Mark looked at the clock: three twenty-two. "Honey, I really need to get online."

His urgency was a red flag to Pam.

"Don't download anything," she warned.

"I promise," he said. "But I need to get on right now."

"Are you researching something?" she called out.

It wasn't research that he was doing, but Mark didn't have time to correct Pam's assumption or explain his latest project. "A used truck," Mark said as he disappeared into the bedroom.

Pam's disposition changed immediately. "That's good. The Jeep is costing too much to repair every month." She wrote the last check from a high pile of bills. "We've been talking about getting a truck for a while." She continued talking as she put away the checkbook and stamps. "Be sure it gets good mileage—maybe one of those new Ford F-150s. Be sure you look at one with leather interior and a navigation system."

When Mark didn't reply, Pam became worried. "Mark?"

Walking into the bedroom, she saw Mark focused on the computer screen. He held up his finger. "Just a second," he said. "Five, four, three, two, one." He hit the ENTER key and new messages appeared. Mark immediately looked at the user name of the high bidder. "We won!" he yelled out. "We got it! This is great!"

"What have we got?" Pam asked.

"You're not going to believe this," he began. "It's a dream come true."

Pam peered. "Whose dream?"

"Well, the Montis dream. See?" Mark pointed to a tiny photograph on the computer.

Pam leaned over her husband's shoulder. "Is that a truck?"

"Isn't she a beauty?" Mark said, beaming. "Let me enlarge it for you."

Suddenly, the picture enveloped the entire screen. Pam was stunned. It was a light green truck, as Mark had said, but it was from another century.

"What exactly is it?" she asked.

"A nineteen-thirty-four Ford Flathead Pickup Model Forty-six," he said, with all the pride of a new owner.

Pam studied the photograph; it was, in fact, a charming-looking vehicle. Reminiscent of the old Model-Ts but with softer lines, it had a graceful running board that began directly over the front wheel, sloped down and then returned over the back wheel. A spare tire was attached to the left grille on the side of the front hood. Although the bed of the truck was no longer than the combined length of the engine and passenger compartment, Pam thought it looked well proportioned.

"It's as if someone took an old Morgan or MG and converted it into a truck," she critiqued.

Mark looked up at his wife, who was still staring at their new acquisition. "Cool, isn't it?"

Patting Mark's shoulder, Pam said, "I have to admit, it's really quite charming. Do you think we could add our Montis Inn logo on the door?"

"I don't see why not," Mark said. "And this saved us a bundle from buying a new truck."

Pam cringed. "Should I even ask how much it costs?"

Mark clicked the computer mouse and brought up another screen, where he pointed to a highlighted field: $3,231.00.

Pam thought for a moment. "Don't you think that seems really low for an antique truck in great condition? Would you go back to the description?"

In a few seconds, the information page filled the screen, and Pam began reading the details.

"We have to pick it up and drive it back," Mark explained. "But Harrison is only two hours from here. We can make a day trip of it."

Pam continued reading. "What is this?" she asked, putting her index finger on the screen. "Under engine it says 'RMV1954.' "

Mark raised his shoulders. "Must be the engine model, I guess. So when can we go get it?"

Pam straightened up. "How about we take off tomorrow morning?"

Mark jumped up and kissed her. "This is going to be great. We'll take the Jeep over and then we'll take turns driving the truck back."

"How fast does it go?"

Mark glanced over at the truck's description. "Probably seventy or something."

"Hello?" a man's voice called from outside.

Pam looked at the clock. "That must be André. Do you want to join us?"

"No, thanks," Mark replied. "I need to get down to the barn."

"Coming," Pam called as she pulled her jacket out of the closet. "If you get bored, you can join us in the kitchen. He said something about rearranging a few things."

Mark followed Pam out the door just as a gust of wind blew through the courtyard. Mark zipped up his coat. "It's really starting to get cold."

Pam watched André as he walked around the building that contained most of the inn's guest rooms. He got credit in Pam's estimation for having a great wardrobe; he was dressed in dark green twill pants, with a green-and-brown-striped shirt under a leather jacket that hung just below his waist. And, of course, he was wearing his trademark: a long scarf that matched his slacks.

"André," Pam called out. "I'll meet you in the kitchen in a minute."

André waved back and headed off toward the dining room.

"Are you sure he's the one you want to hire? He seems awfully"—Mark paused, searching for the right word—"independent—maybe even arrogant."

"Well, he certainly doesn't have a problem with self-confidence," Pam agreed. "But I guess he has good reason to be. I heard that he was flooded with job offers once word got out that Cedar Grove was closing."

"Yeah, but we have to live with the guy," Mark complained.

Pam leaned against her husband's body, trying to get warm. "We just need to work with him," she said. "And he could increase our clientele ten times over."

Mark wrapped his arms around her. "Are you sure we want that many people here? I've gotten used to it being quiet."

" 'Quiet' means no income. We need to start making some money, and he may be the answer."

"If you say so." He pulled her closer and kissed her on the cheek. "You smell nice."

Pam laughed. "You normally say something like that when you're buttering me up."

"No, I'm just really looking forward to our trip tomorrow. We haven't taken a day off in months," Mark said.

Pam pulled her collar higher around her neck. "Does the truck have heat?"

"Oh, sure, it does," he replied, and then gave his wife another quick kiss. "Okay. I'm off to work on the wiring in the new barn. I'll be back in a few hours."

As Mark walked away, Pam called out, "Don't electrocute yourself. If you need help, call Mac."

"You worry too much," Mark said over his shoulder.

"For good reason!" she reminded him.

When Pam walked into the kitchen, André was standing in front of the open wine closet. "We need to move these," he said. "The temperature vacillates too much from the heat of the ovens."

Pam grinned. So much for pleasantries. During her corporate years, she always liked cutting to the chase and getting down to business. And this was a business, she reminded herself.

"We'll have to see where we can make room," she replied.

André looked at Pam. "You don't 'make room' for a wine collection. It should be treated as carefully as your finest crystal."

"That would be ideal," Pam replied, "but as you can tell, we are short on storage space."

André looked around the kitchen. "You have plenty of space. It just needs to be arranged more efficiently."

Pam fought to keep her defenses down. "So, you received our offer letter?"

André pulled an envelope from the inside pocket of this jacket. "Yes, everything looks fine."

"Have you decided if you'll be wanting the upstairs apartment in our main building?"

André didn't immediately answer. "I don't think so," he finally said. "I've been living at Cedar Grove for as long as I've worked there, and I think that might have been one of the problems. I had no time to step away and have a private life."

Pam suddenly realized that they had never discussed anything personal, nor had she been curious about his private life. If she was forced to guess, Pam would have assumed he was single; he had never mentioned a significant other and appeared to have a self-centeredness that quickly changed when one was happily married.

"I can certainly appreciate that," Pam said as she sat on a stool by the island. "Do you think you'll be moving to Lumby?"

"If I can find a quiet rental," he said, slipping off his jacket. "Or perhaps I'll buy a small home."

Definitely no kids, Pam thought. "I'm sure you won't have any problems finding a place." And then she grinned. "In fact," she said, quickly thinking through the idea before saying it, "we might have something that would be perfect, if you want small and private."

André raised his brows. "What's that?"

"We own a stone cottage over on the northeast corner of our property. We think it's as old as the monastery, but we restored it a few years ago when one of our friends moved here from Virginia. It's an easy five-minute walk, or you can drive to it from Deer Trail Lane. It's quite small—about nine hundred square feet, not including a second-floor loft."

"I don't need much room," André said.

Probably not married, Pam guessed. "And the kitchen is simple."

"All I need are a few burners and an oven."

Pam tapped her hands on the island. "Good. When we're done here, I can walk you over so you can see it for yourself."

"Or perhaps I can scout out the cottage on my own," he countered.

"All right," she said. "Let me draw you a map."

"That won't be necessary," André said. "Just point me in the right direction."

Pam stood up and went to the back window. "The path is well marked to the cemetery," she said, indicating the far corner of the backyard. "From there, just bear right and it's several hundred yards ahead. The front door is unlocked."

"Great. But right now, I think all I need is some time to get acquainted with my kitchen. Do you mind if I stay here for a while and get organized?"

Pam was unsure if she was being asked to leave "his" kitchen. "Do you need my help with anything?"

"Not really," André said as he opened the cabinet doors next to the refrigerator. "But if I'm to begin next week, there's a lot of work that needs to be done."

She was a bit dumbstruck and at a loss. "Then that's it, I suppose. Welcome to Montis." She shook his hand. "This is your kitchen now."

Just as Pam was about to go through the swing door, André asked, "If there's any carpentry and cabinetry work that needs to be done, is that Mark's area?"

Pam laughed loudly and shook her head. "Oh, definitely not. You have no idea how dangerous Mark is with an electric saw. But we have a contractor, Mackenzie McGuire, who can do just about anything." Pam looked around the kitchen, which she had renovated so carefully four years before. "Do you think it needs a lot of work?"

"We'll see," André said, with a shrug of his shoulders.

TWENTY-SEVEN

Control

The following morning, Mark had to drag Pam out of bed. Although she was looking forward to their adventure to Harrison, she had been up until two in the morning, watching for the slightest movements in the dining room and kitchen. Finally, at three ten a.m., she saw André walk out with a flashlight in hand and disappear into the woods in the direction of the stone cottage.

"Is his car still here?" she asked before getting out of bed.

"Whose?"

"André's. He was working in the kitchen until early this morning and then he headed off to the cottage."

"That's odd," Mark commented.

"Maybe he's a night owl," Pam guessed.

"Possibly," Mark said, "but it was a great idea to suggest he rent the stone cottage."

"I hope you're right," she said, pulling the covers over her head.

Mark picked up her jeans, which were lying on the chair, and threw them onto the bed. "Hurry up, honey. The guy's expecting us at eleven."

Pam began to dress. "I first need to go over and see what André's done in the kitchen."

"No, you don't!" Mark said excitedly. "You can check it out when we get back."

"But—"

"No 'buts,' Pam. Put on a shirt and we're off."

But Pam couldn't restrain herself. A few minutes later, as she was following her husband to their car, she bolted across the courtyard. Running into the dining room, she froze. Every table had been pushed against one wall, the chairs stacked in disarray on top of them.

She flew through the kitchen swing doors and found total chaos. Most of the cabinets had been emptied, with piles of dinnerware and boxes of cutlery scattered everywhere. The four pantries had also been emptied, and in one closet, the shelves had been removed.

White footprints were everywhere, apparently from a broken bag of flour that had not been cleaned up.

Pam held her hand to her forehead in disbelief.

The only items that appeared to be untouched and intact were the refrigerator and the stove.

"What on earth was he thinking?" Pam said, fuming with anger.

"Come on, honey," Mark called from the dining room door.

She stormed out of the kitchen. "I can't go with you. It's a demolition zone in there and I need to clean it up so I can cook dinner for our guests tonight."

Mark grabbed Pam's hand and forcibly pulled her from the building. "This will only take a few hours, and I'll help you when we get back, but we promised that this was our morning to get away."

Pam looked over her shoulder as Mark escorted her to the car. "You didn't see it in there," she said. "It will take days to straighten up the mess."

He opened the car door and gently pushed her in. "It will take half that time with both of us working on it. Now, let's put it behind us and have a nice day."

After Pam finally accepted her fate for the coming few hours, the drive over to Harrison turned out to be a delightful excursion. Although the air was chilly, there wasn't a cloud in the sky. Pam had brought a copy of *The Lumby Lines,* and read it aloud to Mark.

The Lumby Lines

Sheriff's Complaints

BY SHERIFF SIMON DIXON October 17

5:41 a.m. Moose vs Pickup on Farm to Market Road by the Fork River. Pickup damaged on left side, driver shaken but no injuries.

7:11 a.m. Cindy Watford reported her neighbor was burning leaves in his backyard and some blew onto the roof of her woodshed.

7:20 a.m. Cindy Watford called again—the brush fire appears to be getting bigger.

7:24 a.m. Cindy Watford reported that her neighbor's trampoline is on fire. LFD dispatched.

7:32 a.m. Resident on Cherry Street said that three children's bikes have been on his front porch since last night. Owners unknown.

10:21 Librarian called to report that Hank and mannequin were loitering around the second-floor periodicals table.

11:24 a.m. Jimmy D reported that someone had stuffed pumpkins into his mailbox.

11:58 a.m. Sam called to report that Isabella is at the back of his Feed Store eating grain. Jeremiah is nowhere to be seen.

2:22 p.m. Gas Company reported a potential leak on Loggers Road.

2:32 a.m. Owner of NW Builders reported possible nicking of gas pipe at their construction site.

3:49 p.m. High school reported erratic flushing of toilet caused by water-pressure changes. Water Works notified.

Pam and Mark talked about their plans for Montis and the new barn, the fall cleanup of the orchard and what needed to be done to winter the honeybees. But every so often Pam brought the conversation back to André.

"If you've hired him, let him do what he needs to do," was Mark's repeated reply before changing the topic.

Once in Harrison, which was similar in size to Lumby, Mark followed the directions he had written on the corner of a feed bag. "Does that say Slate or State Road?" he asked, passing the note to Pam, who studied it for a moment.

"It looks like Blake," she said.

"There it is," Mark said, turning right off the main road.

They immediately noticed their new antique moss green truck parked in a driveway a half block down.

Pam leaned forward to get a better look. "I have to admit, it's totally charming."

Mark was glowing. "This is so cool."

By the time they pulled into the driveway, the owner, an elderly gentleman by the name of Bud Harley, was slowly making his way down the front path. "Mark Walker?" he asked in a weak voice.

Mark jumped out of the car and ran up to the man, extending his hand. "That's me. What a great truck!"

Bud looked fondly at the vehicle. "I spent the last forty years working on her," he said with a heavy sigh. "She came between me and the missus more than once—that's for certain. It's a real heartbreak, giving her up."

"She's going to a great home," Mark assured him. From his wallet, he withdrew a cashier's check. "Why don't I pay you?"

The man took the check and stuffed it in his shirt pocket. "Appreciate it."

"You want to go out for one last spin?" Mark offered.

Old Bud half laughed and half coughed. "That's a good one."

"Are there any manuals or paperwork I need?" Mark asked politely.

"Nope," Bud said. "Just the keys, which are in the ignition."

"That's great. Then I guess we'll be off," Mark said, shaking the seller's hand and turning to leave.

"When's your tow truck coming?"

Mark froze in midstep, and then realized the misunderstanding. "Oh, no. We're driving it back ourselves."

The old man laughed weakly. "That's a funny one. I've got to tell the missus."

"No, really, I'm driving for the first half and then my wife wants to try it."

Bud looked at Mark as if he were impaired. "But, son, there's no engine."

For a moment, Mark stared at the man in disbelief. Pulling out a piece of paper from his pants pocket, he unfolded it the best he could. "Your description says the engine is a"—Mark looked down and read the printout—"RMV1954."

Bud Harley shook his head. "Son, that means that the entire engine block was taken out in 1954. 'RMV' is the standard abbreviation for removed."

Mark glanced over at the truck and then at his wife, who was still sitting in the Jeep. "So there's nothing under the hood?" he whispered.

"Not a screw. But it's as clean as a whistle."

Mark's shoulders dropped. "Then how do we get it back to Lumby?"

The man scratched his bald head. "Tow it or put it on a flatbed would be my guess."

"Oh," Mark moaned, "my wife is going to be so unhappy about this."

"Get used to it, son," Bud put his arm around Mark. "This car almost cost me a marriage."

ℰ

The drive back to Lumby was long and silent, with Mark continually checking his rearview mirror to ensure Bud Harley's nephew's tow truck was close behind them. Due to the instability of the rear axle, they could go no faster than thirty miles an hour. Pam constantly checked the clock, concerned about the seven guests who had made dinner reservations for six thirty.

"Mark, can't we go any faster? I have an entire dining room to set up and a kitchen to clean before I even begin to cook."

"Her wheels will fall off if we go any faster."

Just after they passed through Rocky Mount, Pam broke her silence again. "So, what's your plan?" she finally asked. "Where are you going to have him take it?"

"To Montis, I guess," Mark said, knowing full well that would provoke an unpleasant conversation. "Honey, it was an honest mistake."

"I know," she said, patting him on the knee, trying to be supportive. "But what are you going to do with it now?"

Mark thought for a minute. "It's not worth anything to us without an engine. So, maybe we should bring it over to Dakin's Garage and have Jeremy tune it up."

Pam laughed. "I think 'tuning it up' is a bit of an understatement. Do you know how much an engine will cost?"

"It can't be more than a thousand dollars, can it?" Mark suggested as he glanced at Pam. "What do you think?"

"I wouldn't have the foggiest idea. But," she said, turning around and looking at the tow truck following close behind them, "I don't think we have any choice."

~

After dropping off their new used truck at Dakin's Garage just outside of town, and after paying Bud's nephew three hundred dollars for the tow, and after trying to get Jeremy Dakin to estimate the cost of a new engine, which he jokingly promised would be under ten thousand dollars, Pam and Mark finally turned onto Farm to Market Road, five hours later than planned.

"There's no way I can get dinner ready—the guests are going to be there in twenty minutes. Even if André hadn't torn everything up, it's just too late."

"Then we explain what happened and suggest they go up to The Green Chile."

Before Pam could protest, she spotted André's car in the parking lot. "He's returned to the scene of the crime," she sneered. "I wonder what more he's destroyed in there."

Before Mark turned off the ignition, Pam was out of the car and heading for a confrontation with their new chef.

Storming into the dining room, she was about to call out André's name, but then froze. The tables and chairs were not only rearranged, but she saw at once that the new layout accommodated four additional tables, which must have been delivered while they were away. New tablecloths and napkins that better complemented the decor graced each table. Candles held in beautifully forged iron holders were already lit, as were the logs in the fireplace. Classical music played softly in the background, and delectable smells filled the room.

Pam heard humming from the kitchen.

When she peeked in, she first saw André, who was leaning over an open oven door and appeared to be basting a roast. To her amazement, the wreckage of that morning was gone and in its place was an organized, impeccably clean kitchen.

She noticed the obvious changes first: over the island, André had mounted a huge metal grille, from which hung a dozen pots and pans of different sizes. At the food-preparation area, he had installed magnetic strips, to which numerous chef's knives clung. The door and hinges to the wine closet had been removed and the space had been converted into an open pantry for fruits and vegetables, which, in the past, had always cluttered up the counter space.

For some reason, Pam felt she should knock on the door before entering. "André?" she said, just as he was tasting the sauce.

"Welcome back," he said. "I hope you don't mind but I started dinner after I saw the reservations for this evening. Do you normally leave so little time to prepare?"

Pam exhaled loudly. "We should have been here hours ago, but we ran into problems over in Harrison. You've certainly saved this evening from being a catastrophe."

"Glad to help," he said as he withdrew a loaf of bread from the oven.

"It smells divine," Pam said.

"La caille a la genade," André said, pleased with his selection for the evening. Seeing a puzzled expression on Pam's face, he added, "Grilled quail with pomegranate. And for the fish plate, *le saumon de Nouvelle Zealande*—pan-seared New Zealand salmon with caramelized baby arugula."

"I'm not sure if I'm more envious of your skills or jealous of our guests, who will have a wonderful culinary experience."

"I've reserved a table for you and Mark at seven," he said.

"Thank you," Pam said, excusing his presumptuousness. She now concluded that whatever he was lacking in social skills and humility, he more than made up for in culinary talent and efficiency. She continued looking around the rearranged room. "By the way, where's the wine?"

"Out in the cold cellar," he announced. "If you add a few lights down there, it might provide an interesting stroll for your guests. The temperature and humidity are perfect." He turned and stirred a large pot of soup that was simmering on the stove. "So, if you let me get back to cooking, perhaps you want to change before hostessing the guests."

There was no question about it: not only had he just excused Pam from her own kitchen; he had all but told her what to do next.

"Oh, and the cottage is good," André said as Pam was walking out.

"So you found it last night?"

"Actually, I moved my stuff over this morning," he said. "Once I make a few changes, it should work out just fine."

"That's good, I suppose," she replied, but so softly that André never heard.

TWENTY-EIGHT

Drop-offs

Driving with Mackenzie on the road from Lumby to Franklin, Tom slowed the car as he approached the summit's hairpin curve. The guardrails were missing along most sections, and there was a hundred-foot drop-off. Every so often, he spotted the rusted wreckage of cars in the ravine far below. The right side of the road was flanked with steep snow-covered mountains.

"Feel intimidated?" Mac asked as they passed a bent metal sign that read "Bearclaw's Pass."

"From what, the mountains or having you alone in the car with me?" he asked with a grin.

"That," she said, pointing to the winding road with its sheer drop-off.

"It reminds me of Independence Pass in Colorado, treacherously dangerous but manageable if one takes one's time. A little like our relationship," he teased.

Mac slanted a look at him. "So you think I'm dangerous?"

Tom glanced over at her. She was wearing a red rain parka that complemented her green eyes. "Not you. Just what's happening between us." He paused for a minute. "It's been so long since someone has been in my life, and I don't remember all the steps."

"Neither do I, so we can make them up as we go along," Mac suggested.

Ever since Tom had told her about his past, Mac had been acting more cautious around him. Although Tom would have been the first to acknowledge that there were still worlds to be learned about each other, one thing was readily apparent: after his disclosure, a barrier had gone up between them. By asking Mac to drive with him to Saint Cross that day, Tom was hoping to close that emotional distance.

"I've obviously put you in a difficult position," Tom finally said.

Mac sighed heavily. "That you have."

It wasn't Mac's nature to be distant or angry, but Tom's continuing evasions destroyed any hope of their building a relationship. His reticence also drove a wedge that now separated her from her friends and neighbors. And Mac intensely hated secrets.

"You must know that wasn't my intent," he pleaded. "Would you have preferred me to continue the charade knowing that we were getting closer every day?"

Mac had actually considered the question long before Tom had asked it. "No, I don't think so. I mean, of course not. Above all, I want us to be honest with each other. But I would prefer that you tell everyone else so I'm not caught in the middle."

"But, Mac, there's no middle to be caught in if it remains a secret for a while longer."

She nervously rubbed her knees as she continued to stare out the window. "One of the few lessons I learned from my father is that there are no secrets in life—that the truth always surfaces, no matter how hard you try to keep it down."

Tom would have agreed, had he not lived the past fifteen years as someone he was not.

"I just need a little more time," he said.

Mac finally looked at him. "The longer you wait, the longer I'm being dishonest with everyone I know," she said, trying to maintain a steady voice. "I just hope that when the truth is told, all of my friends will understand."

"They will," he said, and placed his hand on Mac's.

She didn't pull it away, but neither did she take his hand in hers. "You don't know Lumby," she said grimly. "There's an unspoken code of conduct among the townsfolk. We may not love everyone, but we're honest with one another."

They drove for several miles in silence and then Tom finally spoke. "Even if I knew how to apologize for putting you in an impossible situation, I don't think I could."

Mac frowned. "I don't understand."

"I've never felt like this for anyone, including Laura, and I'm willing to forgo anything to protect what little I have with you right now."

"Anything except explain yourself to the town?"

"Just not yet," he said firmly.

Mac pulled her hand out from under his. "I hope you tell them soon, because I don't know how long I can take this," she said. "I don't want it to permanently damage the relationships I have."

"It won't, I promise," Tom replied.

Mac flushed with anger. "It infuriates me when men think they can make bold promises that are totally out of their control. You can't promise that the residents of Lumby won't turn their backs on me after you make your final confession."

Tom recoiled, realizing how correct Mac was. "You're right. I suppose I just want to give them and their collective empathy the benefit of the doubt."

"That's a two-way street," Mac said tersely.

Tom heard the animal stir in the large crate that was securely placed in the rear of the car. He adjusted the rearview mirror so he could keep an eye on his valuable cargo.

"Well," he began, wanting to change the subject, "I appreciate your coming to the monastery today."

Mac softened her voice. "The guys are great. It's always a delight to visit the abbey."

As they drove through the small village of Franklin, Tom asked, "So, you know them well?"

Mac nodded. "I spent the better part of two months last summer doing some work for them."

Turning onto the monastery's driveway, Tom stepped on the brakes. "Wow," he said, peering out the windshield. "That's impressive."

"It's a fairly large order of monks. Several of the brothers came from Montis Abbey just south of Lumby."

"The inn that Pam and Mark Walker own? Yes, I was there with Ellen."

Mac pointed toward the fork in the road. "Turn left up there," she directed. "It will take you around to the private entrance."

He put his foot on the brake. "I've never met them and I wouldn't want to be presumptuous. How about going to the front door?"

Mac pointed to the massive double door. "It's right over there," she said, although Tom kept his eye on the chapel. "Are you religious?"

"I was a lot of things before February nineteen eighty-nine," Tom answered somberly.

After parking directly in front of the walkway, Tom got out and opened the back of his SUV, looked inside the crate and gently carried it to the front door. Not seeing a doorbell, he turned back to Mac, who was still seated in the car.

"Just knock," she called out.

Within seconds, a large man in faded jeans and a worn flannel shirt opened the door. "May I help you?"

"Excuse me. Is one of the monks here?" Tom said, assuming that the man was not a brother by the way he was dressed.

"I'm Brother John," he said, first looking at the stranger and then at the animal crate at his feet. Without any further discussion, John said, "Wait one moment, please. You want Brother Michael."

John spoke into the intercom next to the door. "Brother Noah, another delivery for the ark at the front door. Please join us."

Within a minute, a much younger man came walking down the hall. "Where would you like me to sign?" he asked Tom politely.

"Sign what?" Tom asked.

The brother looked out at the car and seemed to recognize Mackenzie McGuire. He blushed. "You're not a delivery driver, are you?" he asked, waving at Mac to join them.

"No." Tom laughed. "I'm Dr. Tom Candor, Ellen Campbell's replacement. This animal arrived in a crate addressed to the Monks of Saint Cross but in care of Ellen. I assumed you would want him as soon as possible."

"Oh, it's very nice to meet you," he said, shaking Tom's hand. "I'm Brother Michael."

Before Michael could look inside the crate, Tom unlatched the door and withdrew a beautiful, docile koala bear, which instantly wrapped its arms around Tom's neck.

Michael reached out and touched the animal's fur. "He's gorgeous."

"And all yours," Tom said, lifting the koala off his chest and passing him over. The slow-moving animal embraced the brother's upper arm and shoulder. Michael was fascinated. "I'm so sorry," he finally said. "I've forgotten my manners. Please come in. If you have a minute, perhaps you can look at a few other animals we have."

"Dogs?"

"If only," Michael said as Mac joined them.

"Let me get my bag," Tom said as he headed back to the car.

Mac hugged Michael as best she could without disrupting the koala. "Wonderful to see you again. Is this fellow your new best friend?" she asked, petting the animal's head.

Michael looked down at the marsupial. "Isn't he wonderful? After getting the snow monkeys, which I assume Tom is now caring for, we've received many additional gifts, and each animal is more fascinating than the next. Come in," he said.

In the community room, Michael handed the koala to Sister Kristina, who disappeared with it down the hall.

Tom and Mac watched another woman cross her path. Over the intercom, a gentle soprano voice rang out. "Brother Aaron, you're wanted on line two."

"This is quite a different place than it was last summer," Mac said with a grin. "Have you guys gone coed?"

Brother Michael blushed. "Oh heavens, no," he replied, then leaned back and gave the question more thought. "Well, perhaps in a way we may have."

"I'm not following," Mac said.

"The Sisters of Saint Amand Abbey are considering moving here from Oregon. They have overgrown their vineyard and their abbey and think, for many reasons, that the property behind our monastery may be an ideal location for them."

Mac raised her brows. "Who would have thought?"

Michael chuckled. "Certainly not us, until the day they suggested the idea."

"And does Brother Matthew think it's a good idea?" Mac asked.

Michael nodded. "More so every day, I believe. He's visiting Saint Amand right now with a few other brothers."

Another sister entered the community room and took a seat at the desk, opening a large journal.

Michael leaned closer to Mac and whispered, "We've already given them your name with high recommendations if they decide to buy the property."

"Thank you," Mac said, watching the nun.

Michael stood up. "Dr. Candor, if it's not too much of an imposition, perhaps you can come out to our dog kennel."

Mac turned in the opposite direction. "I'll join you in a minute. I want to say hello to Brother John."

After Michael led Tom away, Mac walked the long corridors to the kitchen, where she found Brother John standing in front of the stove, stirring a pot of beef stew.

"That smells delicious. May I?" she asked, picking up a spoon to taste.

"Better yet, I already have two bowls on the table for us," the monk said. "Come join me. I've missed our long talks."

"So have I," Mac said, taking the seat she had always used during lunch when she and Terry worked at Saint Cross the summer before.

"And what brings you here today?"

"Tom asked me to come along," she said, circling her spoon through the stew. "He was unsure of the roads."

John noticed Mac playing with her food. "You're usually the first to finish eating. Not hungry today?" he asked.

She looked up, embarrassed that she had gotten lost in her thoughts. "I'm fine. Just a lot on my mind."

John remained silent as Mac put down her spoon and gently pushed her bowl away.

"I'm in quite the predicament," she finally said.

"A pickle," John said.

Thinking John was offering her more food, Mac said, "No, thanks."

John laughed. "No, I mean, you're in a pickle."

"That I am," Mac said, blushing. She played with her napkin while composing her thoughts. "I've been swept away by a man. Is that a bad thing to confess to a monk?"

He had a kind smile. "Not to a monk or a friend."

"The more I get to know him, the more I see that he's everything I admire in a person and everything I hoped to find in a partner. But he has a secret, a past that only I know about. And I've given him my word that I won't tell a soul." She spoke her words softly and quickly, as if she wanted to divulge every detail at once.

"This secret, is it harming anyone?" he asked.

"Him! He doesn't see it, but he's really only hurting himself."

"And now you, apparently," John suggested.

She grimaced, as if stung by a wasp. "Yes, I suppose so. Certainly if I'm put in the position of having to lie."

John studied Mac's expression. "But it's obvious you care for him."

"Much more than I ever thought possible in so short a time," she said. "What's between us is so strong and is moving so fast, it scares me. But then the possibility that I've finally found a soul mate is . . . bliss. I just don't know if any of this is right."

"Why would love ever be wrong?"

Mac looked at her wise friend. "Sometimes I envy you being a monk."

He let out a loud, bellowing laugh. "So you could escape? I'm sorry. It doesn't work that way."

Mac leaned back in her chair. "So, if I can't become a monk, what do you advise?"

Brother John crossed his hands as if to pray. "Be true to yourself and be true to him. All else will follow."

ℴ

Michael led Tom around to the back of the monastery. "So, how do you like Lumby so far?"

Tom laughed as he looked back in Mac's direction. "Challenging but delightful."

"The timing of your visit couldn't be better. I was going to call Ellen tomorrow and ask her to come out."

"She's probably up to her elbows in packing," Tom offered. "I believe she'll be leaving for Greece in a few days."

"Well, we need to give her a call and wish her well," he said.

When Michael opened the door to the dog kennel, Tom was immediately struck by the scents of fresh sawdust and hay. As he walked down the well-swept aisle, he noticed fresh water in all the buckets. The animals were well groomed and either sleeping or eating.

A woman walked up behind Tom. "Excuse me," she said.

Without looking back, he stepped aside, allowing the woman to pass. She led a camel on a rope lead.

"Sister Sara, would you wait one minute?" Michael asked. "Dr. Candor is taking a quick look at our animals."

"Sure," she said, pausing in front of the kennel door. "He's eating well and has gained a few pounds since arriving," she told Tom.

Tom took the stethoscope out of his bag and leaned over the young camel, listening to its heart and lungs. He then felt the animal's legs and looked at each of its hooves. After several minutes, he straightened. "He appears to be in perfect health," he said.

"As we thought. But if you would look at the rhea," the sister requested. "It appears healthy but has dropped a lot of feathers since being shipped here."

"That's to be expected, considering the high stress of being transported across any distance."

"It came all the way from Bolivia," Michael explained as Tom unlatched the kennel door.

The rhea kicked against the stall wall.

"Oh, calm down," Tom said in an even tone. "No need to get so excited." He took the animal's halter and snapped it to a short lead rope secured in a corner of the kennel. Tom walked around the nervous animal. "So much tension for so little reason," he continued, talking to the rhea.

Tom bent under the lead rope and felt the bird's left wing, extending it from the animal's body. He then put the stethoscope up to its chest, closed his eyes and listened, moving the scope a few inches every six to eight seconds. He then moved to listen to the rhea's abdomen.

But as soon as Tom placed the stethoscope on the rhea's underside, the bird jumped up and kicked out with all of its force, striking Tom squarely in the chest. Tom flew backward, crashed against the stall wall and then collapsed in a heap.

"Dr. Candor!" Michael called out.

Dazed, Tom was doubled over in the sawdust. "Don't come in," he groaned. "Don't startle the bird." He tried to catch his breath, but his chest felt like it was on fire. Had the kick been so forceful as to cause a heart attack? "Give me a minute," he said weakly.

The bird craned its neck and looked down at Tom, blinking its enormous eyes with long lashes.

Tom tried to sit up, but the effort was both painful and dizzying.

"Are you all right?" Michael asked from the other side of the kennel door.

"Dandy," Tom said sarcastically.

Sister Sara peered through the chain links from the adjacent stall. "Do you need help?"

"No. I just need to catch my breath."

The rhea continued to blink at him.

Tom looked up at the animal and scowled. "That was *so* not necessary," he said, getting slowly to his feet.

To Tom's credit, he finished examining the rhea and then went on to the other animals, not only in the kennel but also those being kept in the guesthouse and several auxiliary buildings. By the end of the day, Tom had vetted more than a dozen of God's creatures.

ಌ

Meeting Tom back at the car, Mac immediately noticed that he was moving as if in pain.

"You look exhausted," she commented. "Is everything all right?"

"I've had easier days, and I'm too tired to drive. Would you mind?" he asked, handing her the keys.

"Not at all," Mac said, jumping into the driver's seat.

That afternoon, while Tom had been examining the monks' animals, Mac and Brother John had had a long conversation that indirectly touched upon Mac's predicament of knowing Tom's truth. As with all of her talks with John, she came away more clearheaded, with a deeper understanding of her own thoughts and feelings. She was hoping to have a long discussion with Tom on the drive back to Lumby.

By the time they drove through Franklin, Mac had collected her thoughts. "I'm glad we have this time. There's something I need to discuss with you."

She glanced at Tom; his face was turned away. She assumed he was looking out the window.

"Are you with me?" she asked, touching his arm.

His response wasn't at all what she had been expecting: a deep, loud snore.

TWENTY-NINE

Shingled

By seven a.m. the following morning, Tom dragged his sore body from bed. An hour before, two forty-foot-by-sixty-foot white-and-green-striped pole tents had been delivered and raised in front of The Granary. The tents for the shingle party that would welcome the new veterinarian took up every inch of space from the animal clinic's front porch to the street, and could be seen from as far away as Dickenson's Grocery Store on the other end of town.

They were impressive structures. Each tent had three interior posts, fourteen feet high, that were reminiscent of the old circus canopies. Most of the side panels of the tents were rolled up. Where the white sidewall flaps were down, large Palladian windows of clear vinyl offered the grandeur of a large pavilion. Heaters had been placed next to each white aluminum post. With autumn came unpredictable evenings when the temperature could drop below fifty degrees.

Tom was initially impressed with the formidable tents. Curious to see how strong they were, he wrapped his hands around a center post—his ribs and chest muscles screaming—and pushed against it. There was no movement at all, not even a ripple in the taut cover.

"Amazingly stout," Dennis Beezer said, walking up the sidewalk.

Tom looked over his shoulder. "Apparently so. Did you do this?"

Dennis began to untie several straps supporting the rolled fabric of one sidewall. "Not alone. Each of these tents weighs two hundred pounds." When the final strap was released, the sidewall rolled down. "I just heard that it will be cool tonight, so we'll want to turn on the heaters before everyone arrives. The ladies of Lumby are particular about their surroundings when they are in formal attire."

"This will be quite the party, won't it?"

Dennis laughed, thinking back on all the other shingle parties he and Gabrielle had attended. "For the people in town, you could say that. It's a rite of passage, an inauguration into our very small community."

"And every newcomer gets a party like this?" Tom asked.

Dennis shook his head. "Certainly not with such grandeur. This isn't just the introduction of the new veterinarian, but the person who's replacing Ellen Campbell. She's been a trusted confidante and beloved friend to all of us for longer than we want to remember."

"Sounds like big shoes to fill," Tom said as he stepped up onto the porch.

"You have no idea," Dennis replied.

~

By the time Tom reemerged from the clinic, it was late afternoon. He had intentionally stayed in his office all day, hoping that Mac would come by, hoping he could talk with her before the party. When his patience was finally exhausted, Tom called her.

When her voice mail picked up, he said, "Mac, this is Tom. I'm hoping to see you tonight." His mind was racing, trying to keep ahead of what he was saying. He had already apologized for putting her in an untenable position—no need to repeat that. "Please come tonight. I could certainly use your . . . support."

Just as Tom hung up the phone, Jimmy knocked on the front door. "Libations are here!" he called out.

Tom walked out of his office to see Jimmy wheeling in a dolly stacked with cases of wine and soda. He lifted the top case and placed it on the reception desk. "I thought we could set the bar up here."

Tom looked around. "Why not on the porch so there won't be a bottleneck?"

"You're absolutely right," Jimmy said, looking at the front door. "If we have it out there, they can approach it from both sides—perfect. And then Gabrielle can put all the dishes on the tables."

"What tables?"

"Out there," Jimmy said, pointing. "They delivered them about an hour ago. Come see," Jimmy said, swinging the dolly around and pushing it back outside.

As soon as Tom stepped out on the porch, it was obvious that while he had been in the back of the clinic tending to some sick animals, several people had been busy preparing for his shingle party. The tents were decorated with long garlands wrapped around the posts and strings of Christmas lights secured to the canopy. A row of tables had been arranged along the right side of the tent and opposite, in the far left corner, were six chairs.

"For the orchestra," Jimmy explained.

Tom shook his head in disbelief. "There's an *orchestra*?"

"Gosh, no, but that's what they call themselves. It's our volunteer fire department. Some of the guys are pretty good."

"That makes perfect sense," Tom replied, although it actually made little sense to him.

Gabrielle and Dennis Beezer walked up the sidewalk, wearing casual clothes. Each was carrying a large chafing dish and behind them their young son, Timmy, carried napkins and utensils.

Tom looked at his watch: five twenty-five p.m. The party would begin shortly. He cringed at the thought of the questions he would be asked and answers he would have to give. Since hearing of the party, he had struggled to find an alternative or an escape, but there wasn't any. He was absolutely convinced that if he disclosed his past mistakes tonight, the residents of this tight-knit town would never give him a second chance.

Gabrielle looked at Tom standing on the porch. She thought he was an attractive man, but there was a reserve about him that she had yet to understand. "Tom," she said, "you're the man of the hour, so you're not allowed to help with the preparations."

"As dictated by who? The shingle police?" he teased her.

Gabrielle and Dennis both laughed. "You'd be surprised," Dennis warned.

"Why don't you go and get ready?" she suggested. "Everyone should be arriving in about a half hour."

Tom used the opportunity to escape upstairs. If only the rest of the evening would go so easily. Keep all topics of conversation on the guests and their animals, Tom reminded himself as he put on the tuxedo he had rented the day before down in Wheatley.

It had been decades since he'd worn such formal attire, which he used to put on regularly when he and Laura were together. At least every other weekend they would attend a black-tie benefit or philanthropic dinner or even a political event.

After becoming exasperated trying to tie his bow tie, he remembered how it was Laura who had always tied it for him. Funny that one could be divorced for fifteen years and still discover something new that was lost when the marriage ended.

Tom drew back the curtain and looked out his second-floor bedroom window. He immediately noticed that Hank had already arrived, looking smart in his custom-tailored tuxedo. He was standing in front of the bar, waiting to be offered a glass of champagne. How truly odd this town was.

By the time Tom came downstairs, the sky had darkened and someone had turned on the lights in the clinic as well as the Christmas lights around the tents. What an amazing transformation; the entire front of The Granary was ablaze in a warm glow.

To Tom's surprise, Gabrielle was standing by the bar looking ravishing in a floor-length burgundy gown. Next to her stood her husband, also in formal attire. They were talking with another couple, whom Tom didn't recognize. On the far end of the porch, two young boys along with Timmy Beezer were testing the strength and durability of Tom's wooden rocking chairs.

Under the tents, at least sixty people had come to honor him. He quickly scanned the crowd in hopes of seeing Mac, but to his disappointment, she was nowhere in sight. Three couples were dancing close to the band, while many more were serving themselves from a grand buffet of wonderful-smelling entrées and side dishes. Tom recognized Joshua Turner with his wife, Brooke, and Pam and Mark Walker.

He took a deep breath. This was what he had longed for, for so many years: a home, a community and friends who would forgive and forget who he had been a long time ago.

Jimmy came up and patted Tom's shoulder. "Well, congratulations, Tom."

"Thanks, Jimmy," he said, shaking the mayor's hand. "This is a wonderful welcome."

"We have quite a town," Jimmy said proudly. "There're not too many folks who could have come into Lumby and been so well received as you have been. Some townsfolk don't look fondly on outsiders, or flatlanders as they're called. But you've obviously passed the test."

Tom was surprised. "Everyone's been congenial so far."

Jimmy leaned closer to Tom so he wouldn't be overheard. "That's also because they all have pets. After they accepted that Ellen was leaving, they knew they needed a veterinarian in the worst way. Otherwise, there are folks here who would have insisted you be interviewed by the town council."

That idea sent shivers down Tom's spine. "Well, I'm glad we didn't have to go through that formality."

"Absolutely no need to. We could have searched for months and never found anyone as perfect," Jimmy complimented him. "It's a good thing you found us, because I doubt we would have found you in the backwoods of Maine."

Dennis had overheard part of the conversation and joined the men. "It was an amazing stroke of luck that you saw one of Ellen's advertising flyers all the way over in Bangor."

"It was, indeed," Tom said, and took a step away.

"Do you have any idea who sent it to you?"

Tom shook his head. It was an easy and very honest answer. "I have no idea."

Jimmy threw up his arms. "The interview is over. Let's get on with the party." He put two fingers in his mouth and whistled loudly. The band stopped playing, and everyone turned to face the front steps of the clinic.

"Glad you could all come," Jimmy began. "As is the tradition in our fine town, we welcome our newest neighbor, friend, resident and honorable veterinarian, Tom Candor!"

Everyone applauded and some cheered jovially.

"Tom comes with extraordinary credentials and an honest heart to fill the space left behind by our beloved friend, Ellen Campbell."

"Oh, hush, Jimmy! You make it sound like I've died and gone to heaven," a woman said from the back of the tented area.

Suddenly the crowd separated and Ellen Campbell, with Mackenzie McGuire walking by her side, approached.

Tom was mesmerized. Mac looked stunning in a long red gown of soft taffeta. It clung to her body and showed every glorious curve that was usually hidden under her overalls and sweatshirts. Her hair was pulled high on her head, and gold earrings dangled on either side of her sensuous neck.

Even when Ellen began talking, Tom couldn't take his eyes off Mac. And she couldn't stop staring at Tom. She always said that men looked their best in tuxedos, but he went far beyond her expectations. Her heart was racing and she felt light-headed.

"Tom, to be embraced by such extraordinary people is a rare privilege," Ellen began, but quickly noticed she didn't have his full attention. She coughed. "Ah, Tom?"

He heard his name and finally looked over at her. Several folks standing nearby chuckled. Tom blushed. "Yes, Ellen?"

She took her final steps up to the clinic, which she had founded so many years before. "Tom," she said, holding out a large plaque, "I hereby turn over and entrust the residents and the animals of Lumby to your good care."

Thunderous applause rose throughout the crowd.

Jimmy took the plaque from Ellen and, with Dennis's help, hammered it to the siding directly to the left of the front door.

Tom walked up and examined the plaque. It was hand-carved and stained; the background was dark green while the border and letters were silver leafed.

Dr. Tom Candor

Veterinarian

"We can judge the heart of a man
by his treatment of animals."
—Kant

Tom read and then reread the quote, his eyes blurring. He was so focused on the plaque that he didn't notice Mac moving next to him. She read the words as well.

As if she knew exactly what he was thinking, she put her hand in his and said softly, "You need to forgive yourself."

He turned to her. "But . . . ," he began.

She squeezed his hand and nodded. "Like you said, when the time is right."

He turned to face the crowd. "Thank you so much. Your faith in me is tremendously humbling. I can only pray that over time I will earn the trust and friendship that you're offering today."

More applause broke out.

"On with the party!" Jimmy called loudly.

Within seconds, the band was playing and several couples resumed dancing. More guests converged at the buffet line, while others refreshed their drinks.

Tom, still holding Mac's hand, led her to the far end of the porch, away from the crowd and lights. He placed his hand on the small of her back, pulled her close and whispered, "I'm so glad you came." Then he lifted her chin and kissed her tenderly.

Hank, who was standing close to the couple, blushed and immediately took a sip of his third glass of champagne.

THIRTY

Dancing

When the band began playing its own rendition of "Moonlight Serenade," several couples who had been mingling by the bar refilled their wineglasses, kicked up their heels and started to dance the night away.

Watching from the stairs, Mark wrapped his arms around Pam's waist and kissed her on the neck. "You look absolutely gorgeous tonight, honey. Would you like to dance?"

"In a minute," she said, lifting her plate of hors d'oeuvres. "And you're as handsome as ever."

Brooke leaned over to Pam. "Why is it that men look so attractive in tuxedos?" she asked.

"I have no idea, but they really do, don't they?" Pam replied.

"Maybe it's one of the few times that we actually see our husbands cleaned up," Brooke commented.

"They do look pretty rough around the edges when they're working at the inn," Pam concurred.

Joshua looked at Mark and rolled his eyes. "We heard that, ladies," he said.

"Speaking of Montis," Brooke said, "how is everything going?"

"Both the restaurant and the inn are full every night," Mark answered.

Pam continued. "Ever since Christian Copeland endorsed Montis and ran the article in his magazine, we've been booked eight weeks out. I'm glad we could escape for a few hours and come here tonight."

Mark looked at Pam for confirmation. "I don't think either of us ever thought about the amount of effort it would take to run the inn at full capacity, seven days a week."

Pam nodded. "But it's certainly nice to finally show a profit."

Joshua nudged Mark. "Now you can afford an engine for that new truck you've been talking about. You keep saying she's one of a kind."

"Just like my wife," Mark said, kissing her cheek.

"Yeah, old and rusted." Pam laughed.

Brooke put her plate down on a side table. "And how's your new chef?"

"Well . . . ," Pam began.

Mark poked his wife's shoulder from behind. "Go ahead, tell her." Pam shot a glance at Mark. "Then I will," Mark said. "My dear wife is having some control issues and is trying to get used to having someone else in her kitchen."

Brooke laughed. "But, more important, how's his cooking?"

"Extraordinary," Pam said. "If he wasn't so good, I would never think about turning my kitchen over to him."

"But you said you wanted to get out from under the pots and pans," Joshua said.

Mark ran his hand over his wife's hair. "Easier said than done with Pam."

"It will be fine," she said, forcing out the words. "Come on, let's dance."

As Mark was being pulled away, he looked back at his friends and shrugged. "Touchy subject," he whispered.

"Too many cooks must make Pam a nervous woman," Brooke said sympathetically.

Joshua laughed as he watched Mark begin a Fred Astaire imitation as he led his wife onto the dance floor. "It's nice to see two people who, twenty years later, are as in love as when they got married," he commented.

Brooke looked at her husband with concern. "Don't you think we'll be like that in eighteen years?"

He put his arms around her. "I have absolutely no doubt," he said as he leaned over and kissed her tenderly on the lips. "But since you don't see it that often, I find it refreshing."

Brooke, watching Pam and Mark doing their own unique version of the waltz, smiled. "I do too."

Joshua spotted Chuck Bryson standing among the crowd that had converged at the buffet table. "Chuck's back from his trip," he told Brooke, waving to his good friend.

Chuck, looking debonair in white tie and tails, strolled up to the couple.

"Good evening, Mr. Bryson," Brooke said.

"Good evening, Brooke," he said, looking around. "Where's the other half of this dangerous foursome?"

Joshua laughed and pointed toward the band. "Stepping on the toes of all the other dancers."

Chuck scanned the tented area. "Ah, there they are. Very good," he said when he spotted Pam and Mark.

"I thought you were in California until the end of the week," Joshua said.

"Those were the plans, but I couldn't miss a shingle party and I wouldn't have missed this one for anything," Chuck said.

Mac and Tom walked down the porch steps and joined the threesome.

"I haven't seen you in weeks," Mac said, giving Chuck a warm embrace.

"You look radiant, Ms. McGuire," Chuck said, bowing his head.

Mac stepped aside. "Have you met Tom Candor?" she asked.

"Not formally. A privilege to meet you," Chuck said, shaking the veterinarian's hand. "I assume you bought Ellen's practice."

"That he did," Ellen Campbell answered as she walked up behind Chuck. "Lock, stock and monkeys." She put her arms around his shoulders and hugged him tightly.

"What are we going to do after you leave us?" Chuck asked mournfully.

"The same thing Charlotte Ross said about her death: just pour a stiff margarita and continue on without me. I'll miss you, dear friend," she said, kissing Chuck.

"I should have courted you when I had the chance," he whispered.

Ellen beamed. "We wouldn't have made it past one night."

"But what a night it would have been."

"And look here," she said, turning to Tom, "the two Berkeley men finally meet."

"You went to Berkeley?" Chuck asked, taking a closer look at Tom. "Do we know each other from campus?"

Tom froze for a moment. The last thing he had expected was to run into a college acquaintance from his distant past. Chuck was clearly twenty years his senior, but in a long shot, the two of them could have possibly met at the university. "I don't think so. I was there decades ago."

"Probably around the time I joined the faculty," Chuck said. "We must sit down and compare notes sometime. If you and I haven't crossed paths before, I'm sure there are many folks we know in common. It's a big campus, but a small community. I'm sorry. Your last name again?"

"Candor," Tom said, trying not to visibly withdraw from the question.

Chuck looked up at the tent's ceiling and thought for a moment. "The name seems to ring a bell. I'm sure I'll think of it later. So, do you go back to Berkeley often?"

"Not since my graduation."

"A great school—wonderful minds throughout," Chuck commented. "In fact, I was hoping to entice someone from the university to consider buying Ellen's practice, so I hung two dozen of her for-sale leaflets around campus. So how did you find our small town?"

"Someone mailed me a flyer."

Ellen walked over and slid her arm through Tom's. "And a good thing they did. Otherwise I'd be leaving tomorrow with no replacement."

Everyone stared at Ellen, shocked by what she had just said.

"You're leaving *tomorrow*?" Mac cried.

"But we haven't thrown you a party!" Brooke protested.

Ellen looked around at all of her friends, those standing next to her, as well as those dancing to the music of Lumby's fine orchestra. Her eyes shone with joy. "You couldn't have given me any finer or happier memories of my last night in Lumby than this one."

Mac was fighting back tears. "But it's too soon for you to go."

"No, it's not, my dear. And heaven forbid, if I stayed any longer, I might have ended up with that old codger," she said, nodding at Chuck. "Greece awaits and then I will move close to my family and enjoy my retirement."

"Well, the least we can do is buy you another drink," Brooke said, taking Ellen by the arm.

As the women headed toward the bar on the front porch, Dennis and Simon joined the men.

Tom watched Mac as she left with her friends, carefully lifting the hem of her long dress as she gracefully ascended the steps. Such a fascinating contradiction, he thought, that a woman who lifted sheets of plywood one minute could be so sensuous and feminine the next.

"Excuse me," Tom said, stepping away from the growing group of men.

Dennis watched Tom wind his way through the crowd and disappear inside The Granary. A few seconds later, Dennis saw Tom's office light come on.

"Dennis?" Joshua said.

He pulled his eyes away from the office window. "I'm sorry. What did you say?"

Joshua looked toward where Dennis had been staring. "Is something wrong?"

Dennis ran his fingers through his hair and leaned in so as not to be overheard. "Do you guys have a good sense about Tom?"

Joshua was the first to reply. "Other than the fact that we're pretty much opposites in our opinion of genetic engineering, he seems like a nice enough guy."

"Do you have a problem with him?" Simon asked.

Dennis shook his head. "I don't know. I just can't put my finger on it."

"A great education—he went to Berkeley," Chuck said.

Joshua, along with the other men, laughed. "And you're entirely objective about that, are you?" he teased.

Chuck blushed. "Absolutely not. Speaking of which," he said to Joshua, "I wanted to remind you about the symposium there next week. Top scientists from around the world will be on campus for three days."

Joshua nodded. "I remember you mentioning it a while ago."

"I have to return to the university on Monday. Perhaps you'd like to join me and sit in on the debate? It's a closed session, but I know we would be pleased to have you."

Joshua looked over at his wife, who was leaning against a porch pillar. "That would be incredible. Let me talk with Brooke tonight."

"Terrific," Chuck said. "And who knows where that could lead?"

Dennis stepped forward. "If you guys are going to Berkeley, would you do me a favor and ask around about our man, Tom Candor? See if anyone knows him."

"Why the background check?" Simon asked.

Dennis shrugged. "It's just the old reporter in me wanting to know the whole story."

"Well, his name certainly sounds familiar enough," Chuck said, still trying to remember why. "If anyone knows him, it won't take long to find out. I'm acquainted with a few older professors in the school of veterinary medicine."

ꟹ

After the last guests left, Mac removed her shoes and dropped gently onto the soft cushions of the sofa, straightening her long gown. It had been an enchanting evening that she would never forget. Tom looked out the front window one final time before turning off the porch lights.

He walked up behind her and kissed her on the back of the neck. "You looked stunning tonight." He removed his jacket and cummerbund, and then loosened his bow tie.

"And you are dashing," she said. "I think the town has fallen for you as much as I have."

"Hopefully in not quite the same way," he teased, putting his arm around her and drawing her close. "Did you enjoy yourself?"

She kissed him tenderly. "Every minute. It was a perfect dream."

"And dream we will—come with me," Tom said, as he helped her to her feet. Once they were standing, in one fluid motion, he swept her up into his arms.

She wrapped her arms around his neck and kissed him as he crossed the living room with Mac held tightly against his chest.

"I'll never know how you found me in Lumby of all places, but now that you have, I don't ever want to let you go," she said.

The Lumby Lines

What's News Around Town

BY SCOTT STEVENS October 23

A very slow week in our sleepy town of Lumby.

Wanting to put the excess number of large pumpkins to good use, some high school students brought out the catapult and tested theories of weight versus distance. Simon Dixon and Principal Harris have estimated that there are at least eighty pumpkins smashed on the football field (and yes, if anyone is curious, the smallest did, actually, fly the farthest). The recovery of the hardwood catapult is in serious question as it appears to have been crushed under the weight of Jeremiah's winning entry.

Chatham Bank has faced a monthlong mystery as to the origin of a "ghostlike" blur that has been seen each night on the security camera in their locked vault. Many, who have attributed the blur to an apparition of the deceased founder, have withdrawn their monies from the haunted bank, preferring to use their own mattresses until the poltergeist is evicted. Feeling the financial drain, the bank finally sent the surveillance tapes to Washington, D.C., for analysis. Word came back the other day that the ghost was, in fact, a moth walking across the camera lens. The worst of the bank's problems, though, came yesterday when Rob Steadman, president of Chatham Bank, realized that an entire colony of white moths has taken up residence in one of its canvas bags and have been dining on the large-denomination bills inside.

An unprecedented number of rabbits appears to have invaded our small town during the last month, annoying the residents and sending the carnivorous canines into nothing less than a wild frenzy. We were told that the rabbits directly caused one cow to rampage down Main Street the other day. (For those following the story, Max Cooper never did explain why there were pink curlers in the cow's mane and tail, but we are assuming his granddaughters are visiting.) If anyone has any thoughts as to the cause or cure for our hare infestation, please call Chuck Bryson.

And regarding rabbit fur, Brad's Hardware received a nonrefundable order of 1,400 genuine rabbit fur earmuffs, the large quantity the result of a typing error. Brad is now offering a free pair with the purchase of any brand-name chain saw.

THIRTY-ONE

Thrill

Down in the small barn at Montis Inn, Pam paid diligent attention during the seven minutes it took for Mark to explain to her all he knew about operating the motorcycle.

"Release it very slowly," he said, demonstrating the clutch mechanism with his left hand.

"And what is this?" Pam asked, pointing to what looked like a toggle switch.

Mark lifted his shoulders. "I have no idea, but this is for your one headlight."

Pam bent over the seat, looking at the other side. "And how about that switch?"

"Don't have the foggiest."

Pam wrinkled her brow. "Mark, do you think it would be a good idea if we took this back to Dakin's Garage and asked him some of these questions?"

Mark shrugged. "I thought I'd just figure it all out over time."

"Ah," she said, nodding.

"And this is where the gas goes," Mark said, trying unsuccessfully to unscrew the cap. "It sticks a little."

Pam pulled on her leather gloves and clapped her hands together. "All right, I'm ready."

"Ready for what?"

She threw her leg over the seat and grabbed the handlebars. "The keys?"

Mark pulled them reluctantly from his coat pocket. "You're going to drive just around here, right?"

"You sound like I'm going to get arrested," Pam said, taking the keys from him.

"Just be gentle with her," he warned.

"Shouldn't you tell *it* to be gentle with *me*?" Pam asked. "And who are you to talk about gentle rides? You were jumping dirt mounds with this thing yesterday."

"Well, that's different."

"Right," Pam said, turning on the engine. She shifted into first and coasted slowly down the driveway.

Pam soon realized that, because of the sidecar, balance wasn't at all an issue as it usually was on a motorcycle. She weaved right and then left, getting a feel for the steering. At the end of the driveway, she turned around and gave it more gas, so much so that she was going at least twenty miles an hour by the time she passed Mark and drove through the center of the barn.

"This is great!" she yelled, before turning sharply right and heading up toward the orchard.

The last Mark saw of her was when she dropped down from the field and pulled out onto Farm to Market Road, heading toward Lumby.

On a whim, Pam decided to take Yolk, the name she had bequeathed the yellow motorcycle, to town. As there was no traffic in front of or behind her, she used the trip to become more familiar with shifting gears, acceleration and braking.

By the time she reached the intersection of Farm to Market Road and Main Street, she was an experienced Yolk driver, and took the turn going well over the speed limit. Unfortunately for Pam, Simon was standing on the steps of the police station watching her every move.

Pam didn't see Simon waving at her to pull over. She continued down Main Street, where she made a quick, and quite illegal, U-turn in front of Jimmy D's and then headed back to The Green Chile, accelerating all the way.

Gabrielle and Mac, who had been watching through the restaurant window, ran out to the curb just as Pam screeched to a halt. "Look at you, girlfriend!" Mac exclaimed, applauding.

"Am I missing coffee with the girls?" Pam asked.

"Not at all," Gabrielle said. "Mac just returned some serving trays we left at Tom's."

"Oh, running Tom's errands," Pam said suspiciously. "And there's a twinkle in your eye, Ms. McGuire. What exactly have you two been doing?"

Mac beamed. "Having a wonderful time, thank you."

"She looks like the Cheshire cat, doesn't she?" Gabrielle said.

Pam studied her friend. "If you ask me, she looks like she's in love."

"Stop it, both of you!" Mac said, giggling. Under her breath, she added, "But he is unbelievably great."

"I liked him the moment I met him," Gabrielle said. "And he is so handsome."

"Yeah, he is," Mac agreed. "I've just never connected with anyone the way I have with him."

"Feels good, doesn't it?" Pam asked.

"Indescribable. And it's a one in a million that he came to Lumby and that we found each other."

"Well, hold on to him for dear life," Gabrielle said.

"Speaking of holding on," Pam said, revving the motorcycle's engine, "one of you jump in here and I'll take you for a spin."

"Pam!" a man called out.

She looked up and saw Simon jogging across Main Street. She

waved and turned back to Gabrielle. "This is total freedom. Hop in and we can go up to the fairgrounds."

Gabrielle looked back at the restaurant. "Okay, just for a few minutes."

Just as Gabrielle was stepping into the sidecar, Simon raised his hand. "Just one minute," he said, running up to the ladies.

"Good morning, Sheriff Dixon," Pam said with a teasing formality.

Simon circled the motorcycle and then stood directly in front of her.

"I named it Yolk," she said, still beaming from her ride.

"I didn't know you had a license to drive a motorcycle," Simon said.

Pam continued to smile. "Well, Simon, it's not really a motorcycle, per se. It's an old relic Mark bought from the government."

"A relic that you need a motorcycle license to operate," Simon said, dropping his voice.

Pam laughed. "Okay," she said, thinking Simon was teasing her, "I'll put it as a top priority for next year."

"And I notice you don't have a license plate. Is this registered with the DMV?"

"About as registered as our tractor is," she said, winking at Gabrielle.

"The way I see it, Pam, you have at least five violations: driving an unregistered vehicle, driving without a license, driving without a helmet, exceeding the speed limit in town and making an illegal U-turn. That's not including parking in front of a fire hydrant," he said, pointing at the sidewalk.

Pam's smile faded. "So, does that mean I can't take Gabrielle up to the fairgrounds?"

"I'm going to pretend this never happened and escort you back to Montis. The next time I see . . . Yolk in town, I want it to be registered, and the both of you licensed. And," he added, "going less than fifteen miles an hour. And wearing—"

"A helmet." Pam swallowed. "Yes, sir," she said sheepishly.

Simon took out his car keys. "Give me a minute to get the patrol car, and then follow me."

"Yes, sir," she repeated.

When Simon was out of earshot, Pam turned to Gabrielle. "Come visit us tomorrow morning and I'll take you down to Wheatley."

"You're going to end up with a ticket," Gabrielle warned.

"You're right. Give me a day to get a license and registration. Then come down."

Pam turned the key and revved the engine for effect.

"You better get going, Evel Knievel." Gabrielle laughed, pointing at Simon's car.

"I'll call you." Pam waved and then put Yolk into first gear and pulled slowly away.

The drive home was especially slow and boring. And there was no need for Simon to keep his police lights on the entire way. But at least he didn't use the siren.

Pulling into Montis, Pam scanned the courtyard and lower fields of the orchard. To her relief, Mark wasn't anywhere in sight.

Simon leaned out the window as he turned the patrol car around. "Be sure you and Mark take care of this," he advised. "I can't be so lenient next time."

"We will," Pam promised, and parked Yolk next to the only car there.

Just as Simon drove away and Pam was getting off the motorcycle, André came around the corner of the dining room, carrying an empty box. When he saw the bike, his eyes lit up and he beelined directly to Pam.

"What a beautiful machine," he said.

"I almost got five tickets," Pam confessed.

André laughed. "Don't tell me—no license, registration or helmet?"

"Plus speeding and a U-turn," she added.

André ran his palm along the handlebars. "Do you mind if I take her for a spin?"

"Absolutely not," Pam said, assuming André would just drive around Montis.

"Great," he said, taking a seat on the bike. He turned on the ignition. "The engine sounds great."

"Not our doing, believe me. We had it worked on at Dakin's," Pam explained. "Are you familiar with old BMWs?"

"Old motorcycles in general, yes."

Pam put her hand on his shoulder. "When you come back, maybe you can show me what some of these knobs are for."

"Be glad to," André said, already starting to back up. "I'll just run down to Wheatley—be back in about thirty minutes."

He was already pulling onto Farm to Market before she had a chance to stop him.

Pam picked up the empty box that André had left next to his car and read the label: twenty-four kitchen towels. Curious as to why André felt her towels weren't sufficient and more curious to see if he had tossed them away, Pam headed to the kitchen.

Walking through the dining room, she sighed in relief to see that nothing more had changed since the day before, although she had to admit that the small changes André had made in the table settings and linens were all for the better.

When she swung open the kitchen door, she was startled by the brilliant light that filled the room. Blinking several times to allow her eyes to adjust, she finally looked up and saw that André had installed commercial lighting across the entire ceiling. The darkest corners were now bright. Over the stove, in an area that had always been dimly lit, hung a string of four incandescent bulbs. Only after she saw the lights did she notice an electrical-inspection sticker taped to the wall showing that the work had passed code.

Sadly, with André's changes, the kitchen had lost much of its country charm, but Pam reminded herself that Montis was now a commercial restaurant where efficiency was the priority. She was clearly torn between what was her quaint scullery and what André was offering—extraordinary cuisine and the strong possibility of national recognition.

Pam peeked in a brown bag sitting on the island and saw her old towels carefully folded and stacked. Compared to the highly absorbent professional towels that André had hung all around the kitchen, hers looked thin and worn.

Pam jumped when Mark swung open the door. "Hey, honey," he said, kissing her on the cheek on his way to the refrigerator, "I've been looking all over for you. How do you like André's improvements?"

She winced. "I didn't know we needed any *improvements.*"

Mark stopped short of opening the freezer drawer and turned to look at her. "Honey, you need to let go."

Pam took one of her old towels from the bag and began wiping down the granite countertop. "I'm trying," she said.

"This will be great. You'll see. André will change your life."

"I hope for the better," she said gloomily.

Mark retrieved a quart of mint chocolate-chip ice cream. "Let me make you a sundae. Things always look brighter after ice cream."

Pam laughed. "Quite a life philosophy you have."

Mark found two bowls—not an easy feat after André had rearranged everything—and began preparing one ice-cream extravaganza to be shared with his wife.

"So, where did you park the motorcycle?" Mark asked as he rolled the ice cream with the scooper.

"After Simon escorted me home . . . ," she began.

Mark looked shocked. "Why did he do that?"

"Because he didn't want to give me a bunch of tickets. Anyway, André asked if he could take it for a spin."

"What tickets?" Mark pressed.

"We need to register the bike, go to the DMV and get a motorcycle license, and then we need a couple of helmets."

Mark waved his hand as if he were batting a fly. "Is that all Simon is bothered with?"

"Just about," Pam muttered.

"We'll take care of it tomorrow," he said, passing his wife a bowl filled to the brim with ice cream, chocolate sauce and whipped cream. "Enjoy."

~

Twenty minutes later, Mark and Pam were leaving the dining room just as André was pulling into the driveway. In the sidecar sat a teenager with long dark hair. She had her hand on André's leg and was laughing loudly. André jumped off the motorcycle, ran around and lifted the girl from her tight confines. He brushed off the back of her pants.

Pam leaned close to Mark. "Are you watching what I'm watching?"

"The really cute girl with André?" he said.

Pam jabbed him with her elbow. "How old do you think he is?"

"Somewhere between thirty and forty."

"And how young is she?"

"Sixteen, maybe eighteen, I would guess."

"You need to talk to him," Pam said.

"And say what?"

Pam looked at Mark in disbelief. "That we don't want our chef dating a child half his age. No one would approve of that."

"If she's a legal adult, there's nothing to approve," Mark countered.

"Mark, look at her!" Pam exclaimed as softly as she could.

"I am," he assured her.

"And he's moved into the cottage. I don't want him doing whatever with a teenager in our cottage, under our nose."

Mark laughed. "I didn't know you were such a prude."

Pam slapped his arm. "I'm not, but that's just plain wrong."

André had put his arm around the girl's shoulder as he pointed to the different buildings around the old monastic compound. Their intimate familiarity was obvious to any observer.

When André saw Mark and Pam, he took his arm off the teen and waved to them. The closer Pam got, the younger the girl appeared.

"I'm glad you're here," André said. "I want you to meet the lady in my life. Anaïs, this is Pam and Mark Walker, the owners of Montis."

"It's nice to meet you," Anaïs said politely, in a high-pitched immature voice.

Mark waited for his wife to say something, but Pam was speechless.

"Welcome to our home, Anaïs," Mark said. "What a beautiful name."

"Thank you," she said, blushing. "It means 'grace,' 'being in one's favor.' "

André leaned over and kissed her cheek. "And so you are, sweetheart," he said.

Pam jabbed Mark so hard in his side that he grunted and struggled to think of something to say. "So, you two were out for a drive?"

"Your bike is amazing," André said. "It was great trying her out."

The bike or the girl? Pam wondered.

Mark turned to Anaïs. "And did you like riding in the sidecar?"

Her eyes sparkled. "It was awesome. I still can't believe Dad let me do it."

"Next time we wear helmets," André said.

"Your dad?" Pam asked.

"Yeah, but he's a better cook than a driver. He hit a lot of potholes," she said, looking up at André.

He pretended to strangle her. "And all you eat are grilled cheese sandwiches."

Pam exhaled loudly. "I didn't know you have a daughter."

André was surprised. "We never really discussed my personal life. Anaïs lives with her mother just south of Wheatley."

"And with you every other weekend," the girl added with a wide smile.

"I put a bed upstairs in the cottage loft," André explained.

"This is a beautiful inn," Anaïs said. "I like it much better than Cedar Grove."

Mark laughed. "A woman who speaks her own mind."

"It used to be a monastery for an order of monks," Pam told her. "This building was the main abbey."

Anaïs looked up at the roof. "But where is the cross?"

Mark frowned for a moment, thinking back to when they'd first bought Montis four years before. He looked at Pam. "Is it still in the basement?"

"We took it down when we renovated the abbey and had some work done on the roof," Pam said. For the first time, she noticed a small gold chain and crucifix hanging from the girl's neck.

Anaïs looked up at the roof again. "And you never wanted to put the cross back?"

"It was never a deliberate decision," Pam said. "We just haven't gotten around to it." She grimaced when she realized how shallow that sounded, given what she was talking about.

Mark continued to stare at the cupola on the roof, where the cross had originally stood. "You know, honey, I think we should do it. Anaïs is right—we need to replace the Montis cross."

THIRTY-TWO

Ascension

The Lumby Lines

Sheriff's Complains

BY SHERIFF SIMON DIXON October 23

6:50 a.m. Moose damages car on Farm to Market. Moose uninjured but all wheels are punctured.

7:11 a.m. Car almost hits moose on Farm to Market. Same as before.

7:52 a.m. Resident at 4 South Grand Ave requests assistance to get her husband out of his gravity boots. Has been hanging upside down for 45 minutes. EMS dispatched.

7:54 a.m. Rabbit reported stuck in vending machine at gas station. Chuck Bryson called.

8:14 a.m. John Morris reported the misfiring of his musket when shooting at rabbits. Musket was bought last Saturday at Lumby Sporting Goods.

8:26 a.m. Reverend Olson reported large bullet hole in office window at Holy Episcopal.

1:45 p.m. Woman complained of smoke coming from manure pile behind her barn.

3:03 p.m. Deer vs bicycle on Hunts Mill Road. Child and deer both fine.

5:26 p.m. Man reported two draft horses walking down Loggers Road.

October 24

12:28 a.m. JoEllen McKee, 47, arrested for disorderly conduct at Jimmy D's. Bond: $60.

8:14 a.m. EMS responded to call from NW Builders on Loggers Road.

9:42 a.m. John Morris reported several dogs on his property chasing rabbits.

10:06 a.m. Hunter impaled by umbrella stand at Lumby Lumber. EMS will respond.

3:39 p.m. Reverend Poole reported all flowers at the church's cemetery have been eaten. Rabbits are digging holes at gravesites.

4:44 p.m. Cindy Watford complained that a rabbit was trying to have sex with her miniature poodle.

7:18 p.m. Man reported being stabbed in the buttocks with barbecue fork.

Tom Candor rose at five a.m. after a fitful sleep. The day before, he had finished moving the rest of his furniture and personal possessions that had just arrived from Maine into the second floor of The Granary, making it his private residence. Between what he bought from Ellen, and what he had in his prior house, there was ample furniture to fill all of the rooms of his new home.

Although Ellen Campbell had discouraged him from living above the clinic ("You'll never have any privacy," she had warned), his bank account was depleted from the purchase of the business, and buying or renting another house was simply out of the question. Further, he loved living in town as much as he loved the architectural splendor of The Granary.

The front-door bell chimed just as Tom finished shaving. He looked at his watch; it was only five twenty a.m., and the sun wouldn't rise for at least another hour. Pulling on a pair of trousers and a shirt, he was halfway down the stairs when the bell rang again. He turned on the front-porch lights, startling Hank, who was sleeping on the porch. Through the window he saw Chuck Bryson holding an animal in his arms.

When Tom opened the door, Chuck pushed a small goat into his chest.

"Very sorry to be interrupting," Chuck said, "but I found her on Weaver Dairy Road. It looks like a mountain lion got to her."

Tom wrapped his arms around the unconscious goat and immediately noticed the chill of its body. Carrying the animal into an exam room, Tom laid her down on the table and quickly assessed the wounds: deep gouges in her rear flanks and several bite marks in and around her neck. Blood from the wounds was already mostly dry, indicating the attack had taken place many hours ago. Leaning over the body, Tom flashed a small light into each of the goat's unresponsive pupils. He then placed the stethoscope on the goat's chest, moving it farther down its body every few seconds. After a good minute, he straightened up.

"I'm sorry, Chuck," he said. "She didn't make it. There's nothing I can do."

Chuck continued to stare at the goat. "I thought that was the case, but I wanted to give her a chance. Again, sorry for the early hour," he said, embarrassed by the imposition.

"Actually, I was already up and about to make a pot of coffee. Would you like to join me?" Tom offered. "Based on the stories Ellen shared, you're probably more familiar with the kitchen than I am."

Chuck laughed and followed Tom down the hall. "She and I certainly had our share of croissants and coffee over the years. She was quite an early bird."

"Like you must be," Tom countered.

Chuck shook his head. "Certainly not this early on most mornings. But I wanted to help Katie Banks with a fence that came down last night. Have you met her yet?"

"I'm going there this morning. She wants me to look at some of her goats."

"Well, be sure to get an assortment of her cheeses—they're the best in the region."

Tom smiled. "So I've heard."

Chuck took a seat at the table and sipped his coffee. For more than twenty years, he had sat in the same chair at the end of an oak table that his and Ellen's mutual friend had hand-built for her when she first bought The Granary. Chuck had stoked her wood-burning stove almost as frequently as Ellen had on those cold mornings. Chuck glanced around the room and sighed. Ellen's cups, which used to hang under the cabinet, were gone, as was her old cast-iron teapot, which was permanently kept on top of the stove.

Most poignant of all, Ellen was gone.

"Is the coffee too strong?" Tom asked.

Chuck rubbed his eyes. "Not at all. I was just thinking about Ellen."

"I'm sure it's hard not to. That's who everyone thinks of when they come here. It's a hard change for everyone."

Chuck nodded. "Ellen was a large part of what makes our town so special."

Tom sat across from Chuck. "Well, I'll certainly do what I can to fill the void, but it's not easy in such a small town."

"As time passes, the folks will accept you more and more," Chuck advised. "No one here is that enamored of change."

"Nor am I," Tom admitted.

Chuck looked up from his coffee. "What brought you here?"

Tom tilted his head and thought for a moment. "Necessity more than anything. It was time to begin a new chapter."

Chuck smiled. "Lumby provides that for some folks. They find a purpose and a reason here. By the way, Joshua and I are heading over to Berkeley tomorrow. Is there anyone you'd like us to look up?"

Tom chilled when he heard the word "Berkeley," a word from the past that he shunned as much as any because it tied him to Jeffrey Candor, to a man who no longer existed.

After the shingle party, Tom had begun to put a plan together as to when and how he would tell his clients and the residents of Lumby who he had been, but that wouldn't be for a while yet. Even Mac had finally agreed that the townsfolk needed more time to get to know him before he disclosed the worst episode of his professional career.

"Or perhaps you would like to join us?" Chuck offered.

Tom struggled to calm himself. "No, I don't think so," he said, adding a shrug of his shoulder to appear nonchalant. "I'm sure anyone I knew there is long gone."

"Oh, you'd be surprised," Chuck said. "The campus is large, but it's really such a small world. We always joke that it's two degrees of separation, and not six, at the university."

That was exactly what Tom didn't want to hear. "How long are you there for?"

"Just two days. I have some faculty meetings and Joshua is attending a symposium."

Tom stood up, hoping that would bring an end to the conversation.

Just then Mac knocked on the swing door of the kitchen and looked in. "Is there an early-morning meeting I didn't know about?" she asked with a wide smile.

Mac was always a gust of clean, fresh air for Tom, who immediately forgot his worries. He looked outside and noticed the sun was just rising.

"So what brings you here so early, Miss McGuire?" Chuck asked.

"Terry brought a young lady home," Mac said.

"Last night?" Tom asked.

"About an hour ago," Mac bemoaned. "They were making such a racket in the living room that I just wanted to get out."

"The boy seems to be having some troubles growing up," Tom explained to Chuck.

Mac placed a bag on the table, which she had been hiding behind her back. "Fresh biscuits from S&T's to bribe you," she told Tom. "Maybe you can give me some advice as to how I should talk to him?"

"What do you mean?" Tom asked.

Mac opened the bag of pastries. "I'm out of my element when I'm talking to Terry about relationships. He says I don't get it because I don't have a guy's perspective, and since he's an adult, he doesn't need any advice, let alone lame words of wisdom from his mother." She frowned.

"Consider it done," Tom said, hoping to encourage her.

"Thank you," she said, standing on her toes to kiss him. "Okay, breakfast time. What kind of jam do you want, Chuck?"

"As much as I love biscuits," he answered, "I need to head over to Katie's farm and then to Montis Inn. Mark called me last night, asking if I would help him with a project."

"Oh, oh." Mac laughed.

Chuck grimaced and then laughed too. "Wish me luck."

Tom noticed both Chuck and Mac rolling their eyes. "I don't get the joke," he said.

"You'll learn soon enough," Mac replied, laying her hand on his arm. "Mark Walker is a really good person, but the man is a magnet for projects that go awry. He's a danger to himself all the time and to others just some of the time."

Chuck nodded. "Come to think of it, if you're in the neighborhood, I'm sure whatever Mark's planning, he could use an extra set of hands."

Tom looked at Mac, who nodded in agreement, and then said, "I'll try to swing by when I'm done with my rounds."

"Very good," Chuck said. "We'll see you later this morning."

When the two were finally alone, Tom put his arms around Mac. "Good morning." He pulled her closer and kissed her. "You smell like lilacs."

"We'll have to pick this up later," she said, pushing him gently away. "I'm meeting Terry over at the lumberyard so I can finish the back of The Granary today."

Tom let Mac go, but continued to watch her as she placed the biscuits in a shallow bowl on the table. He was always amazed by how delicately she handled certain objects yet had the nerve and strength to single-handedly shingle a roof.

"You're staring," she said, looking out of the corner of her eye.

He chuckled. "That I am."

"So any thoughts as to how I can get Terry back on course?"

Tom dunked a biscuit into his coffee. "I don't think you give yourself enough credit. You don't need to be a guy to teach Terry that there's a moral code in relationships. The core lessons he needs to learn aren't gender specific—what applies to you applies to him."

Mac pulled a chair next to Tom's. "I wish he would see it that way and just, for a minute, listen to me."

"As a friend or as his mother?" he asked.

Mac looked out the bay window as she thought about the question. "Ever since his father left, it's been just Terry and me. And after so many years of being the disciplinarian, I was looking forward to just being friends." She sighed. "After all, he's an adult, as he reminds me every time our heads butt."

"But you will always be his mother, regardless of his age."

Mac patted Tom's arm on the table. "That sounds much easier than what it is."

~

When Tom finally arrived at Montis Inn later that morning, there was so much chaos it was evident that "the project" was well under way. A cherry picker was parked precariously with two wheels on the curb and two on the street. Extending from the crane was a double ladder that reached from the bottom of the two-man basket all the way to the roof. From the end of that ladder, another was laid on the roof that led up to the cupola. Chuck Bryson sat straddling the roof ridge. He was calling something down to another man, perhaps Mark Walker, who was on the lower ladder, perched halfway between the basket and the roof. There was nothing between him and the ground thirty-five feet below. A third man—Tom saw it was Joshua Turner—was in the cherry picker's basket. Pam Walker was standing on the porch, her neck craned with an expression of alarm on her face.

When Tom stepped out of his car, he heard Mark yell, "Bring it up higher, Josh!"

"Not while you've got a hold on the upper ladder," Joshua screamed back.

"Don't worry. It's safe," Mark called back. "Push it as high as it will go!"

Joshua shook his head and forced the lever forward, which jerked the basket up another eight feet in the air.

Suddenly, the ladder shifted sideways and began sliding off the roof. Pam screamed. In a split second, Mark turned and jumped from the moving ladder to the cherry picker basket, grabbing the safety rail just as the ladder slid off and crashed to the ground. Mark held on for dear life, dangling higher than most treetops.

"Get me down!" he yelled to Joshua, who immediately lowered the basket.

When the arm of the crane was eight feet off the ground, Mark's grip gave out and he fell.

Pam ran up to him. "Are you all right?"

Chuck called down from the cupola, "Anyone hurt?"

Joshua waved his arm. "No, he's fine. Just stay put."

With the ladder gone, Chuck was most definitely stranded on the roof. "I don't have much of a choice in the matter," he responded, although no one heard him.

After turning off the machine, Joshua jumped out of the cherry picker and ran up to Mark, who was trying to stand with Pam's assistance.

"Your plan won't work," Joshua said.

"We just need—" Mark stopped to catch his breath. "We just need to secure the ladder on the roof. It will be fine."

"Can I help?" Tom asked as he approached the group. "Chuck told me earlier this morning that you might need a hand."

"Maybe some stitches," Mark said, pulling off his glove. He had a long cut on his palm from a piece of metal that was sticking out of the basket.

Although there appeared to be a lot of blood, Tom could tell it was just a surface wound. "You'll live. Just wash it out really well when you're done. I've got some horse dressing in the truck that we can use in the meantime."

"How appropriate," Pam said sarcastically.

Mark looked up at the cupola. "You okay, Chuck?"

He gave a thumbs-up.

Tom returned and quickly disinfected and bandaged Mark's cut.

"Tom, you need to come by more often," Pam said. "You have no idea how frequently Mark could use your medical skills."

"Can I ask what you're trying to do?" Tom said.

"Mark wants to remount the Montis Abbey cross on the cupola," Joshua explained.

"Here's the plan, Tom," Mark interjected. "We're going to hoist it up on the cherry picker, lean it against the roof and then slide it up to the ridge with ropes from the other side. And then a couple of us will climb up to where Chuck is"—Mark pointed up—"and we'll just slip it into place."

Mark saw Pam close her eyes and shake her head.

"Pam worries too much," he explained.

Tom considered Mark's plan, scrutinizing the cherry picker and then the roof. "It doesn't seem that tough."

Mark's smile widened. "You're my type of man, Tom Candor."

"The cross is four hundred pounds of rusted wrought iron," Joshua said.

"No!" Tom laughed, thinking Joshua was pulling his leg. "Really?"

"At least," Pam said.

"Then you'll need at least another six men," Tom said.

Just then, the Lumby police car pulled into the inn's parking lot and Simon Dixon stepped out. Pam panicked, thinking that Simon had changed his mind about issuing her five different tickets for one motorcycle adventure. Then she saw Jimmy open the passenger door and knew that this wasn't a visit from the sheriff, but from a friend.

"We heard you might need some help," Simon said.

"Some," Mark said cheerfully, holding up his bandaged hand. "Okay, everyone follow me down to the basement."

⁂

To everyone's amazement, the first part of Mark's plan went incredibly smoothly, and within a few minutes, the century-old ornate iron cross was resting on the grass in front of the inn. Most important, there were no further mishaps.

The crew stood around the cross and looked at it in awe.

"This is amazing," Pam said as she bent down and touched the massive cross, tracing the gentle lines with her fingers. "I had forgotten how beautiful it is."

Mark pulled Joshua's coat sleeve. "This is good. He'll like this. And I even bleed and everything."

" 'He'? As in God?" Joshua asked.

"Yeah," Mark whispered. "You know, getting on His good side."

Joshua leaned toward his friend. "I don't think God will give you extra points for cutting your hand," he whispered.

Mark looked crushed. "Maybe not, but if He's having a slow day, He might give what we're doing here a second look." Then, turning to the others, he said, "Now we just have to put it on the cupola."

Everyone looked up at Chuck, who was enjoying the bird's-eye view of Woodrow Lake and the Montis orchard across Farm to Market Road.

The story of the reraising of the Montis Abbey cross would be told and retold countless times in the years to come. If nothing else, it proved the value of divine intervention. For even though the hydraulics of the cherry picker failed when the basket was in midair, and a rope snapped at the roof's ridge vent, and the cupola was all but pulled from its mooring when Mark grabbed hold as he slid down the roof, and Tom's pants were shredded beyond recognition, and the fire department had to be called to rescue Simon, for the most part, everything went as planned. As far as Montis projects went, this one was relatively uneventful. The one incontrovertible fact that Mark repeated when others questioned his tactics was that everyone survived.

THIRTY-THREE

Letters

Running behind schedule that afternoon, Dennis Beezer jogged down the steps of the Chatham Press building. He was to have met Gabrielle an hour earlier for lunch, but had been tied up with a production problem at the printers. Then Scott Stevens, his most senior town reporter, had insisted on recapping the oddities of an iron-cross debacle down at Montis Inn that he happened to have come upon when driving back from Wheatley. As Scott had been known to bend the truth in favor of writing more captivating stories, Dennis didn't believe a word of what he was saying about the raising of the Montis cross.

When Dennis arrived at The Green Chile, he placed the latest edition of *The Lumby Lines* on the back table. "Sorry I'm late," he said, kissing his wife.

One advantage to having a late lunch was that the restaurant was almost empty and Gabrielle could sit down and enjoy some of her own cuisine.

Dennis handed her a postcard. "It's from Brian," he said.

She looked at the photograph—a breathtaking aerial view of Lima, the capital of Peru. She slowly sat down as she turned it over to read her son's note.

hi folks just flew in from bolivia long meetings i think we're finally making some progress so much to do but br matthew would be pleased beautiful but a lot of poverty love you guys brian

Gabrielle sighed. She ran the tips of her fingers over his words, trying to more closely connect with her son, a continent away. Her eyes began to fill with tears.

Dennis put his arm around her shoulder. "Why are you sad?"

"I miss him," she said, turning the postcard over again. "He's so young to be so far from home."

Dennis laughed. "If anyone can fend for himself, it's our son. I think his work with Saint Cross Abbey was a godsend. If it wasn't for Brother Matthew bringing him into their philanthropic foundation, I'm convinced Brian would still be in Lumby, putting his unlimited energy and talents to bad use."

Gabrielle grinned. "He was a handful, wasn't he?"

"He was, certainly," Dennis said. He gave Gabrielle a business-sized envelope. "I also got this in the mail."

She studied it for a moment. The unopened envelope was addressed to a veterinary clinic in Bangor, Maine, and across the left side were large letters stamped in red ink: "RETURN TO SENDER Undeliverable Address," with a small image of a hand pointing to the return address in the upper left corner.

"What's this?" Gabrielle asked.

"I sent a letter to Tom Candor's last employer," Dennis began.

"Why did you do that?"

Dennis sighed loudly, readying himself for a repeat of the same conversation he had had with Gabrielle a number of times since Tom Candor came to town. "I don't fully trust him."

"I do," she interjected.

"He never answers any questions about his past. So, I thought

I'd go directly to the source and touch base with some people he worked with." Dennis took the envelope from Gabrielle. "And the letter came back unopened."

"You probably used the wrong address," she said angrily.

"That's the address Tom gave me."

Gabrielle took the envelope and tore it in half.

"Gabrielle! What are you doing? I need that."

"The mail is always getting misrouted. It was probably a simple mistake at the post office," she said.

"I don't think so," Dennis said firmly.

Gabrielle brushed her hands together as if to clear away her husband's accusations. "I don't know why you don't like him. He's been nothing but kind to us. And he's doing good work in town."

Dennis shook his head. "I know what you think, but there's something wrong. I just feel it."

Gabrielle jumped up from her seat, her voice trembling. "You get me so angry sometimes. You're just turning into one of them."

"One of who?"

"The others who don't like strangers coming to town."

"That's not true!" Dennis snapped. "I just distrust people who can't look me in the eye and answer a simple question."

"Well, he answered all of mine," Gabrielle said as she picked up a kitchen towel from the back of the chair and began to twist it between her hands.

"Did you ask him anything about his past?" Dennis asked. "Where he lived or worked?"

"No, I didn't have to. We talked about the future and what he would do here in Lumby."

"Ellen was in such a rush to leave, she may not have done any background check and just assumed he was telling the truth. We don't even know if he's a licensed vet," Dennis said, knowing how harsh that sounded.

"Ellen would never have done anything that irresponsible," Gabrielle argued.

"She was desperate to sell her business," he countered.

Just then the front door of the restaurant opened and Joshua walked in, holding Brooke's hand.

"Hi, Gabrielle. Are you still open?"

She waved to her friends. "Come in. We're about to eat ourselves, so join us. Maybe you can knock some sense into my husband."

Brooke picked up on the tension between them. "Have we come at a bad time?"

"Not at all," Dennis said. "We were just talking about Tom Candor."

"What a nice guy," Joshua said. "He was a great help to us this morning."

"See," Gabrielle said to her husband.

"Doing what?" Dennis asked.

"Mark got it in his head to remount the Montis Abbey cross on the main building at the inn," Joshua explained. "It was one of our finer moments and not one of us had to go to the hospital."

Dennis smirked. So, Scott Stevens wasn't making up the story after all.

"And Tom helped out, right?" Gabrielle asked.

Joshua nodded. "He broke his back like the rest of us and stayed until the job was done."

"I told you," Gabrielle said to Dennis.

Both Joshua and Brooke looked at Gabrielle, confused by her comment. She explained, "My husband insists that Tom is up to no good."

"That's not true," Dennis corrected her. "I'm just apprehensive. Tom has never disclosed anything about his past. I even tried to contact the last animal clinic where he worked in Maine, to no avail."

"Well, I'm going to Berkeley tomorrow with Chuck," Joshua said. "You never know—it's a large campus, but maybe one of the long-standing faculty members there may remember him."

Dennis nodded. "That would be great if you don't mind."

"Not at all," Joshua said. Turning to Gabrielle, he asked, "Do you mind if Brooke and I take a table in front?"

"Anywhere you'd like. Do you want menus?"

"Your special would be just fine," Brooke said. Sitting down at the table, she leaned forward and asked her husband, "You didn't want to eat with them?"

"No, I wanted to show you something," Joshua said, taking an envelope from his coat pocket. He opened the letter, and handed it to Brooke. "The head of Berkeley's bioengineering department wants to meet with me Thursday afternoon once the symposium ends."

Brooke was visibly surprised. "When did you get this?"

"This morning after you left for work."

She leaned back and stared at the letter. "They want to interview you for a job?"

"I asked that same question of Chuck. He said they read my dissertation and are interested enough to want to get to know me."

"But you didn't apply for a faculty position, did you?"

"Absolutely not! Chuck was talking to a few of his colleagues and mentioned some of my credentials."

Brooke's mind was racing, thinking about what would happen if Joshua were offered a faculty position. She took a deep breath. "But that would mean leaving Lumby."

Joshua laid his hand on hers. "We're not doing anything unless both of us want it," he assured her. "But I'm going to have to get a job at some point."

"But," Brooke began, trying to steady her voice, "I didn't even know you were thinking about a faculty position."

"I wasn't, and I certainly wasn't thinking about California. But, Brooke, there aren't many options in my field. It's that or research, and the thought of going into some stark, windowless lab every day for the rest of my life is so depressing. So, if Berkeley is remotely interested, I think it would be foolish to turn down their invitation to talk. If anything, it may be a good experience."

Brooke was silent for a long time. "I suppose we never really discussed what you want to do after graduate school."

Joshua looked into her eyes. "As much as I hate to admit it, we're there now, honey," he said in a soft, sad voice. "But you need to know that our marriage is the most important thing in my life, so whatever the future offers, we'll decide together."

Brooke leaned over and kissed him and then held his hand to her cheek. "But leaving Lumby? I never considered that possibility."

"Nor had I until this morning," Joshua said, carefully putting the envelope back in his pocket.

ꕤ

The following evening, Dennis was once again on his home computer, trying to uncover the facts about the town's new veterinarian. He began entering different combinations of names and words into Google—anything that might be related to Tom Candor. The significant problem with the inquiry was that the search engine was interpreting the word "Candor" as a noun, so any "Tom" who demonstrated "candor" was returned as hits.

"Tom Candor Veterinarian Bangor Maine" showed no results, nor did "Tom Candor DVM Maine."

Using the same approach he had before, Dennis entered "Tom Candor Veterinarian California" and hundreds of results were displayed. Dennis recalled from his prior searches that the results were for a famous veterinarian, Jeffrey Candor.

He was skimming through the pages, passing over those that referred to Jeffrey Candor, when one title grabbed his attention: "Candor Takes Down Shingle to Join The Park." Opening the page, Dennis read a short article that was again about Jeffrey Candor, but when he paged down, he gasped. There was a photograph of a group of men, all wearing lab coats. The tallest among them, by at least four inches, was none other than Tom Candor. Although he looked much younger, it was definitely the same man.

Dennis read the copy line below the picture: "Dr. Jack M. Thomson, Dr. Barry Douglas, Dr. Jeffrey T. Candor . . ."

Dennis's heart raced. "'T' as in 'Thomas,'" he said aloud, and quickly typed in "Dr. Jeffrey Thomas Candor DVM."

More than ten thousand entries popped up. Looking at the first, a reprint of the cover page of the *New York Times* from February 4, 1989, Dennis confirmed that Dr. Jeffrey T. Candor was, in fact, the same man now living down the street in The Granary.

Through the early hours of the morning, Dennis read a hundred articles, and came to understand who this stranger was, forming a picture of the doctor's past and what he was running from. What Dennis didn't know, since it was never mentioned in the specific articles he skimmed, was the facts related to Laura Candor's car accident. Because Jeffrey Thomas Candor refused to discuss those personal details with the media, many news reports failed to cover that side of his story.

It was four in the morning when Dennis finished. He fought the urge to storm over to the clinic and confront Tom right then and there. But he was certain that Joshua and Chuck would be returning in a few days with the same information, so he decided to wait until he could confirm what he had learned. When there were no remaining questions as to who Tom Candor was, Gabrielle and the others would have no choice but to turn their backs on the impostor.

Had Dennis made his way over to The Granary at that early hour of the morning, he would have found Mac and Tom sitting on the floor in front of a warm fireplace, deep in conversation. In another hour they would fall asleep in each other's arms.

THIRTY-FOUR

Returning

It had been a long drive from Saint Amand Abbey to the small town of Franklin. When Sister Claire approached the entrance to Saint Cross, Brother Matthew asked to be let out so he could stretch his legs and enjoy a moment of quiet before rejoining the community that he had not seen for many weeks.

The sun was just setting, and yellow and pink hues hung in the clouds just over the snowcapped mountaintops. The moon was already out and the stars were just starting to show themselves. As the van pulled away, Matthew lifted both arms and stretched his stiff back, first bending to the front and then arching backward. He inhaled deeply and was invigorated by the familiar scents of the dry air. Although there were many things he liked about Oregon, the humidity and constant drizzle that had stayed with them for most of their visit were not among them.

Matthew looked up at Saint Cross. It was an abbey of impressionable grandeur, and resembled a large church that one would come upon unexpectedly in the English countryside. The lines of the buildings were more graceful than those at Montis, complemented throughout by round arches over the doorways and windows. To the right of the main church were monastic gardens and a cloistered courtyard.

Matthew smiled, thinking how fortunate he and several other monks were to have been able to join Saint Cross when they closed their own monastery in Lumby. Although he would forever miss the Montis orchards, he was home again, and it felt wonderful.

As he began his trek up the long driveway, he buttoned his coat. Although it was still considered fall, cold air was blowing from the north, giving every indication that winter had unofficially begun.

Perhaps that was why the front lawn looked so disheveled, as if a herd of animals had been dining on the last of the fall grasses. Or, Matthew reasoned, possibly the abbey had been invaded by squirrels burying their winter bounty in the most inconvenient places. What he couldn't explain was the muddy hoofprints that he noticed on the driveway.

Matthew looked over at the pond, which had frozen over since his departure. The abundant wildlife one saw during the warmer months had migrated to more southern climates, leaving the pond and its surrounding landscape rather austere.

But all of a sudden, and only for a second, he saw a flash of pink in the brush on the far side of the pond. Assuming his eyes were playing tricks on him after the long road trip, Matthew rubbed them with his fingers. When he looked up, the pink was gone.

It was a time for the earth to replenish itself, Matthew thought. As he came upon the bend in the road, he pulled the collar up around his neck and dug his hands deep in his pockets. The wind was always harshest along this stretch of driveway.

He studied the rolling hills behind the building. The leaves having long since fallen from the trees, he could easily identify the rolling hills that the sisters were considering for purchase. Although the property wasn't marked by a stone wall or fence, Matthew had a good sense of where the boundaries ran from the various tree lines that bisected the land.

He envisioned the transformation that would take place over the coming years if the sisters planted their vineyard there; the forested countryside would be replaced by long trellises that would support hundreds of mature grapevines. What a delight to be able to watch grapes grow ripe and then harvest them each year. To walk down the rows of trimmed branches and smell the earth beneath his feet would be such a joy.

Suddenly, an animal darted past him. The movement was so unexpected and happened so quickly that Matthew almost lost his footing. Seeing only a blurred image of the animal, he assumed it was a deer. But then the creature slowed, turned around and ran back toward him, stopping abruptly ten feet in front of him. It groaned once and then spit.

Matthew jumped back to avoid being splattered.

"What in the world?" he exclaimed.

"Grab his halter," a woman's voice called out.

Matthew turned and saw a nun of Saint Amand running toward him from the direction of the kennels.

"Please," she called out.

Matthew quickly took hold of the camel just as it tried to bolt, pulling him off his feet. But he held firm to the harness and, within seconds, had the animal under control.

"Thank you so much," Sister Kristina said, running up and snapping a leash onto the metal ring on the harness. "I've got him now."

Brother Matthew was so flabbergasted, he didn't know what to say first. "A camel?" he asked in astonishment.

"Isn't he beautiful?" Kristina said, rubbing the camel's forehead. "If you'll excuse me, I need to get him back to his stall."

"Stall?" Matthew said softly, but Kristina didn't hear.

"Brother Matthew!" someone called from the abbey. Matthew saw Brother Michael waving to him from the entrance to the courtyard. He had a large roll of burlap tucked under his arm.

Matthew waved back and cut across the lawn in front of the main church while keeping an eye on Kristina and her charge until they disappeared around the corner.

"Welcome back." Brother Michael smiled. "Did you decide to walk the last mile?"

"I was so stiff from the drive that I needed to stretch my legs. Did you see that?"

Michael was focused on unrolling the canvas. "See what?"

"The camel?"

"A delightful animal, but who would have thought they spat so much?" Michael said, bending over to secure one corner of the burlap to a small stake.

"I think I'm missing the bigger picture," Matthew said.

Just then, a peacock wandered out from behind the courtyard wall and, once clear of the rose shrubs, spread its tail feathers in full glory and emitted a loud mating call.

The younger monk didn't even look up from his work of covering the shrubs in preparation for snow. "Poor fellow. He really needs a missus."

Brother Matthew's jaw dropped. "Would you mind explaining what's going on?"

"I explained in the message I left you at Saint Amand," Michael said. "These gifts keep coming and the sisters are tremendous caregivers. We would be lost without them."

"I never got any message," Matthew said bluntly.

Brother Michael finally looked up and saw Matthew staring at the bird. "So, you must be wondering about all these wild beasts," he said comically, trying to lighten the situation.

Matthew grinned, once again struck by how, as abbot, he was unaware of many of the daily, smaller events of the community he led. "One could say that."

Michael stood up and waved his arms, shooing the peacock back into the courtyard. "Well," he began slowly, "the good news is that we got extraordinary coverage of that phone interview I did a while back. In fact, it was printed in several international publications."

"That's good," Matthew said.

"Not exactly. The highlight of the article, or at least what everyone seemed to focus on, was my comment about the honor and delight we felt upon being given the gift of snow monkeys."

Matthew was confused. "But we don't even have them here. Ellen is taking care of them for us."

"Yes, I know, but I didn't say as much and the reporter never bothered to clarify that detail. It was just about the gifted snow monkeys becoming ambassadors of religious peace," Michael explained. "So to speak."

"So to speak," Matthew repeated.

"So, it was a good trip?" Michael asked, in a bold attempt to change the subject.

"And how many animals are there?" Brother Matthew asked, refusing to be deterred.

Michael thought it best that he get back to work. He leaned over and cut off a long piece of burlap from the roll. "Just a few."

Matthew exhaled in relief. "So then, just the camel and peacock?" he asked as he picked up one end of the burlap and pulled it taut while Michael held the other end. They placed the fabric over four rose shrubs—a task the brothers had performed ever since they had expanded the courtyard's garden.

"No, not exactly," Michael said. "We have a few more in the kennel and then some in the guesthouse, as well as two in another outbuilding." Michael deliberately avoided Matthew's stare by picking up the burlap roll and heading over to the Japanese maple. "So, how was your trip?" he asked again.

"For a moment, it felt good to be back," Matthew said, as if talking to himself.

"Your timing is perfect. You can imagine it's been a little crazier than normal around here."

Two sisters came bicycling up the driveway with grocery bags in their baskets.

"Because of the animals or the sisters?" Matthew asked.

"Oh, no, not the sisters! They've been lifesavers," Michael said quickly.

The sisters waved as they passed, but then what appeared to be an ostrich or an emu darted out from behind the shrubs and seemingly attacked the front wheel of one of the bikes, throwing the sister onto the grass.

Matthew rushed over to help her. "Are you all right?"

Sister Grace jumped up and brushed the leaves off her pants. "I'm fine," she said. "He does that every afternoon. I can't figure out why he gets so upset seeing us on bicycles." She uprighted the bike, mounted it and began to cycle away. "Come on," she called out to the animal, which blinked once and began trotting behind her.

Brother Matthew walked back to rejoin Michael. "And that is another of your herd?" he asked.

"Why does everyone keep calling them *my* animals?" Michael complained. "They were donations to all of us at Saint Cross."

Matthew all but ignored his protest. "It's as if Noah's ark disembarked on our front lawn. What are you going to do with them?"

Having finished covering the last of the ornamental trees, Michael rolled up the remaining burlap. "I was waiting for you to decide."

Matthew laughed softly. "This clearly is not my problem."

The low rumbling of an approaching UPS truck could be heard throughout the grounds. Both men looked toward the monastery's entrance.

"You must be tired, Matthew. Why don't you go inside?" Michael suggested, trying to rush him away. "We can straighten all of this out later."

"Perhaps you're right," Matthew said. "And if you have no objections, I'll call Ellen and ask for her opinion."

Michael was too busy watching the truck approach, and wondering what animal was inside, to hear what Matthew had said. "That sounds good," he replied.

Matthew entered the abbey and immediately made his way to the library. His first phone call was to the home of his old friend Dr. Ellen Campbell, who he was sure would rescue them from this crisis.

Before the phone rang, a recorded message played: "The number you have dialed has been permanently disconnected."

THIRTY-FIVE

Intolerance

On the second floor of the Chatham Press building, Dennis proofread the paper's galley copy.

The Lumby Lines

Lumby Forum

November 8

Can't beat these prices: Stuff for free!

More rabbits have taken up residence in my doghouse. Please help me! Call Cindy Watford. 695-0491.

Mix-breed puppies (2M, 3F) from my golden retriever and Gordy Eller's Alaskan husky.

To a good home. Barron. 5-year-old 172-lb. Great Dane. Easy to keep, eats anything and especially likes children. 925-9951.

Free earmuffs with every chain saw purchase. Brad's Hardware. Main Street.

English writing table suitable for lady with thick legs and very wide drawers. $200 firm. 695-8189.

Swap for winter months: I have one-room rustic cabin. No electricity but extension cord can be run from street post. Outhouse fully operational. Will trade for 1-bed NJ condo. Bath would be nice. Call Phil 925-3928.

Wanted: Female soul mate to come with me to New Jersey for winter. Call Phil 925-3928.

Log splitter for rent or I'll do the work myself. McNear.

Hand-carved four-poster bed and mattress. 92 years old. Perfect for antique lover. Call Joan at Lumby Realty.

Still for sale by owner. Handyman's special cabin unoccupied for 26 years but like new. 4-wheel-drive access. Bring bear repellant. 925-0021.

Honda riding lawn mower—see it in front of Wayside Tavern. Keys are lost. $150 or best offer. See Jeffrey inside at pool table.

Used tombstone. Perfect for someone named Gary Pole. Only one. $50. 925-0021.

Joshua cracked open Dennis's door and stuck his head in. "Am I interrupting?"

"No, not at all. Welcome back," he said, waving in his good friend. "When did you get back?"

"Just an hour ago," Joshua said. "And I thought we should talk."

Dennis raised his brows. "Actually, I've been expecting you."

Joshua nodded. "When Chuck and I were at Berkeley," he began, "we asked about Tom Candor and got some answers we weren't expecting. In fact, we uncovered some pretty incriminating information."

"For one, his name's not Tom Candor?" Dennis guessed.

Joshua was visibly surprised. "Yes. How did you know?"

"I finally pieced everything together a few nights ago." Dennis pulled a manila folder from his desk drawer.

"So you know that he was fired from the American Zoological Park?"

Dennis nodded and withdrew several articles that he had printed during his search. "After a botched operation, his license was revoked for negligence."

Joshua sat down in the chair in front of Dennis's desk. "Have you talked with him?"

"No, I've kept everything to myself, waiting to see if you found out anything more during your trip. Gabrielle and Jimmy think I have some kind of grudge against Tom, so I figured the more evidence I have before talking to Jimmy, the better."

"Well, now's the time to call him," Joshua said.

ൟ

Once Jimmy arrived at Dennis's office, Joshua relayed all the information he and Chuck had collected while on campus. Simultaneously, Dennis was handing Jimmy news clippings, editorials and feature articles about how their new vet had single-handedly killed an invaluable animal and damaged international relations between China and the U.S.

Far more damaging, Tom had lied to the people of Lumby since the day he had arrived in town.

Jimmy's head was spinning as he tried to sort through the information. "So, do you know where he's been since his license was revoked?" he asked.

"I was able to piece some of that together," Dennis said, "and maybe Joshua has more information. It looks like he moved to Colorado and worked for a few nonprofit animal clinics."

"As an unlicensed vet?" Jimmy asked.

"No," Dennis answered. "I have to say, to his credit, he worked as a ridiculously overqualified lab technician in one clinic and as a tech assistant in another."

"And then where did he go?" Jimmy asked.

"Once his license was reinstated, he took and passed reciprocal DVM exams in two states, so I assume he worked in Utah, then in Maine, as he told us."

Jimmy was searching for a thread of hope. "So he was honest about his last job?"

"Initially, I didn't think so," Dennis explained. "I had tried to contact his most recent employer and had no luck, so I assumed he had lied about that too. But, as it turns out, the clinic moved nine months ago, so I was using an old phone number and address."

Jimmy sat back in his chair and rubbed his forehead with his palms. "What a flippin' mess," he said in frustration. "Why didn't Ellen tell us?"

"I'm sure she didn't know," Joshua said.

Dennis added, "She wanted to sell her practice and didn't look for reasons not to. She just assumed he was who he said he was."

Joshua leaned forward. "Not to turn this into a philosophical debate, but was Ellen all that wrong? I mean, Tom never pretended to be someone other than who he is."

Dennis jumped up from his seat. "You're absolutely wrong, Josh!"

"Dennis, the man never actually lied," Joshua argued.

Dennis paced behind his desk. "Omission is the same as lying."

"I don't think so," Joshua said. "Not in all cases."

Dennis stopped and stared in disbelief at his closest friend. "You're a former monk. How can you of all people defend someone who hasn't been telling the truth?"

Jimmy interjected, "I agree with Joshua."

"Because it's an easy out, Jimmy?" Dennis asked. "Do you really think we can just forgive and forget and sweep everything under the rug? The man led us to believe something about himself that was not true."

Jimmy said, "I think you have a lower tolerance for that just because you're in the business of reporting the truth. He intentionally dodged your questions when you interviewed him, but a lot of people would have done the same."

"We should all have the same intolerance," Dennis said, "and not take the low road just because it's easier."

Joshua said, "I just know that there are past actions in all of our lives that, for whatever reason, we want to keep private."

"And if this was about his personal life, I would agree," Dennis said. "But it's about his professional credentials and his skills as a veterinarian."

Joshua shook his head in disagreement. "If he was the director at one of the most prestigious zoos in the world, you can be assured he was one of the top vets in the country. It's to our benefit that a veterinarian with such incredible experience wants to live in Lumby."

"He killed an invaluable animal!" Dennis bellowed.

"Let's calm down," Jimmy said, leaning forward. "Do either of you know if he has a valid license to practice here?"

"Yes," Dennis replied. "I called the regulating board yesterday and confirmed that he is licensed in our state for both small- and large-animal medicine."

"Well, at least he didn't lie about that," Jimmy grumbled.

"We need to talk to him," Dennis said. "He may not deserve it, but it's the right thing to do."

"What do you mean, 'deserve it'?" Joshua said.

"The front page of tomorrow's paper will tell the town the whole truth about exactly who Jeffrey Thomas Candor really is."

"Before you talk to him?" Joshua asked.

"And ask him what he did and why he did it?" Dennis asked sarcastically. "We already know. There are four thousand articles written about him, so there's really not much to talk about. Jimmy, you're the one who needs to come down on him."

"Yeah, I suppose so," Jimmy admitted reluctantly.

Dennis stacked his papers. "Are you coming with us, Joshua?"

"No," he said. "I don't agree with what you're about to do. Also, Brooke's waiting for me at home. A few other surprises came up at Berkeley that I need to discuss with her."

THIRTY-SIX

Retreat

Just down the street from the Chatham Press, Mac carried her coffee mug into Tom's living room at The Granary and sat down on the sofa. The fire that he had started before lunch was still burning strong, helping to counter the strong northerly winds blowing outside.

"It's nice that you have the afternoon off," Mac said as Tom walked into the room.

He laughed. "Let's wait and see if my clients agree with you. I love living in The Granary, but it offers no privacy."

"That's why Ellen moved out," Mac said. "She was living with her work twenty-four hours a day."

Tom sat close to Mac. "I don't mind the emergencies—those are out of anyone's control and it makes living here tremendously convenient. But it's the off-hour unscheduled visits that frustrate me. Someone comes by at eight thirty at night for flea drops, which has happened several times already."

Mac laughed. "Was your outside porch light on?"

Tom looked puzzled. "Yes, I keep it on all night. Why do you ask?"

"It's an unspoken understanding that if your porch light is on, your door is open. Try turning it off when you're done for the day."

"And what about emergencies? They'll need the light to walk up the front steps."

"Ellen had me install night-lights that are motion activated along the soffit of the old barn."

"I didn't know," Tom said.

"Unless you saw them come on, you probably wouldn't because Terry hard-wired them with no switch," Mac explained.

"Speaking of your son," Tom said, "how is that going?"

Mac leaned her head on his shoulder. "Not well. We had a long wait at the lumberyard, so I grabbed the chance to talk about his relationships. It's as if he's deliberately working his way down the list of every young lady in the county and doesn't see a problem with it. Do you have any other suggestions?"

Tom took a deep breath. "I think he needs to stand on his own two feet. He's not feeling the consequences of his behavior, because he can fall back on his relationship with you, which is safe and non-judgmental."

Mac winced from the sting of the truth but remained silent.

"Mac," he said, "I don't know much about parenting, but by not objecting to what he's doing, you're basically saying it's okay."

"I never told him that I approved of how he treated his girlfriends," she protested.

"But you never told him you didn't approve."

Mac buried herself deeper in the sofa. "He's an adult now. He needs me more as a friend than a mother."

"Hogwash," Tom said. "He has lots of friends—in fact, it seems he may have too many for his own good right now. What he needs is your guidance, to know what you approve of and what you don't. Once he starts understanding the damage he's doing, he'll straighten up."

"So, do I just kick him out of the house?" Mac asked sarcastically.

"Tomorrow or sooner," Tom said. "But only after you let him know how you feel about his one-night stands."

Mac couldn't help but come to Terry's defense. "He's not a bad kid."

"I never said he was," Tom replied. "In fact, I think he's a great kid and I also think you're a great mother. He's certainly much more mature than I was at his age. He's just struggling to find out who he is and what a romantic relationship should entail."

Mac looked down at her coffee. "I'll talk to him tonight."

Tom put his arm around her and drew her close, kissing her on the head. "I know it can't be easy."

"It's not," Mac admitted. "I don't know if he still needs me."

Tom smiled. "For guidance, yes, although he doesn't think so. He needs someone to give him a compass so he knows what direction to head in," he added.

Mac took his hand in hers. "When we were talking, Terry asked about us. I had a hard time explaining—I felt a little hypocritical."

Tom was surprised. "Why?"

"I don't know," she replied, shaking her head in confusion. "Maybe because everything is moving so fast between us."

"You know how I feel," Tom said, placing his hand on the back of her neck. "I have never connected with anyone as deeply as I have with you, and that includes my first wife. You are everything that I admire."

Mac rested her arm across his chest. "And I feel the same, but you're just beginning a new chapter. Wouldn't it make sense to keep your life as uncomplicated as possible right now?"

"Are you saying you're complicated?"

Mac tenderly slapped his leg. "You know what I mean. Any new relationship is complicated, especially in Lumby. Right now you're a very important stranger in a lot of people's lives."

"That doesn't sound too friendly," Tom said.

"It's only natural," she said, coming to the defense of the town she loved. "Ellen touched so many lives personally and professionally, the residents want to see if you'll do the same."

Tom leaned back against the sofa cushion. "I'm not Ellen."

"No, but the comparison will be made."

Tom didn't reply.

"You're an extraordinarily good man and a talented veterinarian. They just need time to see that. If you let them know who you are, they can't help but fall in love with you," she said, moving closer. Mac put her arms around his shoulders and kissed him passionately. "I know I have."

Tom and Mac were still stretched out on the sofa when Jimmy opened the front door, triggering a buzzer that rang throughout the house. Tom immediately jumped up. "I'll be back in a minute," he said, leaning over and kissing Mac.

In the lobby, Tom saw Jimmy and Dennis standing by the reception counter. "Hello, gentlemen," he said. "My guess is that you're here to pick up the leftovers from the shingle party."

"No, Tom," Jimmy said. "We're here on business."

Tom looked confused. "Do you have a sick animal?"

Just then Mac walked in from the back hall.

"We need to talk to you in private," Jimmy added cordially.

"Sure, come into my office." Turning to Mac, Tom said, "I'm sorry. I'll call you later."

Jimmy waited until Mac closed the front door behind her before he followed Tom into his office. Just as Jimmy was sitting down, a monkey dashed across the floor and climbed up his leg.

"Oh!" he cried out, shaking his foot. "Get him off me!"

Tom picked up the snow monkey with the same tenderness he would use to pick up a child. "Come on, boy, let's go in back."

Once Tom was out of the room, Jimmy whispered, "That thing could have permanently harmed me."

Dennis shook his head. "Only if it had rabies," he said, taking the other seat in front of the desk.

"Well, maybe he was foaming at the mouth."

"Jimmy, take a deep breath," Dennis advised.

Jimmy looked over at his friend. "I should be telling you the same thing. Remember, we agreed to hear his side of the—"

Tom walked into the room, smiling. "So what can I do for you?" he asked, taking a seat behind his desk.

Dennis stared at Tom. "We know everything," he said as calmly as possible.

That stinging accusation was followed by several long seconds of silence.

Tom looked at each man. "And?"

Jimmy took the deep breath that Dennis had advised earlier. "We wanted to talk with you about your past. To work with you on this problem."

"There's no problem here," Tom corrected him.

Jimmy ignored the interruption. "Our only concern is for the town residents and your abilities to care for their animals."

Tom nodded. "All right. But the two of you can't determine my veterinary abilities—that's totally up to the state board, and it has licensed me for both large and small animals."

"That's not what we're talking about," Dennis said as mildly as possible.

"But that's exactly what Jimmy just said is at issue: am I or am I not qualified to care for the animals that are brought to me? And the answer is, I am. In fact, I am in every state in which I took the exam." Tom pushed his chair away from the desk, as if he were about to stand.

"Okay, wait," said Jimmy. "There's something else."

Tom crossed his arms over his chest. "Which is?"

"You lied to us," Dennis blurted out.

"I *never* lied to you," Tom said in a louder voice. "I never falsely answered a question that was asked of me."

"You didn't disclose who you were," Dennis countered.

"My name is Thomas Candor."

"No," Jimmy said, slapping his hand on the desk. "Your name is Jeffrey Candor. And the last fifteen years of your career have been a mystery."

"Obviously not if, as Dennis said, you 'know everything.' " Angry sarcasm dripped from Tom's words.

"We wanted to hear your side of the story," Jimmy said, trying to leave a door open.

Tom smirked. "Oh, did you really? Well, my version is the same that you probably read in twenty different newspapers the day after the accident at The Park."

"You call it an accident?" Dennis said. "You were found guilty of negligence!"

"I was, and my license was revoked for seven years. But I'm sure you know that as well."

Dennis became furious with Tom's lack of contrition. "So, you're not denying anything?"

That question, which had been posed to Tom endless times during the zoo's investigation, was one he knew to stay clear of. Regardless of the answer, his words would be misconstrued and twisted, making him sound like a sniveling, self-absorbed, irresponsible victim.

Tom glared at Dennis.

"Since you're so sure you have all the facts, I'm not answering that."

Dennis jumped to his feet. "You won't answer *any* question, will you?"

Jimmy stood up, spreading out his arms, as if to keep the two men separated. "Wait a minute. There's got to be a way to resolve this."

Dennis stood straight. "There is, Jimmy. The newspaper is running a full exposé on Jeffrey Candor tomorrow morning."

"You have no right doing that!" Tom yelled. "You don't know—"

"I have all the right I need." Dennis was livid. "You were covered in every major paper in the world for over a week," he said. "It took me less than an hour to sift through the facts. So, yes, I have the whole story."

"And you won't give me the benefit of the doubt? And you actually think I'm a threat to your perfect little town."

This time it was Jimmy who exploded. "You must be kidding!" His face reddened with anger. “These folks deserve someone who didn’t kill an animal and then lie about it for the next fifteen years.”

“So what do you men want, Jimmy?” Tom asked. “You want to run me out of town?”

“Take down the shingle,” Jimmy retorted. “You’re fired!”

Tom couldn’t believe it. He didn’t know whether to laugh or shout. “You’ve got to be kidding. This is a private practice. You can’t fire me.”

“Maybe not,” Dennis jumped in, “but we can make damn sure that no one will ever step foot in your clinic again.”

Tom shook his head. If only Mac were here, she would see firsthand why he had refused to talk about his past. It was clear from Dennis’s and Jimmy’s behavior that they weren’t interested in hearing the truth. Further, the town would draw its own conclusion based solely on whatever slant Dennis put on the story.

“Then there’s nothing else to be said,” Tom stated in a deep, loud voice. He stood up and promptly left his office.

It was such an unexpected and abrupt ending to the confrontation that, for a moment, Jimmy and Dennis stood there awkwardly, wondering what had just happened.

Tom went directly upstairs, where he paced the floor several times before sitting down on the window seat that overlooked Main Street. From that vantage point, he watched Jimmy and Dennis leave The Granary. They paused when they reached the sidewalk and talked for several minutes before parting ways. Dennis headed up Main and Jimmy crossed and walked into Jimmy D’s without looking back.

Tom sat there for several hours, watching the daily panorama of the town below him. He consoled himself with the thought that he had tried his best. And although it didn’t work out as he had hoped, he had had a few amazing weeks in Lumby, which he would always cherish.

But then there was Mac.

Suddenly remembering that word about his past was about to get out, Tom left The Granary through the back door, slipped behind the wheel of his truck and drove directly to Mac's house. She needed to be warned that she had sided with the enemy.

She came to the door as soon as she heard Tom's vehicle pull up. "Is everything all right?" she asked, stepping out onto the stoop.

"No," he said, taking her hand. "Can we talk inside?"

When he walked in, he saw Terry on the sofa. The boy was obviously upset.

"Hey, Dr. Candor," Terry said, without making eye contact.

"Terry," Tom said, nodding. Then, turning to Mac, he asked, "Do you want me to come back?"

"No, Terry and I just finished talking," she said, and looked over at her son. "Terry, I told Joan Stokes you would come by and talk about some rooms she has for rent. Why don't you give her a call and see what's available?"

Terry pulled on his coat. "You know, paying for rent and food is really going to burn up most of my salary."

"Yes, but both of us know it's time," Mac said.

"Welcome to the real world," Tom said, placing a hand on Terry's shoulder as he headed for the front door.

When the door shut, Tom saw Mac wince and immediately went to put his arms around her, wanting to offer his support.

She rested her head on his chest. "That was so hard," she said. "He now knows exactly how I feel. And you were right: he was surprised when I told him that I adamantly disapprove of his behavior, no ifs, ands or buts."

"Good for you," he said, kissing her forehead.

"And we agreed that he needs to own up to the responsibilities of being an adult if he's going to enjoy the benefits."

"You did the right thing," Tom said softly. "He'll be all right."

"I know. It's just so hard letting him go." Mac took Tom's hand and led him into the kitchen. "So, what did Jimmy and Dennis want?"

"To tell me they know about my past. Dennis is running a story in his paper," he said.

Mac appeared stricken. "When?"

Tom cringed. "Tomorrow morning."

Mac grabbed his arm. "Did you explain?" she asked. "Did you tell them about your wife's accident?"

"No, I won't blame my wife for what happened," he said.

"But, Tom, the two accidents were related. You wouldn't be placing blame, just explaining the facts."

"Laura told me never to discuss her accident as part of what happened that day—that the outcome was my doing. And she was right—the few times reporters uncovered her accident, it turned into a sordid, disgusting story." He rubbed his brow in frustration. "And it wouldn't have mattered anyway. Their minds were made up before they even entered the clinic."

"But you could change that," she said. "Tell them exactly what happened."

Tom shook his head and pulled his arm away. "No. I don't want to have to prove I'm a good guy to everyone I meet."

"When people are only given half the story, the only conclusion they can draw is that you were negligent."

"Which I was!" Tom confessed. "And I'm not going to blame that on my wife. I did that once and it was one of the biggest mistakes of my life. Never again."

"But—" Mac began, and then immediately fell silent, deciding to give them both a minute to calm down. "Did Jimmy and Dennis say anything else?"

Tom looked into Mac's eyes. "Yes, Jimmy fired me, literally. They told me to look somewhere else to hang my shingle."

Mac flushed with anger. "But that's not for them to decide."

"No, but the town will draw the same conclusion tomorrow, and then it will be over."

THIRTY-SEVEN

Concealing

"If Pam saw you up there, she'd hit the roof," Joshua told Mark as he watched him trying to regain his balance on top of the tractor's front bucket, which was raised as high as it was capable of going. After several hours of work during the previous two days, they were almost finished erecting the aviary panels that Mark had mistakenly purchased from the U.S. military.

Teetering twelve feet in the air, Mark took a fleeting look over his shoulder at the inn to make sure his wife wasn't in view. "I think she's in the kitchen, talking to André."

Joshua looked nervously up from the driver's seat of the Kubota tractor. "Just put in the last bolt so you can get down from there."

"You know," Mark commented as he glanced toward Wheatley, "there's a great view of Woodrow Lake up here. Just as nice as when we were working on top of the roof of the large barn."

"And that gave me nightmares for days," Joshua said under his breath.

"Okay," Mark said after tightening the last bolt, "bring me down."

Joshua carefully maneuvered the levers, allowing the front bucket to descend slowly. Mark jumped off before it reached the ground and looked at what they had constructed. “Quite the cage,” he said proudly, rattling the chain-link panels.

Joshua studied the massive enclosure. He guessed it to be about twenty-five feet wide, forty feet long and fourteen feet high. They had positioned it close to the new barn so as to allow the convenient movement of animals between the two. With both structures running parallel to each other and the barn being significantly larger, the wire enclosure was surprisingly unobtrusive.

Looking at the empty barn and then at the immense animal pen, Joshua couldn’t help but ask, “What in the world are you going to do with it?”

“I don’t know,” Mark replied, shrugging his shoulders. “But after all the money I paid for it, Pam was getting pretty upset that the panels were just sitting in the barn. For the life of me, I thought it said ‘apiary,’ like in behives.”

Joshua chuckled. “An understandable mistake.”

“Maybe I’ll get a couple of llamas—like the ones we saw on our way to Harrison,” Mark said.

Joshua laughed. “You’ve been talking about that for as long as I’ve known you. With all the open stalls in the barn and now this apiary, you could get an entire herd and you’d still have space left over.”

“It’s a matter of getting Pam’s . . .”

“Approval?” Joshua offered.

Mark bobbed his head. “More like buy-in.”

“You know,” Joshua said, “the problem with our wives is that they are always so darn right.”

Mark grinned. “And they keep us out of trouble.”

“That they do,” Joshua agreed.

“Speaking of staying out of trouble,” Mark said, “can you give me a lift up to Dakin’s Garage? Jerry called me yesterday and said work on the truck is done.”

“You don’t want to go with Pam?”

“No, sirree. I don’t think she should be around when he hands me the bill.”

~

On the drive up to Dakin's Garage, just east of Lumby, Joshua rolled down his window and looked out across Mill Valley. Most of the spectacular autumn foliage had browned and fallen, but the dancing leaves of a few late-turning aspens still showed orange and red.

"They really don't have a fall out there," Joshua said softly, recalling his earlier conversation with Brooke.

"Out where?" Mark asked.

"Sorry," Joshua said. "I was thinking about California. Everything was so different—the landscape, the trees, even the grass."

"Yeah, it's green while ours is covered with three feet of snow." Mark laughed. "How was your trip to Berkeley? You never said."

Joshua turned off the radio. "I'm not sure. The symposium was outstanding—it included some of the best genetic physicists from around the world."

"It's still weird to think that you're in that field, having been a monk and all."

Joshua smiled. "Yeah, looking back, I guess it was an odd choice. But I thought I could make a small contribution back to the world, and never thought of it as going against the will of God." He glanced out at the landscape. "There are so many areas where genomic biology can help if it's being used with nature instead of against it. It could help crops tolerate greater cold or fight off an emerging blight."

Mark cracked his window open. "So, it was a good trip?"

"Not exactly," Joshua said. "Chuck had told several of the faculty that I was to attend the seminar, so they lined up a series of discussions."

"What kind of discussions?" Mark asked.

"That's a good question. After three meetings, it finally dawned on me that they were preliminary job interviews."

Mark almost jumped out of his seat. "You're going to teach there? You're moving?"

"No!" Joshua exclaimed. "No, I'm not." He paused for a moment. "Well, I don't think so."

"I hear a 'but' coming," Mark said.

Joshua shifted in his seat, as if to escape the comment. "But . . . ," he began slowly, "there was enough interest on their side and there are ample openings in the department that . . ." He paused again. "There's a very good chance I could join their faculty next term if I wanted to."

Mark glared at his closest friend. "Why would you want to leave Lumby?"

"I don't!" Joshua said, banging his hands on the steering wheel in frustration. "I never planned to. But I need a job. I need to begin this great career that I've been working toward for the last four years. And to be on the faculty at such a prestigious university would be a tremendous honor."

Mark tried not to sulk. "I didn't know you wanted to teach."

"I don't necessarily, but there are only two areas in my field that are viable: research and teaching. And the thought of going into a lab day in and day out, working on some assigned biological-genome project that might take ten years to unravel, is disheartening. And I know I wouldn't fit into a corporate environment. So that leaves teaching, where I could possibly do some private research that I find interesting. And if Berkeley can offer that, I need to seriously consider it."

"Are you trying to convince me or yourself?"

Joshua shot a glare at his friend. "And the money is great. Brooke wouldn't have to work if she didn't want to."

"But she loves being an architect," Mark countered.

"She supported us for the last four years. It's my turn to give her some options. She's worked almost every day of her life, and I'd like to tell her she can take some time off if she wants and still have a good quality of life."

"Oh." Mark didn't know what to say.

Joshua looked over at him and grinned. "Well, this is a first—you're speechless."

Mark kept his gaze on his friend. "What does Brooke think about Berkeley?"

Joshua cringed. "She doesn't know how serious they are about my candidacy for a faculty position."

"But she has some idea?"

"Yes, we talked about it, and I think she hates it," Joshua admitted. "She doesn't want to leave Lumby. She has no family except you two and she's developed a lot of good friendships here. But she said she would move if it was important to me."

"That's Brooke for you," Mark said. "For the life of me, I don't know why she's head over heels for you."

Joshua smiled warmly. "Me either. Every day I feel so fortunate to be married to her that I find myself considering her preferences more than my own."

"I think that's what a good marriage is," Mark replied.

"Except when it comes to buying old, beat-up cars with no engines," Joshua teased as he turned right onto a single-lane road and then left into Dakin's Garage.

Mark immediately spotted his truck parked out front. "There it is!"

Joshua looked at the row of old cars and trucks. "Which one?"

"That light green Ford pickup," he answered, pointing. "It's a nineteen thirty-four Ford Flathead Model Forty-six."

"Like you know what that means," Joshua teased.

"I know, but it sounds so cool," Mark said just as he was jumping out of the car.

Jerry Dakin walked out of the center bay of his garage, rubbing his hands on a greasy towel. "How does it look?" he asked Mark, who was already circling the vehicle.

"Exactly the same," Mark said, clearly disappointed.

"Then I did my job. The body was in great shape. Didn't want to touch it. Here's the key and the bill," Jerry said, handing Mark a small manila envelope.

Mark opened up the bill and inhaled sharply as his eyes widened in alarm. "This can't be right. It says eight thousand two hundred dollars."

"Yeah, that's right. It should be nine thousand flat, but I took off eight hundred from my standard labor rate. It was great working on the truck."

Joshua walked up beside Mark and glanced at the bill. "You're kidding."

Mark grabbed Joshua's arm. "Okay, here's the deal," he said. "I won't tell Brooke about Berkeley if you don't tell Pam about this bill. I told her it would cost about a thousand dollars."

Jerry looked at Mark as if he were a lunatic. "For a new engine?"

"Well, I didn't know," Mark said.

"When you dropped it off, I said it would be under ten thousand," Jerry reminded him.

"I thought you were joking," Mark said. "Can I give you a credit card?"

Jerry took the bill and wrote "Paid In Full" across the bottom. "I still have your number on file from the motorcycle overhaul. I'll run it through tonight."

"Thanks," Mark said glumly.

"So, how are you going to hide it from Pam if you're putting it on your Visa?" Joshua asked.

"With any luck, she'll fall in love with the truck before we get our next bill," Mark explained.

Jerry slapped Mark on the back. "You wait until you hear that engine purr and you'll know it was all worth it."

Jerry was absolutely correct. Ten minutes later, Mark was driving down Farm to Market Road in a truck that sounded and felt brand-new, but it was a Flathead—the envy of all pickups in 1934. He hoped Pam would feel the same.

When he pulled into Montis, Mark beeped the high-pitched horn that was reminiscent of bygone years. By the time Pam came out of the house, three of the inn's guests were already admiring the truck.

"Want to go for a ride, honey?" Mark said, beaming.

She stood in front of the Flathead, examining its headlights and hood. "It's gorgeous. How far can it go?"

"With a brand-new engine, it could go cross-country ten times and back," Mark assured her.

After he slid over to the passenger side, Pam jumped in and adjusted the old but still working seat belt around her waist.

"How about going down to the Fork River?" she suggested, turning the old-fashioned ignition key.

"That sounds really good," he said.

"Wow," Pam murmured as she pulled the truck onto the road. "This is almost as good as Yolk."

As they approached the north end of Woodrow Lake, Mark pointed to an open field on their left, where a moose was grazing. "There's Howard," he said loud enough to be heard over the noise. "It's not as airtight as our cars today, is it?"

Pam laughed. "I hope I'm in such good shape when I'm seventy years old." She pulled off the road just after crossing over the Fork River bridge.

"To the cove?" Mark asked.

"To the cove," she confirmed.

Gunther Cove, hidden from view of those driving on Farm to Market as well as those on the water, was their secret escape. Mark and Pam had found it while vacationing their first summer in the area, and they had continued to return on a regular basis. But they had not hiked the large boulders down to the cove since much earlier that summer.

As they parked the truck and made their way over the rough terrain, traversing the steep embankment, both found the trek comfortably familiar. Once the cove came into view, Pam saw that it hadn't changed at all—it remained a pristine stretch of white sand no more than a few hundred feet long and thirty feet wide.

"Do you remember the first time we came here?" Pam asked over her shoulder.

Mark kept his eyes on the rocks they were stepping over. "Sure, it was our first real vacation. We checked into Cedar Grove Inn that morning and went exploring that afternoon. And we came back every Sunday morning when we were in the area—to our private church."

Pam made her way over the last boulder and stepped onto the smooth sand. "There are no more duck prints," she commented, pointing where they'd once found animal tracks in the sand.

Mark sat down on a large, flat rock that jutted out over the water. "They've all flown south."

Pam sat next to Mark and put her arm through his. She rested her head on his shoulder. "I love the truck," she said softly.

"Me too. It's perfect for Montis."

"I'm sorry I doubted you," she said, kissing his cheek. "How much did it end up costing?"

Mark winced instead of replying.

Pam looked at her husband. "Mark?"

"Honey," he said, taking her hand and kissing it, "let's not ruin the afternoon."

Pam frowned. "More than a thousand dollars?" she asked.

Mark stalled. "Yeah," he finally said. "But we really don't want to talk about that right now. We have lots of guests and a booming restaurant business—we can afford the truck, I assure you."

"But—"

"Pam, drop it," Mark said firmly. "You really need to learn how to let go sometimes."

Pam knew Mark was right and bit her lip until the sense of urgency to control the situation passed. She struggled to think of something else to talk about. She finally said, "We got a letter from Christian Copeland this morning. He invited us out to his vineyard."

Mark put his arm around Pam's shoulder. "Do you want to take a vacation?"

She was still thinking about the truck bill. "Not really. Certainly not now."

"How about next summer?" Mark asked.

"I was thinking about that the other day," she said, finally becoming interested in the conversation. "Next summer is our twenty-fifth anniversary. I was thinking about having a family reunion. Invite everyone here."

"What a great idea," Mark said, immediately considering the possibilities. "Why don't we do it during the county fair?"

"The one in Wheatley?"

"No, next year it will be in Lumby."

"We can close the inn and restaurant for a week," Pam said, planning ahead.

Mark slid his arm lower, stopping at her waist. "Your customers will knock down the dining room doors."

Pam sighed loudly. "Because of André's cooking, not mine," she said sullenly.

"But this is what we wanted. If it wasn't for André, you'd be in the kitchen right now, preparing dinner for ten or twelve."

"Actually, the dining room is filled tonight from five thirty until closing."

Mark raised his brows. "Really?"

"Another review came out in *Town and Country*."

"Well, that's wonderful. Congratulations, honey."

"You should congratulate André," she said.

"He seems like a nice enough guy," Mark said, finding himself once again coming to André's defense. "And you know you can trust him in the kitchen."

"He's just too independent," Pam blurted out. "We didn't even know he had moved into the cottage until after the fact."

"But you offered it to him," he reminded her.

"I know," she said. "But he's very secretive, always doing things his way."

"And not yours," Mark teased. "But don't you want someone like that—someone quiet and behind the scenes?"

"Not so much so that I don't even know what he's doing," she complained.

Pam suddenly stood up, wanting to change the circumstances of André taking over her world.

All Mark could do was repeat what he had told her a dozen times. "He's a professional chef, honey. He knows what he needs to do and does it."

"I hope so," Pam said as she turned and started the hike up the rocky embankment.

The Lumby Lines

Sheriff's Complaints

BY SHERIFF SIMON DIXON November 11

6:58 a.m. Jogger reported that bear has two hunters up a tree in woods off Deer Run Loop.

7:11 a.m. Car vs rabbits on Hunts Mill Road. Road-kill expected but not counted as of yet. Caller says, "They are heading north from the Feed Store."

7:19 a.m. NW Builders truck vs bear on Loggers Road. Truck dodged bear but hit a parked car.

1:00 p.m. Sara called. Quilters picnic is canceled because of dead skunk in area.

3:32 p.m. Caller reported a grease fire at Trump's Chicken Barbecue stand. LPD displaced.

4:46 p.m. Resident called. Three hikers have not returned from day outing to Eagle Summit. EMS notified.

5:21 p.m. Moose has one hunter up tree close to MM7 on Farm to Market Road. Caller said Moose looked like Howard.

7:55 p.m. Disturbance reported at library on second floor caused by Scrabble Club. Dictionary thrown out window hit pedestrian on shoulder.

8:08 p.m. Moose vs. SUV at MM7 on Farm to Market Road. No injuries.

THIRTY-EIGHT

Departed

For Tom Candor, the past two days had been the hardest in his life since nineteen eighty-nine. The town that had so quickly embraced him had now turned its back on him, with no hope of reconciliation or forgiveness. The seventeen appointments he had scheduled for the day were either no-shows or curt phone cancellations. It was obvious the townsfolk would not accept a man who had indirectly lied to them about his past.

Tom was truly crushed but refused to show his feelings.

After transporting the boarded animals down to a clinic in Wheatley, Tom turned off all the lights in the clinic and brought his bags to the car. Returning one last time to the front porch, he hung the "Closed" sign in the window, locked the door and took down the shingle that had recently been hung with such fanfare. He wiped the front of the plaque with his coat sleeve before turning his back on The Granary.

As Tom drove slowly down Main Street, those who glanced his way quickly looked elsewhere. When one girl pointed in his direction, her mother took her by the arm and headed in the opposite direction. It was clear to all that Jeffrey Thomas Candor was doing what they wanted: he was leaving town.

But instead of turning right onto Farm to Market Road, which would have been the most direct route out of Lumby, Tom drove past the Chatham Press to Mac's home. He ran up the front steps and rang the bell.

Mac opened the door with a smile.

"Come with me," he said urgently.

She was startled by his abruptness. "What are you talking about?"

"Come with me to California," he said. "Today."

Confused, Mac shook her head, sending her red hair in all directions. Over Tom's shoulder, she saw two neighbors staring at them. She grabbed Tom's arm and pulled him inside. "You're leaving?"

"I thought about it all night and there is no alternative for me. I have to leave Lumby just as much as I have to return to California. Everything happened there, and I feel I need to go back to the beginning, to where my life was turned upside down, and put all of these emotions and lies behind me once and for all."

"The town residents will come around," Mac said, only half believing it herself.

"No, they won't," he countered. "And they shouldn't. I got exactly what I deserved."

Mac clutched his hands. "If you would just tell the whole story—"

"So they can take pity on me?" Tom asked. "So they can find excuses and justifications for what happened back then? Don't you see? My guilt would always be there, lurking in the backs of their minds. And do you think they would ever believe me? I don't think so."

"If you give them a chance," Mac pleaded.

"No," Tom said, shaking his head. "It's time for me to quietly leave."

"Why California?" Mac asked.

Tom sat down on a lower rung of the staircase and rested his arms on his knees, clasping his hands together. "I ran as far as I could, to

Maine and then to Lumby, and the past still followed me here. I need to go back and face what happened and get rid of all the demons that have been with me since that horrible night."

Although Mac didn't want Tom to leave, she saw how much pain he was in and knew that his only chance for healing and going forward would require going back to The Park and reopening the old wounds. Perhaps only then would he find the peace of mind he deserved.

Mac sat down next to him and put an arm through his. "I'll miss you."

"But that's what I said." Tom took her hand and held it tightly. "Come with me."

Mac gave the idea only a moment of consideration before practicality set in. "I can't just pack a bag and go to California."

"Why not?" Tom challenged.

"My son, for one thing," she began. "He's going to be moving out. He'll need help."

"He needs to be on his own to grow up," Tom said candidly.

"All right, there's also my job."

"You've been working at The Granary for a month and still have at least another week to go," Tom said. "I'll make you a deal: come with me for the days that you were going to be at the clinic. We can spend a week together, and at any point, if you want to return to Lumby, I'll buy you a plane ticket home."

Mac struggled to find yet another reason not to run upstairs and pack her bags.

He leaned over and kissed her, and she kissed him back passionately. "Why are you fighting this?" he asked. He kissed her again, and Mac abruptly pulled away.

"That's exactly why," she said, jumping up. "The more time I spend with you, the more devastated I'm going to be when it comes to an end."

"It doesn't have to end."

"It does if you're leaving Lumby."

He gently pulled her next to him, wrapping both arms around her hips so she wouldn't bolt again. "Then just consider it a long-awaited vacation. California is wonderful at this time of year. There are vineyards to explore—"

"And ghosts to face," she interrupted.

"Yes, and I want you by my side when I do that," Tom implored. "One week, that's all I ask."

ↀ

"He only asked for one week," Mac told Pam as the two women sat in the kitchen at Montis Inn an hour later.

"It's obvious you're crazy about Tom," Pam said. "I agree it's been a whirlwind romance, but what harm could a short vacation do either of you?"

"My thoughts exactly . . . kind of," Mac said, spreading her hands on the table.

Pam crunched her brows. "Are you trying to convince me or yourself?"

Mac began nervously tapping her palms against the wood. "Aargh," she groaned in exasperation.

"Is there something I don't know?"

How true that statement was! "Going away with him isn't black-and-white. There are plenty of reasons to say thanks, but no, thanks."

"Such as?" Pam asked.

Mac sat up straight, as if getting ready to defend herself. "Okay," she began. "For one thing, the closer we get, the more hurt I'd be when he leaves Lumby."

Pam was confused. "Why on earth would he ever leave Lumby? He just bought a business on Main Street and it's obvious he wants to put down roots."

Mac was totally unprepared to tell Pam about what had transpired in town and Tom's decision to leave, so she backpedaled. "But if it doesn't work out for him here, then where would I be?"

"If you don't go with him," Pam deduced, "you'll be equally miserable without the memory of a great vacation together."

Mac glared at her friend. "You're not making this any easier." She thought for a moment. "All right, how about Terry?"

Pam tried to suppress her laughter. "I'm quite sure the boy will survive. In fact, he'd probably benefit from having to stand on his own two feet for a while."

Mac grimaced. "You sound like Tom."

"Sorry." Pam shrugged. "Sometimes it's easier to see things from the outside looking in."

"Okay, and what about my work?" Mac shot out one last excuse.

"It's *your* business!" Pam countered. "Mac, what's going on?"

Mac took in a deep breath and exhaled loudly, falling against the back of the chair. "I suppose I'm scared. Tom's the first man in my life I really want to be with. And that thought is almost paralyzing because I wonder what exactly I'll have to give up to be with him."

"Why do you have to give up anything?" Pam asked.

"Because I've waited my entire life for something like this, and I know it doesn't happen this easily. A perfect man doesn't just walk into my life without there being a price to pay. But," she said, looking at Pam, "I know in my heart he's the only one for me, even though we've known each other for a short time."

"Does he feel the same?"

"I'm sure he does," she said, almost glowing.

"There you have it. You both love each other, so let your heart rule for a change." Pam stood and pushed her chair under the table. "You need to go home, pack a bag and go to California with a great guy and have a wonderful time."

Mac jumped up, smiling from ear to ear. "You're absolutely right." She hugged Pam. "What would I ever do without a friend like you? I'll call you from California."

The trip out to San Francisco was a fantasy for Mackenzie, who infrequently left Lumby and rarely crossed the boundary of her own state. The drive through the Rockies was breathtaking, as were the miles between the mountains and the Pacific Ocean. Every few hours they would find an exit leading to a country road. There, they pulled the car over, took out their *Sibley Bird Guide* along with two pairs of binoculars and tried to identify local species. For both of them, it was a bird-watchers' paradise repeated over and over.

Although it required an indirect route, Tom wanted Mac to see the Oregon coastline, so first they headed to Portland. From Astoria, located a mile inside the Oregon state line on the north, they followed Route 101 to Harbor, a few miles from the California state line. For those four hundred or so miles, Mac never took her eyes off the cliffs, the rocky shoreline and the infinite ocean. Although it was a route that Tom had taken many times in his youth, he was experiencing it for the first time through Mac's eyes.

Once over the border, they traveled south for another two hours along the California coast, stopping at Redwood National Park. Mac had never imagined the enormity of the trees and the surrounding landscape. They were images that would stay with her for years to come. Those first two days were the happiest in her life.

Just before Arcata, Tom turned east onto Route 299 and headed toward his past, a hundred thirty miles ahead of them in the city of Redding. The scenery was different from anything Mac had ever seen. The terrain was much more barren with fewer hardwood trees. Foothills were thinly covered with scrub brush and small pines, while the distant mountains lacked any vegetation at all. The landscape was austere but beautiful.

On the outskirts of Redding, Tom took several back roads, confident of his destination. Mac noticed a small sign as he turned into a driveway: "Keller Inn." Initially hidden from view by a thick row of native shrubs, the charming two-story California-style home became visible once they passed through the gates. The exterior walls were stucco that had been painted soft beige, and the roof, made of red Mexican tiles, had a large overhang.

"Amazing how different the architecture is here," Mac commented. "Most of the houses seem to be made of stucco."

"Everything is designed for the long, hot summers," Tom explained, as he parked the car. "High ceilings and open verandas."

He carried both bags into the front hall. After waiting a moment, they rang the bell on the counter.

"Coming," a soprano voice called from the second floor. While they waited, Mac warmed herself at the small fire burning in the fireplace.

A woman well into her seventies appeared at the top of the landing and made her way slowly down the staircase, taking one step at a time.

"I know the fire might seem a bit odd," she said, "but it can get quite cool here in the evenings."

"I'm sure it can. And your artwork is lovely," Mac said as she meandered around the living room, appreciating both the paintings and the sculptures on display.

"All local artists," the innkeeper said proudly. "If there is anything in particular you like, I can direct you to that artist's studio."

"Thank you," Mac said. "Perhaps tomorrow."

When the woman reached the bottom tread, she let go of the railing. "I'm Eileen Keller," she said. "How can I help you?"

"We have reservations for a room," Tom said, taking out his wallet.

"Under what name?" Eileen asked as she went behind the registration desk.

"Tom Candor."

Now standing in front of him, the woman studied Tom's face so carefully that the moment almost became awkward. Finally she broke her stare and handed him a registration form.

"Would you fill this out, please? And I'll need a credit card for incidentals."

Tom looked at the form. Questions that would have been easy for a ten-year-old, he struggled to answer. Name? Would that be Tom or Jeffrey Candor? Address? I have none.

"Mac? I'm having a hard time with this," Tom said, releasing the pen that he was clenching. "Would you mind filling it out?"

When Mac began to write her address, it occurred to her why Tom had given her the card. She wished she could ease his pain.

"Your room is upstairs on the right—number two-oh-four," Eileen said with a charming smile. "It has two double beds and a private bath. A full breakfast will be served tomorrow morning at eight." She was still staring at Tom. "Is there anything else you need?"

"No, thank you," Tom said, picking up their luggage. "We'll see you tomorrow."

When they were halfway up the stairs, Eileen remembered something. "Extra blankets and towels are in the hall closet."

"Thank you," Mac said. "Pleasant dreams."

Once in their room, Tom placed the luggage on one bed and they both fell onto the other, exhausted from the long drive. With their arms wrapped around each other, Tom and Mac fell asleep within minutes.

ൿ

The following morning, Tom had already left the room when Mac awoke, still dressed from the day before. After showering and unpacking as quickly as possible, she ran downstairs and found Tom having coffee in the sunroom.

"Good morning," she said, leaning over and kissing him.

"I was about to come and wake you. Breakfast is about to be served."

"Smells delicious," Mac said, drinking a large glass of orange juice.

"I thought I'd be your tour guide today," Tom said.

Before Mac could respond, Eileen walked in, carrying two plates filled with scrambled eggs, bacon, various pastries and fresh fruit.

"I hope you have big appetites," she said in her high voice.

"I do," Mac said, eyeing the plates. "We missed dinner last night."

"Well, this should get you off to a good start."

"I'm going to be shown around town, I believe," Mac said, making pleasant conversation.

"Are you going to The Park?" Eileen said. Suddenly her gaze sharpened on Tom. "That's it! That's why you look so familiar. You're Dr. Candor!"

Tom froze, bracing for an onslaught of questions or, worse, outright ridicule.

"It's a delight to meet you," Eileen said, extending her hand. "My son, Cliff Keller, worked for you."

Tom thought back. "Cliff, yes. He had just taken his board exams when . . ."

"When the panda died," she said, patting Tom's shoulder. "You must have been devastated. I know Cliff was. He always spoke so highly of you, even after you left."

"That's nice of you to say," Tom said, feeling very humbled. "Where is Cliff now?"

Eileen laughed. "Believe it or not, he's still at The Park. Twenty-five years and he's happily married to the zoo and all his animals."

Tom smiled warmly. "That's wonderful to hear. I'm glad he's doing well."

"I'm sure he would be delighted to see you," Eileen said.

"Perhaps we'll find our way over there," Tom said, not wanting to falsely commit.

"Well," she said, gently clapping her hands together, "your food is getting cold. It's such a pleasure to see you back here after all this time, Dr. Candor."

After Eileen left the sunroom, Tom looked at Mac with an expression of disbelief.

She put her hand on his. "If anything, this has got to show you that there are some people who don't blame you."

"Be prepared, Mac," he cautioned her. "Most don't feel that way."

"Time has a way of softening opinions," she said, picking up a croissant.

"I'd prefer not to test your theory any further," he said, wanting to end the conversation. "So, it's a beautiful day out and I thought we would enjoy walking the Sundial Bridge at Turtle Bay."

"Why do they call it Sundial?" Mac asked, tasting the eggs. "These are delicious."

Tom pulled out a brochure he had found in the inn's small lobby and showed Mac a picture. "At one end, there's a 217-foot curved pylon that acts as a huge sundial. It casts a shadow on the tile-covered border of the gardens on the north side."

She looked at the photograph. "That's impressive."

"There's a seven-hundred-foot glass-bottomed pedestrian bridge that crosses over the Sacramento River," he explained. "From there, we can walk through the Turtle Bay Exploration Park and, if you're interested, McConnell Arboretum. For a very private and romantic lunch," he said, kissing her hand, "I would suggest we drive up to Lake Shasta."

"It sounds perfect," Mac said, glowing. "Other than being my tour guide today, do you want to do anything else?"

Tom knew what Mac was insinuating, but he had not yet decided if, when or how he wanted to return to The Park.

"I don't know yet," he answered. "Let's just enjoy the day together."

Mac leaned over and kissed him on the cheek. "I love you for bringing me here," she said softly.

"Enough to share the last of your bacon?"

"Oh, I think more than enough," she said with a laugh.

THIRTY-NINE

Coup

After tying Isabella to the post outside The Granary, Jeremiah hobbled up the stairs and began to open the clinic door as he had done for the past twenty years. When the knob didn't turn, he thought it was simply stuck—just another thing that Ellen needed to grease. He tried again, but still no movement.

Jimmy D, who had been watching from the front of his tavern across the street, cupped his hands over his mouth and called out, "He's not there, Jeremiah."

Unsure where the voice was coming from, Jeremiah turned around and looked out at a blurry image. "Who's that?"

Jimmy thought he was asking "Who's not there?" so he replied, "Tom Candor."

Jeremiah, who couldn't see more than a few feet in front of him, thought it was Tom Candor replying. "Well, come unlock the door then," he said in a frail but demanding voice.

Foreseeing their miscommunication would only worsen if he kept yelling from across the street, Jimmy D ran over to The Granary and joined Jeremiah on the front porch. "Jeremiah, it's Jimmy," he said.

"Well, of course you are. Where's that new vet?"

"He's closed his office and left Lumby," Jimmy explained.

Jeremiah looked around in confusion. "I think Isabella is sick. When can he see her?"

"I don't think he'll be back."

Jeremiah lived a simple life, having no phone and making only limited trips to town, so he hadn't heard about the doctor's abrupt departure. "But Ellen promised me nothing would change after she left."

"She didn't know," Jimmy started to explain as gently as possible. "Tom Candor told us several lies, and when we found out, all of us thought it was best that he not live here anymore."

Jeremiah didn't take what Jimmy said at face value because he couldn't or wouldn't accept the fact that there would be no veterinarian to help Isabella. "But he seemed like such a nice young fellow," he said.

Jimmy shrugged his shoulders. "Appearances are sometimes deceiving, aren't they?"

"I don't know. I can't see," Jeremiah said. "If he doesn't come back, who will help Isabella?"

For the first time since he and Dennis had confronted Tom in his office, Jimmy actually considered the deep personal impact that Tom's departure would have on the community. Had they been too quick to judge? But Tom had lied to everyone. He didn't deserve the trust of the town or of good men like Jeremiah.

"You may have to take her to Wheatley," Jimmy suggested.

Jeremiah looked at Jimmy as if he had suggested Jeremiah grow wings and fly away. "How could I possibly do that? Isabella can't walk that far."

Jimmy held back a grin. "I'm sure Sam would let us use the horse trailer behind the Feed Store. All of us can help you get Isabella down to see another veterinarian."

Jeremiah looked at the blurred image of his mare. "But she's never been in a trailer before. She'd be scared."

A car drove up and stopped in front of The Granary. "You waiting for the doc?" the teenage boy called out.

Jimmy rolled his eyes. "He's gone."

"My dad told me to get some antibiotics for his sheep," the kid said. "Will he be back soon?"

Becoming impatient, Jimmy snapped back, "I suspect he's not coming back at any time."

A woman who was walking her dog toward the clinic heard Jimmy's outburst and quickened her pace. "What do you mean?" she asked.

By then three others had walked over from the Feed Store to watch the commotion. Jimmy threw up his arms. "This is not my fault."

"Did you tell him to leave, Jimmy?" another woman said.

Jeremiah could not see the growing crowd, but he heard their voices. "We need the doctor back. Or Ellen," he said.

"Well, that's not going to happen," Jimmy barked.

"You had no right to run him out of town," the woman said.

"Yeah!" the teenager yelled, just wanting to be involved.

Jimmy was exasperated. "All right! Anyone who has an opinion in the matter can meet me at noon in the theater," he said, before crossing the street and quickly retreating into Jimmy D's.

Once in his office with the door shut, he picked up the phone and called Dennis Beezer. "Your attendance is required," he said, giving Dennis no explanation and leaving him no option but to accept the brusque invitation.

~

Just before noon, Jimmy walked across Main Street. Sam, who had been sweeping loose grain off the porch, paused to lean on his broom.

"They don't look happy," he warned, eyeing the second-story theater.

Jimmy waved off the comment. "I can handle two or three frustrated residents."

"A few more than that," Sam said.

"What? Six?"

"More like *sixty*, and they're stirred up about something," Sam said, laughing. "What did you do this time, Jimmy?"

"Absolutely nothing," he said. "Have you seen Dennis?"

Sam looked down Main Street. "Right over there," he said, pointing toward the Chatham Press building.

Jimmy waved to his friend. "Come on," he called out.

Dennis jogged the rest of the way, and together, they ran up to the second floor of the Feed Store, which served as the town's one and only theater.

As they entered, everyone in the room fell silent. Sam had, in fact, underestimated the size of the crowd, which Dennis guessed to be around eighty.

"Man," Jimmy said under his breath, "word certainly gets around fast."

He and Dennis worked their way slowly to the front of the theater, where they stood on a makeshift stage three feet off the floor.

Jimmy raised his hand. "Thanks for coming," he said too softly. Only the folks in the front rows heard. He took a deep breath. "Thank you for coming," he repeated much louder.

A hush fell over the room. Some people who were standing in the aisles took the few remaining seats. Jimmy looked out at the audience and recognized most of the faces.

"We're here to talk about . . ." As he searched for the right words, he was interrupted by the screeches of guinea hens in the attic. He regretted not having prepared better for the town meeting. "We're here—" The guinea hens shrieked again, louder and longer.

"Sam!" Jimmy yelled downstairs. "Can you do anything about those malcontents in the attic?"

The guineas, seeming to understand the threat, went quiet just as Sam's oldest son reached the top step of the theater. "This will take care of them," he said, holding a shovel in one arm and a large bag of grain in the other.

Jimmy returned his attention to the audience. "We're here to share ideas about how Lumby can find a new vet."

"We already found one!" someone yelled out. "And we need to get him back."

"All right," Jimmy said calmly, "that's one person's opinion."

Jeremiah mustered up all his strength to be heard over so many people. "That's all of our opinions," he said from the front row.

But Jimmy stood firm. "Tom Candor has closed his practice, so I assure you he's not coming back."

"Why not?" a woman shouted from the rear of the room.

Jimmy, totally exasperated, turned to his colleague. "I'll let Dennis explain."

Dennis was caught off guard, and for several long seconds, he glared back at Jimmy. Although he'd been personally involved in the veterinarian's eviction, he had assumed Jimmy would better handle the angry crowd.

Dennis coughed. "Perhaps some of you haven't read the article we printed in *The Lumby Lines,* or don't know the background behind Dr. Candor's decision to leave," he began. "What we learned is that Tom Candor misrepresented himself when he came to Lumby and bought Ellen's practice."

Someone interrupted impatiently. "How did he misrepresent himself?"

"He lied about who he was," Dennis continued. "His real name is Jeffrey Candor."

"I read the article, but it sounded like he changed his name intentionally," another woman said. "And legally."

Jimmy tried to see who had asked the question. "Why would that have mattered?" he asked.

"Maybe he wasn't lying at all," she answered. It was the woman Jimmy had seen at the clinic earlier that day.

"But that's not the point," he replied. "He never told any of us that he was responsible for one of the most infamous veterinary mishaps in our country's history."

Dennis took over, wanting to give Jimmy a chance to calm his nerves. "In nineteen eighty-nine, Jeffrey Candor was the medical director at the American Zoological Park," he explained.

Several "oo"s and "ah"s were heard throughout the crowd, which Dennis decided to ignore as he continued the story. "He operated on an invaluable panda bear that was on loan from China. At the end of the surgery, he injected the animal with potassium chloride, instead of antibiotics, which killed the animal within minutes. The Board of Review found Candor to be negligent and suspended his license to practice veterinary medicine for seven years."

Everyone in the room remained silent.

Thank God, Jimmy thought.

After a moment, Jeremiah spoke up. "So it sounds like he paid the price and accepted his punishment. Who are we to pass judgment a second time?"

Several people voiced their agreement.

Jimmy was getting more wound up. "We're not sending him to jail, Jeremiah!"

"But aren't we?" Chuck Bryson asked as he stood up from the middle of the audience and made his way to the side aisle. From there, he walked toward the front stage. "Isn't banishing him from Lumby similar to issuing a jail sentence? Both take away the freedom of an individual to pursue what he or she wants."

"Chuck, you know this is different," Dennis said.

Chuck turned to the crowd. "Joshua and I were visiting Berkeley University when we stumbled upon Tom Candor's background. The circumstances made it look like he was untruthful both back then and now, but everyone we spoke with on campus who knew him said just the opposite. They believed he was an outstanding vet and a man of strong moral character."

"Well, he wasn't with *us*!" Dennis said bitterly.

Without thinking, Jimmy blurted out, "And he went absolutely nuts when we confronted him. You wouldn't believe how he treated us! He just tore into us. He and his damn monkeys. And we probably don't know the half of it. He could be a fugitive or something worse."

"A fugitive?" an older woman in front asked.

Whispers throughout the room created a low hum in which a few words were audible: "prison," "murder," "robbery." The Lumby rumor mill could be vicious when not kept in check.

"You never know about strangers," a man yelled from the back.

"But Chuck says he's a good vet," a woman argued.

"And Jimmy said he's a felon," another retorted.

Dennis looked at Jimmy, expecting him to correct the hearsay, but Jimmy looked away. He wasn't one of Tom's fans, but Dennis would never stoop to stretching the truth to strengthen his case against the veterinarian.

"The fact is," Dennis said, "he never told us about his past."

"But that was his prerogative," Jeremiah added.

"We need to get him back," a woman said above the chatter.

"Let's write him a letter," someone in the second row suggested. "Invite him to return to Lumby."

"Not if he's a fugitive," the man in back yelled out. "Jimmy's right—he could have killed someone in cold blood."

A woman who had been speaking finally stood up. "Well, I liked him and I don't think he murdered anyone."

"Me too," another said from the side aisle.

The room broke out in unanimous agreement. "Take a vote, Jimmy."

It was obvious what the outcome would be, but Jimmy still went through the motion. It was undisputed that the town wanted Tom Candor back.

Jeremiah added, "We need to give him a reason to come back."

Chuck smiled. "I've been thinking about that. We could offer him a zoo."

"That's ludicrous," Jimmy said.

"Since he was a medical director at the Zoological Park," Chuck explained, "he may be interested in heading up another zoo. A zoo built by our town."

Jimmy laughed at the preposterous suggestion. "And what would be in that zoo? Sam's renegade chickens and a bunch of wild rabbits?"

"I'll contribute two cows," McNear called out.

"This is absurd," Jimmy said. "We can't build a zoo."

"I believe we could," Chuck said. "There's ample property on the north side of the fairgrounds, where we could put up several buildings."

"That would take too long," a woman said loudly. "We need something now."

A man seated close to Jeremiah stood up. "If anyone knows animals, it's Chuck Bryson. So if he says it can be done, then I think it can."

Chuck remained standing. "But Sara has a good point. It would take months to prepare." He thought for a moment and turned to McNear. "Perhaps we could temporarily use part of your farm for the zoo?"

"A zoo at McNear's place. I give up," Jimmy said, throwing his arms in the air and taking a seat onstage.

"I just received another forty head, so my barns are full," McNear said.

Everyone suddenly broke out into twenty different conversations and the noise became thunderous.

"Wait a minute!" Jimmy yelled out, trying to bring order to the meeting.

"You're the mayor, Jimmy," another woman said. "You need to write him a letter."

"A letter would take too long. You need to call him," Jeremiah suggested.

That was the last thing Jimmy intended on doing. "I don't have his number."

Chuck raised his hand. "You can call Mackenzie. I heard she's with him."

"There's a phone over on that table," someone said.

Jimmy looked at Dennis, who noticed the determination on the faces in the crowd. "We may not have a choice in the matter," he said just loud enough for Jimmy to hear.

Jimmy walked over to the front corner of the theater and turned to face the angry crowd. "So, I tell him what? That we're going to have a chicken zoo behind my bar?"

"The Walkers have an open barn," Chuck said. "For now, just tell him that we're opening a national zoo on Farm to Market Road."

"And you're going to talk to Mark and Pam?" Jimmy asked.

"No, *you* are," Jeremiah said. "They're good folks. They'll help out the town."

Jimmy slowly picked up the receiver and began to dial as someone called out Mac's cell phone number.

"Hello?" Mac answered.

"Mac, this is Jimmy D."

You could hear a pin drop in the theater as everyone struggled to listen to what the mayor was saying.

Mac sounded startled to get a call from Jimmy. "Is everything all right?"

"Yes, nothing's wrong," Jimmy said quickly. What to say next? "Are you with Tom Candor?"

"Yes. Why do you ask?"

Jimmy's pause was so long, Mac apparently thought the call was disconnected. "Are you still there?" she asked.

"Yes," Jimmy said. "There are some townsfolk here who think Tom should return to Lumby."

"Where are you?" Mac asked.

"In the theater," Jimmy clarified. "We're having a town meeting."

"So, why are you calling me?"

"Well, for one thing, we didn't have Tom's number."

“Hold on,” Mac said. “I can give him the phone.”

“No!” Jimmy shouted. “That’s all right. Perhaps it’s best if this comes from you.”

“If what comes from me?”

Jimmy glanced over at Dennis, who glared back at him. “The town wants Tom to come back, and to show him their commitment, they’re building a zoo for him to oversee.”

Mac laughed loudly. “A zoo? In Lumby?”

“Yeah, on Farm to Market Road with chickens and stuff, maybe some cows,” Jimmy said, knowing how ridiculous that sounded. “It will show how sincere the residents are about wanting him back.”

“The promise of Lumby is chickens?” Mac asked Jimmy. “I’m sure that will catch Tom’s interest.”

“It will be more than chickens,” Jimmy said, deliberately avoiding any further details. “So you can talk him into it, right?”

Mac’s tone changed. “Jimmy, this is none of my business, and I’m not going to tell Tom what to do,” she said coolly. “But I’ll give him the message.”

FORTY

Solutions

Jimmy yanked Dennis's arm just as he was about to knock on the Walkers' front door. "Why don't you do all the talking," Jimmy whispered. "I'm not at all behind this, and they'll see right through me."

"Well, I'm not a great fan of the idea either," Dennis protested. "I just came along for support. You're the mayor. You need to be the one to take care of it."

"But you're the one who got us into this mess."

Dennis glared at him. "Now it's all my fault that Candor lied?"

"No," Jimmy replied. "But you were the one who really wanted him gone. And also, you have more . . ."

"Credibility?" Dennis offered.

"Yeah, that's it," Jimmy said. "Credibility."

Suddenly the door opened. "Are you two having a meeting out here?" Pam asked. "We saw you drive up a few minutes ago."

"Hey, Pam," Jimmy said with good cheer. "We were just admiring all the work you guys have done around here."

Mark came up behind Pam. "Come on in, guys," he said.

Dennis poked Jimmy in the center of his back hard enough to push him into the kitchen. Dennis was a few steps behind him.

"What brings you two down here?" Pam asked. When neither man answered, she assumed something was wrong. "Is there a problem?"

Jimmy forced a laugh. "No, not at all. We were just in the area and thought we'd see how everything was going."

Pam looked at Jimmy suspiciously. "Everything is great," she said.

Mark refilled his own coffee cup. "Do either of you want some coffee?"

Dennis finally spoke up. "That would be nice, thank you."

Before getting out the mugs, Pam laid several stacked platters on the table. "Dennis, would you mind bringing these back to Gabrielle? To our surprise, our chef bought all new serving plates."

"I heard you have a new cook," Jimmy said.

Dennis added, "Gabrielle is insisting I take her here for her birthday dinner. We're certainly looking forward to it."

"Just let us know when and we'll reserve the best seat in the dining room for you," Pam said as she poured coffee into a mug.

"So, really," Mark said. "What brings you here?"

Dennis looked out the kitchen window, leaving Jimmy to make the next move. "Well," he stalled, "just a social call. Your inn has gotten so much publicity lately."

Pam and Mark continued to gawk at Jimmy. "And?" she asked.

"And . . . how is that new barn of yours?" Jimmy finally blurted out.

Pam and Mark looked at each other. "It's fine. We just connected the electricity a few days ago," Mark said in obvious confusion. "Thanks for asking."

"You still have your draft horse?" Jimmy asked, failing horribly at sounding genuinely interested.

"And a few goats," Mark said warily.

Pam handed Jimmy a mug of freshly brewed coffee.

"You know," Dennis said, as if the idea had just come to him, "I've never seen that barn of yours. How about we take a walk down there?" Jimmy put down his mug without taking a sip. "Good day for a stroll."

Jimmy was out the door before anything else could be said. "Come on, Dennis," he called back.

Pam and Mark exchanged quick glances as Mark pulled on his coat. "Honey, you want to join us?"

Pam was already reaching for her jacket. "Absolutely," she said. She tugged on Mark's coattail. "What's all this about?" she whispered.

"I don't have a clue," he said softly.

As they walked across Farm to Market, the new barn was in clear view. From the lower field of the orchard, when approaching it from the north, the building looked much bigger than if one drove up to it from the dirt access road farther down Farm to Market.

"It's huge!" Jimmy said. He silently calculated how much it would cost to paint "LUMBY ZOO" on the front gable.

Mark beamed, proud of their accomplishment. "It's about two hundred by one hundred with thirty-five box stalls."

Jimmy continued to stare at what might be the solution to his most current town problem. "What are you going to do with all that space?"

Pam glanced askance at Mark, whose smile faded. "I'd like to hear your answer to that as well," she said.

"Llamas," Mark said definitively.

"You could fit a hundred in there," Dennis commented.

"Which we are not going to have," Pam added.

Jimmy quickened his pace. "Is it heated? Do you have a loudspeaker system inside?"

"No and no," Mark answered.

Pam pulled on his coat sleeve again. "Loudspeakers?" He shrugged. Pam stopped in her tracks. "Why all the interest in our barn, Jimmy?"

"No reason," he said. "Just neighborly curiosity."

But even Mark sensed something was up. "We know you better than that," he said.

Dennis nudged Jimmy with his elbow. "Just tell them."

"Tell us what?" Pam said.

Mark suddenly raised his arms. "I know what this is all about," he said. "We still haven't had our final electrical inspection. Is that it, Jimmy? Well, Mac called it in the other day—the guy just never showed up."

Jimmy headed off at a brisk pace. "No, nothing like that."

Pam looked at their good friend. "What's going on, Dennis?"

Dennis called out to Jimmy, who was already ten yards ahead of them. When Jimmy didn't stop, Dennis tried to reassure them. "It's nothing bad. He'll explain in a minute."

Jimmy reached the barn, the other three trailing behind, and opened the massive door to the arena. He took a few steps inside and looked around. Light from the long glassed cupola that ran the length of the roof flooded both the center ring and the box stalls.

Jimmy turned around as the others approached. "If this is what they want, there probably isn't a better place in the entire county."

"What who wants?" Pam said with an edge to her voice, her patience wearing thin.

"Okay, here's the thing," Jimmy began. "You know Tom Candor?"

"Yeah, he seems like a real nice guy," Mark said. "He came here a few times and helped out."

"We just heard a rumor that he killed two people and then escaped from prison," Pam added.

"And when we were eating in The Green Chile yesterday, we heard that he had hijacked an airplane," Mark said.

Dennis rolled his eyes. "Not true. Not true."

Jimmy ran his hand through his hair. "Well, we found out he was lying about his past."

Pam frowned. "We read that in the paper. But he's still a veterinarian?"

"He is," Dennis interjected, "but it's true that quite some time ago, when he was the medical director at the American Zoological Park, he killed a panda that he had been operating on."

"Tough break," Mark said.

"No, it wasn't a tough break," Dennis protested. "It was pure negligence and he lost his license for almost a decade. And then he came here and pretended nothing ever happened."

Pam thought for a moment. "So, it's up to each person to decide if they want to use him as their vet. What's the problem?"

Jimmy raised his hand, as if to stop Pam from drawing any final conclusions. "That's not where the story ends."

"When we got wind of his lies," Dennis continued, "Jimmy strongly encouraged him to find another place to set up practice."

Jimmy's expression darkened. "We *both* suggested he leave."

Pam's face flushed with anger. "You ran him out of town? You had no right to do that!"

"So I've been told," Jimmy said. "We were just trying to protect our community."

"Well, get him back," Mark said.

"Lumby is probably the last place he wants to be right now," Jimmy explained, shifting his weight from foot to foot. "So, some of the townsfolk—"

"Led by Chuck and Jeremiah," Dennis added.

"They want us to basically bribe Tom to come back by building a zoo that he could oversee," Jimmy explained.

Pam burst out laughing. "A zoo? In Lumby? And where would you put it?"

Jimmy looked down at the ground and kicked a stone with his toe. "Right here."

Pam's laughter stopped in a heartbeat. "Here?" she said. "On our property?"

"Only until we build a few enclosures up at the fairgrounds," Jimmy added.

Mark had been silent, but his eyes kept getting wider and wider. "Lions and bears?" he asked.

"We thought we would start with some chickens and cows," Jimmy said.

"This is nuts," Pam said, raising her hands. "After you all come to your senses, come back and finish your coffee." She turned on her heels and walked away.

Once she was out of earshot, Mark assured the men, "Don't worry about Pam. I can talk her into just about anything. And Joshua and I just finished erecting the aviary, so we can have a few birds flying around too. I think having a zoo at Montis is a great idea!" He paused. "You know, I've been looking for a project, and, gentlemen, I've got a feeling this is it. Bring on the wild critters!"

When Jimmy D returned to his tavern, he was handed a note with an urgent message from Brother Matthew at Saint Cross Abbey, asking that he call as soon as it was convenient.

The phone rang only once before it was picked up. "Saint Cross. This is Brother Matthew."

"Brother Matthew, this is Jimmy D in Lumby," Jimmy said, stumbling over his words. For some reason, he was always nervous when he was talking to a monk and especially so when conversing with the abbot of the monastery. "They told me you called."

"I did indeed," Matthew replied. "I have been unsuccessful in reaching Ellen Campbell and I thought you might know how to contact her."

"She left for Greece last week," Jimmy explained.

"Ah, I see. I didn't know she had left," Matthew said. "Brother Michael mentioned someone has bought her practice?"

Jimmy sank into his chair. "Yes, a man by the name of Tom Candor."

"That's it," Matthew said. "He was here not too long ago. But I've been unable to reach him as well."

Jimmy moaned.

"Are you all right?"

Jimmy sat up. "Yes, fine. I think Dr. Candor is gone as well."

"And do you know when he will be returning? We have a rather urgent situation at the monastery."

Jimmy was not very religious, but if there was a God, he certainly didn't want to anger Him any more than necessary by lying to a monk. "I don't think he will be returning," Jimmy said as he exhaled.

There was silence over the phone. Matthew was understandably confused. "But he just bought Ellen's clinic?"

"He did, but everyone thought it best that he not stay," Jimmy clarified, without going into detail. "Is there anything I can do for you?" It was Jimmy's standard question as mayor, and was meant to be rhetorical.

"Perhaps," Matthew said. "We have been given several animals from around the world, in addition to the snow monkeys that we left in Ellen's keeping."

"I heard Tom brought your monkeys, as well as the two chimps Ellen received, down to an animal clinic in Wheatley," Jimmy inserted.

"I'm glad of that," Matthew said. "But, in truth, they are the least of our concerns at present. We were hoping that Ellen or Dr. Candor would assist in finding homes for a number of other animals we now have at the abbey."

Jimmy's eyes lit up. "I have the perfect solution for you. We have just finalized plans for the opening of the Lumby Zoo, and I'm sure we can give your animals outstanding accommodations and care."

There was another pause while Matthew thought through what Jimmy had said. "At the fairgrounds?"

"Not initially. For the grand opening and over the next few months, the zoo will be located at the Montis Inn."

Jimmy thought he heard Matthew laughing. "Mark Walker is running the zoo?" Matthew asked with sufficient skepticism.

"He'll be great," Jimmy said. "He and Pam have a huge new barn there and the Wheatley veterinarian is only twenty minutes away. Mark has everything under control."

Jimmy thought he heard the monk chuckle again, then Brother Matthew coughed gently as if to hide his amusement. "Yes," he said, "I've seen their new barn several times."

"Then you must know that any animal you have can be easily housed there. They have forty or fifty box stalls and an aviary. I'll call Mark to let him know you're coming. Just pack up all the animals you have and bring them over first thing tomorrow morning. Come as early as you want."

"And you're sure the Walkers are in agreement?"

"Oh, they think it's a great idea!" Jimmy said, thinking that it wasn't a half lie, but a half truth—only until Mark could talk Pam into the idea that evening.

"Very well," Matthew said, sounding relieved. "I'll do just that. Thank you very much, Jimmy."

"Glad to be of help," Jimmy said, smiling with relief.

"Jimmy!" the waitress yelled from behind the bar. "We need another keg."

"Coming!" he called back as he jumped to his feet, his burdens behind him.

His problem resolved, Jimmy put the sordid mess out of his mind, so much so that he forgot to place that one important call to his new zookeeper, Mark Walker.

FORTY-ONE

Airborne

The following morning, immediately after matins and well before the sun rose over Saint Cross Abbey, the monks and sisters could be found working side by side in corralling their growing herd and preparing each animal for safe transport. The night before, after Matthew had talked with Jimmy D, the abbot had contacted several local farmers and asked if they would assist by donating the use of their trucks, livestock trailers and delivery vans. By the time the first animal, a sleepy and belligerent young camel, was escorted up the ramp into the first cattle car, eleven trailers were lined up in front of the monastery, with more still to come.

To Matthew's amazement, the loading of the animals went smoothly, except for the rhea, whose strong kick leveled two monks flat on the ground before it was coerced inside the back of an empty milk-delivery truck.

"Well," Matthew said, brushing the dirt off his hands after latching the door behind the last of the boarded animals, "that was quite something."

Michael looked over at the empty kennel. "I'm sorry to see them go," he said. "It was always an adventure when they were here."

"A perfect fit for Mark Walker," Matthew said. "I'm sure he will appreciate any assistance you would like to give."

Brother Michael's spirits didn't change. "That's true. Perhaps I can visit the animals when I go to Lumby, but it certainly won't be the same."

"You did a very good job of taking care of your charges," Matthew said. "Everyone in the community appreciates the fact that you made an impossible situation tolerable."

Michael flinched. "I think they feel I brought it on myself."

"Not deliberately," Matthew said. "I think it has taught us all a lesson as to what can result from one short interview."

"We're loaded up," Sister Kristina said as she joined the brothers. "Do you want us to accompany you?"

"If you wouldn't mind," Matthew said.

She smiled broadly. "I'd like nothing better. I think I'm in the minority who are sorry to see all the animals leave."

Matthew chuckled. "That might only be you and Brother Michael."

~

The seven-truck, three-trailer and four-van procession to Lumby traveled at an intentionally slow pace so that no harm would come to the occupants. Every so often, the rhea kicked at the walls, causing the driver to apply his brakes until the truck stopped rocking back and forth. Sister Kristina, in the front seat, opened the sliding rear window between the passenger compartment and trailer and talked softly to calm the agitated animal.

By the time the caravan had traveled down Farm to Market Road and pulled in front of Montis, it was seven fifteen in the morning. Four guests of the inn, who had just enjoyed one of André's fine breakfasts, were walking through the courtyard when they heard the ruckus coming from the convoy of vehicles. They stopped and stared.

Brother Matthew nodded politely as he hurried toward Pam and Mark's home.

At the sound of a knock on the front door, Mark looked up from reading the paper at the kitchen table. "Come on in, it's open," he called out. Matthew opened the door a few inches and peeked in.

"Brother Matthew!" Mark said in surprise.

"We may be a bit early and I was concerned we'd wake you," Matthew said.

"Not at all. Come in," Mark said, waving his arm. "What are you early for?"

"Our deliveries. You need to tell us where to go."

Mark shook his head, thinking he hadn't had enough coffee that morning. "I'm totally lost. What exactly are you talking about?"

Matthew looked out the window at the caravan. "The animals—they're here."

"What animals?"

Matthew frowned. "Didn't Jimmy Daniels call you last night?"

"Not that I'm aware of," Mark said. "He was here earlier in the day to consider our new barn for a temporary zoo."

"Good." Matthew sighed, relieved to hear that Mark was at least aware of Jimmy's general plan. "So, we have the animals for your zoo waiting outside."

Mark jumped out of his chair and went flying out the door. He came to an abrupt halt on the front stoop. "Really? Where? What did you bring?"

"Mark!" Matthew exclaimed. "You're not dressed!"

Mark looked down at his pajamas. "You're right. I'll be back in a second."

And a second was all it took for Mark to return, Pam close on his heels. When she saw Matthew, she smiled widely and gave him a hug. "Excuse my appearance," she said, knotting the belt around her bathrobe. "What a nice surprise."

"Okay, honey," Mark said as he put his arm around Pam's shoulders. "You know how we said last night that we would go along with Jimmy's plans as long as he gave us some time to prepare? Well, we're opening the zoo a little sooner than we thought." He couldn't contain his excitement.

"But it's still a month or two out, right?"

Mark tried not to grin. "Not exactly." He yanked on his coat. "Matthew has brought one or two animals we need to put in the stalls."

"I'm so sorry," Matthew said to Pam. "Jimmy was supposed to have called you last night. And it's more than one or two, Mark," he warned. "In fact, there are quite a few and they'll eat everything you have." Matthew pulled out papers from his coat pocket. "Here are the feed suppliers that we've been using."

Pam unfolded the pages and scanned the invoices while Mark looked over her shoulder. " 'Two hundred dollars,' " Mark read, looking at the bottom number. "That's not bad for a month."

Matthew cleared his throat. "That's two hundred dollars a day."

"From one of three suppliers?" Pam asked in disbelief.

"Okay, let's go," Mark said, taking Matthew's arm and leading him out the door. He looked over his shoulder. "Honey, would you call Joshua and ask him to come down? Also, why don't you call Jimmy? Maybe he should be involved."

"You think?" she asked sarcastically.

When Mark walked around the corner of the inn and saw the dozen trucks, he finally realized the magnitude of the undertaking. "Wow," he repeated. He pointed to the motorcycle. "Here, get in, Matthew. We'll lead the caravan."

"In there?" Matthew asked, looking askance at the sidecar.

"You'll love it," Mark said. "It will make you feel ten years younger."

Matthew stepped in and wedged himself into the sidecar with his knees to his chest. "Or older," he muttered.

Mark revved the engine and would have done a wheelie out of the drive if it hadn't been for Matthew's additional weight keeping them grounded.

Mark waved one hand wildly to get everyone's attention while he tried to keep control of the bike with his other. "Follow me," he yelled to the drivers.

One by one, the vehicles started up their engines and pulled onto the road.

Mark sped down Farm to Market Road. When they came up to the dirt access road that led to the barns, they were going well over thirty miles an hour. Instead of braking, though, Mark put out his arm to indicate he was turning. He quickly looked over his shoulder to check on the trucks following not far behind him.

As they drove off the asphalt and onto the packed dirt, the front wheel of the motorcycle hit a large pothole, which sent the bike and the sidecar airborne. When they landed, there was such a jolt that Brother Matthew went flying out of the sidecar and landed on his side in the dirt. The bike, with Mark still holding on for dear life, careened into the row of briar bushes that ran along the side of the driveway. A second later, the bike came to a crashing halt on its side with the sidecar suspended over it.

"I'm okay!" Mark yelled.

Matthew, still on the ground, saw a hand rise out of the dense shrubs.

"That could have killed both of us," Mark said from the greenery.

"I think it did," Brother Matthew said, still sitting in the dirt where he had landed.

Mark stumbled to his feet, tripped and then stood again. "Oh, my gosh," he said when he saw Matthew on the ground. "Are you all right?" he asked, scrambling out of the thorny bushes. Mark gave Matthew his hand to help him to his feet.

Matthew glared at him. "Ten years younger, you said?"

"Something like that," Mark replied sheepishly. He brushed off the dust from the brother's coat. "No broken bones?"

Matthew rubbed his shoulder. "I think I'm intact, but I'll walk the rest of the way if you don't mind."

Mark looked over at his crumpled motorcycle. "I don't think we have a choice."

A horn blew behind them. The caravan had stopped and was waiting for the two men to move so they could turn off Farm to Market Road. Mark and Matthew stepped aside and waved them through. One by one, the trailers passed.

"Go to the larger barn," Mark yelled to one of the drivers.

At the end of the motorcade, another car drove past the flipped motorcycle. Joshua rolled down his window. "Should I even ask about the bike and why you two are walking to the barn?"

"He almost killed us," Matthew said under his breath.

Joshua was rightfully concerned. "But are you hurt?"

"It was certainly an experience I don't want to repeat, but I'm fine."

"Matthew brought his animals," Mark explained.

"So I see," Joshua said, studying the long line of vehicles. "Noah's ark delivered in cattle trucks."

"Only first-class accommodations for our charges," Matthew replied.

When they reached the barn, Mark approached the closest truck and unlatched the turn bolt. "So, what did you bring us?" He cracked open the door to peek in.

"Mark! Don't!" Brother Michael shouted, running toward him. One stride behind him was Sister Kristina, holding a rope leash that she intended to use to halter the animal.

Suddenly, there was a deafening crash and the door flew open, hitting Mark squarely in the forehead and sending him backward through the air.

"Don't let the rhea out!" Michael yelled.

But before anyone could respond, the rhea jumped out of its confines, stepped over Mark and bolted toward the orchard.

Joshua watched in amazement. "Was that an ostrich?"

"Something like it," Sister Kristina said. She turned to Michael and nodded up to the hills. "Do you know your way up there?" she asked.

"Pretty well," he said. "Let's go."

Jimmy D, who had just arrived, walked up behind Mark, put his arms around Mark's chest and pulled him to his feet. Mark put his hand over the growing bump on his forehead.

"A little like Jurassic Park, huh?" Jimmy asked.

"Ouch," Mark said, wincing. "What *was* that?"

"An ostrich," Joshua replied.

"More specifically, a cantankerous rhea," Matthew added.

"Well, he's not coming here," Mark demanded. "He could have killed me."

Matthew turned to Jimmy. "Is he talking about the ostrich or the veterinarian? We've heard some wild stories about Tom Candor all the way over in Hamilton, and your name is always tagged on in one way or another."

Jimmy rolled his eyes. "Just huge misunderstandings. No, he isn't a felon or a thief. Just a veterinarian who we are trying to entice back to Lumby."

"Well, not with that bird," Mark interrupted.

"Unfortunately, you don't have much choice," Jimmy told Mark. "I promised Matthew that his entire herd could be moved here."

"But it almost *killed* me," Mark complained.

"Let me show you some of the gentler animals," Brother Matthew said, leading him to the next van.

Joshua unlocked the sliding side door. "Slowly," Matthew warned. "They're all skittish from the trip over here."

Joshua slid the door open no more than six inches, and within seconds, the peacock poked his head through the opening.

"Well, look at that," Jimmy said.

"You can let him out," Matthew suggested. "He's quite tame."

Joshua pushed the door open as far as it would go, but to his surprise, the peacock didn't dash for freedom. Instead, it just stood there, looking out at its new surroundings.

Joshua stepped inside. "Out you go," he said, shooing the bird.

Mark looked at it warily. "Are you sure it's not going to peck out my eyes or something?"

Matthew laughed. "I'm sure." He walked behind the bird and, with open arms, gently nudged the animal into the barn. "Where would you like him?"

"Take the first stall for now," Joshua said. "We'll put the animals in better order once we see what we have."

"Hey, look at this," Jimmy said, finding himself holding the halter of a baby camel that had been given to him by one of the more impatient drivers.

"Now that's more like it," Mark said, walking up to the animal and petting its forehead. "Isn't he a delight?"

But the bewildered young animal was more intimidated than it appeared and proceeded to do what nervous camels do best: spit.

Mark jumped back, but not fast enough. The wad hit squarely on his cheek. "Ugh," he groaned, wiping the slime off his face.

Joshua slapped Mark on the back as he was leading the camel to the barn. "Tough morning, huh?"

Mark turned to Brother Matthew. "Do you have any animals that aren't dangerous?"

"They are all God's beloved creatures," Matthew said, smiling benevolently.

FORTY-TWO

Released

Brooke called out to Pam, who was in the bedroom changing. "How about if I start some pancakes while you get dressed?"

"That sounds perfect. You know where everything is," Pam called back.

A few minutes later, Pam walked into the kitchen, tucking her shirt into her jeans. "We had no idea the monks were coming this morning," she said, still flustered by their unexpected arrival. "We were both in our pajamas."

Brooke laughed. "I'm sure you're not the first woman Matthew has seen in her skivvies."

"I certainly hope so! He's a monk," Pam said. "It was embarrassing."

Brooke grinned. "So Jimmy never called you guys?"

"No. He came down yesterday with Dennis and they talked about the idea of opening a zoo. They said that our large barn would be a good temporary solution for the town. After they left, Mark and I had a long talk and agreed to the idea *in principle,* but we had some concerns and a lot of questions that needed to be answered before we gave the okay." Pam looked out the window. "And less than twelve hours later, vans were pulling up with a herd of animals. I could shoot Jimmy right now."

Brooke cracked an egg and added it to the flour she'd measured out into a bowl. "He certainly isn't the best of communicators. I think his stint as town mayor should be coming to an end. He's stretched too thin."

"I guess I'm more exasperated than angry, but a little warning would have been appreciated," Pam said as she pulled on a wool sweater. "Jimmy just takes over without any forethought. We have so much going on in our lives right now, the zoo was supposed to be later, not sooner."

Brooke heard a harsh edge in Pam's voice and looked up from mixing the batter. "Is everything all right?"

"No, everything is not all right." Pam spoke so softly, Brooke could barely hear her. "And it's really not Jimmy I'm most frustrated with, although he doesn't make things any easier."

"So, what's wrong?"

Pam ran her fingers through her hair. "It's André," she said, and then immediately corrected herself. "No, it's me. I got into something I should never have started."

Brooke tilted her head. "But hasn't André made your restaurant into an overnight success?"

"Yes. We've seen a tremendous turnaround. I would say half our inn guests are coming from out of state just to eat here," Pam said before laying her head down on the table.

Brooke was still perplexed. "So, what's the problem?"

There was silence for the longest time before Pam finally picked her head up. "I want my kitchen back," she said.

"But I thought you liked the freedom he gives you," Brooke said.

"I do," she admitted. "And the additional revenue he's brought in is a godsend."

"From what I hear in town, he's an outstanding chef."

Pam slapped her hands on the table. "As I have been told a thousand times."

Brooke was startled by her friend's reaction. "Do I hear some professional jealousy?"

Pam shook her head. "Absolutely not. I know I'm not even in the same league as André."

Brooke poured a spoonful of batter onto the hot griddle. "Great food, great income and you're free to do what you want. So far, it sounds like a perfect plan."

"I should be the one cooking the meals," Pam explained. "It's my responsibility."

"Then delegate responsibility," Brooke suggested.

Pam glared at her. "It's *my* kitchen," she said, shutting down any further discussion.

Given Pam's insistence, Brooke was unsure if there would ever be a time when Pam could talk about André rationally and objectively. Clearly, for the moment, it was best to change the subject.

Brooke ambled around the room. "It's nice being back here. The last time I cooked you two breakfast was when I was staying here right after you bought Montis."

"Years ago," Pam reminisced. "So much has happened since then."

"Did I ever thank you for bringing me to Lumby?" Brooke asked.

Pam looked up at her, surprised by the unexpected comment. "Many times."

"Coming here changed my life in so many ways," Brooke said as she flipped the pancakes. "I just want you to know that these have been the happiest four years of my life."

"You sound as if they're coming to an end," Pam said as she placed silverware on the table.

Brooke took a deep breath. "You just never know where the next curve in the road will take you."

"What are you talking about?" Pam asked. "Your road is here in Lumby."

Brooke very much needed to talk with Pam but was unsure her friend could face any more turmoil in her life. "You know Joshua and Chuck went to Berkeley for that conference," Brooke began.

Pam nodded. "Yeah, I know Chuck's still on the faculty there and he asked Joshua along on one of his trips. While they were there, they found out something about Tom Candor."

"Well, that's not the only news," Brooke said tentatively.

When she didn't continue, Pam frowned. "What is it?"

Brooke transferred a stack of pancakes from the griddle to a serving plate before continuing. "A few days before the guys went to California, Joshua received a letter from the agricultural department head at the university asking to meet him."

"Why?" Pam asked.

Brooke couldn't look at Pam. "Chuck had told a few of his colleagues about Joshua's doctoral work and they requested an informal talk to see if Joshua would consider a faculty position there."

It took Pam several moments to understand what made no sense to her. She finally unscrambled the words. *"A job in California?"*

"Yes, at Berkeley."

"But, Brooke . . . ," she began. Suddenly and quite unexpectedly, all the glue that had been holding Pam's emotions together melted. She burst into tears. "You're leaving?" she whispered as she slumped into a chair.

"We're not," Brooke said. "At least not for a while. Joshua isn't even sure he wants to begin the first round of interviews. He's uncertain how to begin his career, what he should do next, and we haven't even decided if we're willing to move from Lumby. I'm hoping there won't be any faculty positions open for another year or two."

"But you can't leave," Pam said, trying to regain control of herself.

"I'm so sorry," Brooke said, sitting down next to her friend. "I know this isn't a good time, but I wanted to tell you before you heard any rumors."

Pam took a gulp of coffee and wiped her eyes with a napkin. "I'm sorry," she said, trying to reach deep and find some remaining strength. "I'm really pleased for Joshua. It must be an honor to be considered by such a respected school, but the thought of you two leaving is the last straw. What would happen if you and Joshua moved away?"

Both women looked at each other in helpless dismay.

~

Down at the barn, Mark and Joshua were transferring the last of the arrivals into a box stall at the far end. It had taken over two hours of mishaps, escapes and recaptures to corral the Saint Cross herd into its new home, and about the same time for Brother Michael and Sister Kristina to return from the orchard with the rhea. Jimmy and Brother Matthew were lending a hand when needed.

At the barn door, Brother Michael petted the koala that had wrapped its arms around Joshua's neck. "She's a sweetheart," he commented.

Mark walked by with an alpaca close to his side. "I think you've been giving this guy too many treats. He's really fat."

All of them stared at the alpaca's enormous stomach.

"Mark, he's a she, and she's pregnant," Michael said. "We were told that she was intentionally bred before being sent to us. With a gestation period of about thirty-five days, she's due this Tuesday or Wednesday, so you'll want to check on her throughout the night."

"Pregnant?" Mark repeated. "But we don't know anything about birthing alpacas."

Kristina said, "Just give her ample food and water, make sure she has clean, dry bedding and let nature take its course."

Mark looked apprehensively at Joshua. "You're going to be here, right?"

"If you want," he answered. "Or you can send Pam down at two in the morning."

"Yeah, as if I'm going to ask her to do that," Mark said, looking around. "Where's Jimmy? This whole thing was his idea."

"He's inside, looking at the animals," Matthew said. "Not that we don't want to help, but we really should be getting back to Saint Cross."

Michael walked the rhea into the largest of the box stalls and latched the door behind him. "This afternoon we arranged for a large delivery of food that will take care of all the animals for the next few days," he said. "And then you can arrange your own schedule."

"And the wood shavings for the stall floors?" Joshua asked.

"Should be delivered in a few hours. Just call Woods Farm Supply down in Wheatley," Michael advised.

Joshua turned to Mark. "We'll need more bedding by tomorrow morning."

"But I just had a huge order delivered yesterday," Mark complained, still holding on to the alpaca's halter.

"That was when we had no animals," Joshua said as Jimmy walked up and joined them. "There're six inches of fresh bedding down in every stall. From the looks of it, that's just about the amount we'll go through each day."

"But that order was for sixty dollars!" Mark complained. He turned to Jimmy D. "Mayor Daniels, do you know how much all of this is going to cost?"

Jimmy petted the sleeping koala. "All of what?"

"Shavings and food," Mark said.

"And medicine," Matthew reminded him.

"And electricity," Joshua added.

Everyone was staring at Jimmy.

He winced. "Maybe a thousand a month?"

Mark scowled. "More like three thousand a *week*."

Jimmy waved his hand, dismissing Mark's estimates. "Well, that's nuts. That can't be right."

"Actually, Mark's estimate is very close to what we have been spending," Michael said as he lifted the koala off Joshua's chest and handed her gently to Kristina.

"So, who's going to pay for it, Jimmy?" Mark asked impatiently.

Jimmy took three steps backward. "Well, don't look at me. I can't afford it."

Mark was obviously annoyed. "Pam's going to kill me if this ends up costing us any money. We would never have agreed to it, Jimmy. Since it's a town zoo, the town needs to pay for it."

"No one ever mentioned anything about the cost when they said we should have a zoo to get Candor back," Jimmy said.

"Well, as mayor you need to take care of it," Mark said, "or else these animals will be sleeping at Jimmy D's tomorrow night."

At two o'clock that afternoon, well after Joshua and Brooke had left and Mark had made a sandwich to take down to the barn, Pam finally saw André's car pull in. She had been standing at the window for an hour, rehearsing the words she had secretly scripted the night before. She watched him remove three bags of groceries from the backseat, cross the courtyard and disappear into the dining room.

Before sitting down on the sofa, Pam took out a crumpled piece of paper from her pants pocket. She reread her own words again and again, trying to build confidence in her decision to talk with André. She reminded herself that she would be compassionate, empathetic and most of all appreciative.

After stalling for another twenty minutes, she took a deep breath, stuffed the note back in her jeans and headed over to the main kitchen. When she walked into the dining room, she glanced down at the reservation book—they were fully booked for that night. The room was filled with the rich aromas of the specialties that André was already preparing.

Pam pushed the kitchen door open just far enough to peek in. André was standing in front of the stove, holding a bottle of wine over a large pot. Classical music played over a radio that he had installed the week before.

Pam swallowed hard and stepped into the room. She cleared her throat in an effort to get André's attention, but he didn't look up from the wine he was carefully adding to the sauce.

Pam's nerves and impatience got the better of her. "This isn't going to work," she blurted out.

André continued to stir in the wine.

"I need to make a change," she repeated.

He lifted the bottle before looking over his shoulder. "What is it? Do you think I should use a chardonnay?"

"No, that's not what I mean," she said, abandoning her script. "I don't think you should be here."

André was perplexed. "Tonight?" he asked.

"Any night . . . every night," she said, and started talking so fast, André could barely follow. "I'm so sorry. I thought it was the right solution for our inn, but I just can't stand by and have someone else do something that I feel I should be doing myself. You're a great chef—one of the top emerging chefs in our country. I know I can't come close even with my best meals. But we bought this place as a dream and cooking was my contribution, and if you're here, I can't do what I promised I would do. But you can stay in our cottage for as long as you want." She stopped abruptly when she realized she was talking a mile a minute.

André looked at her in disbelief. "You're firing me?"

Pam fought the urge to continue talking through her nervousness. "Yes, I suppose I am."

André was speechless.

"I'm s-s-sorry," Pam stuttered.

André turned off the stove, folded his towel and laid it on the countertop. Pam stared at him, expecting an explosion.

"If that's your decision," he said in a calm voice as he pulled his scarf and jacket off the coat hanger. The last thing he said before walking out the door was, "I wish you the best of luck."

The Lumby Lines

What's News Around Town

BY SCOTT STEVENS November 9

Trouble in P-A-R-A-D-I-Z-E. Lumby's Scrabble Club is on hiatus from their regularly scheduled Tuesday and Thursday night games until some interpersonal issues are resolved. Further, the club is asking for donations of any dictionaries as most of them were thrown into the library's fireplace during one spelling dispute last week.

Tom Candor would have a doggone fine business if he was here. For the last several days, townsfolk have lined up in front of The Granary with their pets in hand and underfoot as a protest to the veterinarian's departure. Unfortunately, that has caused a slight poop problem on the adjacent sidewalk, which the Parks Department (Harry) will need to address.

Across the street, a bear broke into Jimmy D's stockroom behind the tavern and drank his way through six cases of Heineken. Before rolling over and passing out, he stumbled into the kitchen and demolished one of their two refrigerators.

On the animal front for one more minute, the rabbits have vanished. No sooner did they take up residence at Lumby Lumber than they disappeared altogether. No questions are being asked.

And from all indications our fair town now has a zoo, which is being temporarily housed at Montis Inn while the Parks Department (also Harry) decides how to allocate fairground property for the animal park. However, knowing the bureaucracy of our town council, I wouldn't expect any new developments for another two or three years.

FORTY-THREE

Returning

Tom was up long before the sun rose over California. He had been lying in bed watching the clock since three thirty. Finally, he gave up any hope of falling back to sleep, dressed quietly and left the room. Downstairs in the lobby, he turned on a floor lamp by a large wing-back chair and made himself comfortable. Picking up a regional magazine, he thumbed through the pages, hoping to find anything that would take his thoughts away from the coming morning.

The night before, he had promised to take Mac to the American Zoological Park after breakfast. For the past three hours, he'd been having second and third thoughts about that plan. Although it was his intent to go to The Park at some point, he was thinking later would be preferable. He and Mac were having such a terrific time together, why jeopardize the rest of their vacation by opening a door that should perhaps remain shut?

To Mac's credit, she never forced the issue, but instead, supportively encouraged his return to the zoo. He smiled, thinking how she gently broached the idea. He felt so fortunate to have her in his life, even if it was for only a few more days.

At seven that morning, Tom followed Eileen into the sunroom and helped himself to freshly brewed coffee. When Mac joined him downstairs, he looked drawn and exhausted.

"Are you all right?" she asked.

"Tired," he said, kissing her. "But happy you're here."

"Do you want to change our plans for today?" she asked, offering him an easy out.

"I've been thinking about that since three this morning," Tom confessed. "I don't want to go, but I know I need to."

Mac smiled. "Then we're off after breakfast."

࿐

The side roads near the zoo were what Tom would later describe as "wonderfully familiar." One new neighborhood of middle-priced homes had been constructed a half mile away, and a new gas station and convenience store now serviced thousands of visitors who came to The Park each day, but otherwise little had changed.

Turning right onto Ashgrove Road was more a habit than a conscious decision on Tom's part. This would take them past the staff entrance and ultimately to the east side parking area. As he approached the utility road entrance that he had used for the seven years he worked there, he slowed the car and looked down the side street.

Mac noticed a small sign that read, "Perimeter Road. Keep Out."

The guard gate was obscured by redwoods, which paled in comparison to those they had seen at the national park, but which were certainly large enough to screen the small shack.

Tom stretched his neck, looking for someone familiar; in fact, looking for anyone. But there was nobody in sight and he didn't see the employees' cart that was used by the guard to travel to and from the buildings. Tom quickly glanced at his watch; it was nine twenty-three a.m. During his employment there, it was standard practice for the guard to take three ten-minute breaks during the day. It would appear that that schedule hadn't changed.

"Hold on," Tom said, as he stepped on the gas and turned onto the access road, driving through the open gate at the guard shed.

Mac looked worried. "Should we be doing this?"

"Probably not," Tom answered, but he kept driving anyway.

The access road was just as he remembered it, but the trees were so much bigger that the limbs from either side of the road touched overhead, forming a thick canopy. He instinctively drove to a building on the north side of the complex where he had both begun and, years later, all but ended his professional career: the large-animal clinic.

He lowered his window and inhaled, as he always had on his way to work. It was a smell he would never tire of. "A mixture of fresh straw and pine," he commented to Mac.

The sounds, too, were distantly familiar. The large encaged animals—elephants and large cats—always made the loudest racket.

As they drove along Perimeter Road, he kept an eye out for any law enforcement officers. Most of the cars owned by the staff were known by the security guard and Tom was keenly aware that his out-of-state license plates would draw unwanted attention. The only excuse he could come up with—"Isn't this the road to the giraffe exhibition?"—would be pretty unconvincing. Contrary to the opinion of some Lumby residents, Tom Candor was not a good liar.

After parking the car next to the clinic, Tom took Mac's hand and led her to the side door.

"Shouldn't we be walking a little faster?" she asked, trying to urge him along.

"There are video surveillance cameras throughout The Park," Tom explained. "If we run, someone will spot us immediately. Just act normal."

The gray metal door had an intimidating yellow-and-red sign that shouted, "Private. Staff Only!" Next to the doorknob was a keypad. Tom inhaled loudly, held his breath and punched in a series of numbers he had first set when he became director—051957, his birthday.

There was a loud click and suddenly a green light flashed where there had been red.

"We're in," he said softly, and opened the door for Mac.

Taking her hand again, he led her down a short hall lined with small offices on either side. The last office, closest to the center of the building, was only slightly larger than the others.

"That was mine," he said but didn't slow his pace.

"Stop!" a man's voice commanded from behind them. Both Tom and Mac froze. "Don't move!" he said.

Tom heard approaching footsteps. The man had obviously spotted them from down the hall.

Tom appreciated this man's alarm and forcefulness. Zoos were often targeted by radical animal protectionists who had been known to trespass and release valuable animals. Unfortunately, they didn't understand that the outcome of such a seemingly noble act was the endangerment of the animals since, quite often, they were hurt or worse during their recapture, regardless of how much care was taken.

"We're not here to do any harm," Tom said as he turned slowly around.

The man was now ten feet away. He stopped and tilted his head, looking closely at the trespasser. "Jeff? Jeff Candor? Is that you?"

Tom scrutinized the man's face. "Cliff Keller?"

Cliff smiled broadly. "Well, I'll be," he said, walking up and giving Tom a warm embrace. "You scared the daylights out of me."

"Sorry about that," Tom said.

"My mother told me you were staying at her inn," Cliff said, "but this is the last place I would expect to find you."

"I thought the same thing this morning but was convinced otherwise," he explained, and glanced over at Mac. "Cliff, this is my good friend Mackenzie McGuire. Mac, this is Dr. Cliff Keller."

Mac shook his hand. "I've heard so many good things about you," she said warmly. "And your mother is charming."

"She certainly is a wild one for her age," he said, rolling his eyes.

"Cliff was my right-hand man here," Tom explained. "An outstanding vet all around."

"Thanks. But I wish I had your administrative skills, or at least your patience for all the paperwork. I seldom see the animals these days."

"I understand you're the director now?" Tom asked.

"I am," Cliff said proudly. "I have to admit, it was odd moving into your office. All those nights we sat up together monitoring sick animals . . ."

"We had some good times," Tom remembered. "Well, we're sorry for trespassing. I just thought I would show Mac the place."

"Not a problem. But you could have called me."

Tom dropped his shoulders, trying to relax. "I didn't want to involve you. I'm sure there are folks around here who would prefer I never return."

Cliff looked honestly surprised. "Why would you say that?"

Tom couldn't understand his question when the answer was so obvious to him. "The last day I saw any of you, Ming died and the fallout brought such bad publicity to The Park . . ."

"You didn't come back. We never saw you after you left to go to the hospital emergency room." Cliff's voice was filled with anguish. "I tried to call you a few times and left messages, but we didn't hear from you again."

Tom thought back. "Everything happened so quickly. I was dismissed the following day and banned from The Park. They didn't even allow me to pack up my office."

"I know. They asked me to do it," Cliff said softly.

"And then my license was suspended." Tom dropped his head. "I assumed that none of you wanted to see me again."

Cliff looked confused. "But we all knew it was an accident."

Tom stared at his old friend and colleague. "A preventable one."

Cliff reached out and took Tom's arm. "You know we've all picked up the wrong vial at some point—it's not that uncommon."

"But it's our responsibility to catch the mistake before the syringe is filled," he said.

"Tom, I was there when the call came in from the emergency room. Laura had nearly died. Remember, she was my friend too, and we were all panicked. Any of us could have made the same mistake."

"No," Tom said. "*You* would have looked at the vial before using it."

"It was a human mistake," Cliff insisted.

Tom looked down the empty hall toward the operating room. "Can I walk around for a minute?"

"Be my guest." Turning to Mac, Cliff asked, "Can I offer you a cup of coffee?"

She looked at Tom, who smiled and gave a nod. "I'd like that," she said, and followed Cliff into his office.

Once they were out of sight, Tom walked down the hall. How strange it felt—nothing seemed to have changed. It could have been fifteen years before and he could be about to perform Ming's surgery. The squeak of his shoes on the floor sounded familiar, and the sweet smell of straw was everywhere.

Tom stood in front of the large glass observation window with his arms stretched out on the pane of glass, staring into the dark operating room. From this vantage point he had been observed by the zoo's executive director, curator and chairman of the board. Tom clearly remembered looking up at them before the surgery began, and then once again after the tumor was removed. Had they still been monitoring the procedure when the call came in from the hospital, or had they left feeling confident that Dr. Candor would successfully complete the surgery?

Walking through the scrub room, where he had prepped for thousands of procedures, Tom smelled the mixed odors of surgical soap and disinfectant, and felt as if an electrical charge was running through his body. The hairs on his nape stood up, and his arms were covered with goose bumps. He touched his toe on the floor pedal below the sink and hot water shot from the faucet.

Images of countless successful surgeries rushed in, and he was able to remember all the laughter and closeness he'd shared with his colleagues. How many times had he sat up through the night, hand-nursing a recovering patient?

Out of habit, Tom pushed the swing door open with his hip and walked into the operating room. He turned on the main switch, and light flooded everywhere. The reflection off the stainless-steel operating table was almost blinding. Tom couldn't take another step; he was drenched with sweat and exhausted from the agony he felt.

Looking around the room, he replayed each second of that morning, thinking through every minute detail of the operation. The resection and removal of the tumor had gone so smoothly, and just as he was about to close, the voice came over the speakers.

Tom looked up to where the speakers had been mounted on the wall, but they were gone. Perhaps they'd been removed to ensure that no one else ever got distracted during surgery.

Tom remembered fighting his every impulse to bolt from the operating room when he received the news about his wife's accident. But he systematically stitched each layer of the animal's body. He remembered tying the final knot of the final suture and placing the sterile bandage over the long incision. He even recalled running out of tape on the first roll and Cliff handing him another.

He remembered ripping off his mask because he felt as if he was suffocating, and telling the tech assistant to begin waking the panda. With unbearable pain, he recalled walking over to the drug cabinet, reaching inside and picking up the syringe and vial.

He was then standing next to Ming, gently squeezing her skin as he pushed the syringe into her and pressed down on the plunger.

How he got from the operating room in the clinic to the emergency room at the hospital was a total blur. It was as if his memory jumped from holding the syringe to hearing the words "I'm sorry. She lost the child."

His life was shattered.

"Oh, God," he moaned. "I'm so, so sorry, Ming. I'm so sorry I did that to you. You needed me to protect you and I didn't." And then anger and self-hatred welled up in him and he slammed his fist on the metal table. A crashing sound echoed through the room. "Damn it, why didn't I look?" he yelled out. "Why didn't I grab the right vial?" His anger rose even higher. "Why did she cheat on me?" and then all the other questions poured out: Why did she lie to him about visiting her parents? Why did she have to go and see her lover on that icy morning?

But it was Ming who was the tragic, innocent victim, not him and not Laura.

Tom looked at the far wall and stared at the drug cabinet as he walked over and touched the small countertop directly below. The metal was cold under his fingers. He opened the drawer that held syringes of various sizes. Closing it softly, he then opened the door to the drug cabinet. His eyes blurred as he looked at the vials. Although he couldn't read the labels, the colors were indication enough; the clinic still kept the antibiotics as accessible as possible, placing them on the bottom shelf, the lethal drugs on the top.

He closed his eyes, reenacting each movement as it had happened so many years before. Without looking, he reached up and took a vial on the far-right side of the bottom shelf. Opening his eyes, he looked at the label: Gentamicin, a standard antibiotic commonly used at the clinic. Again and again, he repeated this motion, and each time with the same result.

Contrary to what he had convinced himself every day since Ming's surgery, for the first time, Tom was unconditionally and absolutely sure that he had taken the vial from the bottom shelf. But how, then, did he end up with potassium chloride?

His mind was racing, recalling minuscule facts that he'd long since forgotten.

He gasped in air, his eyes opening wide. Someone had incorrectly stocked the drug cabinet. Someone had placed lethal drugs on the bottom shelf. But who? An intern or temporary worker reassigned from another area of The Park?

Tom felt all the strength drain from his body. He tried to steady himself against the cabinet, but collapsed on the floor, where he sat motionless. He tried to collect his thoughts although his head was pounding.

"Someone misstocked the drug cabinet," he whispered. *"Someone misstocked the drug cabinet,"* he repeated in a louder voice.

But what did it mean? Tom's thoughts scrambled toward the answer, hoping to find a spark of light that could end his torment and make the past understandable.

He buried his head in his arms. *Someone misstocked the drug cabinet,* that much he knew. But who? he asked himself again. But suddenly he realized it didn't matter. The fact that someone had placed the drugs on the wrong shelf didn't absolve him of his actions. He still should have looked at the vial before filling the syringe.

But it made what had occurred understandable and, perhaps in time, acceptable. He was finally able to face his own fallibility. Accidents happened, sometimes for a reason, sometimes not.

In all these years, he had never given that possibility any serious consideration. He had been so tied to the painful reality of Ming's death that he had never let himself imagine other outcomes.

What would have happened if the antibiotics had been where they were supposed to be, or if he had caught the mistake in time? Ming would have lived, but that wouldn't have changed his wife's betrayal. It wouldn't have lessened the sting of his devastating divorce. He would have continued working at The Park, and conceivably, he would still be there.

But instead his life had taken a detour. And on that detour he had found a town called Lumby and, in that town, his soul mate.

A woman he very much loved was waiting for him right down the hall. And the people he had expected to hate him the most, those who'd been most hurt by his actions, showed compassion and understanding.

He took a deep breath and felt something lift from deep inside his heart, and he instantly knew that the weight and burden of guilt were finally leaving his soul.

He stood and looked at the stainless-steel table and then at the drug cabinet. He sighed with the resignation that he was a man who had done the best he could under extreme circumstances, and his best was not enough to save Ming. "I'm sorry," he whispered again. He was now able to forgive Laura, and much harder than that, he had found a way to forgive himself.

When Tom rejoined Mac and Cliff, Mac was flushed with laughter from the stories Cliff had been telling her about Tom's younger days. "I didn't know you were such a hell-raiser," she teased.

He bent over and kissed her head. "I don't know what he said, but it's all lies."

Mac immediately heard a lightness in his voice, and squeezed his hand.

"So, did you have a good look around?" Cliff asked.

"Yes, I did, thanks," Tom said, smiling at Mac. "The ghosts are gone."

Cliff was unsure what Tom was talking about but let it pass. "By the way, did you ever get the flyer I sent you a while ago?"

"What flyer?"

Cliff explained. "The last time I was at Berkeley, I saw a flyer advertising a vet clinic for sale somewhere in the Rockies. It sounded like your type of place, so I called Laura and got your address in Maine."

Tom was stunned. "So, it was *you* who sent that to me? Why didn't you include a note?"

"I assumed you didn't want anyone from The Park to contact you."

Tom thought for a second. "And you've spoken to Laura?"

"I see her every now and again. She remarried four or five years after you left and seems very happy now. Every time I see her, she asks if we've heard from you and is disappointed when I say I haven't. But she was tenacious a few months ago in tracking down your current address for me."

Tom shook his head in amazement. "If nothing else, it's been a day of surprises."

FORTY-FOUR

Commitments

Before dinner that evening, while she and Tom were relaxing in the inn's sitting room, Mac's cell phone rang. Looking at the phone's small display screen, she knew exactly who it was and had a very good hunch as to why he was calling.

"Hello, Jimmy," she said.

"Hey, Mac, it's Jimmy."

"Yes, I know," Mac said, winking at Tom. "What can I do for you?"

"I wanted to give Tom an update on our zoo," he said.

"He's sitting right here—you can tell him yourself. Hold on," she said, about to hand over the phone.

"No! Wait!" Jimmy said, loud enough for Mac to hear.

She put the phone back to her ear. "You don't want to talk to him?"

"Well, it's not exactly that," Jimmy hedged. "It would just be better coming from you."

Mac became impatient. "I already told him about the chicken zoo."

"It's much more than that now," Jimmy said. "We have a rhea."

Mac laughed. "What's that, a bald chicken?" Mac covered the phone and said to Tom, "Jimmy says they have something called a rhea in their zoo."

"Put it on speaker," Tom whispered.

Jimmy heard the click. "Are you still there, Mac?"

"Yeah, I am. Is that it?" Mac asked.

"No," Jimmy said quickly. "You need to tell Tom that we also have a pregnant alpaca and a koala bear."

Mac chuckled. "No doubt stuffed."

"No, a real one from Australia. He almost strangled Joshua when we were unloading all the animals that the monks of Saint Cross Abbey shipped over to us."

Mac couldn't help but notice how intently Tom was listening. "Where did the brothers get the animals?" she asked Jimmy.

"Gifts from around the world, they said." Jimmy then retold the story of Brother Michael's interview and how it had brought in so many unsolicited gifts.

"Where are they now?"

"The monks?" Jimmy asked.

Mac rolled her eyes. "No, the animals. Did you put them at the Feed Store?"

"Sam would never agree to that," he replied. "We're using the new barn at Montis Inn. It's humongous."

Mac looked alarmed. "The animals are in Mark Walker's care?"

"Sure, he's doing a great job."

Mac knew Mark too well. "He can't control the one draft horse he has, Jimmy. How is he going to care for a bunch of exotic animals?"

"Well, he has the best barn," Jimmy retorted.

"Okay, is that it?" Mac asked.

"Yeah," Jimmy said, before putting in a final plea. "And tell Tom everyone really needs him to come back."

After Mac hung up, Tom chuckled. "This Lumby Zoo business just keeps getting better and better."

Mac looked at him in surprise. "I wouldn't have expected you to take the situation so lightheartedly."

Tom held her hand in his. "I suppose you're right. Yesterday, I would have taken it differently."

"What do you mean?"

"I realized something when I went back to The Park today: several bad circumstances led to one very unfortunate outcome, but I honestly did the best I could," Tom confessed. "In those two seconds when I grabbed the wrong vial, regardless of where it was placed or who put it there, I made an irreversible mistake that cost an animal its life. That's what it was: an unintentional human mistake made under extreme duress. And what happened at the hospital afterward was a separate tragedy. But somehow, the two accidents became intertwined with my anger and guilt until they became one catastrophe that was so overwhelming, it controlled my life ever afterward." He wove his fingers between hers. "But it's over and I've come to terms with it."

Mac smiled. She was so proud of Tom and so very happy that he had finally found peace. She took his hand and kissed it. "You're such a good man," she said.

"A happier one, most definitely," he said. "And I've been thinking about the future. As much as I once needed to escape from my life in Lumby, I'm no longer looking for a refuge from my past." He took a deep, calming breath. "There's an organization in Jackson, Wyoming, that specializes in breeding programs for endangered species. I know the executive director and called him this morning. He has a few staff positions open and said I could start anytime." He paused. "It would be a great match for my background."

Mac pulled her hand from his, feeling everything slip away. "Wyoming?" Her voice cracked. "I assumed that after Jimmy's call, you would want to go back to your practice in Lumby."

"Why would you assume that?" he asked.

"Because of what you started there. Because it's obvious they want you back. And because of . . . us." Mac felt as if her life was shattering.

"But it's because of us that I thought of Jackson."

"To be farther away from me?" Mac asked.

"No, to be closer to Lumby. You said you never wanted to be far from Lumby, and Jackson would be an easy drive so you could visit whenever you wanted."

"Visit you?"

Tom laughed, and held Mac's hands tightly. "No, for us, you and me, to visit Lumby."

"You mean I would be with you in Wyoming?" she asked slowly. Mackenzie was so unprepared for Tom's suggestion, her head was swirling.

"Mac, Jackson, Wyoming, is almost as gorgeous as Lumby. The breeding preserve is on the border of Grand Teton National Park."

Mac shook her head, trying to clear her thoughts. "But you're asking me to leave Lumby."

Tom put his hand on her arm. "I'm asking you to spend the rest of your life with me. I love you. You are my soul mate and I can't imagine waking up without you."

"Then come back to Lumby," she begged, tears beginning to roll down her cheeks.

Tom sighed and patiently tried to convince Mac that they could have a wonderful life together elsewhere. "It would never be the same back in Lumby. I don't need to be liked, but I want to live where people trust me."

"In time they will," Mac promised. "And they want you to come back."

"That's where you may be mistaken," Tom said. "What they want is a veterinarian for their animals. They would prefer Ellen, but I'm the next-best thing because I'm their only option. I'm so tired of living a life of compromise in order to hide my past and shield my wounds. I want to make up for all the years I tossed away. And there's not a person in this world I'd rather do that with than you."

Mac couldn't sleep that night. At four in the morning, she slipped on her robe and sneaked downstairs to the inn's study, where she turned on the small television and began to click through the channels. Finding nothing of interest, she turned to the twenty-four-hour news channel, muted the volume, closed her eyes and proceeded to worry. As much as she fought it, her mind wandered back to the same place: Jackson, Wyoming.

After wrestling with her concerns until sunrise, Mac called Terry, knowing he always woke up at five thirty. She prayed a girl didn't answer the phone.

"Hello?"

"Terry, it's Mom," Mac said. "Did I wake you?" She couldn't find the nerve to ask if he was alone.

"No, I was just getting dressed. I need to swing by the lumberyard to put in an order before heading over to Katie Banks's farm. She hired me to rebuild some of her stalls. How's California?"

"Very different. You need to come out here someday," she said.

"When are you coming home?"

"In a few days," Mac answered. "I'll be flying into Rocky Mount."

"Dr. Candor isn't driving you?"

Mac dropped her head. "I don't think so, Terry. He really doesn't want to come back to Lumby." She couldn't disguise the pain in her voice.

There was a long silence over the phone.

"If there's anything I did to make him feel that way, tell him I'm sorry."

"I will. That's nice of you to say." But Mac also heard something different in her son's voice.

"Are you all right, Terry?"

There was another long pause. He finally said, "Remember Cy Johnson over in Rocky Mount?"

Mac thought through her son's friends. "No, I'm sorry. I don't."

"Yeah, you do. He came over the day after graduation and we hung out together," he reminded her

"Oh, right. The football player who's going off to Dartmouth in the fall."

"He was killed in a car accident on Priest's Pass last night," Terry said. "He had been partying and he was driving."

Mac's heart almost stopped. "Was anyone else hurt?"

"Sam, the girl I dated a few times. She's in the hospital. They don't know if she'll be okay."

"Were you at the party?" Mac asked.

"No, I was going to go, but I hung out here instead."

Thank God, Mac thought. "I'm so sorry about your friend."

"Yeah, me too."

"This isn't a good time, Terry, but I wanted to tell you something," Mac began. "Tom has asked me to live with him in Wyoming."

"Oh," Terry said, sounding stung by another life-altering bombshell. "What did you tell him?"

"That I'm unsure," Mac replied. "I'm still in shock."

"Well, if you want to be with him, Mom, then go for it. I'll come visit every couple of months. It would be good to see Tom again too."

"If I do this, we'll have a room for you in Jackson Hole and you can stay with us as long as you want," she said before sending her love and saying goodbye.

Just as Mac hung up, soft laughter came from the lobby. A young couple was checking out to catch an early-morning flight back home. From the snatches of their conversation she overheard, Mac figured it was either their anniversary or honeymoon and they had had a wonderful stay at the inn. She could clearly identify Eileen's high singsong voice, which sounded as chipper at six in the morning as it did at six in the evening.

The front door opened and closed, and then there was silence.

Mac dialed a number on her cell phone that she knew by heart. The phone rang twice. "Oh, please pick up," she whispered, but there were another three rings.

And then a recording came on, in Mark's voice: "Thank you for calling Montis Inn. We're probably in the orchard or the barn, so please leave a message and Pam will call you back really soon." Beep.

"Pam, it's Mac," she said softly into the phone. "Oh, I wish you were there. I don't know what to do. Please call me."

Just as Mac stood up, Eileen walked in, carrying a breakfast tray with two cups of coffee and several muffins.

"May I join you?" she asked.

"How did you know I was in here?"

"I saw the glow of the television," Eileen said, "and you and Tom are now the only guests at the inn."

"I'd love some coffee," Mac said. She gathered together her vibrant red hair and tied it in a knot high on her head. "We met your son yesterday—what a nice fellow."

"He is, indeed," Eileen said with a mother's pride. "I wish he would find someone to be with." She sipped her coffee.

"He seems so happy with his work at The Park," Mac commented.

"But that can't take the place of a human touch or the intimate connection two people make when they are in love, can it?"

Mac looked at the charming old lady, who probably had more wisdom in her one finger than Mac would ever have in her entire soul. Eileen reminded her of her dear friend Charlotte Ross, who had died several years earlier. How I miss her, Mac thought. She would know exactly what I should do.

"You're smiling," Eileen said.

"Just thinking back on an old friend who you remind me of."

"Not too old, I hope," Eileen said, chuckling.

Mac laughed as well. "No, just amazingly wise."

Eileen blushed at the compliment. "I see you and Tom are scheduled to leave soon?"

"I think that's the plan, yes," Mac answered, nodding.

"And are you returning home?"

Mac grinned. "You have no idea how significant that question is."

Eileen didn't respond. Instead she broke off a small piece of muffin and dunked it in her coffee.

"Tom asked me to move to Wyoming with him," Mac whispered, as if making a religious confession. She was not one to discuss personal matters with a stranger, but she needed to find her way out of the fog, and she somehow knew that this charming woman sitting across from her had a flashlight. "I don't know what to do."

Eileen took another long sip of coffee.

"It would mean leaving the only life I've ever known and all of the friends I've ever had," Mac explained as she looked down at her cup. "And my son, who is just beginning his own life." She paused. "But then I think how empty my life would be in Lumby without Tom. And as much as I love everyone there, those friendships couldn't fill the hole that he would leave. And I think it's a void that would be there until the day I die." She looked at Eileen, searching for an answer. "I'm sure I am meant to be with him. I don't think I could make that kind of move alone."

"But you wouldn't be alone, would you?" Eileen asked.

Mac thought for a long moment, then slowly began to smile. "No, I wouldn't," she said. "The man I love is upstairs and he wants to be with me for the rest of our lives." Mac's face lit up and her eyes sparkled. She jumped up and kissed Eileen on the cheek. "Thank you."

Mac wrapped her robe tightly around her torso and ran up the stairs two at a time. When she opened the bedroom door, she saw that Tom was still in bed. He was so still, it was as if he had not slept for the past twenty years, and had finally found the peace he needed to reach a deep, restful slumber.

He woke when the door closed. "Where were you?" he asked drowsily.

"Finding my way home," she said, and lay down next to him.

ꟹ

During breakfast that morning, Mac's cell phone rang just as Eileen was serving beautifully arranged plates filled with eggs Benedict and country potatoes. But instead of an incoming call, it was a text message that included several pictures. She scrolled through them and started to laugh.

"Unbelievable," she said, passing Tom the phone.

Tom first read the message: " 'LIZP is well under way and will be requiring the services of Dr. Tom Candor shortly.' LIZP?" he asked. Mac looked equally puzzled.

Jimmy had attached some pictures taken that morning. One picture, entitled "Rare Poultry Stock," showed the owner of the Lumby Feed Store using a large broom to corral several chickens into a small pen. Another image showed Mark Walker, covered with mud, losing a tug-of-war with a rhea. The next was a photograph of Simon Dixon, Jimmy D and Dennis Beezer entangled in six-foot-high wire mesh as they tried to stretch it between two leaning posts of decayed wood.

The final picture showed the mare Isabella, with Jeremiah standing by her side, holding a sign that read, "Still has the farts and fading fast."

"Do you think he means the horse or himself?" Tom laughed, giving the phone back to Mac. "I think Lumby will be an amazing place for some very lucky veterinarian."

Mac closed the lid to her cell phone, not wanting to look at any more pictures. Her future was sitting next to her and in a place called Jackson, Wyoming. She took Tom's hand and held it tightly. "I've decided to come with you."

Tom wasn't expecting an answer, let alone *that* answer, to his proposal. "Are you sure?"

"I'll miss them," she admitted. "They'll always be in my heart. But I want to share my life with you, and if Jackson, Wyoming, is where you're going, then that's where I'll be as well."

Tom kissed her. "I love you. I can't tell you what it means to me that you're willing to leave all that quirkiness behind. We'll visit often, I promise."

"I know it will work out," she said, before leaning over and kissing him. "But, right now, we need to finish breakfast," Mac said. "My plane leaves in three hours."

"Are you sure you don't want to stay out here for a while longer? I only need two or three days at Berkeley and then we could drive to Wyoming together," Tom suggested.

"You have a life to get caught up on and I have one that needs some wrapping up. It will take me about four weeks to finish a few jobs I had lined up. I'm thinking of letting Terry stay in the house, so I really won't have too much to do other than pack my bags."

The phone rang again. It was more photos from Jimmy D: the first, a koala bear sleeping on Gabrielle Beezer's lap. Mac wasn't sure where the next picture had been taken, but it showed Chuck Bryson holding both snow monkeys inside what appeared to be an aviary. The final photograph was of an exquisite South American parrot. "Wow," Mac said. Upon closer examination, though, she noticed two thumbs at the bottom of the picture and realized that someone had photographed a picture in a book.

A text message followed: "Town wants Tom back. World-class zoological park awaits Tom's return. Jimmy and Dennis sincerely apologize."

"If nothing else, I have to give them credit for trying," Tom said, still laughing at the picture of the South American parrot, which he knew had been extinct for hundreds of years.

FORTY-FIVE

Unloading

The Lumby Lines

Calling All Animals

BY CARRIE KERRY

November 12

The Lumby International Zoological Park and Endangered Species Breeding Society is well under way, having submitted a charter and a list of officers to the town council. The officers for LIZP (pronounced Liz–Pee, for those who were curious) are:

Chairman	open
President	open
VP Park Operations	Mark Walker
VP Veterinary Medicines	Dr. Tom Candor
Secretary	open
Treasurer	open

The Board of Directors includes such prominent townsfolk as Jimmy D, Dennis Beezer, Caroline Ross, Simon Dixon, Katie Banks, Joan Stokes and possibly Pam Walker. Two honorary director seats have been extended to Brothers Matthew and Michael of Saint Cross Abbey.

As Lumby prepares to open LIZP to the public at large, the town is asking for contributions. They include (but are not limited to): money, manual labor, materials for building additional endangered-species habitats, wood fencing, wire fencing, money, chicken mesh, rabbit houses, feed buckets and troughs. Also, vegetation for foreign herbivores, such as bamboo trees, would be appreciated.

Mark leaned against the closed stall door. "That was one of the most amazing things I've ever seen," he said, still staring at the baby alpaca that had been born two hours earlier.

Joshua glanced at his watch. "Are you going to spend the rest of the night here?"

"I think so," Mark said. "There's a cot in the tack room I can use." He yawned loudly. "Thanks again for coming over in the middle of the night."

"I wish I could have helped more, but she did all the work," Joshua said. "If you have things under control, I'm going home for a few hours."

"Are you coming back?" Mark asked.

"I need to drive down to the university for a nine o'clock meeting and then I'll be over."

Mark raised his brow. "An interview, per chance?"

"Not that I know of," Joshua said. "The department head asked if I would come by and talk with him."

"With just two hours of sleep, you're not going to be in top form."

"It's probably about publishing my dissertation with the university press, so hopefully it won't take longer than ten minutes."

The alpaca nudged its baby cria with her nose, waking the young animal. The cria struggled to stand on its shaky legs and, within seconds, was up and drinking milk from its mother. After several minutes, the cria took a step backward, lost its balance and sat down on its haunches. It managed to pull itself up, take several steps forward and fall against its mother.

"I think it's drunk," Mark joked.

The cria was startled by his voice and looked up at the strangers, causing it to lose its balance altogether. Over the coming minutes, the baby alpaca finally began to understand what its legs were for, and it stood up more skillfully. It walked in a circle around its mother, always staying very close to her. After another, wider excursion about the stall, the cria lay down on its side and quickly fell asleep.

Mark smiled. "Pam's going to love this."

"I'm surprised she's not here," Joshua commented.

"She fired André and didn't get out of the kitchen until one this morning," he explained. "We have guests checking out in a few hours, so she might already be back there baking pastries for their breakfast."

Joshua shook his head. "I thought you guys had a perfect opportunity with André. Why did she fire him?"

"It's Pam being Pam," Mark said. "But she's only worsened the situation because now she's working twice as hard in an attempt to equal André's cooking, which was really out of sight."

"Giving up the spatula doesn't mean giving up control of Montis," Joshua said.

Mark stretched his sore back. "I must have told her that a dozen times. But she's never one to shrug off what she thinks are her responsibilities. It's her choice and I'll support whatever she decides."

Joshua patted his friend on the shoulder. "Okay. If you don't need me, I'm off. I'm too old for these all-nighters."

Mark continued to stand at the stall door, watching the cria. "Thanks again for your help. We'll see you in a few hours."

ര

Pam hit her clock when the alarm blared at five a.m. She groaned and covered her head with the blankets. "What a stupid thing I did," she said into the pillow. "Mark?"

She blindly patted the other side of the bed and realized she was alone in the room. She vaguely remembered Mark getting up at two o'clock to check on the alpaca, so she assumed he had fallen asleep down at the barn.

Pam dragged herself out of bed and groggily pulled on her clothes. She needed to prepare breakfast for the Langers, who were departing early, and then serve another eighteen guests throughout the morning. Then, for two hours, she would wash plates, straighten the dining room and reset the tables before going food shopping, only to return to the kitchen to begin dinner preparations. Why hadn't it seemed so hard before André came along? Although she had previously enjoyed hosting the inn's guests, that too had become too demanding.

In the kitchen, Pam's spirits didn't improve. She struggled to invent a new scone recipe that would equal what André had been baking.

An hour and a half later, after the Langers departed, Pam slumped down on a stool at the kitchen island. She rested her arms on the cold granite and laid her head on her hands.

Mark bolted through the door. "Hi, honey! Are those scones? They smell great." He took butter and jam from the refrigerator and began devouring the remaining four pastries. "You really missed something," he said between bites. "The alpaca gave birth a few hours ago and the little cria—that's what Joshua said they're called—is already running around. You should take a break and come down to the barn."

Pam kept her head down.

"Honey? You awake?"

"I'm resting," she whispered.

He ate another mouthful of scone slathered with jam. "These are really good—almost like André's."

"Thanks," Pam said sarcastically.

Mark was as full of energy as Pam was drained of it.

"How does it feel to have your kitchen back to yourself? Must make you happy," Mark said, pouring himself a cup of coffee. "Just like old times."

"Like old times," Pam repeated.

"And I've been thinking. It's okay if we don't make that much money from the restaurant," Mark said, trying to ease any pressure his wife might be feeling. "The money we'll get from the zoo will cover the loss."

Pam glared at Mark from the corner of her eyes. "The zoo is a serious expense."

"Well, yeah, that's what it looks like right now," Mark said. "But I bet you can turn it around just like you turned around the monks' business and we can make a bundle from having the animals here."

Pam looked up. "You don't think we're going to be able to keep the same customers now that André is gone?"

Mark felt himself stepping back into a corner. "No, that's not what I meant," he said. "All I'm saying is that if we do lose some guests, that would be okay with me."

Pam stood up and threw her towel at him. "Well, it's not okay with me."

Realizing he was treading in deep, rough waters, Mark crammed the remaining scones into his jacket pocket. "Well, I have to get back down to the animals. Come join me when you can," he said, slipping out the door.

"Not anytime soon," Pam grumbled.

❧

By the time Mark returned to the barn, two trailers were parked by the arena's sliding doors, and Hank had positioned himself just inside the entry, where he was keeping a close watch over the young cria. He was dressed in overalls, and covering his skinny legs were muck boots. Clearly, he was ready to lend a wing and clean out dirty stalls.

A gray-haired man with a potbelly that threatened to bust out of his buttoned shirt sat on the back bumper of his trailer, gazing up at the orchard.

"Can I help you?" Mark asked.

"Mark Walker? The zookeeper?"

Mark smiled, immediately liking the title. "Okay."

The man spit out a wad of chewing tobacco. "A weird-looking ostrich ran out of here about ten minutes ago. I tried to stop it, but it kicked at me. Could have knocked me down."

"It's a rhea," Mark said. "Did you see where it went?"

"Up there somewhere," the stranger said, pointing up to the open fields by the apple grove.

Mark squinted, trying to see any movement among the trees. He guessed the rhea was already by the beehives or in the fields beyond. When he didn't see anything, he turned back to the man. "What can I do for you?"

"Just want to make my contribution to the town zoo," he said as he dropped the back gate of the trailer.

As soon as the door was down, Mark found himself face-to-face with an enormous bull, staring directly into his eyes.

Mark shuddered. "A bull?"

"Old Jesse. Meaner than a boxed-up rattlesnake," the man said, shaking his head. "Gouged one of my workers in the stomach last month and he still can't eat solid food without throwing up. I was going to take him to the slaughterhouse tomorrow, but Jimmy D told me to bring him down here." The man stood on the bumper and untied the rope that was tethering the animal in the trailer. "Get the other end."

Mark had no intention of coming within striking distance of the bull's eighteen-inch-long horns.

"I don't think we want a bull around here," he said, scrambling for an excuse, "because of children and all."

"Jimmy said you would take him." The man slapped the bull on the shoulder with the end of the rope. "Gid over," he said, jumping down from the bumper.

Mark was surprised by the man's agility, given his girth.

"Here, just hold this." The man tried to hand Mark the rope, but it wasn't long enough to reach where he was standing. "You gotta get closer," the man said, forcing Mark to step up onto the ramp. "He needs some enticing to get out of the trailer."

Mark knew he was in a precarious position. He held the only restraining rope to the bull, standing four feet in front of him.

"Don't worry. It's not the rope that's going to kill you. It's what's at the other end," the man said with a laugh. "Jesse hates walking down the ramp. You're gonna have to pull a little, but I'll give you some help."

The man disappeared into the front of the trailer. The bull snorted and Mark was sure he saw fire in its eyes.

"Just let him know who's boss," the man yelled, "and hold on."

Suddenly the truck's horn blasted, startling both Mark and the bull, which bolted from the trailer, missing Mark's chest by inches and ripping the rope out of his hands.

The man came running up to Mark. "I told you to hold on."

Mark stared after the rapidly disappearing bull in disbelief. "He almost gored me to death!"

Jesse's owner spit another wad of tobacco. "Jesse's only done that once before."

"Escape or kill a man?"

"No, he escapes all the time. You won't see him for weeks now."

"What a shame," Mark said facetiously. "We really don't want a wild bull running around our orchard, so why don't you go on up and get him and take him somewhere else?"

"Can't do. Told the missus I'd be back for breakfast," he said, climbing into his truck. "Oh, and Jesse likes rock music played in the barn."

"Like that's going to happen," Mark said under his breath.

Mark turned his attention to the second visitor. A dozen crates and cages were roped down in the back of an old pickup. A young woman in her twenties jumped down from the driver's seat.

"This is the Lumby Zoo drop-off, right?"

"So far," Mark said.

"Jimmy D sent me over. I've got a few animals for you," she said cheerfully.

Seeing the size of the crates, Mark assumed this would be far easier than dealing with the bull. "What do you have?" he asked.

"Let's see," she said. "Two porcupines, a couple of squirrels, one beaver with missing front teeth, three possums and an owl with a broken wing."

Mark spotted a raccoon that had extended its arms through the cage bars and was playing with the door latch. "And a raccoon," Mark added.

"Right. I forgot Rocky," she said.

"Where did you get all these?"

"Animal wildlife rescue west of Wheatley. If you show me where your pens are, I can move my truck closer."

Mark rubbed the rope burns on his palms. "Sorry. We don't have any pens, just stalls and a large aviary."

She looked at him as if she didn't understand. "But where are the small animals?"

"We don't have any," Mark said. "Maybe this is a large-animal zoo."

"That's crazy. All zoos have small animals."

Mark looked at her with a blank expression. "But we have no place for them."

"Well, Jimmy said—"

"You know what?" Mark said, trying to control his temper. "I don't care what Jimmy said. If you have any animals that can be safely kept in a twelve-by-twelve box stall, we've got plenty of those. Or there's the aviary, but the peacock is in there during the day."

"The article in the *Wheatley Sentinel* said you were taking all kinds of animals," she complained.

"The article was wrong," Mark said. "What can I say?"

The woman turned on her heels and opened the driver's-side door. "Well, I'm going to go and see Jimmy D right now."

"Great!" Mark said. "Tell him to get down here and clean out some stalls."

From the way the woman spun her tires as she drove off, it was obvious she couldn't be counted as a satisfied customer. Hank blinked at the woman's rudeness.

~

By midafternoon Mark was exhausted from the onslaught of county residents who thought they'd found the perfect haven to unload their unwanted animals. One couple had the audacity to bring a litter of twelve-week-old rottweiler pups, nine in all. The wife complained that they had tried to find owners, but no one was interested and the pups were starting to eat them out of house and home.

Joshua arrived just as the couple pulled away with their pups jumping all over the backseat. He found Mark slouched down on the ground, resting his back against the barn door. "How's it going?" he said.

"Don't ask," Mark moaned. "We've become the dumping ground for every rejected animal in the state."

"It can't be that bad."

"Pam came down an hour ago. Some kid came by on his bicycle and left his ant farm on the front porch of the inn."

Joshua chuckled. "Well, that sounds harmless enough."

"And would you say the same about a two-thousand-pound bull with full horns running loose in our orchard?" Mark asked. "Oh, and before you answer, good old Jesse has already gored one man to death and another near to death. Who knows? Maybe the bull has already speared the rhea."

"They're both up there?" Joshua asked in alarm.

"For most of the day," Mark admitted. "This isn't going very well and I want to strangle Jimmy D."

A Ford Explorer's horn honked at the end of the dirt driveway.

"Speaking of the devil, Jimmy's waving to us," Joshua said, lending Mark a hand to get up. "Sorry I'm so late," he said as they started down the drive to meet the mayor. "I got tied up at the university."

"Anything important?" Mark asked.

Joshua kept his head down, kicking at stones. "Actually yes," he finally said. "It seems one of the faculty at Berkeley is school chums with the dean at the university in Wheatley. They were talking the other day and my name came up in conversation. Dean Fulton asked if I would consider teaching here in Wheatley."

Mark's face lit up for the first time that day. "That's great! You said yes, right?"

Joshua dug his hands in his pockets. "I said I would be interested in talking to them about it at some point. But it turned out they wanted to talk to me sooner than later, so I ended up meeting with a half dozen folks today."

"Did they offer you a job?"

"Oh, definitely not," Joshua said. "But I think they might if I submit an application and go through the process."

Mark looked over at his close friend. "So, why don't you sound happier?"

He raised his shoulders. "I'm not unhappy, just . . . dispassionate."

"Well, then, keep on working here," Mark proposed.

Joshua slapped his friend on the back. "As much as I love Montis, I need a more substantial job."

"More substantial as in better paying?" Mark asked. "Because we can talk about increasing your salary."

Joshua appreciated how Mark was trying to help in his own unique way. "Substantial as in being on staff. In fact, I just turned down a really interesting part-time offer yesterday."

"For what?"

"Caroline Ross and her husband, Kai, were over last night for dinner. You know she heads up the Ross Foundation. Well, it seems that Ross Orchards is now the single-largest fruit producer in the

Northwest and is pouring money into her foundation. The Board of Directors wants some genetic research done on a few of the diseases that have been hitting their crops pretty hard the last five years. They already talked with Monsanto, Dow and several other chemical companies, but the project isn't big enough for a major corporation to take on."

"Is it big enough for one person?" Mark's eyes opened wide. "Like you?"

"Boy, that would be a dream come true," Joshua said, his face lighting up for a second. "But I'm afraid not. They're starting small and only investing enough for part-time research for the next six months."

"What's wrong with that?"

"Maybe if I was single and twenty years younger and had no responsibilities, but, Mark, I need a real job, with a solid income. So, I told Caroline thanks, but no, thanks. You just don't turn down a faculty position with possible tenure for a part-time unknown, even if it is the best job in the world, working with people you like." He paused. "Although the university here is only the satellite campus, it's a good school that could offer job security, and we could stay in Lumby, which would please Brooke no end."

Jimmy honked his horn again and Mark waved to him. "Coming," Mark yelled. "So, what are you going to do?" he asked Joshua.

His friend looked up at the sky. "Take the mature, responsible road and interview at the university even though it's not really what I want."

"What's taken you guys so long?" Jimmy said. "We've got to get the sign up before the sun sets."

"The last thing we need right now is a sign, Jimmy. You've got to stop sending people here," Mark said. "I was buried all day with people trying to dump their unwanted pets on me."

"Well, the more animals the better!" Jimmy said.

"We don't have cages for them!" Mark insisted. "So no small animals until *you* figure out where they go."

"Well, just to let you know, I've got a plan that covers all the animals. Once Tom Candor comes back, we can give them all to the state zoo, which is only about an hour from here. I've already called the zoo's director and he thinks it's a great idea. And Brother Matthew is okay with the monks' herd going to a well-run zoo. Not that this isn't that."

Mark glared at the mayor. "Jimmy, it's just a barn. You know it and I know it."

"Let's just get Tom back here. I've been sending Mac pictures on her cell phone and I thought this would be the clincher." Jimmy opened the back of his SUV and pulled out a spectacular black-and-gold etched wooden sign.

Lumby International

Zoological Park

FORTY-SIX

Introduction

At Saint Cross Abbey the following evening, the monks fended off cold autumn winds as they walked from the annex to the small church, which was protected by a surrounding cypress grove. In preparation for vespers, Brother Michael, who had found himself with ample free time since the animals left, had already lit the two hundred candles that adorned the private chapel.

Those who crossed the chapel's threshold were transported into another world of deep prayer and Gregorian chants, all for the glory of God. In earlier days, the wooden pews of the one-room chapel were usually half empty, with two or three seats in back taken by visitors or residents of Franklin. Since the sisters had arrived, the intimate sanctuary was almost always full.

As bells rang out across the monastery grounds, indicating that vespers would begin in five minutes, Brother Matthew pulled open the heavy wooden door, the old hinges creaking in the silence. Most of the members from both communities (since the sisters wished to be called their own community) were already seated.

During matins and vespers Brother Matthew sat in a pew and had no unique responsibilities. On that evening, he found a seat in back next to Sister Megan. She smiled as he sidestepped into the pew. Her familiarity was unnerving, but Matthew had racked his brain trying to remember where he had met her, without success. Even her voice in song was vaguely recognizable but so distant in his memory that he was unable to make the connection.

During the first chant, Matthew closed his eyes and couldn't help but smile. He had heard nothing but male voices fill the chapel for so many years, and the women brought both lightness and depth to the singing. Now layered over the lower octaves were almost angelic high notes.

Matthew stopped singing to hear better; the voices of two religious orders were becoming one. And five harmonic tones—the basses, baritones, tenors, altos and sopranos—weaved an intricate dance as they all sang to their one God.

There was, indeed, much for which to be thankful.

⁂

As Matthew had done most every day during his years at the monastery, after vespers he walked to his bedroom for a short period of meditation before supper. He was exhausted from a week of long discussions with the other brothers. After the last opinions were voiced, it was unanimously agreed that the sisters would make a welcome addition to the Saint Cross order.

Although Brother Matthew closed his eyes for only a minute, he woke an hour later. Seeing the time, he donned his sweater and rushed downstairs to meet Sister Claire. "I'm sorry I'm late," he said as he walked into the community room.

Sister Megan was seated in an armchair across from Sister Claire. "We've been enjoying the fire," Megan said.

Matthew sat on the sofa facing both women. "Last night, our community voted on the proposal that the sisters of Saint Amand Monastery join with the monks of Saint Cross Abbey, and it was unanimously agreed that we should. Although many details must be worked out, there wasn't a dissenting voice within our community."

"That's wonderful!" Claire said. "We feel the same. And the final evaluation report on the soil came back today."

Megan continued. "We are all but assured that the land behind your monastery would produce an excellent-quality grape."

"And that comes on good authority?" Matthew asked.

Claire smiled. "Megan has friends in high places."

He couldn't help but laugh. "Well, I thought I did too. So how high are your friends?"

"Well, it's not from Him." She blushed, looking upward. "My father is Christian Copeland, the owner of Copeland Vineyards."

Claire added, "Her father owns one of the largest wineries in Sonoma Valley."

"Of course!" Matthew said, smiling. "That's why you look so familiar. You used to write a feature in your father's magazine with your photograph at the top of the column. And you were on his television commercials."

Megan nodded. "Yes, before taking my vows and assuming my new name, I was Laura Copeland. I called my father a few months ago when we began considering a move to Franklin. He's been here several times since then, looking at the terrain and collecting soil samples."

"In fact, during one of his visits," Claire interjected, "he returned a stray animal to the monks, but never introduced himself."

"My father will be delighted to know that his magazine is read here at the abbey."

Matthew nodded. "And appreciated by all of us."

"Mr. Copeland has a vested interest in our success," Claire said. "He is a silent investor in Saint Amand wine. Depending upon the year and the harvest, we also trade grapes with his vineyard."

Sister Megan laughed softly. "Our wines go up against his in national wine-tasting competitions each year, and although he frequently wins, we are becoming a formidable challenger."

"So, you feel confident that moving your vineyard here is the right thing to do?" Matthew asked.

"We do, thanks to Mr. Copeland," Claire said, and then turned to Megan. "We really need to thank your father for his assistance."

"There's no need," Megan said. "He was delighted to help."

Matthew leaned forward. "Perhaps he would like to visit again, and this time meet the community?"

Megan gave a sly smile. "In truth, he wouldn't like anything more than to be personally invited to Saint Cross by the abbot himself."

"Well, I think that can be easily arranged." Matthew winked at both of them. In his eyes there was a twinkle that the sisters had not seen for weeks.

Welcoming Christian Copeland to Saint Cross Abbey several days later was, for Brother Matthew, like embracing a visiting brother from another monastery. Christian was genuine, kind in spirit, soft in voice, entertaining with stories and, above all else, respectful of the monks' lives and surroundings.

When Christian heard the legal papers had been finalized for the sisters to acquire the adjacent property, and when Sister Claire suggested an impromptu groundbreaking party, he graciously insisted on hosting a "small gathering." All he asked was that the brothers invite whomever they wanted.

The first call Brother Matthew made was to Pam and Mark Walker at Montis Inn, and the second was to Joshua and Brooke Turner. Matthew went so far as to ask Joshua to invite all of the monks' other friends in Lumby as well. That afternoon, Brother Michael drove into Franklin and invited parishioners and townsfolk alike.

Few people had the connections and the clout to pull together a party for several hundred guests at the drop of a hat, but Christian Copeland, using his company's resources, was one of them. The following afternoon, just hours before the party was to begin, large trailers arrived at Saint Cross Abbey and were discreetly parked behind the guesthouse.

Returning to the abbey after daily chores, the monks were astounded by the transformation that had taken place in the community room and adjacent parlors. The catered food was some of the finest cuisine that many had ever tasted, and the wine was a reserved merlot from the private cellar of Copeland's own vineyard. Fresh flowers adorned the tables. A wind quartet played soft Renaissance music in the background.

Thirty minutes before guests were to arrive, Brooke and Joshua knocked on the back door. When no one answered, they peered in. Immediately hearing the music and smelling the aromas, they knew the festivities were about to begin.

As they let themselves in, Brooke pulled on her husband's sleeve. "I didn't see any other cars out there. Are we too early?"

"Matthew called and asked if we could come by before the party started. He probably needs help setting up."

When they turned the corner and stepped into the community room, though, they realized that no help was needed—the monastery was already transformed into a picture-book setting for a memorable celebration.

"Come in," Matthew said, waving to them. He was standing next to a distinguished-looking man with short gray hair and a closely trimmed beard.

Brooke gave Matthew a hug. "It's been too long since I've seen you."

"Thank you for coming a little early," he said. "I'd like you to meet a friend of ours, Christian Copeland. Christian, this is Brooke and Joshua Turner."

Brooke couldn't help but stare at the man's intense blue eyes. "Nice to meet you," she said, shaking his hand.

He smiled warmly at both of them. "I've heard so much about you in the last few days," he said, shaking Joshua's hand as well, "that I feel I already know you."

Joshua squinted his eyes at Matthew. "I wouldn't trust anything he's told you," he teased.

"He said you almost became a monk," Christian said.

"Oh, that part is true," Joshua said. "But I wouldn't be so sure about anything else."

"Brooke," Matthew said, touching her arm as if to lead her away, "perhaps you would like something to drink?"

"The nicest offer I've had today."

As Matthew and Brooke wandered off, Christian picked up two glasses of white wine from the side table and offered one to Joshua.

"Are you a wine drinker?"

"Not seriously," he replied, taking the glass offered to him. "The only time I became interested in wine was in an academic setting. During my graduate work at the university, we used grapevines to test the chemical residency of different strains of some bacteria. To make it easier to identify the infected plants, we altered the genes so that the grapes with the bacteria glowed fluorescent green under a black light."

Christian laughed, imagining a dark laboratory filled with radiant grapes. "Did it alter their taste?"

"Not that I know of, but nor were we successful in eradicating the microorganism."

"Well, perhaps this sauvignon blanc will change your perspective." He lifted the glass to his nose and smelled the delicate bouquet. "It is one of our finest vintages."

Joshua studied the labels on the wine bottles lined up down the table: Copeland Vineyards. "Ah, you're a vintner."

"Yes. In my humble opinion, we are fortunate to be one of California's finest."

"We?" Joshua asked.

"Hundreds of people contribute to Copeland Vineyards. I'm just the president and one of the more recognizable faces."

For the next ten minutes, Christian gave Joshua a brief history of his business and an introduction to the fine art of growing grapes. Joshua listened with keen interest, and since the topic dealt with horticulture, which was akin to his expertise of agriculture, he posed insightful questions.

"There are still vast opportunities to improve our crops and create hybrids that have better taste and are not as susceptible to the cold," Christian said. "In fact, my daughter and the other sisters of Saint Amand will be facing some unique challenges when they plant their new vineyard here in Hamilton."

"I heard that they were joining Saint Cross with cross and wine in tow."

Both men laughed easily.

"Which brings me to why I asked Matthew to invite you here before the crowd arrived."

Joshua looked up in surprise. "You?"

Christian nodded. "Matthew told me about your work in genomic biology."

"In truth, I'm surprised you know that term."

"I'm in the business of growing grapes, and genetic engineering has already taken us one small step closer to our goal of consistently producing high volume without compromising the quality of our grapes. So, yes, I follow your field very carefully."

"Well, my field is genetic manipulation in agriculture, in field crops, and not horticulture, which is focused on gardens and orchards."

"But wouldn't you agree that the two are almost inseparable when it comes to the theories of gene management?" Christian asked.

Joshua nodded. "I agree. The theories as well as the practice are highly transferable."

"Then we may have a proposition for you. Besides having a personal connection, I'm heavily invested in Saint Amand, so their ability to grow world-class grapes in a northern climate is of interest to me. Also, two years ago, we lost close to sixty percent of our California crop due to an unexpected freeze that hit five weeks before harvest."

Joshua's thoughts began to spin a mile a minute. "You're looking for a frost-resistant grape?"

"I doubt we could ever reach that point," Christian said. "But if we could hybridize a variant that could sustain temperatures just six degrees lower than they do now, it would have a tremendous impact on my vineyard and the entire industry."

Joshua was speechless.

"What we are initially looking for is a commitment from someone with your knowledge and experience to work with our grapes for at least a year so you would be involved through the entire growing cycle. We would find you sufficient research facilities either in the private sector or at a local university."

"In California?" Joshua asked.

"Oh, no, here. Or in Lumby, if you prefer," Christian answered. "We want this very low-key, and I would expect you would need to be at Saint Cross a day or two a week, but that would be your decision. It would be very autonomous—you would be responsible for planning and managing your research and fieldwork. My job is to get you whatever resources you needed to reach your goal."

Joshua stared at the man, and for a second, he wondered if he was dreaming.

"Joshua?" Christian asked.

"I'm at a loss. I don't know what to say."

Christian was unsure what Joshua was thinking. "Would you be interested in joining the Copeland Vineyards team?"

Joshua was so excited he felt himself trembling. "I would be more than interested. It sounds like a once-in-a-lifetime opportunity."

Christian put his arm on Joshua's shoulder. "It's a business of passion and life and earth and growing. I guarantee it will so far exceed anything you're thinking that you won't want to leave, and we have enough work to keep you busy until you're an old man. We'll get together tomorrow and go over some details."

Joshua beamed. "Thank you. I hope I can meet your expectations."

Christian smiled. "Matthew assured me that's one thing I'll never have to worry about if you join us."

FORTY-SEVEN

Celebration

Brother Michael opened the front door of the monastery. "The Montis contingent has arrived!" he exclaimed, smiling from ear to ear. "Come in! Come in! The party's already begun."

"You look happy," Mark said, lugging in a case of champagne.

"Life is good," Michael said. "What's the champagne for?"

"There's so much to celebrate," Mark answered.

Pam sneaked away from her husband and headed toward the community room. Weaving her way through the crowd of guests, monks and sisters, she first spotted Brooke and Joshua standing by themselves, close to a window. Even from a distance, she could see that Joshua was grinning like a Cheshire cat. Suddenly Brooke threw her arms around her husband's neck and kissed him. As Pam began to make her way toward her friends, she saw Brother Matthew wave to her.

"Join us," he said, as she approached. "Let me introduce you to Christian Copeland. Christian, this is Pam Walker."

Christian shook her hand. "It's good to see you again, Pam."

"Christian?" Pam said in disbelief. "What are you doing here?"

Matthew looked as surprised as Pam clearly was. "You know each other?"

"On my first trip to the area, I stayed at Montis Inn, where Pam and Mark were perfect hosts," Christian explained.

"Ah, that makes sense," Matthew said, with a smile. "Several of the brothers mentioned that Montis was on the cover of your magazine last month." Michael gently tugged at Brother Matthew's elbow to get his attention. "If you would excuse me," Matthew said as he stepped away.

Pam hugged Christian. "I'm still in shock. You know the monks?"

"My daughter is Sister Megan," Christian said, looking over at a small group of people standing by the fireplace. "So, how have you been?"

Pam grimaced. "Have you spoken to André recently?"

"He called the afternoon you . . ."

"Fired him? What an absolute mistake that was," Pam admitted.

Christian narrowed his eyes. "So, why did you let him go? He could have been an outstanding complement to your inn."

"If I didn't know it then, I know it now," Pam said. "I just couldn't turn over the kitchen to someone else. It had always been my responsibility, and its success or failure was my own doing."

Christian grinned. "You couldn't give up control," he guessed.

Pam looked down and swirled the wine in her glass. "I suppose not, which is pretty embarrassing to admit."

"Why?" Christian asked. "I believe being accountable is one of the most honorable traits a person can have. We don't see enough of it today."

"But it has obviously been my own undoing," Pam confessed.

"It's easier to accept the consequences when they're a direct result of our own actions. I have firsthand experience of that," Christian said, laughing at his recollection. "Quite some time ago, more years than I care to admit, I began my vineyard with three acres. I insisted on doing everything myself—I planted, harvested, blended, bottled and then, at night, I set up floodlights and pruned the vines. Two results came out of all that hard work: I destroyed my marriage and made mediocre wine. The more I tried, the less fantastic the results." He took a sip of wine. "It took a few years for me to smarten up and create a team in which each person was an expert in his or her area. Copeland Vineyards became a success not because of me or *them* but because of *us*. As time passed, my confidence in my employees gradually increased, so I loosened my management style. Mistakes are still made, but they're rare and easily corrected."

Pam, who had listened intently to every word Christian said, leaned closer to him so no one else would hear. "I don't know how I would ever get him to come back. I doubt he'll talk to me again."

"Sure he will," Christian said. "André!" he called out, and waved his arm.

To Pam's horror, André walked across the room toward them.

"What's he doing here?" she whispered.

"He's a good friend," Christian replied.

When André joined them, Christian embraced him like a son he hadn't seen for a long time. "You look dashing as always."

"And you look far healthier than the last time I saw you." André laughed. He turned to Pam. "Bad oysters in Seattle, if I remember correctly," he explained.

"Indeed," Christian said. "Now, if you will excuse me, I need to talk with my daughter."

Pam stood awkwardly next to André. "I don't know what to say," she said hesitantly. "I'm so sorry."

"No apologies are necessary," André said in good humor. "You and Mark need to do what's best for Montis Inn. I fully understand."

"But . . . ," Pam said slowly, carefully choosing her words, "I made a mistake. What's best for Montis is for you to be our chef." She looked up at him and tried to smile.

"Ah, but is that also what's best for you?"

Pam nodded. "It needs to be," she said, before taking a gulp of wine. "Would you consider coming back?"

André smiled sincerely. "Of course I would. And if it eases your concerns, I think what you're going through is very understandable.

Cedar Grove fired me three times in the first month as they struggled with entrusting another person in their kitchen."

"It's something I'm not good at," Pam admitted. "So, be patient. But I very much want you back."

"Then I'll be there at six tomorrow morning."

"You will?" Pam asked in surprise.

"I'd be honored."

Pam laid her hand on his arm. "Thank you, André. Thank you."

She was unsure if she should kiss his cheek or shake his hand. Instead André put his arm around her shoulder, shook her slightly and laughed. "You really need to relax some and not take everything so seriously. Let me refill your glass," he said, as he took her crystal tumbler. "I'll be back in a minute with more wine."

As André walked off, Pam made her way over to Brooke and Joshua. "When did you two arrive?" she asked Brooke.

"A while ago," Joshua replied.

Pam looked at Joshua and then at Brooke. "Okay, both of you look like you just won the lottery and are bursting with excitement."

"We sort of did," Brooke said, squeezing Pam's arm. "Joshua just accepted an offer to work for Christian Copeland. He'll be doing research and fieldwork on the sisters' vineyard right here in Hamilton."

Pam hugged her dear friend. "So you're not moving? I'm so relieved," she said, fighting back tears of happiness.

Matthew clinked his glass to get everyone's attention.

"I'll tell you all about it later," Brooke whispered.

It was seven o'clock, and most of the two hundred guests had already arrived.

"If all of you can brave the cold for a few minutes, the sisters would like us to gather outside."

To everyone's surprise, the weather was cooperating and warmer winds were blowing in from the southwest. With the light from the lanterns that several of Christian's employees had set up around the monastery grounds, Matthew led the group to the base of the knoll, where the sisters' land began. Claire was holding a shovel, and the other sisters were standing close to her, each grasping a lit white candle.

As the visitors approached, they formed a circle around the women. When Claire spoke, her voice rang out. "God has led us to a new home. May the vines we plant grow strong and may our faith and understanding deepen as we become one monastery."

She dug the spade deep into the ground and lifted the shovel full of dirt.

"We are home," she said, to the cheers of all.

FORTY-EIGHT

Howard

After saying goodbye to Mac at the airport, Tom Candor returned to Redding to bring closure to the last fifteen years of his life. One delightful surprise of his last days in town was a pleasurable dinner with Cliff and Eileen Keller at the inn.

Even more renewing was lunch the following day with his ex-wife, Laura. After all that they had been through, both together and alone, they were able to find a middle ground that moved from cordiality to genuine friendship. As Tom would explain later to Mac, it was the last step in asking for and offering forgiveness to the woman he had once loved.

When Tom Candor finally turned onto Route 299, he looked in his rearview mirror and silently said goodbye to his past. Heading northeast, he passed the town limits and smiled. What an amazing turn of events he had seen in his life, he thought, and credited much of it to Mackenzie McGuire. By the time he drove out of the state of California, he was racing twenty miles over the speed limit just to see her that much sooner.

During the journey, he thought about little else except how they were about to begin their lives together in Wyoming. He had to correct himself several times—their lives together had already begun in Lumby, but that chapter had ended.

Tom's cell phone rang. "Hello?" he answered.

It was a poor connection. "Tom? It's Mac."

He smiled broadly. "I was about to call you."

"Is everything okay?"

"Better than okay. I miss you, I love you and I'm on my way."

"I love you too, and I'm working as quickly as I can," she said. "Where are you now?"

"In Oregon," he said. "About thirty minutes from the Idaho border."

Mac so wanted to be with him at that very moment. "You're getting close."

"I'm driving as fast as I can to you."

"To me?" Mac asked. "I thought you were going directly to Jackson."

"Lumby's not far out of the way," Tom explained. "There are some things I could use from the clinic."

Mac had expected Tom to ask her to bring whatever he needed from The Granary so he wouldn't have to come back.

"Oh, that would be wonderful! Everyone has been asking about you."

Tom chuckled. "I'm sure."

Mac paused for a moment. "They know everything about that day. Everything," she said, "including your wife's accident. Chuck Bryson heard about it when he was at Berkeley, but he kept it to himself out of respect for your privacy. But when he and I talked the other day, and I told him that we were going to Wyoming, we thought that it wouldn't hurt anyone if he shared what he knew with the town residents. So, when the town asked you back two weeks ago, it wasn't out of sympathy."

Tom no longer felt hurt by the residents of Lumby. In fact, he thought kindly of the townsfolk—they had done the best they could under the circumstances, and had behaved better than he would have if faced with the same situation.

"That's nice to hear," he said.

"And when you arrive, you have to see the zoo." Mac laughed. "Even though everyone knows we're leaving, they thought the zoo would be a good enticement for another vet who might consider moving to Lumby. Anyway, it really is something that needs to be experienced firsthand."

"Should I ask?" Tom asked.

"Oh, definitely," Mac said. "It has tripled in size in the last week alone. Katie Banks donated three goats. And Simon Dixon contributed a wild goose that broke its leg last year."

"Wonderful!" Tom chuckled.

"And, I know this sounds nuts, but someone put a wildebeest in one of the pens."

"A wildebeest? I seriously doubt that."

"Well, that's what Mark is calling it."

The harebrained craziness of Lumby never ceased to amaze Tom, but what attracted him more was how comfortably Mac seemed to adapt to its quirkiness with such style and finesse.

"Yeah," she continued. "No one knows where it came from, but they had an article on the front page about it laying a football-sized egg."

Tom laughed even harder.

"And little Tommy Beezer, Dennis and Gabrielle's son, brought over his fish tank. I think it was more of a bribe—he's still hoping you will talk his parents into allowing him to get a puppy."

Tom grinned. "There's always a hitch with an eight-year-old."

"Tom," Mac said, becoming more serious, "I'm glad you're coming to Lumby, if only for a few hours. You might not want to see anyone, but there are a lot of folks here who want to apologize."

"There's no need," he said. "They're good people. Anyway, I'm going to drive for another hour and then find a hotel. I'll call you then."

~

Tom checked into a small hotel west of Boise, and after talking to Mac for an hour on the phone, he got a restful night's sleep. The following day, he reached Wheatley early in the afternoon and gave Mac a quick call to let her know he would be arriving shortly.

On the north side of the small city, Tom turned right onto Farm to Market Road, pulling in behind a large flatbed farm truck that was creeping along at twenty miles an hour. Seeing it was going to be a slow, boring drive for the last thirty miles of his trip, he fiddled with the radio, trying to find a decent station to pass the time. When the truck's loose hay began blowing, it obscured Tom's vision, so he slowed down and kept ample distance between the two vehicles.

Rounding a bend at Woodrow Lake, Tom noticed that a dilapidated truck with out-of-state plates was traveling in front of the flatbed, and was actually responsible for slowing the traffic. Although Tom wanted to pass, the time needed to skirt by both the flatbed and truck made it too dangerous.

Unfortunately, the driver of the car behind him didn't think so.

As the caravan reached a short straightaway on the north side of Woodrow Lake, the driver of the sports car behind Tom veered into the other lane and stepped on the gas. Seeing that the car was about to pass him, Tom looked ahead and saw an old man walking his horse along the opposite side of the road. Oddly, twenty yards behind them, a moose was following, keeping the same distance.

Tom heard the sports car's engine roar, and then it took off at full speed. It rocketed past the flatbed, but another bend in the road was approaching. There wasn't enough time to pass the first truck, but there also wasn't enough room between the flatbed and pickup for the car to return to the right lane.

As they started into the bend, the front truck, oblivious to the passing car, swayed slightly into the left lane, pushing the car onto the far left shoulder. The car was now heading directly for the old man and his horse.

Just before the inevitable impact, the driver yanked the steering wheel and the car veered to the right, avoiding the pedestrian and his horse, but colliding with the front fender of the flatbed. The collision of metal on metal sent the car ricocheting across the road and over the shoulder, where it skimmed a ditch and jettisoned into the air before landing. The moose that had been following the man and the horse was unable to get out of the way in time, and the car's front end caught the animal's hind legs, flipping the terrified moose onto its side.

The car came to rest deep in the underbrush twenty yards from the asphalt. The truck with the flatbed had already slammed on its brakes, as did Tom and the three cars behind him.

Tom jumped out of his vehicle and ran up to the old man, whom he immediately recognized. "Jeremiah, are you all right?" he asked.

Jeremiah appeared to be unharmed. He was so blind that he never saw the car careening toward him. He nodded his head. "I was walking Isabella down to Wheatley to see a vet," he explained.

Tom glanced up at the mare, which was standing on all four legs with her head hanging low. He put his hand on the old man's shoulder. "Bring her in to see me when you get back to Lumby."

"Over here!" yelled out someone standing by the moose.

"I'll stop traffic," the truck driver shouted, and ran up the road to flag down oncoming vehicles.

When Tom got to the moose, it was lying flat on its side, unconscious. Tom opened its eyelids, examining the pupils. It was obvious that the animal was in shock.

Tom bent over and put his ear on the moose's chest and listened to its heartbeat—weak but regular. He palpated the rib cage and immediately felt several fractured ribs. Just below that area, a twelve-inch laceration oozed a fair amount of blood. Tom took off his jacket and pressed it firmly on the cut to slow the blood loss.

"Get the flatbed over here," Tom shouted.

One man had already begun directing the flatbed to the side of the road. A dozen people were crowded around the injured animal.

"It's Howard!" one of the ladies cried. "You can tell by the antler he broke fighting the tricycle."

Tom didn't have time to ask questions. "We have to lift him up. Do any of you have a tarp?"

"I have a couple of twelve-inch-wide hauling straps," the truck driver said, grabbing them from the backseat and passing them out the window.

"I've got to get him to my clinic in town. His left rear leg is broken, so be careful," Tom told the crowd.

After maneuvering the straps under Howard's body, Tom explained how he needed everyone to help lift the moose. "We all have to work together so he's kept level as we gently lower him onto the flatbed."

A dozen people circled the unconscious moose, with eight grabbing the ends of the straps and the others holding his legs, neck and head. "On three," Tom said. "One, two, and three."

It wasn't a pretty sight, but Howard was lifted high enough to be laid on the flatbed.

"Go!" Tom yelled and the truck took off. "Drive directly to my clinic."

Tom jumped in his car and speeded behind them, keeping an eye on the moose. The last thing he needed was for Howard to wake up during transport. In his rearview mirror he saw that Jeremiah had turned around and was walking along the road back toward Lumby with several people assisting him. He was quite sure that Jeremiah would make it safely back home and, with some medical attention, Isabella would be no worse for her travels.

Immediately before passing Montis, Tom couldn't help but notice a black-and-gold sign announcing the Lumby International Zoological Park. As he sped past, he looked down the dirt road and saw the two red barns. A short distance farther, out of the corner of his eye he saw a rhea loose in the orchard, pecking at the last apples on a tree.

Within minutes of arriving at The Granary, and with the help of several people who had followed him to town, Tom converted the clinic's new horse stall into a large-animal emergency operating room—very standard "barnyard surgery," as he would later describe it. The stall was far from an ideal environment, but it offered the moose its only chance for immediate treatment.

After many bystanders helped move Howard from the flatbed to the horse gurney that Tom had rolled into the center of the stall, Tom adjusted the lights and closed the door. He immediately administered an injectable anesthesia, thankful that the animal had not woken up since the accident. After setting up an IV drip, which offered a mixture of saline, anesthesia and antibiotics, he got down to business and began taking a closer look at Howard's injuries.

The moose had suffered several fractured ribs on his right side. Further palpation indicated that there was some bleeding in the chest, but his lungs sounded clear. Tom hoped the internal hemorrhaging would stop on its own as he turned his attention to the laceration.

The cut was long and deep and filled with dirt, twigs and broken glass. Tom repositioned the lights and began the long process of cleaning out the wound.

During the operation, news of Tom's return ricocheted through town and even made its way to Saint Cross Abbey, where the monks listened with rapt attention. Since Tom Candor might play a significant role in caring for the monks' animals, Matthew took a personal interest and immediately headed off to Lumby.

Hank was the first to arrive at The Granary, wearing disposable blue surgical scrubs, a surgeon's cap and a mask covering his protruding beak. From his neck hung a stethoscope and on his feet were disposable paper overshoes. A first-aid box lay on the ground not far away.

It was another hour before Tom was packing fresh dressing on Howard's sutured cut. Tom then carefully inspected the rest of the animal, but didn't find any other traumatic injuries. Returning to the chest area, he once again listened to the heart and lungs. Confident that he had done all he could, he adjusted the IV drip so the moose would slowly regain consciousness over the next several hours.

As Tom began to clean up after surgery, his thoughts kept circling back to Lumby, back to The Granary and always back to Mac. The more he contemplated each one, the farther away Wyoming seemed to fall. Lumby had not turned its back on him. In fact, just the opposite: the townsfolk had gone to extreme lengths, all of them extraordinarily unusual, to show their desire to have him in their lives. And, after all, Dennis and Jimmy had apologized for their initial judgment and overreaction.

And The Granary—how he loved the old place. It was the perfect small-town veterinary clinic at a time when private businesses were fading too quickly from the landscape.

And finally, there was Mac, who loved him enough to leave Lumby. Were his own love and faith strong enough to allow them to stay?

When Tom finally emerged from the operating room, the bystanders who had originally helped him were long gone. But when he walked around to the front of his clinic, he was stunned by what he saw: a huge crowd filled the west end of Main Street. Clamorous applause and cheers rose from a hundred people, who had been waiting for him. Even some people he had never seen before were waving to him and calling out his name.

"How's Howard?" one man yelled.

Tom stepped up on the porch and raised his arm. "He's just coming out of anesthesia, but he should be just fine," he said to the crowd.

"What happened to him?" another called out.

"He's got several fractured ribs and some internal bleeding and a deep laceration. He'll be staying here for at least three weeks and then we should be able to turn him loose."

Tom's announcement was followed by even louder cheers.

Mac ran up the stairs and threw her arms around him, giving him a big kiss, which elicited more ovations from the growing crowd.

"Did you see what they did?" she whispered in his ear, pointing to the front door. The old plaque had been rehung on the siding.

Dr. Tom Candor

Veterinarian

"We can judge the heart of a man
by his treatment of animals."
—Kant

"I'm home," Tom told Mac with a broad smile.

"For good?" she asked.

He squeezed her hand. "Forever and then some."

Mac beamed with happiness. "Then we will be here, together."

Across the street, Mark and Pam stood next to Brooke and Joshua, watching as their good friend turned the next page and began a new chapter in her life—one that would always include a veterinarian named Jeffrey Thomas Candor. Brother Matthew stood behind them, smiling.

"What a great ending," Mark said, and tightened his arms around his wife's waist.

"For them or our zoo?" Pam asked.

Mark gestured with his arm. "To all of it," he said. "We're so fortunate."

"We are indeed blessed," Brooke said, holding tight to Joshua's hand.

Gazing fondly at his good friends, and then at Mac and Tom, Brother Matthew said, "Faith, hope and love, and the greatest of these is love."

The Lumby Lines

What's News Around Town

BY SCOTT STEVENS November 14

A very slow week in our sleepy town of Lumby.

Reverend Poole of Lumby's Presbyterian church will be facilitating an open discussion with both the parish and the public regarding the church's plan to install a lightning rod on the roof of the main sanctuary. After initially hearing the idea several months ago, many parishioners complained that such an action would show a lack of faith where it should be most evident.

After several months of disorganization and occasional "lighthearted" combativeness among its members, the Lumby Scrabble Club has thrown away its dictionaries and been renamed the Lumby Checkers Club. Any donations to support their new pastime would be appreciated.

Anomalies in the voting tallies for our recent town seat elections revealed that many residents registered their cows as independents, artificially increasing the town's population by 894. As the practice appears to be widespread, no action is being taken against the violators. However, all poll results are being thrown out and a more secure method of voting will be implemented before reelections take place next month.

The last of the animals have been transported to our state's largest zoo, and LIZP has permanently closed its barn doors. Many thanks to Mark and Pam Walker of Montis Inn for donating their time and facilities to such a worthy cause.

Some of you may have noticed that the divider line painted on Main Street has changed from fluorescent yellow to bright chartreuse. An investigation by this reporter of what was assumed to be graffiti has revealed that a new Department of Transportation employee misread the color mixture when blending the paint. DOT says that it will return in a few days to repaint the lines and apologizes for any inconvenience.

Godspeed to all.

Photograph by Claire Donley

Gail Fraser has written *The Lumby Lines, Stealing Lumby, Lumby's Bounty* and *The Promise of Lumby*. She and her husband, folk artist Art Poulin, live with their beloved animals on Lazy Goose Farm in rural upstate New York. Gail and Art feel fortunate to be down the road from their close friends at New Skete Monastery, authors of *How to Be Your Dog's Best Friend*. When not writing, Gail tends to her heirloom tomatoes, their orchard and beehives. Or she can be found in her pottery studio.

Prior to becoming a novelist, Gail Fraser had a successful corporate career, holding senior executive positions in several Fortune 500 and start-up corporations and traveling extensively throughout the world. She has a BA from Skidmore College and an MBA from the University of Connecticut, with graduate work done at Harvard University.

Please visit www.lumbybooks.com and join Lumby's Circle of Friends.

CHATHAM PRESS
NOTES
LAWYER

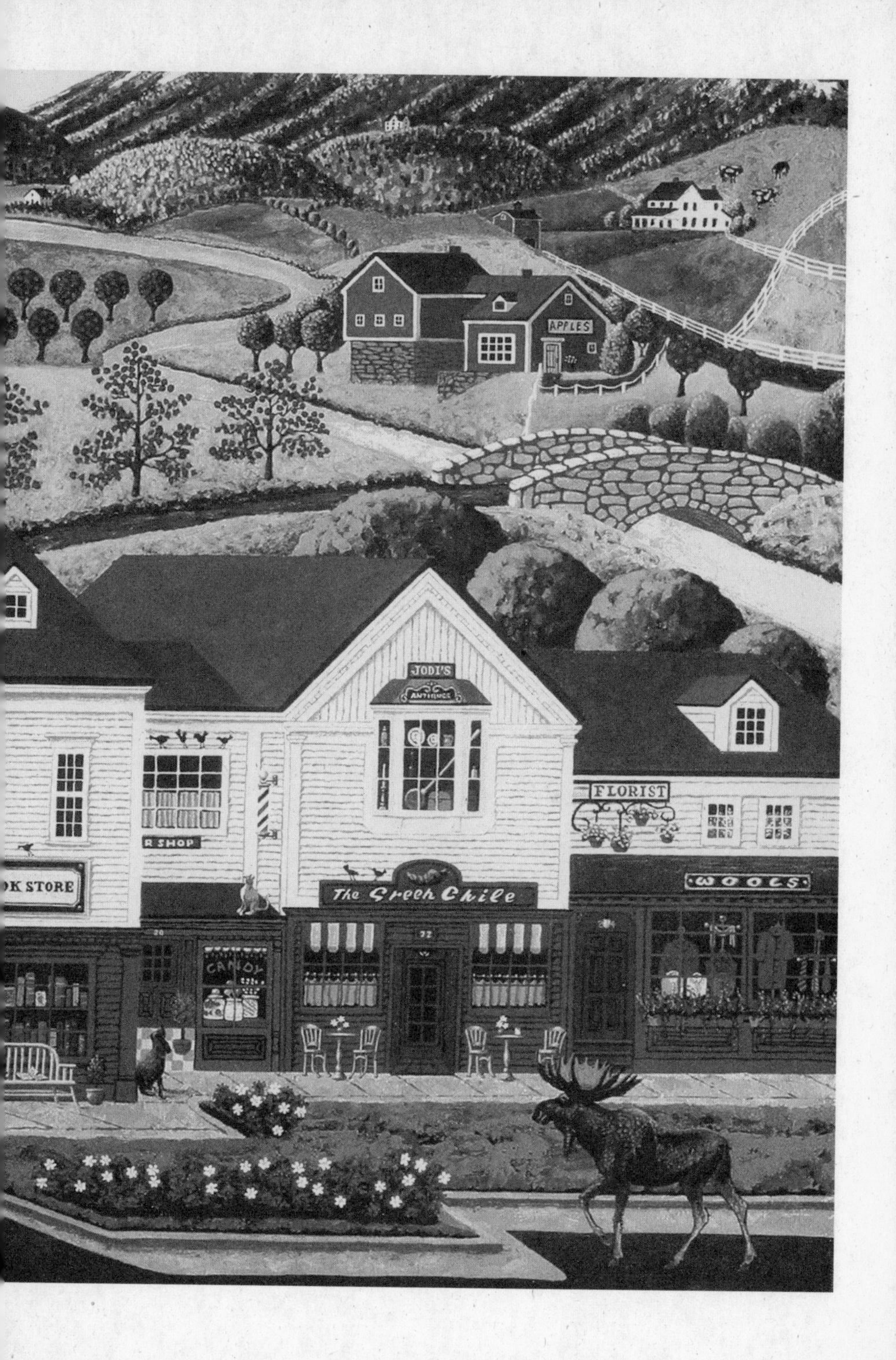

APPLES
JODI'S
FLORIST
R SHOP
OK STORE
The Green Chile
WOOLS
CANDY

THE LUMBY READER

Spend more time with your favorite Lumby characters.
Discover new wonders of the Lumby lifestyle.
Share your Lumby experience with friends and family.

At Home with Hank and the Author

Just outside a small town in upstate New York, and nestled at the end of a long dirt driveway that goes over the river (well, stream) and through the woods, several brightly colored buildings form the heart of Lazy Goose, a gentleman's farm that Gail and Art have been developing for the past several years.

Close to the main house and easily accessible from Gail's office is their orchard of apple, pear and cherry trees. At the far end of the field, tucked in a protective bend of blue spruce, are three active beehives. Below that, terraced lawns lead to a large trout pond. On the other side of the compound, close to the barn, are raised beds of verdant vegetables. Berries and lilacs abound.

Art spends most days painting in Studio 2, a vibrant red two-cupola artist's haven with immense north-facing windows. A short distance away, Gail can usually be found writing in her office. But the weather during the past few weeks was hot and dry, so today she's out watering the tomato plants.

Hank, having recently returned from a long sojourn, is wearing a pair of navy Dockers shorts and a pale-yellow-and-navy-striped short-sleeved shirt. As he relaxes in a wooden Adirondack chair in front of the barn, he surveys the changes that were made to the property since his departure last summer.

hank: you're not saying much.

Gail: You're a flamingo. What should I be saying?

hank: a fl-fl-fl-flamingo? i think not. i am a raptor, a noble bird of prey, a bald eagle that has come home to roast.

Gail: Roost.

hank: whatever. i've been gone a year. at least you could ask how my world tour went.

Gail: Fire away.

hank: the world adores me.

Gail: I hope so. We spent a fortune sending you first-class FedEx.

hank: eagles don't exert themselves unnecessarily.

Gail: Fine. Well, go use those talons of yours and catch some trout for dinner.

hank: but the snapping turtles . . .

Gail: Easy prey for a bald eagle with chicken legs.

hank: they just look that way because i've gained a few pounds recently. in fact, i've decided to go on a diet.

Gail: You hate fish and lettuce and you've been grazing on guacamole and chips all afternoon.

hank: and that presents a problem?

Gail: I would think so.

hank: i'll start tomorrow. so, the suspense is killing me. where, exactly, is my new abode?

Gail: What new abode?

hank: my chalet—hank's villa—the one i was returning to after my world tour.

Gail: You were in Newark most of the time.

hank: among other places.

Gail: Yes, I know. Rochester and Detroit and . . .

hank: and great towns they are. i naturally assumed you and art would build my new accommodations before work began on his studio.

Gail: Sorry, but you assumed wrong.

hank: i'm fl-fl-flabbergasted. then we have some work to do this summer, don't we?

Gail: When you earn it, we will build it.

hank: build it and i will earn it.

Gail: This isn't your field of dreams.

hank: so where am i to sleep?

Gail: The same place you always have.

hank: with *camille* in the *barn*? how can you suggest that i, hank, sleep with a cat now that i'm an internationally recognized icon?

Gail: Better than sleeping with a mannequin from Lumby Sporting Goods, I would think.

hank:	jealous?
Gail:	Why don't you actually do something useful and pull some weeds.
hank:	i think i'm above that now.
Gail:	Do tell.
hank:	they cheered me in newark.
Gail:	No, they were cheering because the garbage strike just ended.
hank:	well, they gave me a ticker-tape parade upon my arrival in new york city.
Gail:	Hank, as a joke someone duct-taped you to the tire of one of the Macy's Thanksgiving Day Parade floats.
hank:	humph. and my red-carpet reception in hollywood?
Gail:	That was the Emmy Awards.
hank:	naysayer.
Gail:	Dreamer.
hank:	is or is not the world knocking down your door to meet me?
Gail:	Not.
hank:	perhaps you need to write more novels.
Gail:	You have two invitations—Flint, Michigan, and somewhere in the bayous of Louisiana.
hank:	cajun cooking—my favorite. crawfish étouffée, jambalaya and f-f-f-frogs' legs.

Gail: Interesting diet.

hank: yes, and it begins with smothered pork chops. when do i leave?

Gail: We think you should stay around Lazy Goose for a while.

hank: grounded?

Gail: Yes, until the next book is released.

hank: lazy goose is great. but for a fl-fl-fl-bald eagle, it's on the boring side.

Gail: It's perfect. It's exactly what we want.

hank: it's lumby.

Gail: Just about as close as you can get. Wasn't that your last stop before coming home?

hank: the town residents embraced me. they're insisting that i run for councilman and go to washington.

Gail: Great, that's all we need: you on Capitol Hill working on our federal deficit.

hank: i'm a shoo-in.

Gail: But you only got eighty votes last time you ran for mayor.

hank: excuse me. eighty-seven.

Gail: Well, you might as well unpack and put on your dungarees. The compost pile needs to be turned.

hank: i'm speechless.

Hank continues his world tour and will next be traveling to Vancouver to spend some time with his Canadian fans. If you would like to host Hank for a week or two, or if you would like him to come to your book club meeting, please e-mail hank@lumbybooks.com so we can get that on his schedule.

Notes from Lazy Goose Farm

Far from the city, where dirt roads and one-lane bridges are more common than not, is our home on forty acres demarcated by a two-hundred-year-old stone wall. It is where our deepest roots grow and where our respective passions—painting for my husband, Art Poulin, and writing for me—find expression. And Lazy Goose Farm is the source of endless stories about nature and wildlife; a moose not so different from Howard regularly crosses our property.

A few miles from Lazy Goose is the small town and heart of the community to which we belong. As average and American as the town is, I'm still amazed on a daily basis by some of the oddities I encounter, from being assigned the town garage as our official voting location to having our main street closed due to an unexpected cow crossing.

Lumby readers frequently ask where I find fodder for my novels, and I'm proud to admit that I need only look at our lives here at home. Perhaps these notes from Lazy Goose will give you some idea of how we spend our days . . . and how some of these relationships and events provide inspiration for the Lumby series.

Does That Come with a Deed?

At my book signings and speaking engagements readers ask, "So, where do you get all your funny ideas?" to which I always respond,

"Everyday living in a small town." Case in point: last night, Art and I went out to dinner with some neighbors. On our drive down to Eagle Bridge, we took several country (read "backwoods") roads, as there are no major streets between here and there. Approaching Eagle Bridge, we passed a small cemetery with a rotted sign tied to one of the gravestones: "Lots for Sale Cheap Call Leon." Below that was a faded phone number. And on the third line, "Two-for-One Sale." A hundred yards farther, there was yet another posting, "10% If Used Before Christmas." Too funny, I thought, and then, as always happens, the questions started flooding in: so how much would a lot cost? Do lots vary in size or are all sized to fit a standard coffin? Does a deed come with the lot? Is Christmas a reasonable target? And . . . who is Leon?

One could write a book about what I don't know about graves. And so begins my research. Be assured that there will be a graveyard subplot in one of my future novels. . . . The possibilities are endless.

When a Reporter Comes Knocking, Comb Your Hair

As most of you know, I'm a relative newbie writer standing on the edge of the broader literary world of bestselling authors. But, to one degree or another, we all must walk the same road, which includes publicity. So, being a good trouper, I agreed to have a reporter from the local paper and her sidekick photographer come over to Lazy Goose. Unfortunately, preparations were not going well.

Because of our recent snow, the driveway to Lazy Goose was all but impassable except for those prepared to compete in the Iditarod, so a call of desperation was put in to our snowplow man. He was stranded with a blown transmission. We soon learned how long it takes a good-natured man (Art) to shovel a one-third-mile-long driveway.

My hair looked like it hadn't been cut in months, because . . . well, it hadn't been. So that morning I put in another call of desperation to my hairdresser, who, I found out, was on vacation. I had no choice but to go against my better judgment and agree to have "Bunny" cut it. Bunny dropped out of beauty school and was very excited about her first week of work. An hour later, my right ear was covered with hair but my left wasn't. I kept pulling it but it wasn't growing out any faster.

During the thaw before the snow, Emma and Yoda had dragged in nineteen pounds of mud from the orchard and had smeared it on every inch of our hardwood floors. To ensure coordination, they had dabbed plenty of the walls with their ever-wagging tails.

Finally, hank was frozen in the ground over the gas tank with a G-string hanging from his. . . . He was a gift from a fan when *The Lumby Lines* came out, and was subsequently dressed by one of our feral friends in a leopard-skinned G-string. We had anchored him over our buried gas tank to guard off any construction trucks. He was in so deep that I couldn't pull him out, but Art promised to dig up his legs after he was finished shoveling.

Good Thing They Didn't Serve Bloody Marys

Following up on an invitation I accepted several months ago, this morning I headed toward Vermont to join a book club at their monthly breakfast meeting. As with many of my author events, it was an opportunity for lessons learned:

1. On Route 32, don't be driving twelve miles over the speed limit when you pass Stewart's, a mile out of town.
2. Using the "I'm good friends with the owner of the tractor store" line can't get you out of every tight bind.
3. When all else fails, offer an autographed copy of each of your books.
4. There is a 1.3-mile difference between "East River Road" and "River Road East."
5. When someone describes their club as "average size," don't be surprised to see forty-two members waiting for you to arrive.
6. Before removing your blazer, first check to see if the dry cleaners somehow forgot to iron the right shirtsleeve.
7. The strawberries in the center of the eggs Benedict serving plate are tasteless because they're fake.

8. And, finally, for those who haven't read *Lumby*, first explain who Hank is before suggesting he take the mannequin from Lumby Feed Store to the movies for a romantic rendezvous.

Other than that, I had a delightful time with some great folks

Planning Ahead: Their Christmas Lists

Camille (our resident studio cat and Art's constant companion while he paints) gave us her Christmas list just as we were leaving for PetSmart this morning. Other than the fact that it's the middle of summer, she has an excellent sense of timing. Her requests:

A heated bed to be placed under my Ranchette Retreat, a multi-stationed bird feeder
Two servings of your friend Beth's meat loaf
Fourteen plastic balls with those silly little bells inside
A grow light for my catnip plant that is wintering in the barn
Feline booties with snow treads
A deluxe chipmunk feeder to quickly attract quarry
More of Beth's meat loaf
Andrea Bocelli's CD to give to Mom as apology for eating her birds
Christmas elf that will take those crazy canines, Emma and Yoda, to the North Pole
Unescorted visit to Friskies factory
Bridge built over koi pond for easy fishing
Six gallons of Beth's gravy

The next day, we found a note scrawled by Emma, taped to my desk.

Santa, I was as nice as possible this year. Yoda says he was nice too. So, I think I deserve the following presents under the tree:

Water heater for trout pond so we can swim year-round
2-lb. block of Cabot cheese
Liver
Liver on Cabot cheese
One Nylabone Wishbone (maybe another one for Yoda)
Ten feet of snow to play in
Fluff bed in the back of Dad's ATV so I can ride along to the top of the mountain
Bulldozer to accidentally knock over beehives
Lesson on opening lever doorknobs with nose, like Yoda does
Yoda says to add: Two minutes alone in the barn with Camille
Another 2-lb. block of Cabot cheese with peanut butter
Two thousand peanut butter–and-banana cookies

My Undoing

I was suffering from terminal spring fever and, against my better judgment, was following through on some of my warm-weather adjustments, although it was only nineteen degrees that morning. It was our first spring at Lazy Goose so, naturally, it was also our first April and I was very excited. Also, change was at our fingertips with Studio 2 finally under construction. I would say I was "impatious," putting me somewhere between impatient and anxious.

But it was the "premature execution" (as it could be coined) of my change-of-season rituals that was my undoing:

First, I lowered the temperature on the hot-water heater by ten degrees, prompting Art to wake me up at four forty-five that morning asking if we had a plumbing problem. (No, honey, we didn't.) Also yesterday, I packed away all of his sweatpants and fleece sweatshirts and replaced them with T-shirts and shorts. I assure you, he was less than impressed by my diligence when he went in search of his clothes after getting out of the rather chilly shower. And I was less than overjoyed when he woke me up yet again to explain why he couldn't wear Bermuda shorts for his quick stroll to the studio. Poor honeydew.

The next morning, I changed the wild-bird feed to a summer

mix but not one feathered friend showed up to feast. Finally, a few days ago, under blue skies and balmy 42-degree weather, I brought out our Adirondack lawn chairs only to drag them back into the barn because a snowstorm was heading our way that would leave us with at least four inches by morning.

My Top Ten Excuses for Missing My Publisher's Deadline Today

10. Staples ran out of computer paper.
9. J. K. Rowling called this morning to discuss the theological character threads of the monks of Saint Cross Abbey.
8. The same dog that ate my sixth-grade math homework ate most of my manuscript last night.
7. I accidentally burned my thesaurus.
6. Oprah interviewed me as the first author chosen for her "Series of the Month" book club.
5. I ran out of Visine and Tylenol.
4. Had to participate in a conference call with Steven Spielberg and Tom Hanks to finalize casting and filming location for *The Lumby Lines*.
3. A national-grid two-day power outage in upstate New York.
2. The Pope swung by Lazy Goose on his way to JFK.
1. My husband would have rightfully divorced me if he had to build the raised beds for my heirloom tomatoes by himself.

Some Things Just Can't Be Rushed

I never considered myself a berry-loving person, until a few weeks ago, when we discovered Winnies, a pick-your-own-blueberry farm a few miles from Lazy Goose.

We've returned twice a week since then for the best berries I've ever tasted, and they're only two dollars a (very generous) pound. The owners have several hundred blueberry shrubs, so one never needs to hunt very hard—there are always plenty for the picking.

Three things I have learned about blueberries of late:

1. After picking, the blueberries need to be given about forty-eight hours to "plump out" and sweeten up.
2. The best blueberry pie I've ever made was from a recipe from New Skete.
3. And, finally, one can't rush when picking berries.

Regarding the last aha, yesterday a friend called and asked Art and me over for lunch. I offered to bring a pie for dessert. As soon as I hung up, we were off to the berry fields. However, a huge storm was on the horizon: thunder with distant rain but no lightning. Grabbing our little blue plastic buckets, we ran between the rows toward the most distant shrubs, which offered the plumpest berries. More thunder. We could see the rain approaching, so Art and I agreed to pick as fast as we could for five minutes and then bolt back to the car.

When all was said and done, squished berries were everywhere! In the buckets, in Art's shirt pocket, on my glasses, between the car seats, even in my hair. But we ate a handful on the way home, and they were just as delicious as the ones we'd picked on our first trip there.

But What About . . . ?

My new plan to limit time allocated for nonwriting projects failed miserably today—not that I wrote too much, but instead, I wrote too little. . . . All right, I didn't write at all.

Today's project was to prepare the beehives for new colonies. But first I had to find our apiary tools, which were in the barn buried under our winter equipment, which really needed to be prepared for summer storage. Five hours later, the barn was a bit more organized and somewhere along the way I found it necessary to run to our local hardware store twice and Millie's, the family-run garden store, once. Good accomplishments, but I haven't seen a glimmer of either the beehives or chapter 40, which I should have been working on since seven o'clock this morning.

For more Notes from Lazy Goose Farm, please visit the Lumby Circle of Friends Bulletin Board on www.lumbybooks.com.

Lumby Living: Tips from Home

Recipes for Your Kitchen

Welcome back to Lumby Living: Tips from Home. In this issue, we offer a collection of simple and savory recipes, courtesy of Montis Inn, The Green Chile, Saint Cross Abbey and a few of Lumby's Circle of Friends.

The townsfolk of Lumby are always looking for personal favorite recipes and well-kept secrets, so if you would like to contribute your own tips from home, please visit www.lumbybooks.com and join the Lumby Circle of Friends. There, you may add your contributions, share your thoughts on a variety of subjects and chat with others who have embraced Lumby.

From Montis Inn

Pancetta Egg Bake

When Pam and Mark first arrived in Lumby, they regularly enjoyed an S&T's egg-bake breakfast made by Libby Nessle, a longtime town resident. Pam loved the simplicity and layering of the dish, but added her own flair by using two of her favorite ingredients: pancetta and Gruyère.

- 1½ cups cubed or chopped pancetta
- ½ cup chopped onion
- 2 cups washed and sliced baby portobello mushrooms
- 8 eggs
- ¼ cup half-and-half
- 1 large package crescent rolls, room temperature
- 1 cup grated Gruyère cheese

Preheat oven to 350 degrees F. In a large fry pan, brown pancetta. When cooked, remove with slotted spoon and drain on paper towels. Then transfer to mixing bowl and set aside. Place onion and mushrooms in same fry pan and cook in remaining pancetta grease for 5 minutes. Remove with slotted spoon, allow to drain on paper towels and add to pancetta in mixing bowl. Discard grease.

In a separate bowl, whisk together eggs and half-and-half.

Carefully unroll crescent rolls and form a single layer in the bottom of a large 9 × 13-inch (or equivalent) baking dish. Spread pancetta, onion and mushroom mixture evenly over dough. Pour egg mixture over that, and sprinkle with grated Gruyère cheese. (Do not add any salt because of high salt content in pancetta.) Bake for 30 minutes. Serves 4 to 6.

From Montis Inn

Prosciutto Spiral Appetizer

Pam's love of Italian hams shows in this classic spiral appetizer, which she serves at all her wine-tasting parties. It's also a perfect hors d'oeuvre to complement any meal or can be served along with a cup of soup for a lighter lunch.

1 pound thinly sliced prosciutto
1 pound softened goat cheese
1 cup chopped pine nuts
2 tablespoons extra-virgin olive oil
2 cups steamed spinach leaves
2 cups roasted red peppers, cut into thin slivers

Working on a large piece of parchment paper to simplify the rolling process, lay out one slice of prosciutto. Gently and evenly spread two tablespoons of goat cheese over the ham. Sprinkle 1 teaspoon of chopped pine nuts on goat cheese and then dash with olive oil. On top of that, add a single layer of spinach leaves, followed by a single layer of sliced red peppers, using about an eighth of a cup for each slice of prosciutto. On top of the peppers, place another slice of prosciutto, another layer of cheese, nuts, olive oil, spinach and roasted red peppers.

Starting at the long side of the stacked prosciutto, carefully roll prosciutto, forming a jelly-roll-shaped log. Wrap tightly in plastic wrap. Continue making additional rolls using remaining ingredients. Refrigerate for at least 12 hours.

When ready to serve, remove plastic wrap and slice each roll into ¾-inch pieces, laying each on its side so guests can see the colorful spiral.

From Saint Cross Abbey

Craisin Chicken Salad

Since the monks cook for twenty to forty community members and guests on any particular day, the ease of changing proportions and quantities is an important factor in the dishes that they prepare in the abbey's kitchen. Using apples provided by Montis Inn makes this recipe all the more delicious.

2 pounds boneless, skinless chicken breasts

¾ cup mayonnaise

1 tablespoon lemon juice

salt and pepper

1½ cups peeled and diced Granny Smith apples (or any crisp, mildly tart apple)

1½ cups seedless grapes, each grape cut in half

1½ cups Ocean Spray Craisins (or homemade dried and sweetened cranberries)

In a large pot, cook chicken breasts in boiling water for approximately twenty minutes, until no pink remains and juices run clear. Drain and cool. Dice chicken into ¼-inch cubes and place in large mixing bowl. Add mayonnaise and lemon juice, and mix thoroughly, allowing the chicken cubes to break down slightly. Gently fold in apples, grapes and craisins, mixing thoroughly. Add salt and pepper to taste. Cover and chill for several hours. Serve on a bed of mixed greens or between slices of bread of your choice. Serves 6.

From Saint Cross Abbey

Fresh Corn Pudding

During the summer months, the monks get their fresh produce from local farms in Franklin. Among their favorite places to shop is Cold Creek Farm out on Eddie Road (where Gabrielle also buys many of her vegetables when she visits the area). The monks believe their corn is the finest in the county, if not the state, and makes their corn pudding absolutely heavenly.

8 eggs, separated

4 cups fresh corn kernels (score corn before cutting off cob, and drain any liquids)

2 cups heavy cream

2 teaspoons salt

½ teaspoon pepper

2 tablespoons sugar

2 tablespoons flour

Preheat oven to 350 degrees F. In a small bowl, beat egg yolks together until smooth. In a separate bowl at high speed, beat egg whites until they form stiff peaks. Place fresh corn kernels in a large mixing bowl; then add and blend together egg yolks, cream, salt, pepper, sugar and flour. Fold in beaten egg whites. Immediately pour into well-buttered casserole dish. Place casserole dish inside larger pan in which an inch or two of water have been poured. Bake for 30 minutes or until set. Serves 6 to 8.

From The Green Chile

Smothered BBQ Burgers

When Gabrielle first opened the doors of The Green Chile by holding a Main Street barbecue party, town residents Diane and Dave Nelson contributed their delicious smothered BBQ burgers from a personal recipe that they had refined over the years. The burgers were a smashing success, and have since been enjoyed at all of Lumby's town festivities.

For the onion sauce:

- 1 18-ounce jar of your favorite barbecue sauce
- 1 12.5-ounce can of beef broth
- 1 13-ounce jar of spaghetti sauce
- 6 pounds sweet onions (approximately 20 medium-sweet or 10 Vidalia onions), peeled and cut into ¼-inch slices, then separated into rings

For the hamburgers:

- 2 pounds ground hamburger
- 1 6-ounce box of your favorite seasoned stuffing mix
- 2 large eggs
- 1 envelope (1 ounce) dry onion soup mix
- 2 cubes beef bouillon dissolved in 1 cup water
- salt and pepper

For the onion sauce: Combine all sauce ingredients in a large saucepan. Stirring intermittently, simmer over medium to low heat for four hours, until the onions are thoroughly cooked. While the sauce is cooking, in a large mixing bowl, combine all ingredients for the hamburgers. Mix well. Form meat into 4- to 5-ounce patties and fry to medium-rare (the hamburger will continue to cook later in the oven). When patties are done, set them aside to cool.

Preheat oven to 325 degrees F. In a 9 × 12 inch or comparably sized Pyrex or aluminum baking pan that's several inches deep, spread 2 cups of onion sauce evenly over the bottom. Add a layer of hamburgers, placing them loosely next to each other. Then add another layer of sauce, using about 2 cups, and then more hamburgers. Continue layering to the top of the pan, ending with a layer of sauce. Place pan in oven and bake for 45 minutes. Serve the hamburgers on buns or hard rolls, with additional sauce on top. Add salt and pepper to individual hamburgers to taste. Makes approximately 10 to 12 hamburgers.

Note: This is a great recipe to make in advance and freeze. Allow contents of the baking pan to thaw in the refrigerator for 24 hours before baking. Leftover sauce can be reused on other dishes. Enjoy!

From The Green Chile

Corn and Avocado Gazpacho

Gabrielle remembers, as a child, watching this soup being made by her grandmother in Vera Cruz. Although corn is not usually added to traditional gazpacho recipes, Gabrielle's family grew several types of yellow and white corn in their large garden, so corn became a long-established ingredient in many of their personal recipes.

4 large heirloom tomatoes (about 4 pounds in total), cored

2 cucumbers, peeled

2 green peppers, stems and seeds removed

¾ small sweet onion, outside layers removed

3 stalks celery, leaves removed

4 cups tomato juice (or mixed vegetable juice)

2 cups drained, canned corn

salt and pepper

two avocados

croutons

Dice tomatoes, cucumbers, peppers, onion and celery into 1- to 2-inch pieces. Combine ingredients and blend in food processor for 10 to 20 seconds or until chunky. Depending on the size of your food processor, this may need to be done in two or three batches. Pour into large bowl. Stir in tomato juice and corn. Cover tightly and refrigerate at least six hours and up to two days. Before serving, add salt and pepper to taste. Prepare garnish by peeling, pitting and thinly slicing avocados. Serve in large soup bowls and top with avocado slices and croutons. Serves 8.

From Saint Cross Abbey

Fresh Berry Pie

When first exploring the monastic grounds, the sisters of Saint Amand found an acre of wild berry bushes of various kinds just behind the small church. So they treated the monks to one of the finest pies they'd ever tasted. Although the sisters prefer to use a combination of blueberries and raspberries, this recipe can be made using all blueberries (early in the season) or all raspberries (in late summer) or some of both combined with loganberries and blackberries.

For the crust:

- 9 graham crackers
- 2 tablespoons sugar
- 5 tablespoons butter, melted

For the filling:

- 2 cups fresh and cleaned blueberries (divided into ½-cup and 1½-cup portions)
- 2 cups fresh and cleaned raspberries (divided into ½-cup and 1½-cup portions)
- 1 cup sugar
- ¾ cup water
- 3 tablespoons red currant jelly
- 3 tablespoons cornstarch
- ¼ teaspoon salt
- ¼ cup water
- whipped cream

Preheat oven to 325 degrees F. Place graham crackers in a food processor and mix until fine, about 20 seconds. Transfer to a bowl and stir in sugar and melted butter. Transfer crumbs to a 9-inch pie plate and press crumbs evenly into bottom and sides. Bake for 16 minutes.

While the pie crust bakes, prepare the filling. In a large saucepan over medium heat, combine ½ cup blueberries, ½ cup raspberries, sugar and water. Cook for ten minutes until fruit is soft. Stir in red currant jelly and lower heat to simmer. In a small bowl or cup, combine cornstarch, salt and water to make a paste. Add paste to berries and continue cooking over low heat until mixture is well thickened. Fold in remaining fresh berries and heat through, approximately 2 minutes. Pour mixture into cooled crust. Loosely cover pie with plastic wrap and refrigerate for several hours. Serve with whipped cream. Serves 6 to 8.

From The Green Chile

Chicken and Artichoke Chili

This recipe was originally passed down from Dennis Beezer's great-grandmother, with each generation adding something unique to the soup. Now it's a town favorite at Gabrielle's restaurant, where Dennis enjoys it every Sunday evening with a glass of pinot grigio.

4 tablespoons olive oil

2 pounds boneless, skinless chicken breasts, cubed

1 cup chopped onion

4 garlic cloves, minced

2 cups vegetable broth

2 14-ounce cans artichokes, drained, patted dry and loosely chopped

2 teaspoons parsley

2 19-ounce cans cannellini beans, not drained

salt and pepper

Asiago cheese, grated

1 baguette

In a large 3-quart saucepan, heat 2 tablespoons of olive oil over medium-high heat. Add chicken and cook about 5 minutes, stirring often. Remove chicken and set aside. Add remaining 2 tablespoons of oil and reheat pan. Add onion and cook for 2 minutes over medium heat, and then add garlic and cook for another 2 minutes. When onion is tender, stir in vegetable broth, artichokes and parsley. Reduce heat and simmer for 10 minutes. Stir in cooked chicken and beans and simmer for another 20 minutes. Add salt and pepper to taste. Garnish by sprinkling grated Asiago cheese on top, and serve with warm baguette. Makes 6 to 8 servings.

From Montis Inn

Vegetable Soufflé

A staple recipe that André brought to the Montis kitchen, this vegetable soufflé is so versatile it can be made in any season using a variety of fresh or cold-stored vegetables. André advises using the richest butter and Gruyère available to ensure outstanding results.

3 tablespoons butter
3 tablespoons flour
1 cup half-and-half
1 teaspoon salt
½ teaspoon pepper

⅔ cup blanched fresh vegetables cut into 1-inch pieces—you can use anything that's in season, such as zucchini, broccoli, asparagus, or mushrooms

½ cup grated Gruyère cheese
4 egg yolks
5 egg whites

Preheat oven to 350 degrees F. In a saucepan over medium heat, make a simple roux: melt butter, blend in flour until smooth and then, stirring constantly, add in half-and-half, followed by salt and pepper. Continue to stir until sauce thickens. Remove from heat. Quickly beat in egg yolks one at a time. Fold in your choice of vegetable(s). In a separate bowl, beat egg whites until stiff peaks form. Fold egg whites into vegetable mixture. Pour into well-buttered soufflé or baking dish. Bake undisturbed for 35 minutes, or until top is nicely browned and center has set. Serves four.

Questions for Discussion

1. Dr. Campbell has worked very hard her entire life and, at the beginning of the book, has her eyes set on retirement, which will begin with a long vacation in Greece, after which she will move closer to her grown children. Do you have a similar dream, and where would you go if given the time and resources?

2. The veterinarian clinic is a prominent setting in the novel, and the animals play a key role in people's lives. Is that true in your family or in your own town?

3. The importance of honesty and truth-telling is a central theme in the story. Are there times when choosing not to disclose the full truth is understandable, even preferable? And have you ever been in a position similar to Tom Candor's, wanting to withhold details for fear of being judged or misunderstood?

4. Hank is always a supportive, benevolent character who seems to be nonjudgmental. Is there anything the town residents can learn from him?

5. Are Jimmy's and Dennis's reactions to Tom's background justified? What are their different reasons for so quickly and, some would say, harshly judging Tom's actions?

6. Do you think Jimmy's time as town mayor is coming to an end? If so, whom would you like to see as mayor of Lumby?

7. Brother Michael's innocent comment about the snow monkeys that the monks were given as gifts, which receives wide distribution via a magazine article, produces unintended consequences. Have you ever faced unintended consequences from something you've done?

8. Do you like the idea of uniting Saint Amand and Saint Cross Abbeys, and how do you think the nuns will change the monks' community?

9. How does Mark's unrestrained excitement and occasional impulsiveness both help and hurt his relationship with his wife and what they are trying to accomplish at Montis Inn?

10. What are your opinions of André and Christian? Is there still some mystery about them, and would you like to see them in future books? Do you think André is committed to staying at Montis?

11. Initially, Tom and Mac seem to have common interests, but they are quite different people. Do you think they have a chance for a successful long-term relationship, and do you hope to see them married?

12. Brooke and Joshua consider the possibility of moving away from Lumby, as does Mac. How should couples balance different priorities and desires, and when should they uproot their families?

LUMBY LUMBER
WOODSMITHE
COUNTRY FURNITURE
To THE
BARNS
Lumby Lumber
WOODSMITHE

If you enjoyed your visit to Lumby,
read on for an excerpt from

LUMBY'S BOUNTY

Available now from NAL

Lumby sits quietly on the northern rim of Mill Valley, a lush vale of rolling pastures, rich agricultural fields, and grasslands dotted with white farmhouses. To the west, protecting both the town and the valley, are densely forested hills and low mountains. Beyond those rise the vast and majestic Rockies.

The natural beauty of the surroundings can be appreciated throughout the year, with each season revealing a new wonder. Summer offers the sights and smells of verdant croplands, while autumn brings the colors of a painter's palette, splashing brilliant yellows and oranges across the landscape. When cold winds sweep down from Canada, the first winter snow settles on the jagged mountain ridges and then slowly descends onto the town.

In spring, though, the streams swell and the trees bud along Main Street, officially named State Road 541 but frequently referred to as Old 41. Charming storefronts and small cafés line sidewalks of raised flower beds, scattered fruit trees, and brightly painted benches. As the temperature warms, yellow-, blue-, and green-striped awnings are rolled out with their edges flapping in the breeze.

Simon watched Jimmy enter the Chatham Press building, which

housed one of the oldest family-run businesses in Lumby. The enterprise consisted of the town's bookstore, a bookbinding concern, and a substantial printing operation that published the local newspaper, among other periodicals and flyers.

Woodrow Beezer, who built the three-story stone office at the turn of the twentieth century, began the family enterprise, which was, in time, passed on to his son, William Beezer. William was a hard man who kept a keen eye on the bottom line and grew the business tenfold. After William's unexpected death two years ago, his estranged son, Dennis, followed in his footsteps.

Jimmy looked at his watch and walked inside, jogging up the stairs two at a time.

At the top of the stairwell, he heard a loud voice. "What the heck have you done?"

And then silence.

Entering the publishing floor of *The Lumby Lines*, he first noticed Dennis's assistant, Kim, working at her desk, her head lowered. She looked up and quickly pointed to Dennis Beezer's office. As did everyone in town, she knew that Dennis was a good man with a long fuse, but today something—or someone—had obviously set him off.

Through the frosted glass of his office door, Jimmy saw Dennis pacing back and forth, occasionally frowning at the person seated in the chair in front of his desk.

Jimmy considered leaving—this was obviously very bad timing indeed.

Just then Dennis slammed open the door. "Kim," he said, forcing calm into his voice, "would you please get Jimmy on the phone?"

"He's standing right there," she said, pointing.

Dennis waved him over. "I was just calling you," Dennis said, shaking the hand of his close friend.

"So I heard," Jimmy said cautiously. "What's up?"

Dennis ran a hand through his hair in frustration. "I think you need to come in and sit down."

Walking into the private office, Jimmy saw Dennis's nineteen-year-old son, Brian Beezer, slumped in the chair. His head hung low, his dark brown hair mostly covering his handsome, angular face. His long legs were outstretched, with his feet knocking against each other.

Dennis handed a piece of paper to Jimmy. "Read this advertisement that was faxed over to us this morning. It's to be run in *The Lumby Lines* in a few weeks."

"Why are you giving it to me?" Jimmy asked.

"Please read it," Dennis said, turning with annoyance toward Brian.

Jimmy scanned the copy, taking note of the critical words: Balloon rides . . . Regional Balloon Festival . . . Lumby.

When Jimmy had digested its meaning, he started laughing. "Well, this is clearly a mistake, Dennis. We don't have any hot air balloons in Lumby, so it would make no sense that we would host a hot air balloon festival." He held out the fax. "I'm sure someone's just pulling your leg. That, or whoever submitted this just faxed it to the wrong local paper in the wrong town."

"No, they didn't," Dennis said, glaring at Brian.

Jimmy saw how angry his friend was. "What's going on?"

"Tell him," Dennis told his son.

Brian slid farther down in his chair. No one could do sullen better than the son of the newspaper's editor.

"Brian, tell him," he repeated.

"Well," Brian said at last, "Terry and I were looking at some magazines a few months ago, and saw this thing . . ."

"What thing?" Jimmy asked.

Brian hesitated. "An article. Anyway, it said they were—"

"Who?" Jimmy continued to press for clarity.

"The U.S. Hot Air Balloon Association. They were looking for a town to host this year's balloon festival." Brian continued to stare at his knees, which were nervously moving back and forth. "And we thought it would be cool if it was here, in Lumby. So we pooled some money at school."

Dennis was ready to explode once again. "How much?" he demanded.

"Two hundred and fifty dollars."

Both men looked at the teenager in disbelief. How could high school kids collect that amount without parental involvement or even awareness?

"Go on," his father said.

"We filled out the application and got a money order." His story abruptly ended, and after a few moments it was obvious that Brian had no intention of continuing.

Jimmy coaxed the boy. "And?"

Brian twisted in his chair. He went on very reluctantly. "Well, they wrote back several times asking for more information, and then about a month ago they sent us a contract."

Jimmy leaned forward, visibly confused. "Why would they possibly send a contract to you?"

Brian looked up at his father, hoping he would end the interrogation, but his father just glared back. When he saw no escape was possible, he lowered his head still farther down on his chest so he could barely be heard. "I told them I was the mayor."